He stared at her in shock, as if it were the first time he'd realized Crystal was a woman.

The white wash of moonlight bathed her face clearly, her lashes dark smudges above her cheeks. Startled, Travis stared at her smooth skin. He was wrong about her age. He leaned closer, really looking at her. With her hair down, she was transformed; her pale skin was smooth. The woman was far younger than he had guessed. She must be only twenty-three or twenty-four, he decided.

If she had let down that mass of hair once or twice and let the men of Cheyenne have a glimpse of it, she would have had more proposals than his to consider.

Travis sat down gently and stretched out, trying to avoid disturbing her.

The bed creaked as he straightened and shifted. Suddenly she sat up, gasping and scrambling away from him.

"Crystal," he said quickly, taking hold of her arm lightly, trying to reassure her. "It's Travis. Remember?"

She blinked and stared at him. She looked young, frightened, and *pretty*. He realized he was staring and checked the urge to reach out again and touch a silken curl. He became aware of his fingers closed around her slender wrist.

"The ground is wet and I came in here to sleep."

BOOK YOUR PLACE ON OUR WEBSITE AND MAKE THE READING CONNECTION!

We've created a customized website just for our very special readers, where you can get the inside scoop on everything that's going on with Zebra, Pinnacle and Kensington books.

When you come online, you'll have the exciting opportunity to:

- View covers of upcoming books
- Read sample chapters
- Learn about our future publishing schedule (listed by publication month *and author*)
- Find out when your favorite authors will be visiting a city near you
- Search for and order backlist books from our online catalog
- Check out author bios and background information
- Send e-mail to your favorite authors
- Meet the Kensington staff online
- Join us in weekly chats with authors, readers and other guests
- Get writing guidelines
- AND MUCH MORE!

**Visit our website at
http://www.zebrabooks.com**

COMANCHE EAGLE

Sara Orwig

Zebra Books
Kensington Publishing Corp.

http://www.zebrabooks.com

ZEBRA BOOKS are published by

Kensington Publishing Corp.
850 Third Avenue
New York, NY 10022

First Printing: August, 1998
10 9 8 7 6 5 4 3 2 1

Printed in the United States of America

With thanks to Val and Rick Rothwell, Cheryl Goudge,
the Wyoming Chamber of Commerce, Mary Hartman,
Shirley Flynn. Thanks, too, to Kate Duffy and
to Maureen Walters.

Author's Note:

   In 1869, in a unique moment in history, years before women won the right to vote in the United States, the Territory of Wyoming passed laws giving women full voting rights along with the right to hold office and the right to serve on juries. In 1870, in South Pass, Wyoming, Esther Morris became the first female justice of the peace in the United States.

One

Cheyenne, Wyoming Territory
1871

"How does the defendant plead?"

"Not guilty, ma'am." Andrew Cain shuffled his feet.

Summer wind swept through the windows, stirring a faint breeze in the stuffy courtroom that adjoined the Cheyenne jail. A few spectators, along with three males waiting to have arraignments, sat on rows of benches. At the front of the room behind a table, Justice of the Peace Crystal Spencer sat with her shoulders squared as she looked at the blond man facing her.

With a conscience that was as cool and collected as her demeanor, Crystal relished both the June weather and the dispensing of justice. She had never met the charged, Andrew Cain, who could barely answer her and looked like a whipped mongrel. As far as Crystal was concerned, guilt was written all over his pale countenance. Judging his age to be less than twenty years, she felt a faint stirring of sympathy that she crushed immediately by recalling his misdeeds.

"What do you have to say for yourself?"

With his blue eyes darting around the room, the slender man nervously twisted his hat in his hands. "Ma'am, I didn't mean no harm."

"Your Honor," came a deep voice. Along the front row, boot heels scraped. A tall, black-haired man stood and moved forward.

She recognized Travis Black Eagle, farrier and owner of one of Cheyenne's livery stables. As he strode toward her, her gaze flicked over him and her composure frayed. She was merely a nodding acquaintance with Mr. Black Eagle, but the man made her nervous. From a headband an eagle feather dangled down over his shaggy black hair. Broad-shouldered, he looked as if he were holding raw power in check, and his piercing dark eyes seemed to see too much. He looked as if he needed to be out on the plains on the back of a horse instead of abiding in the community. In a rare experience in her courtroom, she became uneasy.

Hoping she hid the trepidation she felt, Crystal gazed up at Travis Black Eagle. For the first time she felt at a disadvantage by being seated and having to look up. He stopped in front of the table and stood beside Andrew. Most of the men who faced her looked embarrassed or pleaded innocent or occasionally gave her a surly stare. None made her heart trip in anxiety like the man staring at her now. He wasn't moving or speaking, yet she felt a contest of wills, and she felt buffeted by his male presence.

"I would like to vouch for Andrew's character," he said firmly in a voice that was low, husky, and ran over her nerves like a brisk summer wind across her bare skin. "He's in my employ and he's a good worker and a fine man."

"Mr. Cain was inebriated and disorderly." Knowing she should sound more forceful, she took another breath and started again. "He caused a fight in Brewster Worth's saloon, breaking

Mr. Worth's window and causing Jasper Simmons to lose three teeth in a brawl.''

"I believe Jasper was also involved in the brawl. He was not an innocent bystander.'' Travis Black Eagle's voice was quiet, yet it held authority. She felt the familiar surge of anger over lawlessness, and it fueled her resolve.

"I am here to uphold justice and see to it that Cheyenne enjoys law and order.'' Looking at Andrew Cain, who immediately, and to her relief, glanced at the floor, she rapped her gavel. "Five dollars in fines and eight dollars in court costs.''

Andrew's head snapped up and his fair complexion became snowy as he swayed. "I don't have that much money!''

"If not, you will spend the time in jail.''

"Jail!'' Andrew gasped.

"You will spend the time in jail,'' she continued solemnly, "at the rate of two dollars per day until you work out the time. In addition, you must replace Brewster Worth's window. Jail will give you time to consider the evils of hard liquor and brawling, Mr. Cain.''

She rapped the gavel. "Next case.'' She felt eyes boring into her and struggled to avoid turning her head, but the compulsion was too strong. Her gaze slid across Andrew Cain to Travis Black Eagle. He stood with one hand on his hip, his dark eyes stabbing into her, pinpoints of fiery anger in their depths. She raised her chin. She had sworn to uphold the law, and no harsh looks were going to deter her from doing her duty.

Black Eagle stepped forward and, for a fleeting second, she almost flung herself out of the chair and ran. His hand jammed into his hip pocket, causing his black pants to pull tautly across his narrow hips. She yanked her gaze back up to his face and then down again as he tossed money onto the table.

"Here's Andrew's fine.''

"You may pay the clerk. Mr. Cain can contact Mr. Worth about replacing his window.''

Her gaze met Travis Black Eagle's again, and she clampe

her mouth shut, feeling a shiver of fright as his dark eyes
stabbed into her before he turned and strode from the room.

"You were a little harsh, Sister, on poor Andy Cain yesterday. They're talking about it at Worth's."

"I would think Brewster Worth would be thankful he'll get
his window replaced," she said, glancing at her brother as he
smoothed his auburn hair. He stood in front of a mahogany-
framed oval mirror that hung near the front door of the small
house they shared on the edge of Cheyenne. Her gaze ran over
her brother, noticing the small black threads standing up along
the collar of his black coat, the shiny material wearing thin at
his elbows, his scuffed and worn boots.

"Worth won't get his window replaced until Andy can earn
the money."

"If Mr. Cain doesn't cooperate, he'll go to jail."

"He won't be able to repay anything if he languishes in jail.
And Travis Black Eagle would be minus a helper."

"Andrew should have thought about that before he became
so besotted!"

Ellery Spencer turned, focusing on her with eyes that were
the same deep green as hers. "There are worse crimes than
liquor, Crystal. You won't win support by putting your constit-
uents in jail. The governor appointed you this time, but in three
years you'll have to have the approval of the public for him
to appoint you again."

Raising her chin, she felt a surge of defiance. She moved to
the tall rosewood piano that she had brought to the Territory
from the Baltimore family home. Her fingers brushed the polished wood lovingly before she glanced again at Ellery. "People
need law and order. You told me only two years ago Cheyenne
had mostly vigilante justice. And before that, the town was
almost lawless.

"Those days are over. And you don't have to bring law and
order all by yourself. Leave that to the sheriff."

"Ellery, let's go to California!" She blurted out her longed-for dream, knowing his feelings.

With a sad smile he shook his head. "Sister, I can't leave these folks. They need me and I need them. You'll like it here as time goes by."

"The wind blows constantly. Unless you have your own well, water is as precious as gold. The town is filled with rough men. California would be warm and beautiful and we both could follow the tasks we love."

"I can't leave and you know I can't," he said quietly. Ellery placed a battered broad-brimmed hat on his head. "Take care."

Her anger evaporated, replaced by worry. "Ellery, will you be gone long?"

His smile revealed a missing eyetooth. "Don't concern yourself about me. I shan't get involved in any brawls." He straightened his black coat and swept out the door and she sighed, knowing there was no way to stop her worry about him.

"You're too much like Pa," she said quietly, dimly remembering their gentle, besotted father. Ellery was her only living relative now and she worried about his vices. He tried to hide his gambling and drinking from her, but it was impossible for her to avoid hearing him stumble into the house and shut himself away in his room. And he had to confide in her about money, although he tried to hide the extent of his debts. She worried, too, about his practice. He criticized her for being so harsh. Yet she knew he should stay sober to take care of his patients.

She moved to a window and lifted a lace curtain, looking down the wide, hard-packed dirt street at the nearest small frame house that belonged to the Shaffers. Ellery was already out of sight down the street, and Crystal let the curtain fall and moved away, her thoughts shifting to her dream of California and a warm, sunny place where she could grow flowers and continue to work in law or teach piano. If only she and Ellery could save enough to go. And if only Ellery *would* go. Yet she knew why he clung to this outpost on the frontier, a terminal for the Union Pacific railroad—the town needed a doctor, and out here people were willing to overlook his drinking.

As she crossed the room, she paused in front of the oval mirror in the hallway and felt a surge of pride when she looked at her reflection. Justice of the Peace. Judge Crystal Spencer. Drawing herself up as tall as possible, she smiled. She was upholding the law, doing something important and vital, the first woman in Cheyenne to become a justice of the peace.

That was the best thing about Wyoming Territory—they had recognized women in a manner beyond any place she had ever heard of. Nowhere else in the States did women have the vote and the right to hold office and the right to serve on juries. Nowhere else could she be justice of the peace.

As she studied her reflection, the silence of the house wrapped around her, pulling her attention from her image and thoughts of court. She became aware of the emptiness, the lonely hours that stretched ahead. She rubbed her forehead and hurried to the small kitchen to start a supper that she knew Ellery would not come home to eat. Pausing, she glanced through the window at the rolling land behind the house and the mountains so far in the distance. The town nestled on the high plains with unending vistas and magnificent sunsets; yet when the wind howled across the land, it reminded her of her solitary life. She would always be alone except for Ellery. Painfully alone. Something tightened and squeezed inside her, a fleeting pain of longing that she tried to shake away.

Six hours later, during the night, Crystal's eyes flew open and she stared into the darkness and wondered what had awakened her. An insistent, loud banging on the front door made her jump with fright. Her heart thudded as she thought of Ellery.

Swinging back the covers on the bed, she grabbed up her blue cotton wrapper. Pulling it over her gown, she rushed from the small bedroom to the front door. In the parlor a lamp still burned for Ellery and it shed a faint glow. She yanked open the front door and gazed up into dark brown eyes.

Bringing in a swish of cool night air, Travis Black Eagle brushed past her into the house. He smelled of leather and was even more imposing than he had been in her simple courtroom. He wore black from head to toe, and she felt as if she faced the devil. His coattails spun out behind him as he swung around. "Where's your brother?"

"He's not here," she answered. "He's probably at Worth's."

Travis Black Eagle whipped past her, charging through the door and across the porch. She rushed after him. "When Ellery returns—"

"I'll find him. I need him. Our baby's coming," came the terse reply.

The image of Elizabeth Black Eagle came to mind as Crystal watched Travis leap into the saddle and gallop up the street. How such a sweet, dainty woman could fall in love with a man so forceful, Crystal couldn't imagine. She remembered the last time she had seen Elizabeth Black Eagle in town. Elizabeth was a beauty with silky blond curls and flawless skin.

Would Travis Black Eagle find Ellery at Worth's? Heaven hope Ellery was sober, yet babies seemed to come into the world without too much fuss and bother. Most of the time. Remembering how petite and delicate Elizabeth Black Eagle was, Crystal frowned. "Please, God, let Ellery be able to help." She envisioned Elizabeth with Travis. The devil and the angel. Crystal shrugged and returned to bed, shaking her long braid of auburn hair behind her shoulders.

She was too busy the following day to worry about Ellery. When night came, she felt the first prickling of worry, yet she reassured herself that first babies were sometimes long in arriving. She slept fitfully and rose early Monday, beginning to watch the wide lane for any sign of Ellery when she stepped out of the house for morning chores. She milked Buttercup,

Ellery's peaceful cow, a chore Crystal was becoming accustomed to far better than cooking.

By midmorning she could hardly keep from thinking about Ellery and was tempted to put on her bonnet and call on the Black Eagles. Yet if it were a difficult delivery and Ellery was busy, she did not want to get in the way. And she was loathe to have to talk to Travis Black Eagle, knowing he would be more on edge than ever.

Stepping outside, she picked up the bucket of water she had saved from the last washing and poured it on the pots of flowers on the porch. Usually caring for the bright yellow daisies and purple columbine lifted her spirits, but today she barely noticed them. She moved to the side of the porch to pour a gray stream on the pink primroses that bloomed beside the house.

When she finished watering the flowers, she looked down the wide street. At this end of town the houses were spread far apart. The Shaffers' had a white fence around their yard that was similar to the picket fence around Ellery's house to guard each family's vegetable gardens from roaming pigs and chickens. A few blocks up the street she could see the false-fronted buildings, the solid structure of the bank that had been built since the fire last year that had destroyed so much. For a while a log cabin on Thomas Avenue had been used as a jail for petty offenders. She knew the Black Eagle livery was on the other side of town, to the northwest, along the road to Fort D.A. Russell.

If she went searching for Ellery, she would have to ride farther than the livery, something she would not do. The Black Eagles had moved several miles west of town because Travis Black Eagle was raising cattle and horses now, along with his livery business.

"Get the Black Eagle's baby delivered and come home, Ellery," she said quietly, reminding herself it was foolish to worry over Ellery because he came and went as he pleased.

Hugging her waist even though the June sun was bearing down with a reassuring warmth, she walked around the house that was atop a hill and she could see the blue mass of mountains far in the distance. Her red calico dress swished around her legs, stirring the warm air.

Going back inside, she did her morning cleaning and then sat at the desk in the parlor to do bookkeeping. As she pulled out the straight-backed wooden chair, she glanced at Ellery's gunbelt hanging on a peg above the desk. She must remember to talk to Ellery. Law and order had come to Cheyenne, but there was still an outlaw element that appeared occasionally. The Union Pacific had created the town; and as long as gold was hauled by rail, there would be scoundrels willing to risk all to gain fortune by robbing the train.

Hoofbeats and voices approached the house. With relief sweeping over her, she pushed back her chair. Ellery was home. She rushed to the front door and swung it open, stepping onto the porch and stopping in shock while her heart began a thunderous pounding and her blood turned to ice.

Four men, including Sheriff Wade Hinckel, climbed down off their mounts, but it was the riderless roan led behind the last man and a travois pulled behind one of the horses that held her attention. A blanket-covered mound that looked like a body was strapped to the travois.

Her hand flew to her mouth as Sheriff Hinckel strode toward her. His blue eyes were filled with pity, and she felt her head spin.

"Judge Spencer, I'm sorry." He stroked his brown mustache nervously. "Your brother—" The sheriff clamped his lips closed and shifted his weight from one foot to the other as he paused at the foot of the porch steps. "Someone found Ellery on his way back to town. He's been shot. Ellery's dead."

"Ellery, I miss you. What will I do?" Crystal Spencer wiped her eyes as she ran her slender fingers over the rosewood piano. Aware she would never hear an answer from her brother again, remembering the bleak little funeral fourteen days ago, she shook her head.

Tears blurred her eyes and spilled down her cheeks, dropping unheeded onto her stiff black cotton dress. She moved restlessly around the small parlor that held, along with her piano and Ellery's desk, two overstuffed chairs, one marble-topped table and her glass-fronted bookshelves that held the precious English Common Law books, Blackstone's Commentaries, that had been passed from generation to generation.

On the desk, Ellery's papers were neatly stacked in the manner she kept them. On a peg beside the desk hung his gunbelt and revolver where they had been for the past month. As she looked at the revolver, she shuddered, rubbing her upper arms. If he had been wearing the gunbelt, would he have survived? Would he have defended himself against Travis Black Eagle, who had coldly killed him? It was like Pa all over again—standing defenseless while someone shot him.

She clenched her fists. Sheriff Hinckel had said it was robbery, a stranger who had ambushed, shot, and robbed Ellery. But Crystal thought differently. Travis Black Eagle had reason to hate Ellery, and Black Eagle looked capable of the temperament and strength to take someone's life in anger. She had heard about the death of Elizabeth Black Eagle. And Crystal had heard the whispers that came behind her back when she had been in the general store, that Ellery had been too befuddled with whiskey to tend Elizabeth and had let her bleed to death in childbirth.

"Oh, Ellery!" Crystal covered her face with her hands. Then she wiped angrily at her eyes and drew herself up. Crying never solved anything—she had learned that truth back on that disastrous day in Baltimore. Crying would not return Ellery to her or help in her dilemma. She needed to think clearly about her future.

For one more day she would not face the future. Tomorrow, she would have to make decisions. Today, she didn't want to think about her future. She was alone. Totally alone in the world. She had no one to go to, no relative to care about her. Not even a friend to help. Maybe she should have tried to make friends with Mrs. Shaffer or some of the town ladies, but she knew little about socializing. She needed Ellery badly.

Fear crowded in on her. Ellery's debts loomed like a hulking monster waiting to devour her. She had had no inkling of the enormity of what he owed. Her justice of the peace salary and her tiny savings for California might save the house, but it would take all her money and leave nothing for living or paying the men who had come by to tell her how much her brother owed them. Perhaps she could give music lessons. The thought nagged at her that she might have to sell her piano, and tears filled her eyes as she ran her hands over the smooth ivory keys.

She heard the clop of hoofbeats and paused to listen because the horse seemed to be approaching the house. Her first thought was Ellery. And then she remembered he would never come riding home again. With curiosity she wondered if someone were coming to call and could not possibly imagine who it would be unless it was Mr. Holder, the barber, who had buried Ellery.

Moving to the window, she gazed through the lace curtain, and her heart jumped as she watched the rider dismount. Travis Black Eagle! A black hat sat squarely on his head, and he wore his usual black clothing. His long legs ate up the ground as he stormed toward the house. His back was ramrod straight; his face was in shadow beneath his wide hat brim. Watching him stride toward the door, she felt threatened. He looked like the devil himself, coming to claim her soul.

Whirling around, she ran across the room to pick up Ellery's revolver. Her hands shook so badly she could not extract the heavy weapon from the holster. She had never held a revolver in her life, much less fired one.

The door crashed open, slamming back against the wall, rattling windowpanes. She screamed, shaking violently, trying desperately to hold the gun. The broad-shouldered silhouette in the doorway took her breath. As he stepped into the room, her heart thudded in her chest. His dark eyes were filled with fury, and he looked as if he wanted to wrap his hands around her throat and take her life.

"Stay there or I'll shoot," she stammered with the force of a frightened rabbit.

"Put that damn gun away before you do shoot me with it!" he snapped. He seemed to fill the small house as he kicked the door closed behind him and strode toward her.

"You killed my brother. Have you come to kill me?"

"No! I'm not going to kill you. Put down the gun."

"Get out of my house," she ordered, backing up until she bumped the desk. Her heart hammered against her rib cage.

"It isn't your house," he said flatly, and her head spun. How did the odious man know Ellery's business? *Her* business? Did the whole town know Ellery had mortgaged the small house?

The gun waved wildly, and her wrists ached holding it. She had no idea how to fire it. Why was Travis Black Eagle here? To kill her in a blind rage was the only answer she could come up with in spite of his denial.

"Give me that gun!" he snapped again, walking directly toward her.

"Stop or I'll shoot!"

"The hell you will." Facing the muzzle of her gun, he crossed the room.

Terrified, she closed her eyes and squeezed the trigger. There was a click. She opened her eyes to face him, feeling his anger beat over her in waves. Ellery's gun wasn't loaded!

Travis Black Eagle yanked the revolver from her hands, tossing it onto the desk. It landed on a stack of papers with a thump that was as loud as her heartbeat.

She wanted to fling her hands over her head, close her eyes, and sob, but she wasn't going to give him the satisfaction. Instead, she drew herself up and glared at him. Fear poured over her like ice water. The man was a fright. She knew he was a half-breed. There was always talk in town about his lineage. Now he looked wild and savage, as though the veneer of civilization had been ripped away.

His eyes were red with dark circles making shadowy smudges above his prominent cheekbones. Beneath a wide-brimmed black hat, his black hair hung down in a wild tangle, looking uncombed and unwashed. He was broad shouldered, a look of solid strength about him that made her shaking knees even weaker. Yet he had tossed the gun aside. For the first time, she saw he held a tiny bundle in one arm. Her gaze went back to his eyes that were the color of midnight, the devil's own fires raging in them.

"Let me give you some advice, Judge Spencer," he said in a quiet voice that was as sinister as his appearance. "An unloaded gun is about as much protection as a gnat's tooth. If you want to defend yourself, keep it loaded."

"What do you want?" Her voice was breathless and shaky.

"I'm here because I have a new baby to care for and I can't do it." He ground out the words as if he were in dreadful pain, and she felt a wrench of sympathy. "I need someone to care for him. This is your brother's fault, Judge."

"And you killed him for it!" The moment the words were out, she wondered if she had sealed her own fate. She wanted to scream at the man—and how she wished there were solid proof of his guilt so he would hang for his deed.

"I didn't kill your brother, but I damned well would have liked to," Travis Black Eagle said with chilling conviction. "I would've killed him if I could have, but he was dead long before I had a chance to go after him."

Startled, she almost believed him. Almost. He sounded full of regret that he hadn't been the one to do the horrible deed.

"Stop your swearing under my roof," she snapped perfunctorily, her thoughts tumbling in confusion. She couldn't follow the turn in the conversation, and the man still terrified her. There was no way to get past him to the front door to escape. "If you're not here to take my life, what did you come for?"

She wished her voice sounded firmer and she tried to hide her trembling hands in the folds of her black skirt.

He shuffled his feet and stared at her. He seemed at a loss for words, and she felt even more puzzled. "Why are you here?" she repeated.

"You're going to marry me and take care of my son."

Two

Stunned, Crystal stared at him, finally realizing her mouth had dropped open. The man's mind had snapped. Ellery had said men who experienced great tragedy sometimes began to imagine things.

Closing her mouth, she backed up a step and drew herself up. "I *what?*"

"You're going to marry me," Black Eagle repeated grimly as though he were announcing she was to pick up the gun and shoot him.

"I certainly will do no such thing!" she sputtered. He was raving, and she couldn't imagine how she could get him out of her house.

"While I don't like it either," he said firmly, "it seems the best solution to both our problems. You have nowhere to go, no family. You can't stay here alone."

"Of course I can!" she snapped, beginning to shake again, knowing what he said was the bald truth, yet hating to hear it.

"No, you can't." Moving a step closer, Black Eagle loomed over her like a giant. His bloodshot eyes looked as if he had missed sleep for weeks. His rage was palpable, assaulting her like flames leaping from a fire. "In the first place, this house doesn't belong to you. It belongs to the Cheyenne Territorial Bank and your brother is months behind on his payments."

"You needn't remind me," she replied stiffly, hating the man for reminding her of her predicament. "I was in hopes the bank would give me a little time." She felt hot and then cold. She had pushed aside worries while grief was uppermost, knowing she would soon have to face the dilemma she was left in by Ellery's demise. Now Travis Black Eagle was thrusting all her concerns in her face.

"In the second place," he continued, ignoring her reply, "you wouldn't survive a month here alone."

"Of course, I will. I am doing fine, and everyone has been courteous."

His derisive snort made her jump. "Why do you think your besotted brother always sobered up on Saturday nights and sat home with you?"

She blinked in uncertainty. It was on the tip of her tongue to retort that Ellery enjoyed her company, but she knew better than that. He shut himself into the back room and buried himself in his books. And he didn't always stay absolutely sober, but she wasn't about to reveal that to Travis Black Eagle.

"I'm sure he wanted to stay home," she said, knowing that wasn't the case, but unsure exactly *why* Ellery had spent every Saturday night at home.

"Damn, you don't even know," Travis Black Eagle muttered in disgust. "He wanted to make certain your virtue was protected. Saturday is the night the cowboys come to town and cut loose. Men come to Cheyenne to wait for the train and they have idle time on their hands. Our town is thriving, but it's the male population that's large. There are damned few women. You're not safe here alone on Saturday nights."

"Except for grief, I've been perfectly fine the past two weeks and haven't given a thought to being alone." The words sounded stiff and false.

"Townsfolk know you just lost your brother. The sheriff has warned men to leave you be, but it will last only so long and then life will return to normal. Strangers will come to town who don't know our sheriff or care. You know a woman can't stay out here alone."

"I'm safe," she said stubbornly.

"You weren't safe when Ellery was alive. How safe do you think you'll be on Saturday nights with your brother dead and gone and you here alone? How about when the next cattle drive pushes into town? How safe will you be then with the place overrun with rowdy cowmen?"

"As safe as I would be with you!" she snapped, yet a tingle of fear ran down her spine.

"You're safe with me. I don't want your body, Lord knows."

"Watch your language, sir! Don't be disrespectful of the Lord," she admonished him, feeling her cheeks flush. She knew men didn't want her body, but it was embarrassing to have it so emphatically announced by one. She couldn't imagine what kind of woman would be attracted to him. Her mind stopped abruptly because a sweeter, prettier woman than Elizabeth Black Eagle couldn't be found. Downright dazzlingly beautiful, so maybe that was what put a hint of agony in his voice. He had good reasons to be distraught just losing his wife in childbirth.

"You're not going to reform me," he said. "You damn sure couldn't reform your brother."

"I'm not going to try, Mr. Black Eagle," she replied, hoping her voice was growing stronger, "but my brother had the courtesy to refrain from foul language or taking the Lord's name in my presence."

"I don't have your brother's courtesy or his drunken ways." Black Eagle leaned closer. "I know I've startled you, but I'm desperate. And I know you soon will be. I'll get Preacher Nealy to marry us." Travis Black Eagle started to turn away.

"I won't marry you! And it's only your word that you didn't murder Ellery. Townspeople say you did."

Travis Black Eagle whirled around. "I didn't kill Ellery," Black Eagle snarled, his black eyes blazing into her with such fire that she tried to take another step backward. She pressed firmly against the desk, unable to put any more distance between her and Black Eagle.

"Ellery let my Elizabeth bleed to death because he was too blind drunk to do what he needed to do," Black Eagle said in a quiet voice that held such fury she shivered. "I wish I could bring Ellery back so I could send him to hell myself. And you're going to marry me. You don't have any choice. You can't stay here alone. You've made enemies with your fines and jail sentences. You don't have family. The bank will take the house. You don't have money to go anywhere."

"How do you know that?" she gasped, shocked, terrified that a man like Travis Black Eagle would know the full state of her affairs.

"Your brother talked. What money you came out with from the States, he drank up."

"There are other women in this town you can propose to," she reminded him in desperation, realizing the man meant what he was saying .

"The whores and Agnes Blair or Myrtle Hastings."

"There's Genny Branham, too. Marry one of them," Crystal implored, insulted by his foul language in her presence. How she detested this town and every man in it! Particularly the man standing before her.

"I gave it thought," he answered solemnly and, again, his voice carried the ring of truth. "The whores I know are drunk too much of the time to take responsibility for a baby. I've lost one person I loved to whiskey. I don't intend to lose the other person I love to it. Agnes Blair's father would not let her be courted by a half-breed. Myrtle Hastings and Genny Branham all have regular beaus. Louella Lee Anderson is thirteen. That's just too young, and her pa would never consent."

"There's Eloise Knudsen. She's a beautiful young woman and just the right age."

"You know women like the ones we've named won't marry a half-breed," he declared bitterly.

"No one would marry you, looking the way you do. You have to court the ladies, Mr. Black Eagle."

"I don't have the time or the inclination for courting." He ground out the words with anger. "The marrying ladies in town I might want either don't want a farrier or their fathers won't allow them to associate with a half-breed."

For just a moment he sounded so pained, she felt another stir of sympathy. It vanished as his dark brows drew together in a frown and he leveled another one of his piercing looks at her.

"No, Judge, you're it."

"I'm too old to be marriageable."

"Ma'am, I don't give a hang if you're older than Abraham. You're female. That's all I need."

"Get a mail-order bride like Mr. Holder did."

"Look what he got. She doesn't speak English; he doesn't know whether she even has good sense. She's a child. And it took him three months to get her here. I can't wait three months. You're going to marry me. You have no choice."

Shivering, Crystal knew the man was right, but he frightened her senseless. And he was incredibly insulting. Yet he knew whereof he spoke. She had no money to go anywhere, no way to escape Cheyenne and its inhabitants. But the thought of marriage to the forceful, powerful man standing in front of her turned her veins to ice water. "No. Marry one of the . . . the soiled doves. They can make you happy and I can't."

"You'll make me very happy if you care for my son. And I don't want your body. I'll go to one of the saloon women if I want pleasure. I swear with absolute honesty that there is no lust in my heart for you, Judge. This marriage will take care of my son and, in turn, marriage to me will give you a home and protection."

"I'm justice of the peace."

"I'm well aware of that, Your Honor," he drawled in an

insolent tone that lashed her with his contempt, and she remembered their courtroom confrontation that now seemed ages ago. "You can continue the job for the rest of your term. It takes you from home only one day a week."

"Your proposal is incredibly foolish," she argued, feeling as if she were mired in quicksand, slowly sinking into a morass that was closing over her shoulders and neck, sucking her down until she would be suffocated and cease to exist. "Suppose you fall in love with someone—"

"Elizabeth is the woman I love, the only woman I'll ever love," he said hoarsely, his voice losing all its anger. Such a look of pain came to his dark eyes that this time she couldn't fight back a wrench of sympathy. The man must have some warmth buried deep within him. It was obvious he had loved Elizabeth deeply. "I will never love again," he said with so much conviction, she knew that argument about his falling in love was futile.

"I do have money and I'm going to California," she exclaimed in desperation.

"Show me this money you have," he said, narrowing his eyes while her heart began to thud again because that was probably the first lie she had told since early childhood. "Ellery told me that you only have a little money saved and he had damned big debts."

"Stop swearing, Mr. Black Eagle," she ordered in a panic. Had Ellery told *every* secret? Had he told men about her life in Baltimore?

"So where is this money you have?"

Forgetting Baltimore, she felt her cheeks flame and hated to admit the truth as much as hating that she was caught up in a lie. "I don't have it," she admitted. "But I can try to earn it."

The bundle he held so easily in the crook of one arm began to move, and suddenly a wail came from the small shape. An arm appeared, flailing the air.

"Oh, Lord!" Travis Black Eagle looked stricken. She could understand why. She had never been around babies and she knew nothing about them. And the few times when she had been with church people at socials, when any of the babies had begun to cry, no one had ever put a child in her arms or her care. Never did new mothers pass their babies to her. She wrung her hands while she watched the flailing arms become more agitated.

"I'll get his bottle." Travis Black Eagle placed his son on the settee and raced outside.

Moving closer cautiously, she stared at the infant, whose red face was screwed up in anger, his little arms beating the air. How could something so tiny make such furious noise? she wondered.

Slamming the door behind him, Travis Black Eagle returned. The bang of the door made her jump, and she realized how tense she was. In long strides he crossed the room, scooping up the babe and thrusting a whiskey bottle at it.

"Mr. Black Eagle! Whiskey—"

"Keep your apron on, woman. It's cow's milk in this bottle. The bottle is a way to get milk down him. Spooning it in is the devil to do." The baby screamed, his little face turning a bright red while Travis struggled to try to get him to drink. The two seemed engaged in a strange wrestling match. The babe's tiny arms and legs waved while both of their faces turned deep red. "Here, Son," Travis Black Eagle muttered to no avail.

"For heaven's sake," Crystal said, her patience and nerves frayed. Impulsively, she stepped forward and took the baby and the bottle from him. Tucking the little fellow in her arm close against her body, she touched his cheek with the strange looking covering that resembled a bit of pigskin. The baby turned his head, his lips smacking, and then his rosebud mouth closed over the covering and he began to suck.

Silence descended and along with it came a greater feeling of accomplishment than Crystal had ever felt in her life, even more than she had after her sessions dispensing the law. For an instant she forgot Travis Black Eagle.

Tucking his blanket back around him, she watched the baby suck. As he drank, she tilted the whiskey bottle slightly, aware of the warm bundle pressed against her heart. She knew this fragile little person didn't know or care about her, yet, like flower petals in summer sunshine, something tight in Crystal's chest seemed to loosen and unfurl and warmth spread to her heart.

She looked up at Travis Black Eagle, who was studying her with those unfathomable dark eyes.

"I can't marry you," she repeated. "Marriage is impossible."

"No, it's not. You can't live here alone. No one else has proposed to you. You have no money to leave; as a matter of fact, your gambling brother left debts. I'll cover what he owed as part of our bargain."

She blinked and stared at Travis Black Eagle, unable to resist letting her gaze slip to the desk to the small pile of notes that men had given her, showing her the amounts Ellery owed them.

"You don't have that much money!" she blurted out, thinking the man was half savage. How could he earn enough to do all he was promising?

"I think I do. If I don't, I can get credit."

Travis Black Eagle was offering her survival—an answer to her nightmare of worries and debts. For the first time, she began to consider Black Eagle's offer. Amounts of money owed the bank and others in town spun in her head. The bleak possibility of selling her piano and belongings to raise money tormented her. She glanced down at the babe in her arms and tightened her arm slightly before looking up. She met Travis Black Eagle's gaze unflinchingly.

"My body is not part of the bargain?" she asked, feeling as though her face were on fire, hating that she had to deal with this man.

"Absolutely. I want a woman to take care of my son. That's all. I loved Elizabeth. I don't want a woman to fulfill wifely duties to me."

"You could pay me to be a housekeeper."

"No," he answered flatly. "I want a mother for my son."

Wanting to rub her eyes, Crystal wished she could wake up and find all this had been only a wild dream, but the man standing before her was as solid and real as the floor beneath her feet. She could feel her dreams of a life in California—living by the sea in a sunny land where flowers bloomed year round and finding some way to continue her fight to uphold justice—shredding, ripped to pieces by the determination of the man facing her.

The amounts Ellery owed danced in her mind along with the bleak truth that she could not repay them even if she sold her piano. Her four-year term as judge would be up in two more years, and if she lost the house and her possessions, she would never get the position again.

She stared into eyes as black and as unsettling as midnight. And she knew she had only one choice.

"Very well, it's the devil's own bargain, but I will marry you, Mr. Black Eagle."

Three

Travis tried to curb his impatience. He couldn't feel elation with her acceptance, only a faint relief. Far stronger was the urge to reach out and wring her scrawny neck. And he knew his anger was not actually with Judge Spencer, or Judge Spinster, as townspeople called her. His rage lay squarely with her drunken, irresponsible brother.

Travis stared at her, looking at his son and then raising his gaze to hers again. "I've startled you with this proposal; but if you give it thought, you'll see that it's the best solution for both of us."

She stared at him with her huge green eyes for a long moment, and then she returned her attention to his son.

Travis knew many of the people in town shunned him because of his Indian blood. He had everyone's business, but he was never asked to socialize with a growing element in the town. He did not know whether Judge Spencer disliked him for his heritage or simply because she seemed to dislike the entire male population of Cheyenne. Nor was she particularly friendly with the females. Ellery had worried about his unsocial sister who, had she unbent even a fraction, would have had proposals regularly.

Women were incredibly scarce in the Territory, and they could pick and choose a man—usually. Judge Spencer kept a wall around herself that no one bridged except her brother. Yet she would do for his purposes, Travis reminded himself. He looked at her holding his son and momentarily felt better. The infant was tucked against her, sucking happily at the improvised bottle of nourishment. Judge Spencer had some womanly ways after all. She seemed to take to his son naturally, and the sight of the two of them in harmony helped soothe Travis's frayed nerves.

Trying to give her time to think, he waited and mulled over their conversation. He saw no choice except what he proposed. God knows, if there had been another choice, he would have taken it. No, this was right, he reassured himself.

And thank heaven her brother had talked when he was soused. Ellery Spencer had talked openly about his debts and mortgages and love for gambling. He had told too much about his spinster sister and his worries over her welfare. Keeping silent, Travis shifted impatiently, letting her think about his proposal. It was the only solution for both of them. He was certain marriage was as odious to her as to him, yet they should be able to make a union workable.

He glanced around the parlor and noticed it looked tidy and pleasant. And that was good enough for him. Lord knows, he cared little about his surroundings. His gaze fell on the gavel on the desk and he remembered her appointment by the governor as justice of the peace; he felt a faint stir of apprehension. Everyone knew the woman had no tolerance for anyone outside the law. He shrugged away the thought. The past was no concern now.

Trying to give her time to think, as well as feed his son, Travis moved to the window to stare outside. With Judge Spinster's acceptance of his proposal, what was a concern now was his Comanche blood.

Elizabeth had never cared, yet he had been determined to

build a life for her that would earn the respect of others so Elizabeth would never be shunned. And now he had to do the same for his son. He turned around to study Judge Spinster. He didn't know her given name. Ellery referred to her as Sister as if that were her name. Travis's gaze raked over her while she shifted his son in her arms. Her red hair was pulled tightly into a bun behind her head; a few wispy tendrils escaped and curled around her face. The plain black dress was no enhancement to her pale skin, and a faint smattering of freckles dotted her nose. She was a tall woman, scrawny with somewhat of a bosom. Her appearance was of no consequence. He turned to stare outside again, telling himself this was the only solution.

Waiting another few minutes, Travis Black Eagle turned to look at her. "I've given you a little time to think about my proposal. You still agree to accept?"

While she stared at him, the silence between them lengthened. A slight frown creased her brow, and she looked angry and frightened at the same time. He felt a rising panic that she was going to say she had changed her mind. Her lips thinned, and she drew herself up.

"There's one thing. I want to go to California. It's a dream I've had."

"You can't go now anyway because of your debts here—and you're not the type to leave them unpaid," he drawled. He stood in silence, mulling this new obstacle in his path. "Marry me and when my son is old enough, thirteen, I'll pay your way to California and you'll be free to go."

Her eyes widened and she blinked and he could see she liked the idea. Thirteen years sounded as far away as one hundred to him, but by that time he could deal with his son without her help. By that time, his son should be working beside him every day. Maybe she came to the same conclusion because she nodded her agreement.

Relieved, he squared his hat on his head. "I'll get Preacher Nealy. He said the words over your brother for the burial so I assume he'll be acceptable to marry us. I already have a license because I knew I would marry within the next few days. We just need to fill in your name.''

"Reverend Nealy will be fine," she answered.

"I've asked in town, but I want to know absolutely—do you drink like your brother did? I want the truth.''

His eyes pierced her like knives, and Crystal felt as if he had reached out and wrapped his hands around her throat while he waited for his answer.

"I have *never* touched whiskey, sir!" she replied, outraged. "Nor will I ever.''

He shrugged. "I don't insist you be that strict about it, Judge. A drink or two now and then can pass your lips without disaster. I'll go now." He crossed the room toward the hall.

"Mr. Black Eagle.''

Crystal's heart pounded in fear as he swung around. "I have some requests. I brought my books and my piano and my bookcase with me from Baltimore. Those items were not mortgaged to the bank. I want my things moved to your place and, particularly, I want my piano moved without scratching it.''

"Yes, ma'am, but my boy's not growing up playing a piano. He's going to work alongside me.''

She bristled. "It wouldn't hurt you to have a little culture in your background," she snapped, aware she had no idea what kind of background the man had.

"We're out West, where it's important just to survive," he answered flatly, but his face flushed. "Culture doesn't put food on the table or protect a man from lead.''

She didn't care to argue with him, thinking of a verse that said not to cast pearls before swine. Something else was bothering her and she was uncertain how to put it into words. "You said we won't—" She felt fire rising in her cheeks and she couldn't get out the words, but she wanted absolute reassurance from him about the physical part of their agreement.

"No, we won't," he stated bluntly, as if he could discern her thoughts before she spoke. "I don't want your body.''

She should have felt relief, but the words hurt. No man had

ever wanted her, and she should be enormously thankful this one didn't.

He placed his hand on his hip and studied her and her stomach knotted as she wondered what he was getting ready to announce.

"I have a small house," he said in a determined tone of voice, "so we have to sleep in the same bed because I can't work all day and sleep on the floor at night, but I won't touch you."

In the same bed! She felt her cheeks burn as she stared at him. She could not imagine being in the same bed with the man standing only yards from her. Ellery had been six feet tall. Travis Black Eagle looked a good three or four inches taller than that. His shoulders were broad, his skin dark, but it was the male aura about him that was so different from her brother. Ellery had moved about the house quietly, drinking and working soundlessly. He seldom talked, and they had spent hours without a word passing between them. When he shut himself in his office, she often forgot he was home.

From her brief encounters with Travis Black Eagle, she already knew he was a man who banged doors and rattled doorknobs and spoke forcefully. She knew she would be aware of him, intensely aware of him, every second he was within a quarter of a mile of her, much less shut up together in a tiny house. In the same bedroom, in the same *bed*, she could not even imagine.

"I have a bed!"

One black eyebrow arched in a sardonic manner. "Did you bring the bed with you from Baltimore?"

"No," she answered, flushing, knowing why he was asking.

"Then I believe that bed belongs to the bank."

She clamped her jaw tightly closed. Knowing it was useless to argue, she decided she would worry about the bed when they got to his place.

His gaze swept the room. "I've talked with Sherman Knudsen at the bank. This house and all of Ellery's belongings are mortgaged. Your brother might have mortgaged your piano."

She had never thought of that possibility. Shaken, she glanced at her beloved piano that she had struggled so hard to transport to Cheyenne.

"I'll see about it. If it isn't mortgaged, I'll move it," Black Eagle said.

She nodded, and he strode to the door. Now that his piercing dark brown eyes weren't stabbing into her, she took a long look at her husband-to-be. His black shirt that was worn thin at the elbows pulled across his shoulders and was tucked into a narrow waist. A gunbelt wrapped around his hips, the butt of a big revolver showing. Black denim pants rode low on his slim hips and covered long legs, the frayed pants ending above worn black boot heels. With each step, his boots scraped the bare plank floor.

"Mr. Black Eagle." He turned again. She looked down at the baby. "What's your son's name?"

There was a moment of silence, and she glanced up to see Travis Black Eagle's brow furrowed. "I haven't named him. Elizabeth wanted to wait to pick out a name and then she didn't get to. I just call him Son."

"I don't know one thing about babies."

"It looks to me that you're doing fine," he said flatly and turned to leave, slamming the door behind him, but not as hard as before.

Still in shock, Crystal walked to the window to peep through the lace curtain. He slipped his foot into a stirrup and swung his long leg over the saddle, settling with ease, turning his bay toward town. Frightened, she looked at Travis Black Eagle's broad shoulders and long, muscled body.

"Oh, Ellery, what did you get me into? Why did you have to drink so much?" she whispered. And suppose she was marrying Ellery's killer?

Regret swamped her. She knew she had little choice about accepting the proposal, but suppose Travis Black Eagle was the man who had killed Ellery? Suppose Black Eagle had a violent temper, violent enough to kill? He looked quite capable of it, and his rage this morning had been frightening.

A warm wetness spread over her arm, jerking her thoughts back to the infant. Startled, she looked down at him. His eyes were closed, long dark lashes feathering over his rosy cheeks while he sucked happily at the bottle.

"My goodness!" She held him away from her and was appalled to see her dress as well as the blanket the baby was wrapped in were soaked. "Great heavens, we have to do something about you."

She looked around helplessly. Clamping her jaw closed, she hurried to her bedroom and placed the baby on the bed, taking the bottle from him. He kept sucking while she undressed him. Beneath the knitted blanket he was wrapped in a man's shirt, and as she undid the shirt, she found a scrap of a sheet folded over and over around his tiny hips and bottom.

"You poor thing."

Big dark eyes stared up at her solemnly, and then his fist touched his cheek and he turned his head to suck on his fist.

"Let me wrap you in something dry and change my clothes and I'll give you the rest of your bottle."

She tossed his wet garments and blanket in a heap, going to the kitchen to get a towel made from flour sacking. She hurried back to fold it into several thicknesses. Then she wrapped it around his tiny bottom and secured it with pins. To her dismay, when she picked him up, it fell off.

"Oh, my!" Crystal placed him on the bed and began again. After four tries, she wiped her brow and stared at him in consternation. There had to be a way to keep him wrapped. How could such a tiny little person be so noisy and difficult to deal with?

She bent over him and tried again, securing the cloth in place. She held him up and with great relief and a surge of satisfaction she saw the cloth remained secure around his tiny bottom.

"There!" she exclaimed, placing him on the bed. "Now, let me change quickly and then I'll give you your milk."

As if in protest, his face screwed up again and he began to scream, his legs and arms waving in the air. She rushed to change her damp clothing, talking to him, uselessly trying to cajole him while she dressed. As she fastened the buttons to her only other black dress, a high-necked, long-sleeved garment, she glanced at herself in the mirror.

Tendrils of red hair had come loose from her bun. She pushed them in place and thrust a few more pins into her hair. She remembered Elizabeth Black Eagle's big blue eyes and golden hair and rosy cheeks as she looked at her own image that was quite plain. Well, the man was not marrying her because of her looks or her body. She raised her chin and turned to get the squalling baby.

In minutes she was seated on the straight chair in the parlor, singing softly while she held the baby in her arms. As she studied him, gazing down into his deep brown eyes, she wondered what change her life would take.

Panic swept over her at the thought of living constantly with a man like Travis Black Eagle. As her sense of desperation grew, she considered running away. She could grab a few clothes and the little money she had hidden beneath the horse-hair mattress, take the horse, and go. Black Eagle wouldn't come after her. The bank would take the house . . . her piano. She loved the piano—her tie to childhood and a blessed time. The tall rosewood piano symbolized the solid things in life, the order she believed in, the quiet home she had known as a girl in Baltimore. She would have to leave behind her job as justice. Cheyenne's first woman justice ever. She had a duty to help bring law and order to Cheyenne. She would not run like a renegade.

Oh, Ellery, if you just hadn't gambled! If you had taken payment for your doctoring, we could have gone to California and had a fine life. A fine life. Abruptly she changed her thoughts, knowing the futility of such wishes. She looked down.

The baby's round face was beautiful, with a tiny button nose, thick black lashes, creamy skin, and rosy cheeks. He had his father's black hair and his mother's curls. Marveling at this tiny person in her arms, Crystal touched his head. As she curled black locks of his hair around her finger, she saw his pulse beating in the top of his head. An aching void in Crystal, a part of her that she had kept shut away for years, began to fill with warm feelings for the tiny infant. "Sweet, sweet baby," she whispered.

A pang of sadness stung as Crystal thought about Elizabeth Black Eagle. Ellery should have sobered up and taken care of the young mother so she could have known and enjoyed her little babe. Crystal raised her head and looked at the wide dusty road. How long before Travis Black Eagle returned? Was she absolutely certain she couldn't do anything except marry him? This would be her last chance to run.

Two blocks away, Travis Black Eagle rode along one of the main streets of Cheyenne. Houses became numerous and then false-fronted buildings were interspersed with more recent, solid structures. Laid out like a grid, Cheyenne had sprung up overnight with word that the Union Pacific would make the town a terminal. He had heard of the wild early days, the town that had mushroomed to four-thousand population with saloons and bawdy houses and a wild lawlessness. And then after the train had come through and tracks were built beyond Cheyenne, the wild element had moved on to the next new town. The population dropped and life was less unruly. Now, Travis knew, Cheyenne's population was less than half of what it had been before. Streets were named for the engineers, retired Union officers who had laid out the railroad.

A breeze tugged at his hat brim. He liked it out West. Men didn't ask questions. They left their past lives behind and could start anew.

He rode past the Golden Bear, a two-story saloon and sporting house with upstairs rooms where two of the town's most favored soiled doves, Delilah and Fancy, plied their trade.

Feeling the warmth of June sunshine on his shoulders, Travis spotted Delilah sitting on an empty whiskey barrel in front of the Golden Bear Saloon. His gaze traveled up over her trim ankles. Her thin, blue cotton dress clung to her long legs and strained over an ample bosom that threatened to spill out of the low-cut gown. Regret filled him because she would warm a man's bed nicely. His gaze rose higher to the thin cheroot between the fingers of one of her hands and the whiskey bottle in the other hand, and his regret changed to certain knowledge he had done the right thing.

Judge Spencer was plain and tall, a gaunt, dried-up old spinster without any feminine appeal and unbending in her enforcement of the law, but she was better educated than most women in the territory. Ellery had told Travis about his sister's two years at Mount Olive of Maryland Normal College for Women. With her drab black dress and her hair pulled tightly to the back of her head and rolled into a wad, the judge looked as if she could be anywhere from twenty-eight to thirty-eight. He was twenty-eight. Her age did not matter; he was marrying her for other reasons. And she had damned little choice. At least she had some backbone, holding a gun on him. He had not expected her to pull the trigger. Next time he would remember not to be so foolhardy—and he would remember not to leave a loaded revolver lying around.

He had scared her, but in spite of her fear she had stood up to him and Travis felt a little better about her bravery. Educated and brave—that was preferable to what he'd find at the Golden Bear. Delilah and Fancy were a mile prettier, eager and willing in bed, but there it ended. Right now the thought of bed with any woman besides Elizabeth made him feel sick inside with longing.

He shifted his thoughts back to Delilah and Fancy. The whores had no more education than he did, and if he had stormed in on either one of them as he had Judge Spencer this morning, they would have capitulated at once. Brains and bravery were more important to him for the mother of his child than carnal delights.

He caught Delilah's eye. Usually she flashed him a big smile, in spite of knowing he wouldn't stray from home after he married Elizabeth. This morning, however, she was staring at him with a peculiar, speculative look. Then he realized why. She thought he had murdered Ellery Spencer. According to Judge Spencer, most of Cheyenne thought he had murdered her brother. At least Sheriff Hinckel didn't think he had, declaring that Ellery had been ambushed, robbed, and murdered.

Even if people thought he had murdered Ellery, would anyone blame him? They would all know Ellery had been drinking and his neglect had caused Elizabeth's death.

Travis had intended to ride straight to find the preacher, but curiosity got the better of him and he halted at the hitching rail in front of the quiet saloon. "Good morning, Delilah."

"Mornin' to you, Travis. I'm sorry to hear about Mrs. Black Eagle. But I heard you have a fine new son."

"That I do and I thank you for your condolences." As he dismounted, Delilah held out the bottle. Wordlessly, he accepted it, tilted it up, and took a long drink, handing the bottle back to her and wiping his mouth with the back of his hand. The liquor burned a fiery trail down his throat. He wished he could drink himself into oblivion, but the mere thought of whiskey brought back memories of Ellery and Travis was loathe to take another drink.

"I didn't kill Doc Spencer."

"Everyone thinks you did," she said. "No one blames you. That Injun that works for you came to town to get Preacher Nealy. Turtle River said the doc neglected your wife and she bled to death."

Travis winced, hating to hear the words said aloud, feeling pain cut into his chest like a saber plunging into him. "That's right." He leaned down, tilting Delilah's face up with his finger beneath her chin, taking one long last look before he totally committed himself to old Judge Spinster. Now he couldn't even remember what color hair the judge had. She had big eyes; he had noticed that much. Big green eyes that looked like a terrified deer facing a wolf.

Delilah's whiskey breath hit him and she blinked drunkenly, smiling at him. A few teeth were missing, leaving dark gaps between her yellowed teeth.

He leaned closer. "I didn't kill the doc. If I had gotten the chance, I would have, but I buried Elizabeth and took care of our new son and by the time I was ready to go after Doc, Turtle River told me that Doc was dead. Said he was shot and robbed going home on the trail after he left my place. I wish I had been the one. He deserved a shot right in his irresponsible heart!"

Delilah blinked rapidly and licked her lips. "I think I almost believe you. 'Cept there was no one else hated Doc enough to shoot him. You had reason."

"I told you, he was also robbed. There's a reason."

"Sure 'nuff is," she agreed solemnly and then burped.

Travis removed his hand from her chin and looked around. Two men stood in front of the general store talking to the owner, Clem Mandeville. All three men were watching Travis. Two were cowboys and friendly enough to him. And Clem was one who saw no barrier of race either, viewing anybody who could breathe as a potential customer for his store. Travis looped the reins over the hitching rail and turned toward the store. "See you later, Delilah."

"Anytime, Travis. You're good anytime. Now I'll be seeing more of you."

When hell freezes over, he thought, and then felt another stab of pain so swift and intense it almost doubled him over. His instant reaction to her remark was denial because he was married. Only he wasn't married any longer. Elizabeth was gone forever, but it was incredibly hard to accept. He clamped his jaw closed and strode toward the store. The men shifted. Thrusting out his hand, blond Tom Yiblonski gave him a nod.

Tom had immigrated to the States only three years earlier and held no prejudice about the color of a man's skin. Logan North stared at him as he shook hands, and Clem smiled. "Morning, Travis," Clem said.

"Good morning," Travis replied, shaking hands with all three of them. "I might as well still some rumors as much as I can. I didn't kill Doc Spencer. I wanted to, but someone beat me to it."

"Heard there have been robberies in the area. Maybe someone waylaid him," Logan suggested, as if that ended the matter.

"I wish it had been me," Travis said. "If I'd had a chance, I would have done the deed for his neglect of Elizabeth."

"Sorry, Travis, about Elizabeth," Clem said, and the other men chimed in with the same words.

"Thank you," Travis answered quietly, knowing nothing would stop the pain he felt.

"Hear you have a son now."

"That I do and he's a fine one. I'm amazed you haven't heard him crying."

They chuckled, but then Clem sobered. "Are you going to keep a baby at the stable with you?"

"No. I can't do that."

"You and Andrew gonna take turns keeping the little fella? Or will Turtle River take care of him?"

Travis shook his head and realized he might as well tell them his plans because the news would be all over town before sundown.

"I intend to marry."

"You should," Tom said. "Tyke needs a ma."

"You'll be better off as well as the babe," Clem added with a nod. "Are you going to send off for a mail-order bride like Elmer did?"

"Lordy, I hope you get something better!" Logan rubbed his black beard with a grimy hand. "And one that speaks the same language you do."

"This man doesn't need to get a mail-order bride," Tom

drawled dryly. He shifted his booted feet and spat a stream of tobacco juice into the street. "There are some nice-looking women in Cheyenne now. Marrying age. Look at—"

"It's a bit soon for me to marry," Travis interrupted," but I have a baby to care for and I can't handle him alone. I need a wife now."

"Sure you do," Clem said earnestly while the other two nodded. "No one out here waits a year in mourning. A month, two months, that's plenty long."

"I can't wait that long. I swear there's no disrespect for my Elizabeth. I'm marrying today," Travis said. The words were difficult to pronounce; his throat felt as if it were coated in sand. All three men were staring at him, Tom and Clem both with open mouths.

"Gawdamighty, *today?*" Logan asked.

"That's right. I need someone to take care of my boy and I can't wait."

"Where'll you find someone to marry today? I'll bet it's pretty Miss Hastings," Clem speculated.

"No, it's not. As a—"

"Lord-a-mercy, you're gonna take Delilah or Fancy from us!" Tom snapped before Travis could answer Clem's question. "Hold on. Maybe we could work something out where you could bring the little tyke into town and the girls could look after him all day, sort of take turns."

"You can't take Delilah or Fancy. They're the best Cheyenne has," Logan added swiftly, none of them giving Travis a chance to speak. "Try Miss Knudsen or Miss Branham. They're marrying age and as pretty as a new filly."

"Lordy, don't take one of the sunshine girls," Clem said.

"I'm not about to," Travis said forcefully. "Look at Delilah." He jerked his head in her direction. "Do you think she's sober enough to care for a baby? Whiskey is what killed Elizabeth. That drunken fool Spencer let her bleed to death!" Travis snapped, his fists clenching as he fought a wave of emotion that tightened his throat. He locked his jaw closed tightly while the men shuffled their feet and looked away.

"Maybe some of us that work in town could look after the tyke during the night, and the girls—maybe one of them could stay sober—during the day," Clem suggested.

"Maybe you could get Elmer's wife, pay her, to look after him during the day."

"In the first place, I don't think Caterina has the capabilities. Elmer's looking after *her*. She must be thirteen years old herself. I don't trust Fancy or Delilah to care for a baby. Eloise Knudsen is the banker's daughter. He wouldn't allow me to court her."

"Well, who is the woman then?" Logan asked in an exasperated tone. "Who are you marrying?" All three men focused on him.

Why did he dread announcing his intended bride? Travis wondered as he forced the words out. "I'm marrying Judge Spencer."

Once again Clem and Tom stared at him openmouthed. A grin split Logan's face as he let out a guffaw and slapped his thigh. Travis's gaze swung to him, and he bit off the smile instantly, his laughter ending.

"You can't!" Clem said, glancing down the street. "Judge Spinster?"

"That dried-up old maid. She'll be like marrying a post," Logan said.

"Although Rupe Peters in a drunken fit last night said he might propose to her, he hasn't mentioned it since he sobered," Tom added. "Lordy, that woman won't give an inch when she thinks she's right."

"Cheyenne's got women. You should be able to find someone besides that old spinster," Clem remarked.

Travis shook his head, depression filling him. "No. I'm marrying her and I'm going to get the preacher and do it now so she can take care of my son."

"Has she agreed to this?" Clem persisted.

"Yes, she has. She doesn't have much choice either. Since her brother's death, she's all alone."

"Judge Spinster," Logan said quietly. "Imagine that. Never would have guessed she would snag a husband even as likely as it should be out here. Ellery said he knew she would be a spinster and live with him for all their lives."

"It's impossible to predict our tomorrows," Travis said glumly, hurting and knowing he needed to get the deed done. "I'll see you boys later." Travis turned to walk away.

"Good luck, Travis," Clem called after him quietly.

"Yeah, good luck," the other two chorused.

Travis gave a wave of his hand in acknowledgment, striding along the wide boardwalk. He moved into another block, passing the glass windows of the bank. A buggy slowed to a halt in front and a man in a black suit with leather gloves stepped down. Tall with thick black hair and a full black beard, Sherman Knudsen glanced at Travis and nodded curtly.

"Morning, Mr. Knudsen," Travis said.

Staring straight ahead, Knudsen strode into the bank.

Travis looked through the window at the man, knowing that when Knudsen's horses were ill or needed shoeing, he would talk and greet Travis cheerfully. Or when Travis came to the bank to deposit his money. Travis thought about Knudsen's daughter. Eloise was black-haired and, with the exception of Elizabeth, the most beautiful woman in Cheyenne. Eloise had been educated one year back East, and she was more than happy to talk to him—or she had been until he'd married Elizabeth. She would never be allowed to marry him, Travis knew. And he also knew she was not the woman he needed. He couldn't give a woman his heart again. It had been buried with Elizabeth. The judge would never expect love and would never be disappointed. And a woman like Eloise Knudsen deserved a man who adored her just as he had adored his Elizabeth.

Clamping his jaw shut, he tightened his fist. Determination filled him to succeed, to establish himself in the town so that

men like Sherman Knudsen would speak to him. One thing—
Sherman Knudsen was bound to respect the judge.

Travis strode past a dry goods store, the land office, and
the courthouse that held the sheriff's office, Judge Spinster's
courtroom, and the jail. Along the outside wall of the courthouse
wanted posters of outlaws fluttered gently in the breeze, and
Travis scanned them. He kept his features impassive, looking
away as he strode past the building. He headed toward Church
Corner, nicknamed that by the locals because a church stood
on each of three corners.

Four

A white spire thrust toward the deep-blue sky and the branches of newly planted aspens framed Reverend Nealy's church. Travis felt a twist of impatience. He wanted this done and over. His heart was leaden, and he wondered if life would ever seem right again. Swallowing hard, he forced his thoughts from Elizabeth to Judge Spencer and their son. For his son's sake, Travis swore silently that he would build a life for the three of them.

He found the short, muscular minister chopping wood behind the church. His curly red hair made a fiery halo around his head.

"Preacher."

"Ah, Mr. Black Eagle." He lowered the axe, wiping his brow. His shirt sleeves were rolled high; his collar was gone. He gazed up at Travis with curiosity in his blue eyes. "How are ye and the babe faring?"

"Not too well."

"Sorry to hear that."

"Want some help?"

"Aye, that would be good now," the minister said, stepping back and handing the axe to Travis.

Wrapping his fingers around the worn wooden handle, Travis hoisted the blade high and brought it down, splitting a log. Travis worked in silence while Nealy moved to the pump to wash his face and then to take a long drink of water. The chopping was a release for Travis's pent-up anger, and he momentarily forgot his purpose as he let his body settle into a rhythm of swinging the axe. When he was ready to stop, he slammed the blade into a log and straightened to look at the minister.

"There's a few more logs for you that you won't have to cut yourself."

"Thank ye." He received a grin as the preacher sat on a stump and waited patiently.

"I want you to come with me now if you will. I want to marry. I need a woman to care for my baby."

Preacher Nealy's brows arched. "Isn't this rather sudden?"

Travis took a deep breath. "No more sudden than Elizabeth's death."

"I suppose," the stocky minister replied. He rubbed his jaw as he stood up. "This is a harsh land and it makes harsh demands on us. The land also holds large rewards for us. Let us hope this union ye're about to enter will hold rewards for ye and yer intended."

"My son is the one who should benefit."

"Aye. 'Tis a good thing. And this woman who has agreed to this union—she must love the little tyke?"

"It's Judge Spencer," Travis said, falling into step beside the minister as they started toward a shed. The minister stopped and turned to stare at Travis.

"Judge Spencer?" The preacher's sandy brows arched.

"That's right." Travis felt a twinge of impatience. Was he going to have to explain this union to every man in town?

"Judge Spencer is older and beyond marrying age. She has

shown no particular fondness for children. This is a decision made in haste, Son.''

"I know what I need. I have damned few choices, sir.''

Blue eyes studied Travis, and Travis gazed back without flinching. He had been over and over this in his mind and he knew she was the only choice not just in town, but for miles around in the Territory.

"Maybe ye should reconsider.''

Travis's stomach fluttered as he shook his head. "No. I know what I'm doing, and she'll be a fine wife.''

"I would give this thought.''

"You wouldn't if you had a baby screaming for care,'' Travis retorted. "I need a woman and there aren't many in the Territory who aren't already taken.''

"Unfortunately, that's true. Very well. You know what you want to do. I should wash my hands and face and change shirts and then we'll go.''

Travis nodded, taking little offense at the minister's frank comments. Preacher Nealy always spoke his mind. A reason, Travis decided, the man might be settled in a frontier town where people often accepted behavior they might not back in the States.

Ten minutes later, he walked down the street with Reverend Nealy beside him. Perfunctorily, he continued to argue with the preacher about marrying Judge Spencer without waiting several weeks. Travis's thoughts drifted as the minister talked about the vows of matrimony being forever binding and Travis should give more thought to what he was doing. The only person who had known about his plans and had not tried to talk him out of them had been Turtle River. When he had told the Cheyenne, Turtle River had remained silent and looked beyond him as if he were having one of his visions. Travis had become accustomed to Turtle River's silences, so Travis had waited without talking. Turtle River's gaze had returned to Travis and Turtle River had nodded.

"It is a good thing,'' he had said in a tone indicating that was the only comment on the matter that Travis would get. Either Turtle River approved of Judge Spencer or he approved of Travis's need for a woman to care for the babe or he felt marrying the judge sufficient revenge for Doc Spencer's carelessness.

As they approached the store, Clem was no longer in sight, but the other two men still stood talking.

"We'll need witnesses," the reverend remarked.

"Tom, Logan, come be witnesses to the wedding," Travis called. "I'll get my horse and join you," he added to the preacher and strode toward the sporting house. While the men fell into step, Delilah watched as Travis approached.

"Who's getting married?" she asked, studying him with narrowed eyes.

"I'm marrying Judge Spencer, Delilah. I need someone to take care of my son."

Delilah nodded solemnly. "That's a good thing. Miss Spencer is all right."

He was surprised that Delilah would approve of Judge Spencer. He was certain the opposite would not be true.

"She's a real lady," Delilah said with a wistful note coming into her voice.

"Yeah," Travis answered, wondering how much Delilah would consider the judge a real lady if she knew Judge Spencer had tried to shoot him this morning.

"You're marrying today?"

"Yes. Reverend Nealy's going to marry us."

She shrugged. "Too bad it's so soon. Since you're between wives, you could have come up for a little fun. It's been a long time," she said, running her tongue across her upper lip, her voice becoming coy.

For just an instant Travis wished he could drink himself beyond thought and go upstairs and bury himself in Delilah's soft body and her loving arms. He glanced at the waiting men and then stepped closer to Delilah, tilting her chin up again.

"Someday, Delilah. I'm not marrying Judge Spencer because I'm in love with her."

"Yeah, Travis," she said, lapsing into more familiar terms with him. "But I know you men of honor. Once you're married—"

"Not this time," he said, feeling the hurt come. He straightened up. "There isn't a shred of love this time. And she knows how it is, so honor doesn't even come into it. This is a bargain between us."

"She's damn lucky," Delilah said solemnly.

"I'll be back." He turned and led his horse, falling into step next to the Reverend Nealy again.

"Thank heaven you're not taking Delilah or Fancy," Logan said with feeling. "Don't know what we'd do without the two of 'em."

As Travis and the other men approached the small white house, Travis wondered how Miss Spencer had fared with his son. The little fellow had a mind of his own and he could set up a fearsome howl when he was not satisfied.

They reached the end of the street. Travis looked at the simple house made from the wood of packing boxes. Sunlight brightly reflected off the flattened tin cans that shingled the roof. Travis knew from Ellery's talking that the place had only one bedroom. A little over a year ago after the death of their only other relative, their grandfather, Judge Spinster had come West to join her brother. Ellery had given her the bedroom and moved himself into the small room that was his office.

Two pots of flowers bloomed on the porch, one filled with delicate lavender columbine, the other with bright yellow daisies. A riot of primroses peeked over the edge of one end of the porch. Although little more than a shack, the house looked tidy and welcoming. He was certain it was Miss Spencer's touch and not her brother's. If she wanted, he would move her flowers along with her other things. A piano . . . about as useful out here as toenails on a snake.

In silence the men walked to the hitching rail, and Travis

looped the bay's reins around the rail. Reverend Nealy turned to him, his eyes filled with unspoken questions. Wind ruffled his curly hair as he studied Travis, who gazed back at him steadily. "I think ye should reconsider what ye are about to do."

"I know what I'm doing," Travis said quietly, aware that he had not convinced Reverend Nealy of the need of this union. "She can take care of my baby. I need her; and she has no one now with Ellery gone, so she needs me," he insisted again.

Reverend Nealy shrugged.

Logan scratched his chin as he stood beside them. "Too damn few good women out here. That's the drawback. Man has a chance to build something, to make something of hisself, but it's damned lonesome without women. Delilah and Fancy are good company, but sometimes they're not enough. And it ain't the same when you share them with every man here."

"No, it sure as hell isn't," Travis said. "Pardon me, Reverend."

"Well, if yer mind's set this is what ye want to do, let's begin," Reverend Nealy said, turning toward the front porch. He glanced at the two witnesses. "C'mon, boys."

"Hey, Travis," Logan said softly and Travis turned. "You can still back out."

"No. I know what I'm doing," he answered grimly, thinking about the hellish past two weeks when he hadn't known how to take care of his son and he'd had to bury Elizabeth and deal with his grief. He strode across the porch and knocked on the door.

"Come in," came a lilting voice from the other side of the door. How he wished that voice belonged to one of the women he had known in his lifetime! He opened the door and paused, feeling momentarily better than he had all morning.

Holding his son in her arms, Judge Spencer was rocking her body and his baby back and forth on a straight-backed chair. The baby was asleep again, looking angelic, and the judge looked as if she had handled babies all her life.

"Judge Spencer, I brought Reverend Nealy to marry us," Travis said.

"Good morning, Judge Spencer," Reverend Nealy said politely, doffing his hat. "Logan and Tom are here as witnesses." As Travis closed the door, she rose to her feet as gracefully as if she didn't have her arms filled with a sleeping infant.

"Good morning, Mr. Nealy, Mr. Yiblonski, Mr. North."

As soon as greetings were said, the men viewed Travis's tiny son. "Little fellow," Tom said.

"He's already grown a bit since I last saw him," stated the reverend. The men shifted their feet and gazed out the window while an uneasy silence fell.

"Let's get on with it, Reverend Nealy," Travis said, tossing his black hat on the settee.

"Very well. If ye two will stand in front of me."

Crystal held the sleeping baby and stood where Reverend Nealy directed. Her palms were wet and perspiration dotted her brow. Hurtful memories of another time in Baltimore plagued her, and she tried to close her mind to the bleak past and the frightening future.

She did not look around, but she was aware of Travis Black Eagle moving to her side. She could feel the warmth from his body, and she was conscious of his height. His black clothes were a solid bulk in the corner of her vision.

Her stomach fluttered and churned at the prospect of tying her life forever after with this tall, wild man who was completely foreign to all she had ever known. He was Indian, perhaps her brother's killer. A chill ran down her spine and her breath came in short, fast gasps. Yet what choice did she have? The man had offered her hope.

"We'll begin," Reverend Nealy announced. "Folks, we are gathered together in the sight of God and these witnesses to join together this man and this woman in the bonds of matrimony. Travis Black Eagle, do ye take Crystal Spencer for yer lawfully wedded wife?"

"I do," he answered in a deep, firm voice, and she glanced up at him. He was formidable, a fierce determination in the set of his jaw and his dark eyes. Sunlight streamed through the window, falling across Travis Black Eagle, revealing blue-black highlights in his hair and throwing his cheeks in shadow.

"Do ye promise to love—" Reverend Nealy cast a worried glance at Travis. "Promise to honor and keep her so long as ye both shall live?"

"I do."

Feeling as dazed as she had the first few hours after she had learned about Ellery's death, Crystal listened to the vows, wondering how this could be happening to her. And then Reverend Nealy was staring at her.

"Crystal Spencer, do ye take Travis Black Eagle for yer lawful wedded husband?"

"I do," she replied, her heart hammering. She felt cold, and she was trembling again. Travis Black Eagle looked fierce and male and angry. How could she spend the rest of her life with this man?

"Do ye promise to honor and obey him so long as ye both shall live?"

"I do."

"Very well, repeat after me. I, Crystal, take thee Travis—"

"I, Crystal, take thee Travis," she repeated, glancing up at Travis Black Eagle. His dark eyes were on her, and she felt ensnared. In their depths, pain and anger were raw and unmistakable. There was a masculine force in his gaze that was tangible, an intensity in his dark eyes that made her tremble and want to flutter her hand over her hair.

"—to be my lawful, wedded husband. To have and to hold for better or for worse, for richer, God willing, or for poorer until death do us part. I hereby plight thee my troth."

Crystal repeated the words, her voice barely a whisper now, her mouth and throat feeling as if they were filled with cotton. She had played the piano at enough weddings and married enough people as justice of the peace to know Reverend Nealy was leaving the word love out of the vows. He was leaving out other things, too, but love was consistently omitted. Which was appropriate under the circumstances. This was the devil's own bargain, she thought again.

The babe in her arms stirred, and she looked down in surprise. She had forgotten him during the ceremony. His round face was serene, his tiny mouth pursed, and her fears fell away as reassurance filled her. He was a tiny being who already needed her and accepted her without reservation or reproach. If only she could properly take care of him! A fleeting panic seized her because she knew nothing about babies and she suspected she would be in charge of this one most of the time.

"Travis Black Eagle, repeat after me: I, Travis Black Eagle, take thee Crystal Spencer, to be my lawful wedded wife."

Travis looked into her wide green eyes and he hurt so badly he could barely whisper the words. Not so very long ago it had been Elizabeth gazing up at him with love shining in her beautiful eyes. His throat closed up and he couldn't get out the words. He tried again, and his words came out in a rasp. Shifting his gaze to his son, he took another breath and got through the vows.

"Let us pray."

As she bowed her head, Crystal said her own silent, heartfelt prayer. *Please, God, give me strength for what I have to do. Help me be a proper mother. And keep Travis Black Eagle busy with his livery stable.*

"Amen," Reverend Nealy intoned. "Do ye have a ring?"

To her surprise, Travis Black Eagle turned to take her hand and he held a plain gold band in his other hand. His fingers were warm against her cold ones, his hand rough from work.

"Repeat after me," Reverend Nealy said. "With this ring, I thee wed."

"With this ring, I thee wed," Travis Black Eagle said in a tight voice, and she cast a surreptitious glance at him through lowered lashes and received another shock. His head was bent over their hands, but she could swear his eyes were filled with tears. Was she wearing his Elizabeth's ring?

"I now pronounce ye man and wife," Reverend Nealy announced cheerfully. "Ye may kiss the bride."

She stiffened, feeling cold and frightened. Then Travis Black Eagle bent his head and brushed the most fleeting kiss across the top of her head. It was the faintest touch, yet she was keenly aware of him. She caught the cotton scent of his shirt, a faint odor of sweat. She had seldom felt dainty around men, but she did next to this one. She looked up at him as he stared at her grimly.

"That's it. I'll be back with the wagon to get you and your things this afternoon," he said, taking the baby from her. "Thanks, Reverend Nealy." He handed the reverend money.

"Congratulations," Reverend Nealy said perfunctorily. The men said goodbye as if they couldn't escape fast enough, and in a minute Crystal was alone. She stood at the front window while Travis Black Eagle talked briefly to the three men, and then he mounted up, tucked his baby close against his body, and turned his horse toward the west. She touched the gold band that circled her finger and a tremor shook her. She was Mrs. Travis Black Eagle now.

Two hours later, she heard a commotion in the yard and went to the window. On his dancing bay, Travis Black Eagle rode into the yard. A wagon pulled by a lively team of black horses slowed and stopped in the road. Stepping over belongings she had readied for the move, she went to the door and opened it, crossing the porch as Travis Black Eagle stood beside the wagon.

She had heard Ellery talk about Turtle River, the full-blood who worked for Travis Black Eagle. The Indian had driven the wagon and he handed down Travis's son and then jumped to the ground. With his babe in his arms, Travis turned to the house and the two men approached. Turtle River was slightly shorter than Black Eagle, but both men looked as if they belonged with their own people out in the wilds of the land. They both had long black hair—Travis's was a wild tangle while Turtle River wore a braid with an eagle feather in his hair. He wore a leather vest, but was bare-chested beneath it. He wore buckskins and moccasins. He was solemn, his eyes almost as dark as Travis Black Eagle's. Both of them looked wild and savage. They were coming to take her away with them. Her heart thudded and she wanted to run inside, bar the door, and scream at them to go away.

She touched the ring on her finger, a tiny band that lawfully bound her like chains to the man approaching her.

The two men paused at the bottom of the steps. "Crystal, this is Ma' inoypo' hi, Turtle River. Turtle River, my wife, Mrs. Black Eagle." The last words were pronounced stiffly, and they raked over her raw nerves. "My wife." She couldn't believe the words, yet they were true. She felt caught in a nightmare. Travis's features were unfathomable. She shifted her gaze to Turtle River to receive another impassive stare.

"How do you do?" she asked politely. He nodded in return, and she thought he was as inscrutable as the man she had married.

"We brought the wagon to get your things. If you'll watch my son, we'll load up," Travis announced, moving past without waiting for a comment from her. She followed him into the house. "I've been to the bank and settled your debts," he said. "I have a list of the furniture that belongs to the bank. They own your bed, but they sold me your mattress. The piano and bookcases are yours."

She nodded, her thoughts churning over the bed. "The bedding is mine and I have it folded and packed in my trunk."

He nodded and strode through the hall, disappearing into the bedroom.

For the next hour she directed the men, following them, carrying the baby until he fell asleep. She placed him on the

bed and continued to trail after the men, holding her breath
when they hoisted her beloved piano and went out the door.

"Careful! Watch the steps," she cautioned and received a
quelling look from Travis Black Eagle. She raised her chin.
"Watch out where you place it so it won't get scraped badly,"
she said, not caring if she annoyed him with her instructions.
She would rather caution him and have her piano cared for
correctly than sit back with her mouth closed while he wrecked
it. She trailed after them as they set the piano down beside the
wagon. Travis Black Eagle had shed his hat and rolled up his
sleeves.

"We're going to have to pick it up and lift it over the side.
We can set it on top of the trunk and then move it."

Turtle River nodded.

"Now," Travis said and bent down to grasp one end. Muscles
bulged in his arms as he lifted the piano. Her gaze ran across
his back where his shirt pulled tautly and along his arms. She
felt a shiver run through her at the display of his strength. What
if he turned that brawn on her? *Had he turned it on Ellery?*

Raising their arms, both men hoisted the piano up over the
side of the wagon. She forgot her beloved piano as she watched
the flex of Black Eagle's powerful muscles. They released the
piano and climbed into the wagon to move the piano next to
the trunk.

"You'll have to set it where it can't fall over," she said,
shading her eyes.

Securing the piano with a rope, Black Eagle turned around
to look down at her. He was a dark silhouette against the
afternoon sky. In the bed of the wagon, he towered over her.
Locks of his dark hair tumbled across his face. She saw that
his shirt was open at the neck and his muscled chest was
partially exposed. His legs were spread, his hands braced on
his hips as he glared down at her. He looked more the wild
savage than Turtle River. "We'll get your piano packed," he
said tersely.

"Thank you. It was part of our agreement," she answered,

hoping she sounded collected. Feeling ruffled, unable to rid herself of the image of his rippling muscles and fit male body, she returned to the house to gather more of her possessions together and to sort through Ellery's belongings.

It took less than an hour for the two men to load her things and what she had kept of her brother's. Black Eagle swiftly dug up her plants and placed them in the wagon, and she felt better, being able to take her flowers with her.

Turtle River helped her into the wagon and placed the baby in her arms. The infant had been fed and changed during the time the men were loading the wagon and now he slept peacefully.

In minutes Travis Black Eagle closed the door of the house and mounted up to move ahead of them. Turtle River drove and Crystal rode in the wagon with the baby. The cow and Ellery's roan were tied to the back.

Her gaze went to the small house she was leaving. A vision of home flashed through her mind—of Baltimore streets, the bustle of people, of their two-story home with tall sycamore trees and the oval bevelled glass in the front door, the delicious dinners of golden chicken or thick roasts that their servant Addie used to cook.

Crystal felt a pang for what she had lost. How had she gone from that to this wild town on the frontier? And now she wouldn't even live in town, the last tiny vestige of civilization.

She touched the wedding ring. For so long she had expected to live in Baltimore with her mother and work for her grandfather in the family law office. Then life had changed drastically and nothing was left for her in Baltimore, and she dreamed of California, a new life in a better place.

Instead, here she was in a wild land, married to a tough, hard man who did not love her. A man who, in spite of his protests, was most likely Ellery's murderer. She would live with strangers and a tiny baby. At the thought of the baby, she looked down at him beside her and lightly touched his soft cheek. She didn't know anything about caring for him, but she would give him love. Mr. Black Eagle would have to think of a name for his child. *Son* wasn't sufficient. The boy needed a name.

As the wagon swayed, they rode through Cheyenne. The small town had been built in the bend of Crow Creek. They passed buildings, the false-fronted shops built after the 1870 fire, the building that held her courtroom, the wooden Territorial Assembly building on Seventeenth Street and Carey Avenue where the men of the territory had passed the laws that enabled her to become a justice of the peace.

The wagon rolled through town toward Fort D. A. Russell and soon drew in sight of the Cheyenne Livery Stable that belonged to Black Eagle. They stopped while he dismounted and strode toward the stable.

Andrew came out to meet him and the two men stood talking. In minutes Black Eagle mounted and they continued, passing houses and then heading west toward the mountains. A woman hanging out wash paused to wave, and Black Eagle waved in return. Minutes later they passed another house where a man straightened from pumping water. He waved and the greeting was returned by Black Eagle. What kind of man was her strong new husband? So fierce in his beliefs, yet friendly to towns-people—how would he be with her?

Soon they were following a rutted trail through short grass across the high plains that ran for miles to the slopes of the Laramie Mountains. Puffy white thunderheads drifted across a deep-blue sky and the smell of wild summer grass filled the air, stirred by the sigh of a breeze. A hawk circled on wind currents high above.

Born and raised in Baltimore, accustomed to the bustle and refinement of the city, Crystal gazed around her with awe and fright. She felt diminished, as if she might dwindle to nothing and blow away on the wind that swept constantly over the rolling land.

They were alone in this expanse of nothing but sky and land and grass. The path they followed was little more than wagon ruts through a vastness of green. The wagon bounced and she clutched the seat with one hand, tightening her hold on the sleeping baby with the other. She wanted to go back to town, back to people and even the small grip on civilization that Cheyenne held.

Her gaze shifted, and she studied Black Eagle again. Straight-backed, he rode ahead. She noticed the butt of the big revolver that fit snug against his hip. This was a strong man who would not hesitate to defend himself and his child. But would that be enough in this harsh land?

And somewhere along these tracks, someone had murdered Ellery. She scanned the grassy plains. No man could slip up on another sight unseen. Ellery had to have known someone was coming. He was shot twice in the chest, she remembered grimly. He had faced his killer. Had it been someone he trusted? Her gaze rested again on Travis in speculation. Was she going to live in isolation with a man whose fiery rage might cause him to kill? While the summer sun beat hotly on her shoulders, she shivered.

A quarter of an hour later, they turned a bend to follow the road down a slight incline and ford a narrow creek. Travis held up his hand to halt and he swung his leg across the horse and dropped to the ground. Turtle River stopped, and then she saw why.

Cold stark horror filled her as memories of her brother surged in her brain. She looked at a body sprawled ahead near the wagon ruts.

Five

Crystal's horror grew. She had never seen anyone who had been beaten, and the boy's battered, torn body made her stomach churn with queasiness. He was a pitifully thin creature; yet judging from his long legs, she guessed him to be thirteen or fourteen years old. The welts across his back were clotted with dried blood and his shirt was matted against his body. Flies swarmed over him and Black Eagle swung his hat, shooing them away. She pulled her handkerchief out to place it over the baby's face, afraid the body was long dead and a stench would soon reach them.

Black Eagle felt for a pulse and then strode back to his horse to get a canteen. He knelt beside the boy, lifting and turning him slowly, taking great care to avoid his torn back.

She saw the boy's blue eyes flutter open. Black Eagle yanked off his bandanna and wiped the boy's face, shoving long straight locks of brown hair from his forehead, and then held the canteen to his mouth. The boy drank deeply until his head lolled to one side.

Black Eagle picked him up gently and headed toward the

wagon. She realized he was going to place the boy in the wagon and she moved quickly to make a place for him.

He stirred again as Black Eagle and Turtle River lifted him. Groaning, he looked up at Black Eagle.

"What's your name?" Black Eagle asked.

"Zachary." A mere croak. His eyes were blackened and he had cuts on his face, but it was the welts across his body that made Crystal feel sick. How could anyone have beaten him so badly? He was too young to be traveling alone, yet where was his family? Had they been killed? Thank heavens Ellery hadn't been beaten before his death.

"Where's your family?"

Crystal stood close enough to see the blue eyes focus on Black Eagle with a look that was so filled with hatred she was startled. "I ran away from home." The words were little more than a whisper. Black Eagle's jaw knotted while anger darkened his eyes.

"I'll take you home with me until you get well."

As the boy's eyes closed, Crystal didn't know whether he had lapsed into unconsciousness again or was merely accepting what Black Eagle had told him. Black Eagle lowered him to the bed of the wagon and turned him on his chest. Taking off his hat, Black Eagle handed it to her. "Keep the sun and flies off him," he said as she took the hat from his hands.

She nodded and watched him jump down while Turtle River moved up front to drive again. She hoped the boy lost consciousness because the constant jiggling of the wagon would only add to his misery.

It was another half hour before a dark speck in the distance gathered shape and form and she saw a house and a barn. When they drew near, she looked at a sturdy house built of pine logs. A porch ran across the front beneath a sloping roof, and two steps led down to the ground. The mountains were not as distant now, and she could see their tall peaks and had to admit they were majestic.

Her gaze returned to her new house. To her relief, it looked larger than the one she had shared with Ellery in Cheyenne. Aspen and spruce had been planted near the house, and the young trees gave meager shade. To the west beyond the house was a makeshift shed that probably held equipment; another shed that was merely a roof; and beyond the shed, a pen where half-a-dozen horses milled. Lumber was stacked near the shed and she wondered if Black Eagle intended to build a barn.

Outbuildings flanked the house, and several yards beyond the buildings was a slash in the earth where a creek cut across his land. South of the pen was a small cabin, and near the cabin was a tipi.

Her heart jumped when she saw the pump in front of the house and a well to the side. They would have their own water! What a luxury! Water was a precious commodity in town. There were artesian wells, but anyone unfortunate enough not to have a well, had to buy water and conserve it carefully.

The house looked promising, but her growing sense of approval vanished beneath concerns about her new status.

Crystal twisted in the seat to look back the way they had come, wishing she could see Cheyenne. How alone they would be! For a moment she considered telling Travis Black Eagle that she wanted to go back, to get this false marriage annulled, but she reminded herself that she had nothing to return to except a mountain of debts she didn't know how to pay.

When they halted, she swung her foot over the side to climb out of the wagon. Clinging to the rough wood, she stepped down on a spoke of a wagon wheel.

Strong hands closed around her waist and swung her to the ground. Startled, because she was so rarely touched by any man, she looked up at Travis Black Eagle, who climbed past her into the wagon and placed his hat on his head again. "Here, I'll hand you some things to take inside. I'll carry Zachary." Black Eagle gave her a bundle of clothing. "Judge Spencer—" He clamped his jaw closed for an instant. "Crystal," he pronounced with deliberation, and her name said in his husky voice stirred an unaccustomed heat in her. "I'm not an orderly man and the past two weeks have been particularly bad."

"I understand, Mr. Black Eagle," she said perfunctorily, still hearing her name said in his deep voice.

"You might as well call me Travis."

She nodded, but it was difficult to imagine addressing him as anything other than Travis Black Eagle or Black Eagle, as Ellery had always called him. As she took the bundles and set them on the ground, she couldn't imagine any kind of familiarity with the man, even to saying his first name. "Give me your son and I'll carry him."

"I've got him," Black Eagle answered easily. She watched him pick up the small baby, and the fierce look on the man's face softened as he held the infant.

"How many men work for you?" she asked, noticing how thick Black Eagle's dark lashes were.

"Just Turtle River. Sometimes he'll eat with me and sometimes he comes up to the house and gets food to take back to his tipi. Turtle River stays to himself."

She suspected Travis Black Eagle stayed to himself as well.

Holding his baby, Black Eagle strode into the cabin. She picked up a bundle of clothing and followed him along a dirt path. Crossing the porch, she stepped inside the open door and blinked while her eyes adjusted to the darkened interior. As she looked around, shock immobilized her.

Shirts, pants, boots, blankets, and dishes were strewn over the cabin along with tools and utensils. Pans and buckets were stacked on the furniture. Two-by-fours leaned against the wall. It looked as if wild animals had been making the place their habitat. There were few places where the plank floor peeked through. Crystal stared in dismay. Order had always been a part of her life. Even in the last months of Grandfather's life when they had begun to sell their household things, they had kept order. And finally when she had had to dispose of everything and the house to pay family debts, she had done so in an efficient manner.

Now she looked at her new home in stunned disbelief. The cabin was one large, undivided room. Directly across from her was a stone fireplace with a rifle above it and a shirt draped over a corner of the mantel. To her left she spotted an iron stove stacked with unwashed pans. Shock transformed to anger as she looked up at her new husband.

"Sir, I cannot live in this!" she exclaimed, waving her hand in the direction of the cabin.

He placed his fists on his hips and he stood too close to her. She wanted to back up, but she was determined the man would not intimidate her. She took a deep breath and glared at him.

"You're my wife. This is home, whether you like it or not. I know it's bad, but you'll just have to deal with it."

"You should have warned me," she said in a low voice. She could not recall losing her temper in years, but she felt on the verge of it now.

"What would you have done if I had told you this morning that my place needed cleaning?"

"Cleaning is an understatement," she protested. "It is a rat's nest." She stared at him, knowing there wasn't anything she could have done but go right ahead and marry the man. "I'll clean it, Mr. Black Eagle, but then you're to cooperate with me in keeping it clean."

"Well, ma'am, I'll do my damnedest to cooperate, but I might not be quite as neat and tidy as Brother Ellery." Black Eagle turned on his heel and strode across the room, stepping on whatever lay in his path. With a sweep of his arm, he sent clothes and tools scattering. He yanked a blanket from a chair and folded it to make a pallet on the floor.

"We'll put the boy here."

She heard the baby cry and looked around, unable to spot the infant. She could hear the cries that were loud enough to carry across the prairie, yet she could not find the baby.

"He's crying," Black Eagle snapped, striding past her.

"I can't find him!"

Black Eagle snatched up the child from behind a pile of

clothing and she stepped over a wheel to take the baby from him.

"Here's his cradle. There's a springhouse out back, and I keep the milk for him there. I'll fill the bottle."

"Thank you. Is there a chair in this place?"

Black Eagle looked around, scratched his head, and then pushed lumber and clothing aside and pulled a rocking chair toward her. He used his foot to shove bedding and clothing out of the way and waved his hand, motioning for her to sit.

"Thank you," she said frostily, wondering why she had worried about getting into a bed with the man. They would never find the bed by nightfall.

She hunted until she found something suitable to use to diaper the baby and then Black Eagle reappeared with a bottle of milk. She sat in the rocker and fed the baby and watched Black Eagle return, carrying Zachary in his arms as if he were no more burden than his son.

Black Eagle knelt, lowering Zachary to the pallet, and she heard the boy groan. Black Eagle strode to the mantel, picked up a jug, and carried it back to Zachary, popping a cork. "Drink this," he urged. "It'll ease the pain and help you sleep."

Black Eagle lifted the boy's head and held the jug to his lips. Zachary drank, then coughed and moaned, but turned to drink more.

"Turtle River is getting medicine to put on your back. I'm going to have to cut your shirt away for him to put the salve on you."

Crystal drew a deep breath and wished she could take the baby and run from the room. What Black Eagle had to do would be painful for Zachary, and she wished she didn't have to be within hearing distance, much less view the procedure.

Turtle River entered carrying a pot in his hands, and she closed her eyes, clenching her teeth, thankful they hadn't asked her to help.

"Take another long drink, Son. It'll help you," Black Eagle said gently and held the jug to the boy's lips.

What a strange man was her new husband! She had seen his fiery temper, knew his strong will, and suspected his murderous capabilities, yet here he was being as tender and caring to a complete stranger as anyone could possibly be. Could he be the same man who murdered Ellery?

She remembered his hot denial and affirmation that he wished he could have had the chance to kill Ellery himself. As she watched him gently lower Zachary's head to the pallet, Crystal decided this man was not Ellery's killer. Her anger with Travis Black Eagle abated, and as it diminished, the barriers around her heart went down. She stared at him, seeing a man who had been devastated by loss, yet could be deeply kind to someone in need.

"Let's move a few things inside and give the whiskey a chance to take hold," Black Eagle said. "On his empty stomach it ought to hit hard in a few minutes."

The two men left the cabin. Zachary's eyes were closed, his cheek against the pallet. Her attention shifted to the baby, keeping her gaze on his tiny face as he stared back at her. The world and the cabin and Travis Black Eagle vanished from her mind. This tiny little person became her world. The wonder of him filled her with awe and a blossoming warmth. This baby would grow up as her son. She tightened her arm, pulling him closer while he sucked intently on the bottle, his tiny fingers moving back and forth over the glass. Every inch of him was beautiful. She had never really noticed children before, but now she realized they were miracles of perfection.

Finally he finished drinking and drifted to sleep. She heard a bump and the sound of a note of music. Looking up, she watched Black Eagle and Turtle River carry her piano into the cabin and set it down inside the door.

"My piano blocks the doorway!" she cried, wondering if he intended to leave everything in the haphazard manner he had placed it.

"We'll get to your furniture when I can, but I've lost a lot of work time." He turned and left, and silence descended except for the rhythmic squeak of the floor as she rocked back and forth. She looked at the piano. Her three-legged stool was turned upside down on top of the piano. Clothing stuck out beneath it. She still had not spotted any sign of a bed. Remembering their home in Baltimore with her mother's crystal and the polished floors and rosewood furniture and even the neat little house in Cheyenne she had shared with Ellery, she was swamped with sorrow.

For a minute she yielded to the unhappiness settling over her, then Crystal took a deep breath. The cabin could be cleaned and she had a home now and a man to protect her. And he was not going to put any physical claims on her—at least he had promised he would not. She suspected he had meant what he said. She was not a woman men desired.

Best of all, she had a baby that was going to be hers! As of this morning, she had become a mother—something she had decided would never happen. And caring for the infant was not the terrifying, impossible task she had deemed it to be. It was a labor of love because he was an adorable little person.

Black Eagle and Turtle River returned and went to Zachary. Black Eagle pulled out a knife. As he cut away the shirt, Zachary moaned. In seconds Black Eagle stood and Turtle River moved closer, cleaning the wounds and then spreading a paste on them. A strange leafy odor came from the paste.

"You hold him and I'll bind this up."

Black Eagle helped Zachary sit up. His face was chalky and his mouth shut grimly and she hurt for him, wishing there were some way they could deaden his pain. Turtle River worked with care and in minutes they eased Zachary to the pallet.

"I'll build a fire in the stove and put meat on to boil. We need to get some broth down him as soon as possible. He looks starved," Black Eagle said, glancing over his shoulder at her.

He rummaged for a pot. He went outside to the pump and returned, setting the pot of water on the iron stove. Soon he had a fire going. He moved with deliberation and purpose and

Crystal wondered whether the man ever relaxed. She could not imagine laughter coming from him.

"I'll unload the rest of the wagon, and then I have to feed the animals. I'll be back as soon as I can."

She nodded again and continued to rock. Her gaze ran over the room and she spotted the bed beneath mounds of clothing, bedding, boards, and tools. The man must not sleep in the bed, she wondered if he expected her to have it cleaned off tonight. The baby pushed the bottle and she readjusted it, looking at him.

She held him up and kissed his soft cheek, cuddling him against her heart. When he snuggled against her, she felt her spirits lifting. She was a mother now. As the shock wore off, reality set in, and with it, a sense of wonder at her new status and the baby that had been entrusted to her.

"I will make a home here for us," she whispered to him. "And someday, my little love, I'll teach you to play the piano. When your papa hears you, he will be glad you know how to play."

She held the baby tightly while she rocked, taking another look at her surroundings. How could one man create such havoc?

She looked over her shoulder at the stove piled high with pans that had food caked on them. Nearby, draped over a pile of clothing was a blanket. As soon as the baby was asleep, she carried him to his cradle.

"Now, my love, you sleep and I will begin to make a home for you. A real home," she said with a little awe, touching his soft dark curls. He was the most beautiful baby she had ever seen, and she drew her fingers over his cheek lightly.

With a determined sigh, she turned to study the cluttered bed. She suspected by nightfall, she would be exhausted enough to sleep in it even if Travis Black Eagle were only a foot away.

* * *

Travis turned his horse, heading north to check on his cattle. The cows were calving and he needed to make certain they were all right. His gaze went over his land without really seeing it. The smell of grass filled the air, heat rising from the ground. Turtle River rode several yards ahead.

Travis didn't want to think about this morning, yet it nagged at him. His jaw was clamped so tightly it hurt, and he still felt a knot in his throat that had been there off and on all day. Elizabeth. He had been through rough times before when he'd thought he had been hurt as badly as a man could be. He'd found out there was a worse hurt. The only person he would ever love again was his son. His and Elizabeth's baby. Love was an incredible risk and thus far had brought him unbearable pain. Never again did he want to risk his heart. His life would be dedicated to making a place for his son.

He knew Judge Spencer didn't want this union any more than he did, but he was absolutely certain he would never regret it because of falling in love again. Love meant pain and loss and being vulnerable. And he would keep his promise about Judge Spencer's body. He saw her only as a woman who could care for a baby. Right now passion had been replaced by sorrow and when time began to heal the wound, he knew he could satisfy his body's needs with Delilah or Fancy.

The only sure thing in the world was land. In the white man's world, land and money meant respect.

Long ago, through no choice of his own, he had taken the white man's road. He lived in the white man's world now. He couldn't go back to his people because he would only bring the soldiers and grief to them.

Travis ground his jaw closed, determination filling him. He would build his ranch and his business until people in town would accept him and his son. He would do everything in his power to protect his son from the prejudice that had tormented him all his life.

Travis glanced at Turtle River. The stoic Cheyenne kept his hurts to himself. Travis rode over a rise and down through the swift-running creek. He remembered Elizabeth riding here with him, remembered her in his arms. Swearing under his breath, he rubbed his eyes angrily.

One bright spot in the whole miserable day had been the judge's care of his son since she had stepped forward and taken his son out of his arms. She had asserted herself then, taking charge as if she knew what she was doing. She might be plain and prim, but she was not timid. As far as he could see, she had done just fine in caring for his baby.

He didn't want night to come; he didn't want to have to go back to Judge Spencer and the cabin that was filled with painful memories that were too fresh. And he tried to keep the thought out of his mind that it was her brother who could have saved Elizabeth.

Hours later as the sun neared the western horizon, Travis wiped his brow and straightened from bending over a newborn calf when Turtle River approached. "It is night. The first night your woman is here."

"She'll be all right," Travis said, dreading returning, wanting to work himself into exhaustion. Nights were a torment, nightmares plaguing what little sleep he got. "We need to keep searching for any other cows about to drop calves. I want to get these two back with the herd so predators won't get them."

With a shrug, Turtle River returned to work. An hour later Travis's stomach churned with hunger. He needed to get home to feed the young boy. At the thought of Zachary, Travis felt a deep burning anger, wondering if the boy's father had inflicted the beating. Zachary was young and would mend if fever and infection didn't set in.

At dusk Travis motioned to Turtle River and the two started back. At the pump in front of the house Travis stripped off his shirt and washed beneath a full, bright moon that was rising over the horizon. As he dried his face with his rumpled shirt, he raised his nose in the air. He smelled beef cooking, yet his appetite was gone. When he thought of going inside, sharing a table with the judge instead of Elizabeth, the thought of food made his stomach churn.

"Come join us for dinner," he urged Turtle River.

"I will come later. You should be alone with her first. This is new to her. I'll bring medication for the boy."

"Fine," Travis answered, his curiosity rising about Crystal. He half-expected to come back and find her ready to take another revolver to him. If she had been the type for tears, she would have yielded to them this morning. The woman had grit and that was good as long as she didn't shoot him or treat the babe harshly.

He had carefully placed Ellery's revolver on a high shelf. The only other revolver on the place was on his hip and he had unloaded his rifle when he arrived home. He was going to have to hand a gun over to her soon for her own protection when she was left alone, but he thought he would give her a few days to become accustomed to her new life. And time for him to get to know her better before he placed another revolver in her hands. With resignation, Travis strode into the cabin.

"Evening," he called gruffly. The piano and stool blocked his way. He stepped around it and paused. She stood in front of the iron stove, a spoon in one hand and the baby on her shoulder, held by her other hand. Tendrils of her hair had come loose from her topknot, wispy locks twisting down around her face. The underarms of her dress were soaked with perspiration and her forehead was beaded with it. There was a smudge of black across her cheek. In spite of her disarray, he liked her better this way because she looked less spinsterish and remote. Her eyes widened, her gaze dropping to roam over his chest while color flooded her cheeks and he remembered he carried his shirt in his hand. He pulled it on, wondering whether he had shocked her. A spinster lady out in the wilds of the frontier with two men was probably in for a lot of shocks, he thought wryly as he crossed the room to Zachary.

"How's the boy?"

"He's burning with a fever. I've been putting a cold, wet cloth on his head," she said, motioning to Zachary with a jerk of her head, "but I had to stop to feed the baby."

Travis knelt and placed his hand on Zachary's forehead, touching hot, dry skin. He saw the pan of cold water and a cloth hanging over the side. He dipped the cloth, wringing it out and bathing Zachary's face with it. "I'll get Turtle River."

Black Eagle strode out of the room, and Crystal watched him go, noting how his shirt pulled across his back with the swing of his shoulders and remembering in absolute detail his bare chest. Heat burned in her at the memory, a different heat than the one she had experienced all evening from the warm cabin. She had never seen a man's chest like his, bare and bronze, the smooth skin taut over solid muscles. She fanned herself with her hand. The man was incredibly disturbing. How long would it take for her to become used to him?

The baby wiggled and she patted his back. He had been awake the longest stretch since this morning, his dark eyes bright with curiosity as he kicked and cooed and gurgled. The cabin was hot from the boiling stew. She wanted to feed the men and crawl off alone and sleep for days.

Every bone in her body ached and exhaustion made her feel faint. She wanted to stretch on the bed and sleep forever, but she hadn't had time between tending Zachary and the baby to get the bed cleared off. She felt on a ragged edge, tears threatening that she refused to yield to.

The men returned, working over Zachary, spooning more liquid from the stew down him and getting him to eat a few bites. They joined her and ate, all three sitting in silence, and she wondered if she would go through years of silent meals with taciturn men.

As soon as they finished, Black Eagle returned to Zachary's side to dip the cloth in the basin of cold water, wring it out, and place it on the boy's forehead again. Turtle River watched solemnly and then turned and left.

After cleaning the pot and dishes, she removed everything from the bed, realizing Black Eagle must not have slept on it since his wife's death. And as Crystal removed a large washtub and piles of blankets, she discovered why he had brought her mattress. His bed was merely a frame without a mattress. She glanced across the room at him as he sat beside Zachary and guessed he had probably destroyed the mattress he had shared with his wife.

She moved across the room and knelt down beside him, feeling as if she were drawing dangerously close to a wild, unpredictable animal.

"This house is all one big room."

He raised his head, and his dark eyes bore into her. She wished he had continued leaning down over Zachary because it was less disconcerting to look at the top of his head than into his eyes.

"I would like you to string a line so I can hang a blanket up in one corner. It would give me some privacy for dressing."

"Fine," he said, bending over Zachary again. "I'll try to do it tomorrow. In the meantime, I'll turn my back and Zachary is lost to the world tonight."

It wasn't quite the same, but she knew it was useless to argue with him. "Thank you. I'll keep Zachary bathed off and cool. I have one more request. Will you carry my mattress to the bed?"

Nodding, Black Eagle moved away while she sponged Zachary's face, praying that the boy didn't die in the night. In a few minutes when she glanced around, Black Eagle was nowhere in sight, but her bare horsehair mattress was on the bed.

She tended Zachary until the baby stirred. She fed the infant, and as soon as he was down again and asleep, she returned to bathe Zachary's face once more.

She heard a rustle and saw Black Eagle had returned. His

shirt was gone and she drew a deep breath, something tightening inside her as she looked at his broad chest. How could he be so powerful? Realizing she was staring, she turned away with burning cheeks.

Minutes later she heard him approach and kneel beside her. His hand closed around her wrist and she looked up in surprise. His touch was light, his hand warm—a meaningless gesture, yet the moment his fingers locked around her wrist, tingles of awareness danced from his hand along her arm and into the rest of her. She was acutely conscious of his nearness, the warmth of his body, the bareness of his chest.

She didn't know where to look because his dark eyes were disturbing, his chest unsettling. She gazed up at him, aware of his physical presence in a way she had never been aware of a man before. She tried with all her will to keep her gaze lifted, but in her peripheral vision she was too conscious of his body. As if she had no control over her muscles and eyes and mind, her gaze drifted down. He was only inches away, his chest a solid bulk that looked hard and strong and strangely reassuring. And she felt a maddening urge to place her hand against him. She balled her fists in her lap and looked at Zachary, flushing with embarrassment.

"How is he?"

"Still burning. How could anyone beat him so badly? Do you know his family?"

"No, but if the father did this, he'd better not come here after him."

Startled by the harshness in his voice, she looked back at him. "If his father comes for him, he has to go with his father."

Black eyes bore into her and she felt the familiar clash of wills that made her want to flinch. Instead, she lifted her chin, refusing once again to let Travis Black Eagle see that he alarmed her. "Even if his father was the one who inflicted this? You would hand the boy back to him?"

"By law he belongs to his parents until he's of age. You know that."

"You see the law as black and white with no shades in between?"

"You can't see the law in shades," she replied, wondering again about this strong man who had so little regard for law.

"So you would hand him back to the man who did that and let him inflict more pain?"

She looked at Zachary and felt a strange bewilderment. Usually the law was clear and right and good. It was reasonable, a way to bring order and justice. "He belongs to his parents," she whispered. "Surely his own father never did this to him," she added, but she remembered the fiery blaze in Zachary's eyes at the mention of his family.

"You heard him say he ran away. In this condition, if someone else had beaten him, he would have run for home." Black Eagle's fingers caught her chin and turned her face up to his, his eyes boring into her. "Would you give him back to the monster who nearly killed him?"

Emotions churned inside her. Why did Travis Black Eagle constantly challenge her? "It would be unlawful not to," she answered, searching her heart and realizing she had not encountered a situation before where she felt the law was wrong.

"I pity you, Judge. And heaven help you if you ever lay a hand on my son like this."

She drew herself up. "I wouldn't think of hurting a child!"

"No, I don't think you would. But the day may come when your view of law and life is going to tear you apart. The law isn't always on the side of justice."

She jerked her chin from his grasp and narrowed her eyes. "The law is meant to be upheld, and if it is a bad law, then it needs to be changed."

"And in the meantime, if that sorry bastard comes to get this boy, he'll answer to me and you won't hand over his son. You get me, and I'll face him."

"Don't use foul language," she said perfunctorily, thinking about what Black Eagle had just ordered her to do. "You will have to curb your tongue unless you want your son to say the same things you do.''

Black Eagle blinked, and she realized it hadn't occurred to him the child would pick up his words. ''I'll watch what I say when my son starts talking.''

She held out her hand, her thoughts returning to their marriage. ''Am I wearing your wife's ring?''

''No. I have gold at the livery stable. I made the ring for you.''

Astonished, she touched the smooth golden band. ''How did you know what size to make it?''

''I remembered your slender fingers from that day in court with Andrew.''

Amazed, she turned the band. He strode outside, and she wondered if he were gone for the night.

Mulling over their argument, she bathed Zachary's forehead. A monster had given the boy the beating, yet the law was what everyone had to obey and live by. And as a justice of the peace, she had taken a vow to uphold it. It was clear and unyielding and she prayed no one came to take Zachary home.

When the baby stirred, she left Zachary to take care of the baby. When she returned the baby to his bed, she went outside to the privy, washed and returned to the cabin. The moment she stepped through the door, shock struck her again at the swift change in her life.

Too nervous to sleep, Crystal worked diligently, trying to bring some order to even a corner of the cabin. Now that night was here, she viewed the bed with trepidation. Earlier she had thought she would be too exhausted to care that she had to share the bed with Black Eagle, but her nerves tingled and she knew that if she worked straight through the night and into the next one, she would not be too exhausted to notice him.

The man had married her because she was the only available female. He merely tolerated her, yet she was acutely aware of him. And she knew Travis Black Eagle was hurting badly. As odious as this marriage had seemed this morning, it would take care of her future. Now she had a baby; and if Travis Black Eagle came through the door right now and said he had changed his mind and if she wanted an annulment he would consent, she would say no.

He might come to regret this marriage someday when time healed his heart. And she knew he would heal. He was too full of energy to go through life in mourning. The day might come when he would fall in love again, but he had committed himself to her today and given his son into her care in a truly legal and binding marriage.

And in all her folding and picking up of his clothing, she had not come across a nightshirt. Her insides fluttered at the thought of Travis Black Eagle in a nightshirt or, worse, not in one. She suspected he would find a nightshirt an unnecessary encumbrance. Her cheeks burned and she busied herself stacking up more pans, arranging them on a shelf next to the stove, hanging two on hooks on the wall.

Crystal turned her back to the bed and cleaned furiously, trying to stop the pictures of him that danced in her mind. In all the images that flickered through her thoughts, there was none of the man laughing. Even though he did soften when he talked to his son, she couldn't imagine him smiling or laughing.

She wondered if he would sleep outside. Was he out there mourning his wife or trying to cool his rage that he had had to marry a woman he didn't care a whit about? She walked to the bed. As she sat down on the bare mattress, she intended to pause only a moment before getting the bedding and making up the bed, but she stretched out, closed her eyes, and oblivion came.

During the night Zachary's fever broke and Travis sponged the boy's face and then moved to a chair to stretch his long legs in front of him. When the baby stirred, Travis fed him without waking Judge Spencer. She was lying half on the bed with her feet dangling over the floor. Moonlight spilled over her and he looked at her face. She looked younger in repose. His gaze slid away and he tried to avoid memories, getting up and moving restlessly outside. He yanked off his shirt, wiping his damp forehead, thankful for the cooler air outside the cabin.

He felt he shouldn't stray far in case his son stirred. Travis didn't think even the screams of the baby would wake the judge this night.

Six

The next morning Crystal's eyes fluttered open, and she stared at the rough-hewn logs overhead. Disoriented, she sat up and groaned. Her arms ached and she was horrified to see her dress rumpled, and clinging damply to her. She met Black Eagle's unfathomable gaze, which startled her but brought memory tumbling back.

"I thought you needed the sleep. I've fed my son."

"It must be late." She stood, blushing, embarrassed that she had slept in her clothing. Her black dress was a mass of wrinkles and her hair felt matted, her mouth dry. Feeling uncomfortable under Black Eagle's steady stare, she rushed across the room toward the door. "I'll wash and be right back to take the baby."

She fled, thankful for the cool morning air. Crystal washed her face, trying to freshen up. The moment she re-entered the cabin, Black Eagle stood.

"Zachary's fever has broken, and he's sleeping quietly. Turtle River was here this morning and we changed the boy's bandages. He should be better today. I'm leaving now." He studied her as if something else were on his mind and he didn't

know how to broach the subject. He reached behind his back
and pulled out Ellery's revolver.

"When we get a chance, I'll show you how to use this
properly; but until then, all you have to do to summon me is
fire two quick shots. I know you can do that."

She blushed, guilt swamping her as she remembered firing
at him and realizing that if Ellery had kept a loaded weapon,
Travis Black Eagle would be dead by her hand and the baby
would be an orphan. She nodded as he moved toward the door.

"I'll place the revolver on the shelf by the door." His gaze
slid past her to the sleeping boy. "Don't turn him over to his
father without letting me know. The man who inflicted that
beating needs to answer to someone."

"You can't take the law into your own power."

His dark eyes met hers, and she felt another clash of wills
with him. "You are not to turn him over to his father without
trying to summon me."

Praying she didn't have to make that decision, she followed
him to the doorway and stood in the cool breeze. He strode to
the barn where the bay was saddled. With ease he mounted
and turned to ride away, sitting tall and straight.

Crystal bathed and changed the baby and then began to clean,
singing to him as she worked. Sweat poured off her body and
dust made her sneeze, but bit by bit the cabin became neater.
While she worked, she was conscious of moving tools, buckets,
Black Eagle's clothing; but Elizabeth's belongings were gone
and she wondered what he had done with all her things until
she found a small trunk.

Crystal opened it and saw the keepsakes that had belonged
to his wife—small tintypes, a locket, a crystal vase, a set of
china. She closed the trunk and wondered if he had burned the
clothing and bedding and mattress. Her gaze ran over the cabin
and her curiosity grew about Black Eagle.

A few minutes later, she opened a cabinet and found the
only belongings that indicated the nature of the man. She pulled
out a shield that had a sun and a buffalo painted on the hide

with two eagle feathers attached to it. She ran her hands over it, wondering about his past life. An eagle feather headdress lay beside the shield. Was he a man of importance in his tribe? A bow and quiver filled with arrows lay on the shelf and she picked them up, feeling as if she touched Black Eagle when she touched his things. How easily she could imagine him in the life he'd once led. There was still a wild air about him. She ran her finger along an arrow and touched the bow again. These had to be ties to his past, yet why had he left his own people?

She found a necklace with a golden locket and assumed it was Elizabeth's. A long-bladed knife lay on the shelf, a leather pouch. With care she returned the knife to the shelf and closed the cabinet.

As she continued to clean, she mulled over what to do if Zachary's father came for him. Never before in her life had she felt the law was wrong, but this time she did. Yet even if it were wrong, it was still the law. No matter how dreadful, she felt she would have to uphold it and she prayed his father did not find him.

If the man came, she knew she would not fire the gun to alert Travis Black Eagle.

She moved pans and clothing away from a chest and opened the top drawer to find Black Eagle's clothing tossed inside. She folded a shirt and placed it in the drawer. Curious, she opened the next drawer and saw more of his clothing; she touched it lightly, drawing her fingers over denim pants, again feeling as if she were touching the man and not merely his belongings. In the corner of the drawer were two metal boxes. She opened the top one. Stacks of gold coins gleamed dully in the light and took her breath.

Shocked by the amount of money he had in the box, she stared in amazement. She closed the box and looked in the one beneath it. Both had keys in the lock, but neither were locked. The second held more gold, silver, greenbacks, and papers that she assumed were deeds to his land and the livery stable. She was amazed at his wealth and stared outside, not seeing the rolling grassland, but thinking of the man she had married. Now she knew why he had made such a generous offer to pay Ellery's debts. She looked at the gold coins, closing the box carefully, mildly surprised that he trusted her with the money. He could have easily locked the boxes, pocketed the keys, and she would never have known their contents. However, since he knew her staunch feelings about the law, why wouldn't he trust her with his money?

She looked in the bottom drawer and found it empty. It must have held Elizabeth's things, but now it would have to hold hers, Crystal decided.

She moved to a crate and picked up the delicate green music box that she had brought from Baltimore. Winding it up, she listened to the familiar tinkling notes of a waltz.

"Morning."

She whirled around to see Zachary trying to stand.

"Let me help you," she said, rushing toward him, but he waved her away.

"I can stand," he said and grinned at her, looking younger than before, yet he was inches taller than she would have guessed. His teeth were crooked with a slight overbite; his brown hair stood up in tangled bunches, and bruises colored his face with blue and brown patches almost hiding his freckles. "I need to get out. Nature calls."

"Oh! The privy is that way," she said, motioning. "Don't you want help?"

"No, ma'am." He closed his eyes, and she thought he was going to faint. She started toward him again, but stopped as his eyes opened and he shook his head. "I'm all right. Just need to move around."

"I have cold meat from yesterday."

"Yes, ma'am. When I get back, I'll eat." He slowly eased his way across the cabin; and although she wanted to help him, she knew her aid wasn't wanted. Quiet descended and he was gone so long, she wondered whether he had run away or fainted. When he returned to the cabin, she smiled with relief.

"Now, I'd be real grateful for some of that food."

His hair was wet and slicked back from his face and she guessed his age fifteen. Still young enough to belong to his parents. She sliced the thick beef from the stew and got out cold biscuits to place them on the table. She poured a large glass of milk and set the baby where he could watch Zachary.

"Your son is a cute little fellow."

"He's not really my son," she said quietly, and Zachary shot her a quizzical look as he sat at the table and took a bite of biscuit. He closed his eyes and chewed and then drank the entire glass of milk and wiped his mouth. "Ma'am, the food is heaven."

She had to laugh. "That's the first time anyone ever described my cooking in such a manner!" He grinned as she poured more milk and brought it to the table. "I'm Crystal Spencer."

"I'm Zachary North."

She smiled and then remembered her married name. "Actually, I'm Crystal Black Eagle, but it's difficult to think of myself as a married woman," she admitted. Crystal sat down and related briefly how she had come to be Black Eagle's bride, leaving out most details, including Ellery's drinking and Black Eagle's forceful proposal. "We found you along the trail."

"I remember. Two men."

"My husband and Turtle River, the man who works for him."

"You folks saved my life and I'm grateful."

She nodded, getting up to fetch more beef and biscuits. After Zachary had eaten, he began to make feeble efforts to help her restore order to the cabin until he tired and sat on a chair, propping his arms on his knees while he watched her work.

Later he moved around again, doing simple chores to help, and she was amazed by his resilience. His fingers brushed over the keys of the piano. "My grandma had a piano. She said I play by ear." He grinned. "I really don't. I play by hand."

She laughed, feeling more lighthearted with Zachary seeming to get better by the hour. He sat at the stool and played a simple melody that she recognized, the lilting chords of the fighting song reminding her of the war years and home in Baltimore.

Crystal sang as she worked while Zachary played a few more tunes and then returned to either helping her or getting down on his knees to play with the baby.

In late afternoon she left him to watch the baby and went to the stream, meandering upstream until she found a deeper spot. On impulse she stripped and bathed, shivering in the icy water, but thankful to get clean. She washed her hair and returned to the cabin.

Zachary and the baby were at the pen where the black horses were, and Zachary waved to her as she returned. She changed, reaching for her other black dress, then paused. She pulled on a blue cotton that was far cooler. Her hurt over Ellery's loss hadn't changed, but it was senseless to wear the hot, black dresses for mourning when no one saw her except the men and the baby.

She braided her hair, letting the long braid hang down her back, and built a fire to cook their supper, wondering if her cooking would make Black Eagle wish he had found a different bride.

Zachary was outside with the baby when Black Eagle returned in early evening and she heard the two greet each other. She busied herself getting supper, but she was aware of the deep rumble of Black Eagle's voice as he talked quietly.

She heard the steady squeak of the pump and the gush of water. Curious, Crystal peeked through the open door. Black Eagle was bending over, pumping water over his back and head. Zachary was out of her sight.

Unobserved, Crystal watched transfixed, staring at the ripple of muscles in Black Eagle's back as he straightened and ran his fingers through his thick, black hair. Water glistened on his back and shoulders, and she felt that same tingling awareness of him that she had experienced before. The man was powerful, healthy, intensely male. He turned his head and she met his gaze. Heat flooded her cheeks, and she stepped away quickly, embarrassed at being caught staring at him.

She smelled something burning and discovered smoke rising from the slabs of meat she had placed in the large iron skillet. She grabbed the skillet, removing it from the fire as it sizzled. Crystal bit her lip, staring at the charred meat, ready to throw up her hands in exasperation. Supper was ruined, but it was all they had to eat. In defense, she reminded herself that this marriage had not been her idea. Nor had he inquired about her cooking abilities before he proposed.

As if her thoughts had conjured him up, Black Eagle stepped inside. Instantly she became aware of him and of herself, aware of wisps of hair curling around her face that had escaped from her braid, aware of perspiration dotting her face and making her dress damp. He looked over the room and she wondered if her changes annoyed him.

Travis paused, staring at his orderly home. The bed had a cheerful blue-and-red quilt. A bouquet of primroses decorated the center of the table that was now spread with a lace cloth.

The piano had been moved against a wall; clothing hung on hooks, and the floor was swept. For an instant he saw it as Elizabeth had kept it, remembering their golden moments that were filled with joy and wild lovemaking. His insides knotted and he gritted his teeth, clenching his fists and trying to control his emotions. How long was the hurt going to keep hitting him like this, a staggering pain coming out of the blue? He ran his hand across his forehead; he would have to stop thinking that way. Elizabeth was gone forever. He clamped his jaw closed and glanced at the smoking stove.

Crystal waved her hand over it, her face screwed up in a frown. If it had been any other woman, he would have braced for tears, but he didn't think the judge knew how to cry. He moved to the cradle and the moment he picked up his tiny son, Travis's anger and hurt vanished.

The tiny baby was a miracle and he loved his son without

reservation. The baby's brown eyes sparkled and he cooed and kicked as if that were his welcome home to his father. Travis swung him gently in his hands and talked softly to him.

"How's my boy?" Travis began to chant an old Comanche song. He caught the judge watching him, and she turned her back swiftly. Once again, he wondered whether she disapproved of him because of his race.

When she announced that supper was ready, the men sat down to eat. As Crystal busied herself getting steaming dishes on the table, Travis picked up a bowl of potatoes. He stuck a fork into one, and it fell apart in mushy pieces. He fished some onto his plate and passed the bowl to Zachary while Crystal poured cups of hot coffee.

Travis tried to saw the slab of burned meat into pieces.

"It's going to be tough," she said, her brow furrowed as she sat down.

"I can eat it if it's as hard as this table," Zachary said cheerfully. "The supper tastes wonderful, and I thank you all three for taking me in. You've saved my life."

"Turtle River has good medicine," Travis said, wishing Turtle River had been caring for Elizabeth, yet knowing the Cheyenne's natural medicines wouldn't have saved her.

Travis sawed off another bite of meat and chewed it, hoping he didn't break a tooth.

"This meat is dreadful," Crystal said, flushed and embarrassed.

"It's edible," Travis remarked and cut another bite. "Did Ellery cook?"

"As a matter of fact, he did the cooking a great deal of the time," Crystal admitted. The supper was a disaster, she knew, but Travis Black Eagle seemed to want to eat anyway. She was certain the man would not take one bite out of politeness or to spare her feelings. She glanced at him as he took a sip of coffee and saw his brows narrow as he set the cup back on the table.

"Something's wrong?" she asked.

"That's Yankee coffee," he said in a derogatory tone. "I

drink mine stronger." He stood and crossed to the counter to the coffee grinder. He dropped grounds into his cup, stirred them, and sat down again to saw at his meat.

"I would think *you'd* cook," she said.

"I have cooked when I had to."

At his shuttered look, she inferred that he was thinking about his Elizabeth. The angles and planes of the man's face, his prominent cheekbones, and his firm jaw gave him a rugged air that was heightened to a fierce wildness by his thick hair, stubble of beard and bloodshot eyes.

"I'm surprised you didn't learn to cook at home," he remarked.

"We had a servant who cooked until the last few months when I was all alone."

He paused with his fork in midair as he studied her along with the other two males who stared at her.

"You've always had servants until you came out here?" he asked.

"Yes, we did until the last month before I came West. My father was shot and killed when I was thirteen. My grandparents lived with us, and I sold everything when Grandfather died and paid his debts."

"You must have lived in a big house," Zachary said, awed.

"It was two-storied with a large porch that ran around two sides and fancy woodworking on the porch. We had a flower garden and an iron fence around the yard. Baltimore is a beautiful place."

"Do you want to go back there?" Zachary asked with rapt attention.

"No. Baltimore is far away and out of my life. All my family is gone now," she said, uncomfortable because that was not the reason she did not want to return to Baltimore. As she glanced at Black Eagle, she thought of the gold in his drawer. If she were unscrupulous, she could take it and flee to California. She glanced up again to find him still watching her. One look

into his dark devil-eyes and she knew she would pity anyone
who tried to take something from him against his wishes.

The men became silent. Zachary ate every bite on his plate
and had another helping, which made her feel slightly better.
The boy must have been famished. She couldn't bear to eat
the tough meat, but she ate potatoes and drank the coffee.

"Do you live near here, Zachary?" Black Eagle asked.

"No, sir. Closer to Laramie."

"How old are you?"

"Seventeen."

Crystal was surprised to discover he was that old. Next to
Travis Black Eagle and Turtle River, the slender boy looked
like a child.

"You can have a job if you want to stay for a while,"
Black Eagle added. His offer was a bigger surprise to her than
Zachary's age. Crystal studied Black Eagle, amazed by his
kindness. She wondered where Zachary would live. Would he
continue to share the cabin with them?

"You mean that, sir? I'd like that. Thank you!"

"There's a small cabin not far from this house where you
can stay. There's not much furniture—just a bed and chest of
drawers—but you can eat here with us."

"That would be fine," Zachary said, relief plain in his voice.
"We both stay in the cabin?" he asked Turtle River, who
shook his head.

"No. I have my tipi."

Black Eagle placed his fork on his plate and studied Zachary.
"Will anyone come looking for you that I should know about?"

Zachary's smile vanished. "Someone might, but it shouldn't
concern you, sir."

"It will concern me if it places any of us in danger," Black
Eagle said solemnly, and Crystal saw the blink of surprise as
Zachary's brows arched. He flushed and looked away.

"If my pa comes for me, he won't give anyone else trouble.
Leastwise, not the two of you," he added, looking at Turtle

River and Black Eagle. "He's a coward when someone is his own size."

"I don't want my son to be in danger," Black Eagle added. Crystal felt no surprise that he didn't mention her welfare because she knew he didn't care for her in the least, but she was curious about Zachary's answer because she didn't want the baby in any danger either.

"A baby won't be in danger. Besides, I'd go with him before I'd let him bring trouble or hurt to any of you."

"You won't go with him unless you really want to," Black Eagle said emphatically, turning to look into her eyes. She knew what he was telling her, but she had sworn to uphold the law and that is what she would have to do.

As soon as they finished eating, all three males left to look at the cabin for Zachary while she cleaned dishes and fed the baby. None of them returned, and she stretched on the bed, still wearing her dress, expecting to have to get up again with the baby. The next thing she knew it was morning and the little fellow was screaming and kicking.

That night Turtle River and Zachary came to eat after dark.

"Your husband is tending an ailing cow. He will be here when he can," Turtle River said.

"Supper smells wonderful," Zachary said, heaping food on his plate.

She enjoyed their company, Zachary keeping up a constant chatter and wanting to know about her life in Baltimore. Turtle River warmed and asked a few questions, listening attentively and nodding as she talked. She wondered about the laconic man's past. Why wasn't he with his own people? For that matter, she wondered the same about Travis Black Eagle.

When the men left, she cleaned, leaving beef and potatoes for her husband. Later she changed behind the makeshift blanket he had hung. She slipped into her white cotton nightgown and blue wrapper. An hour later she decided Black Eagle would not return at all, wondering whether he slept outside or at the cabin where Zachary stayed.

For the next two days, she didn't see him. He ate and left before she was awake, not coming back at night. The temperature climbed, but the nights stayed a cool relief.

One night, hours after Turtle River and Zachary had eaten, the door swung open and Black Eagle entered. He was bare-chested, wet from washing. In spite of his muscles and fit body, he had dark smudges beneath his eyes and his cheeks had a hollow, gaunt look. She wondered how much he had slept or eaten since the death of his wife, and her sympathy went out to him.

"Evening. Supper might still be warm. It isn't burned tonight."

"I'm hungry enough to eat it raw." He raked his hair from his face with both hands. "Cows are dropping calves, and I've been busy the last three days. We need rain desperately, but thank heaven I have water on this land," he said, sounding distracted and concerned about his ranch. "How's my son?" he asked, crossing to the cradle to pick up the cooing baby. She watched Black Eagle's features soften as he talked to the infant.

"I was just getting ready to feed him," she answered, putting down the bottle while she served a plate for Black Eagle. She placed his food on the table and took the baby from him, sitting down on one of the straight-backed chairs.

Her fingers brushed Black Eagle's, and she was aware of his broad bare chest as he sat facing her.

She saw no reason to try to make conversation. She knew Travis Black Eagle was not interested in her trying to entertain him. As he ate, he seemed to forget her presence completely. When he finished, he carried his dishes to the washpan. He moved around the room, hanging his gunbelt on the bedpost, looking at the baby, and finally settling down at the table with tools and a hinge he was mending.

"Mr. Black Eagle—"

"Travis," he corrected without looking up.

"Travis," she said, blushing, wondering if he thought she

was the silliest woman he had ever had to deal with. As she watched his hands moving over the broken hinge, she felt a strange tingling awareness of him. His fingers were blunt, his hands well-shaped, and she remembered the moment his hands had closed around her waist and he had lifted her down from the wagon.

"There's something I want to talk to you about," she said.

He paused to look at her. "What's that?"

"You need to give your son a name." Again the shuttered look distanced him from her, and his stony countenance made her want to drop the matter, but she persisted. "I've been thinking about it. You can't name a boy Elizabeth, but what about Elizabeth's father's name?"

A muscle worked in Travis's jaw and he stood up abruptly, walking to a window to stare into the darkness, and her gaze drifted down over his back to his trim hips, the dirt-smudged denim pants that hugged him snugly. He had long legs and stood with them apart as he stared outside.

"Elizabeth and I talked a little about it," he said gruffly. "She preferred Jacob or Joshua."

"And what do you prefer?"

With an angry scowl on his features he turned to look at the baby in her arms. "Elizabeth's father's name was Irwin. I suppose Jacob Irwin Black Eagle." His dark gaze swung to her and silence spread between them.

"Jacob is a fine name," she said emphatically, pleased by his choice. "Jacob Irwin Black Eagle. Would you prefer the name of a relative of yours?" she asked, wondering about his heritage. "What about your father's name?"

His dark eyes stabbed her, and she felt a shiver slither down her spine.

"My father was Tall Bear. Tall Bear Black Eagle would sound too strange for him to be accepted anywhere. I will give him my name—Black Eagle. Jacob Irwin Black Eagle. It would please my father for him to be called Black Eagle."

"Is your father living?"

Travis shook his head. ''No. He was killed by soldiers years ago. My mother was a captive, but she came to love my father. When I was twelve, soldiers raided our camp. They took my mother and Brett, my brother, and me back with them. I never saw my father again, but I heard when he was killed.''

''So you lived all your early years with your father,'' she said, easily imagining him in that life. She placed the sleeping baby in his cradle. ''Good night, little Jacob Irwin Black Eagle,'' she said softly, kissing his cheek, happy with the name. ''We should have Reverend Nealy christen him.''

Travis's gaze shifted to the cradle and the sleeping baby. ''I'll speak to him when I go to town.''

A mental list spun in her mind of more things she wanted Black Eagle to do, but she had pushed it far enough for one night. Every bit of conversation from him seemed pried out against his will. He rarely gave her a direct look, and she sensed he was holding himself in check; yet he didn't look like a man who would give in to his emotions easily.

She watched him. Had she married a man who had had too many losses? Maybe it wasn't just Elizabeth's loss that had made him so hard and angry. Still, there was no point in offering consolation. She suspected the less she said, the better he would like it. She knew she wasn't the woman he wanted helping him name his baby.

She folded clothing while he mended broken tools, and finally he leaned back in the chair and stretched. She glanced at him as he held up his arms, her gaze sliding over the bulge of his muscles and the veins standing out in his forearms. His long legs were stretched in front of him, and he seemed to radiate power just sitting still in the chair. Again, she felt fluttery, a strange sensation she had every time she gave him her full attention. She went back to folding and stacking clothes that she picked up from the floor.

She turned as he strode across the room and buckled on his gunbelt. He jammed his hat on his head and his dark gaze swung to her.

"I'm going out and I'll sleep outside. Go ahead and go to bed and sleep in your gown. It's too hot to sleep every night in all your clothing. I won't be back tonight." At the door he paused. "Crystal," he pronounced grimly as if reminding himself that she was now his wife. "I won't notice whether you're in a dress or a gown and I won't care. I feel as numb as this damn door." He clamped his jaw closed and left, slamming the door behind him.

She blinked and let out her breath, her heart hammering from his words and the fierce look he had given her. He might be numb, but she wasn't. Great heavens, how could she go around in her nightgown in front of a man whose looks stripped her to her soul?

As if fleeing a monster, she rushed to the cradle and knelt beside it, reassuring herself with the sight of the baby. *Her* baby now. Jacob Irwin Black Eagle. It was a fine, strong name and she liked it. "Jacob," she said quietly. "My darling little Jacob." She leaned down to kiss his soft cheek and then stood up, going to the crate that held her clothing.

She pulled out her nightgown and wrapper and took her hair down, brushing it, her thoughts on the strong man she had married. Her gaze ran over the cabin and she felt a rush of satisfaction. Travis Black Eagle was a tiny part of her life and he was keeping his bargain. She had a home and was no longer in debt. She had a baby who would know her as his mother. Zachary was a cheerful friend and Turtle River in his own quiet way was becoming a friend. The only enigma was the man she had married.

She stretched on the bed and was asleep in minutes.

The next morning dawned with sunshine and blue skies, but by noon the air was heavy with heat. They needed rain and whenever she stepped outside to the pump, she scanned the horizon. By midafternoon heat lightning streaked the sky and dark clouds gathered along the horizon. Crystal prayed the rain would blow their way.

She unfastened the top buttons of her red calico dress and

pushed the neck open, fanning herself. She stood outside, digging a small garden and watching the approaching storm while the baby slept blissfully in his cradle only yards away from her.

When lightning popped and crackled close at hand, she picked up the cradle and carried Jacob inside, setting him down and fetching a cool wet rag to wipe his face and then hers.

Lightning zagged across the sky, streaking to the ground with a pop. It struck in the field of grass stretching away to the west from the cabin.

Crystal stretched high, getting down a large iron skillet from a shelf, dreading building a fire in the already-stuffy cabin. She stepped outside on the porch to get kindling for the firebox and glanced in the direction of the storm clouds.

Across the field that stretched away from the house to the west, a bright orange tongue of flame flickered in the dry grass.

Crystal gasped, terror galvanizing her into action as she raced into the cabin. Wildfire!

Seven

Panic swept her as swift and hot as the tongue of flame already dancing across the grass. She remembered the terrifying fire that had swept Cheyenne last year, burning most of the town.

Grabbing up her skirts, Crystal ran to the door, standing on tiptoe to retrieve the heavy revolver. She rushed outside, firing two quick shots, and then she dashed back to return the revolver to the shelf. Jacob slept undisturbed through both shots, and she prayed that the men had heard them.

She picked up the cradle and carried the sleeping infant to the porch. Then she ran to the shed to search for anything to beat out the fire. She found two buckets and gunnysacks and raced to the pump to fill the buckets.

The line of fire had spread with terrifying speed. As she pumped she looked at the dark clouds building in the sky and she willed rain to come. Lightning popped, causing her to jump. She tossed the sacks across her shoulders and carried both buckets, water sloshing as she hurried toward the flames that were too close to the cabin. She would have only minutes to fight the fire before she would have to get Jacob and flee.

Ignoring an urge to run, she moved as close as she dared and set down the buckets. A fierce need to protect the cabin gave her the courage to fight the flames. This was her home now, and little Jacob's, and it was worth fighting to save. Shaking with worry, she dipped a sack in the water and beat the flames.

Almost immediately her arms ached and smoke stung her throat. The wind blew the flames toward the cabin, and she struggled desperately to stop their hungry path.

Beyond the dancing flames dark forms loomed into sight, and her heart jumped as she saw the men riding toward her. Travis reined his horse and leapt down.

"Where's my son?" he shouted.

"He's on the porch, asleep."

"Take the horses to the house. Get them away from this. Take the baby and get away from here!"

She grabbed the reins and mounted, swinging her leg across the saddle to sit astride, forgetting her dress was hiked up to her knees as she turned the big gelding and gathered the reins to Turtle River's pinto. At the shed she saw Zachary jump off a horse and run to help fight the fire.

The storm clouds had darkened the sky and rain was coming, but would it reach them soon enough to save the cabin? Debating whether to take Jacob and flee now or go back to help, she tethered the horses beyond the house. With another look at Jacob, who still slept peacefully, she decided to stay.

She grabbed a pot from the house and pumped more water, rushing to carry it to the men, who beat wildly at the flames. While thunder rumbled and the wind tore at her, dark clouds covered the sky. Curling flames and sparks blew across her, and black smoke stung her eyes as she swung a wet sack.

The brilliant orange flames were bright against the black clouds, billowing and growing, inching closer to the cabin.

Travis had shed his shirt and worked in a steady rhythm,

beating flames, muscles rippling in his back. She dipped a sack into the water, turning to beat at the flames, when she heard a hissing sound.

Beyond the line of fire a sheet of gray rain and white bits of ice pounded the earth. Her heart leaped with relief. *Rain!*

"Rain!" A jubilant cry from Travis echoed her thoughts. He flung the wet sack in the air. "Run!"

She raced for the house, trying to hold up her skirts as the hissing changed to a roar. She covered her head with her arms when stinging pellets of hail stung her.

Strong arms swept her up, wrapping around her. She was pulled close against Travis's broad chest and she wrapped her arm around his neck, clinging to him and turning her face and upper body against his bare chest. She knew he was protecting her from the hail, but the reason was of little consequence compared to the feelings that raced through her.

Tiny shocks were more disturbing to her system than the storm pouring over them. It was the first time she had ever been held in a man's arms, and she liked it. She was aware of the solid beat of his heart, his masculine scent, the warmth of his body.

All her life she had had to take care of others, to take care of herself, but for this brief moment she felt protected and cared for. He had no love for her, but he was considerate and his care set her heart racing. She liked being in his arms, and she savored the feeling of closeness. His chest was solid, hard, feeling so good against her.

Never before had she been as aware of a man or as tingly around one. And it went deeper than that. When he married her, she had seen only a wild, angry and strong-willed man. But in the days since they had said their vows, she had seen that he had a kind and gentle side. He could be protective, generous to Zachary, loving with his son. Yet along with his kind side, he had a forcefulness that she found exhilarating. All her life she had been surrounded by weak men—her father,

her grandfather, Ellery. This man was strong, decisive, power-ful—a challenge and a temptation at the same time.

Long ago she had decided she would never know a man's love and she had felt she would have a fulfilling life anyway; but now during the wild storm as Black Eagle raced toward the house with her held close in his arms, a longing for more blossomed within her.

He leapt to the porch and set her on her feet, laughing as Zachary and Turtle River ran past to get the horses to take them to the animal shed.

She looked up at Black Eagle and shock riveted her. The man could laugh! Laughter transformed him from the solemn, angry man she had always known to a man whose white teeth were a bright contrast to his dark skin and whose brown eyes sparkled with triumph. He was handsome and she stared trans-fixed, her body still feeling the warmth of his, her memory still fresh with how it felt to be carried in his strong arms.

He had a tiny cut on his cheek where a hailstone must have struck his cheekbone. She reached up and lightly wiped away blood. "You're cut," she said, conscious of brushing her fingers against his face.

"It's nothing," he replied, giving his cheek a swipe with his hand. He knelt beside the cradle, his wet denim pants pulling tautly and molding his muscled legs. "Look at him sleeping through it all!" he said, laughing at his son. All she could do was stare at the father.

Don't fall in love with him.

The words came out of the air, startling her, popping into her mind; and instantly she gave a shake of her head as if she were arguing with herself. The notion was ridiculous; why was her heart racing madly?

How in heaven's name, in the space of minutes, had she gone from a woman knowing her own mind to one who no longer knew her own heart? Black Eagle faced her, placing his hands on his hips, and it took all her self-will to keep from letting her gaze drift down over his bare chest.

"Thankfully, we were close in when you fired the shots." He draped his arm across her shoulders and turned to look at the blackened circle of burned grass. "What happened?"

"Summer lightning," she said. Although she understood that he thought nothing of draping his arm around her, she was acutely aware of standing close enough to him to feel the heat of his body and she was conscious of his strong arm across her shoulders. The realization that she wanted to move closer to him frightened her. Feelings she had never known before were beginning to stir inside her, and curiosity and a desire that she had never experienced disturbed her. When she moved away, he dropped his arm to his side.

"Thank heaven the rain came. I'm surprised the fire went so fast," she remarked, barely aware of her words, too conscious of him.

"The grass was dry out there. The house would have been in the fire's path. As it is, the patch of burned ground will be covered by new growth in no time ... especially with this rain." He ran his fingers through his hair, sweeping the long black hair sleekly away from his face and changing his appearance again. With his hair pulled back, his prominent cheekbones stood out starkly, his nose had just enough crook to give him an air of arrogance. She could imagine him as a warrior with streaks of paint on his face and a lance in his hand. Now he looked fully the dominant, determined male she had clashed with too often.

He gazed at her solemnly. "If there's ever a fire again, you take my son and get him out of here."

"When it got closer, I was going to go."

"You might not judge correctly. You go," he said with a firm stare. "But you were a big help this afternoon, Judge," he added quietly.

His praise fueled satisfaction in her. When his brown eyes swept over her, she knew she looked like a bedraggled, half-drowned rat. It really didn't matter how she looked; he wouldn't care. She suspected he didn't even really see her, and the knowledge hurt.

"This may settle into a long night of rain, and God knows, we need it desperately. I'll head out to see about the horses." He jumped off the porch and ran to the shed. She watched his long stride cover the ground swiftly. Why hadn't he returned to his own people? He looked like that was where he belonged. She thought of the shield she had found in his cabinet. If he saved a shield and a headdress, then his past was important to him. Why had he chosen the white man's life?

Now, bare-chested, with his black hair flying as he ran, he looked like a fierce warrior. She remembered the powerful muscles in his back as he swung the sack, beating flames. He was a magnificent specimen of manhood, virile and powerful. Her memory shifted with startling clarity to how it felt to be carried in his arms.

She went inside and threw open her trunk, rummaging through the belongings she had not unpacked. She found a small mahogany-framed oval mirror that she pulled out and held up, looking at herself. Her face was smudged with black streaks, and locks of wet hair hung around her face. She looked soggy; but in her best moments, she would never look like his Elizabeth, who had been breathtakingly beautiful.

Setting aside the mirror, Crystal unbuttoned the wet dress and stepped out of it to dry and change to a cotton dress with a white bodice and a black skirt.

That night she cooked more stew because she was less likely to burn it. While a light rain came down steadily, the thick stew bubbled away in a pot on the stove.

All three men came to eat, and for the first time, Travis seemed less tense and withdrawn. And she was more aware of him than ever, conscious every time his solemn gaze rested on her. The men played with the baby and while they ate, talked about the fire and the rain and the new calves. As always Zachary told her how wonderful the supper was.

It amazed her to watch both Black Eagle and Turtle River

around Jacob. Black Eagle became tender, caring, laughing with his son, fascinated by the baby. It surprised her that he had a gentle side. Turtle River was even more amazing. The stoic Indian was as giddy as a new father, babbling with Jacob, talking to him about hunting, telling tales the infant could not possibly understand. Zachary, who was as friendly as a puppy, was the least interested in Jacob, but she guessed it was not unusual for a young male to have little interest in a baby. With his back healing, Zachary worked now as long as the other men. His brown hair was slicked down and parted in the center, but sprigs of hair stood up in the crown. His skin had grown darker with the past days of working in the sunshine.

When she stood to clean, Zachary moved to her side swiftly, taking dishes from her hands. "Let me help you, Judge."

"Zachary, just call me Crystal."

"Yes, ma'am," he said, smiling. He helped while Turtle River and Black Eagle went outside, taking Jacob with them.

Once the dishes were washed and dried, Crystal was done with evening chores and Zachary motioned toward the piano.

"Play something, Crystal. I want to hear you play."

She went to the piano that she hadn't touched since Ellery's death. She sat on the stool and uncovered the keyboard, striking a chord and then playing an old familiar hymn. To her delight Zachary began to sing, his tenor voice carrying, and she joined him as they went from one song to another and she wondered about Black Eagle, who sat on the darkened porch with Turtle River and Jacob.

Eventually he came inside, carrying the cradle and setting Jacob down. In her peripheral vision she could see Black Eagle standing and watching her. Then he disappeared, and she heard him moving around.

"I'd better be going, Crystal," Zachary said. "Turtle River must have gone already."

"It was fun, Zachary. I haven't played in a long time."

"Yes, ma'am. It was fun," he said, gazing at her so intently

Crystal was startled. He had pulled a chair close and she slid off the stool and moved away.

"Night, ma'am," Zachary said quietly and then left.

She closed the piano and looked around, half-expecting to find Black Eagle gone as usual, but the rain must have driven him inside. He was stretched on the bed, still dressed, and he had fallen asleep as she had the past nights. She looked down at him. Even in sleep he looked masculine and powerful, and all her fluttery feelings returned.

Curious, she moved closer, studying him with a slow thoroughness that she could never do when he was awake. His lips were well-sculpted, his lower lip full. She studied his mouth, her own lips tingling while questions swirled. The only kisses she had ever known were Harvey Goodwill's, and she suspected Travis Black Eagle's kisses would be vastly different. Hot and disturbed, she stared at Black Eagle's mouth, imagining the feel of it against her own, and she suspected it would be nothing like the kisses from Harvey that she never wanted to recall.

Another deep pang of longing swept her like the one she had experienced in Black Eagle's arms in the afternoon. When there had been no man in her life, she hadn't given it much thought; but now, with a vital, forceful man with her daily, she was conscious of what she was missing. She reminded herself she should be thankful for what she had with Black Eagle. If he hadn't come along, she would be alone and facing immediate payment of Ellery's debts.

Reluctantly, she faced the stark fact that she was locked into a loveless marriage and she would never know a man's love and kisses and care. There never had been a man who had loved her, she reminded herself. It wasn't as if she had given up her chance for happiness with this marriage.

She knew she should move away and not stand staring at him, but she was fascinated. His chiseled features were exotic to her, so different from the men she had known. His deep-brown skin was smooth over prominent cheekbones. The dark fringe of lashes shadowed his cheeks. He had the faint line of a scar along his temple and his dark brows were straight. His chest was bare and her body tensed and heated more as she let her gaze stray slowly over the powerful muscles, and dark nipples, down over his flat stomach to the wide belt and the tight denim pants that hugged his narrow hips. His hipbones pushed against the denim, and the worn fabric bulged over his maleness. She flushed as her gaze rushed back to his face.

She had to admit that she was physically drawn to him, but she reminded herself sternly that he was not drawn to her, nor would he ever be.

How long she stood staring at him, she didn't know, but Jacob stirred and she went to change and feed him. When Jacob finally went back to sleep, she stared at the bed. Exhaustion filled her, but she didn't want to climb into bed beside Black Eagle. The mere thought made her nervous. At the same time, she didn't want to spend the night in a chair and she knew he would think she was incredibly foolish if she did so.

Reluctantly, she went to the opposite side of the bed and lay down, staying fully dressed. When she leaned forward to extinguish the lamp, she glanced at him one more time. The glow from the yellow flame gave burnished highlights to his skin. Remembering him carrying her in his strong arms, she put out the lamp.

Every inch of her skin prickled with awareness that he was stretched out only inches away. She closed her eyes, listening to the rain but thinking of Black Eagle, hearing his quiet, deep breathing, trying to avoid staring at him more.

Why did he have such an intense effect on her? Never had she been so conscious of a man or of herself around a man. How long before she grew accustomed to him and lost all her jittery awareness? And what would happen if she did love him? He would never love her in return. She would open herself to hurt. She turned on her side with her back to him, but her skin still prickled and she was as conscious of him as ever. And she vowed to guard against letting her affection for him grow, because her love would never be returned.

* * *

Tomorrow was Friday, her day in court, and as they had done the week before, Travis would take her, taking Jacob with him to the livery stable. For once, she didn't look forward as eagerly to the court day because it meant being away from Jacob. All the same, she loved her work, and it was only one day out of the week. As she left the house she carried Jacob. Her hair was braided and rolled into a bun behind her head and she wore a black bonnet that she was certain did little to help her appearance. She could still hear her grandmother's voice telling her, "You are a plain woman, Crystal, so you should learn to take care of yourself and use your mind."

What would Grandmother say if she knew about this marriage? She would probably be horrified that Crystal had married what Grandmother Spencer would call a savage.

Travis stood waiting beside the wagon, and even though she knew it was foolish, she felt nervous under his scrutiny. Beneath a wide-brimmed black hat his dark hair was pulled behind his head and tied with a strip of rawhide, and he wore a black shirt and black denim pants. He looked formidable and handsome while she felt hot in her black dress and as plain as a mud hen. Until the past couple of days, she had not thought of the man as handsome. Overwhelming, yes. Powerful, yes. But *handsome?* When had her reaction to him shifted and why did her heart race every time he was nearby?

He had a holster buckled around his hips, and she thought of Ellery and the dangers between here and town. Riding beside Travis Black Eagle, she would feel no fear for her safety or for Jacob's safety.

The day Black Eagle had proposed he had been wearing black, and all she had been able to think of was a devil of a man; but now she no longer thought of him that way. Too conscious of his gaze on her, she hurried her step. When she looked directly into his chocolate-colored eyes, her fluttery feelings deepened.

"Sorry to keep you waiting," she said perfunctorily, uneasy in the silence. "If you'll hold Jacob, I'll climb into the wagon."

Instead, Black Eagle swept Crystal up in his arms and swung her up onto the wagon seat easily. Time stopped. She was aware of being in his arms again; aware of how easily he could carry her; conscious of his warm, strong body, his face only inches from hers . . . his clean, male scent. Then he placed her on the seat and released her. He went around and climbed up to sit beside her.

Flustered, she looked at the cooing infant, smoothing black curls from his face. With a creak of wheels, the wagon began to move.

"You think you can tend him while you work?" she asked, concerned about the baby at a livery stable with only men to watch him. "Perhaps on my court days we should get a nurse."

"There are no nursemaids to hire," Black Eagle replied bluntly; and she realized if there had been, he would not have proposed marriage to her. Crystal was aware of him seated close beside her, his booted feet propped up on the wagon and her skirt against his long leg. "I'll take good care of him," Black Eagle added, amusement in his voice, and she was embarrassed that she had implied she was afraid he couldn't. She looked at Jacob, who stared back at her. He had won her heart so swiftly. Such a tiny person, yet he was already more important to her than anyone else.

As they rode away from the log house, she glanced back, thinking how her life had changed. She had dreaded coming to live here, been terrified of the responsibility of a baby, defiant toward and frightened of her new husband. Now, in such a short time, how different she had come to feel about the union! She loved Jacob fiercely and she was no longer alone. She would repay Travis Black Eagle every cent, but she was free of debt to the bank and to the men Ellery had owed.

Out of the corner of her eye she looked at the tall man beside her. He sat straight, staring in the distance. Had he been this quiet and uncommunicative with Elizabeth? Crystal doubted it. She remembered the moments yesterday when he was filled with easy laughter, jubilant over the rain. Charm had radiated from him like rays from the sun . . . briefly.

"Are you Shoshone or Cheyenne?" she asked, her curiosity about him running rampant. She had heard of Shoshone, Arapaho, Bannock, Cheyenne, and Sioux, although most Indians Ellery had talked about had been Cheyenne or Shoshone.

"Comanche."

Puzzled she rolled the foreign word on her tongue. "I have never heard of the Comanche."

"Most of them live on the southern plains now. My people are in Texas."

His answer shocked her. He was as far from his home as she was from hers. She thought of Texas as a wild place, hundreds of miles south and more of a lawless frontier than Wyoming. The cowboys who rode into town bringing cattle up from Texas were a wild bunch. Why hadn't Travis Black Eagle returned to Texas?

"You said your mother and your brother were taken by the soldiers. Where's your mother now?" Crystal asked, prying, but too curious to keep quiet.

"She died before the war and my brother and I got separated during those years."

"So you fought in the war?"

"Yes, for the Confederacy, but no one out here asks."

She became silent for a few miles. People on the frontier didn't ask questions that they would have back home because too many people on the frontier were hiding or fleeing from something they had left behind. Plagued by curiosity about Black Eagle, she wondered what he had fled from. She couldn't imagine him hiding anything; he seemed too direct and forceful. And she didn't want questions asked about her own past, so she felt uncomfortable asking him, although her curiosity persisted.

"It wasn't your war. I'm surprised you got involved in it instead of returning to your people," she murmured. He stared ahead, his profile to her, and as her gaze ran over his features, she remembered him stretched beside her on the bed last night.

Shifting his weight, Travis stared at the wagon ruts ahead that cut two swaths through the short grass. The clop of the hooves of the horses blended with the creak of the wheels. The judge was filled with questions, and he could give her the answers he had concocted years earlier. It had been so long since anyone had asked him about his past that he wondered if he remembered the story he had usually given.

"By then my father had been killed and the government was taking land from my people and trying to move them. Our way of life was disappearing and I could see that once the war was over it might vanish completely. We lived near a fort and I saw the weapons and the supplies the soldiers had."

"The Confederacy wasn't as well off."

"Maybe not, but by joining them, I had a chance to fight the soldiers who had torn my family apart and taken my heritage from me."

"Were you a scout?"

"No," he answered, amused. Of course she would think the only thing an Indian would be allowed to do was scout. He caught her looking at him, her green eyes wide in surprise, her cheeks pink with embarrassment. "I was a captain when the war was over," he answered dryly.

"My goodness!" she exclaimed. "A captain!"

"You didn't think it was possible, did you, Judge?"

"I'm just . . . surprised," she answered and fell silent.

He felt a ruffle of anger over the prejudice that he always faced, but shrugged away the irritation. Crystal was not as biased as many people. He suspected she held more grudges against men in general than Indians in particular. And he suspected the judge was not only a stickler for law and order, but was also honest to a fault. What in her life would she have ever had to hide?

His thoughts drifted to his land and the livery stable. He needed to spend more time in town next week. The stable was lucrative while his cattle business was just starting. Turtle River was as reliable as a man could be and Zachary was learning fast.

The past three weeks of married life had been strange, but not as bad as Travis had expected. He reflected on the nights when he had sat on the porch in the gentle rain and listened to the judge play the piano and sing. Her voice was flawless with a beauty to it that eased away the worries of the day. It was good to hear a woman's voice lifted in song. And she seemed attentive and captivated by his son, Jacob. He would have to remember to think of the baby as Jacob now and not merely Son. Jacob Irwin Black Eagle.

Travis liked the name and he knew Elizabeth would have approved. He glanced at the judge who sat fussing with Jacob, her black bonnet hiding her face from Travis's view. Her fingers were long and slender and looked delicate as they fluttered over the infant. He had made a good choice, she was going to be a good mother. She had grit and he admired that. He had already known she had grit, but it had surfaced again yesterday when she kept a cool head about the fire. Thank heavens he had been working close by.

The moment he'd heard the shots, his fear had been that something had happened to Jacob. And then as he raced home, he'd seen the gray plume of smoke curling and known it was fire, but he'd been terrified Jacob might have been caught in it. Then he'd seen the judge swinging a wet sack, beating the flames as vigorously as possible.

Travis glanced at her again. She should have married some man who would have loved her, but how would she find that out here? Most men he knew were scared of her or disliked her intensely, disapproving of a woman serving office and sitting in judgment over men. Most of the men he knew disapproved of women having the vote or being able to hold office, even though few ladies wanted to hold office. He admired strong women, although there were moments he wanted to give the judge a good shake because of her stubborn, blind-to-reason views on the law.

His people's women were strong. Comanche women had to be strong to survive, and sometimes the elders asked their opinions and accepted them, but most white men he had encountered didn't want a woman to have power over them. Most of the men around here resented her being a judge.

She was smarter than half the men in Cheyenne—if not more than half, Travis thought uncomfortably. He himself could do a lot of things—take care of animals, run the ranch and stable—but he had only a couple of months of schooling.

They rode in silence, finally drawing in sight of Cheyenne. He glanced at her again, unable to see her face for the bonnet. He knew she was eager to get back to town and to her courtroom. He preferred his days at the ranch to the ones at the livery stable, but the stable was supporting the ranch at this point and Turtle River could run the ranch.

Travis stopped in front of the courthouse and jumped down, going around to help her. She had placed Jacob in the cradle in the bed of the wagon and he was protesting, his cries carrying loudly and drawing the attention of people along the street. Travis swung her down easily. She was far taller than Elizabeth, but willowy and as easy to lift as a child.

She blushed anytime he touched her, and he thought of her Judge Spinster nickname that still seemed to fit even though she was now officially Mrs. Black Eagle. And Judge Black Eagle. That would never cease to amaze him.

"What time will you be finished here?"

"At the end of the day. I'll walk down to the livery stable."

He nodded and climbed back into the wagon, lifting Jacob into his arms before picking up the reins to drive away. "Try not to hang 'em all, Judge," he said lightly, touching the brim of his hat with his finger in a farewell salute.

Consternation filled her as she stared at his broad shoulders. Did the man have such a low regard for the law that he could be so flippant about her task? She took a deep breath and went inside, suddenly feeling more sure of herself and at ease in the familiar building that was Cheyenne's courthouse.

By the end of the day Crystal was thinking about Jacob and longing to see him. She called forward the last name on the docket.

Gower Colby was charged with intoxication, brawling, disturbing the peace, and attacking Deputy Thomas. She listened attentively to the deputy's testimony as Clarence Hoyt prosecuted the case and then she heard one of Cheyenne's lawyers, Elwood Briarly, plead Gower's case.

When she levied fines and sentenced Gower, he suddenly stood, pushing back his chair and knocking it to the floor with a bang that made her jump.

"No! No damn squaw is sending me to jail!"

Shocked, Crystal banged her gavel. "Sit down, Mr. Colby, before I fine you for contempt of court!"

Elwood Briarly and Deputy Thomas got Colby back in his chair and she restated the sentence and fines, banged her gavel, and dismissed court. Swiftly, she left the courtroom.

As she removed her robe in the tiny room that served as her office, she heard a knock at the open door. Sheriff Hinckel stood there. A full six inches shorter than her husband, the sheriff still seemed imposing to Crystal. As he entered her office, his bulky shoulders almost brushed both sides of the door.

"How's the new bride?" he asked.

"Fine, Sheriff."

"I heard Gower Colby. I was in the hall."

Embarrassed, she shrugged. "He's in jail now and that's that."

"Judge, I was a friend of Ellery's and I've known you since you moved here. You don't have your brother now, so I'll speak frankly to you in his stead. Your new husband is a half-breed, and a lot of people in town don't like redskins. Gower isn't going to be the only one to give you trouble."

Dumbfounded, she stared at the sheriff. "My husband being a half-breed, has little to do with me," she said stiffly. "I was born and raised in Baltimore and am as civilized as anyone in this wild town."

"I know you're civilized, ma'am," he remarked patiently, shifting tobacco from one cheek to the other. "But your husband's heritage has a lot to do with you since you married him. You heard Gower. There's a lot of people here who, from now on, will see you as a squaw. Nothing else."

"That's absurd! Mr. Black Eagle lives the same kind of life most of the people here live. He left his people a long time ago to follow the white man's way."

"He's Indian, and that's all some people see. You married a redskin, so you're a squaw."

"I just can't believe that!" she exclaimed, certain the sheriff was wrong.

"Ma'am, if I were you, I'd use your maiden name—Judge Spencer, not Judge Black Eagle. People will take more kindly to it. And you're going to find a problem when you go into town to shop. Wilbur Throckmorton won't allow Indians or their families in his store, so the dry goods will be closed to you and your husband."

Shocked, she stared at the sheriff. "You mean I can't purchase material from Mr. Throckmorton any longer? That's impossible."

"I thought I might save you some embarrassment. It's Wilbur's store, and he can refuse anyone he wants."

"Mr. Throckmorton won't refuse my business. He's always been friendly."

"Don't push things, Judge. You'll just get that new husband of yours into a fight ... or worse. And he needs business at his livery stable. After all, his isn't the only livery in town and he isn't the only smithy. First ripple of trouble, and your husband's business will be gone."

She ran her hand across her head. "I can't imagine . . ."

"If you can't, then you have less prejudice than a lot of people. Ellery didn't care about the color of a man's skin, so I suppose it's natural that you don't either; but that's not the case with a lot of folks. Some of these people have lost their families to Indians. They hate a redskin more than anything on earth. Ask your husband. He'll tell you. He's a damned good farrier, so people tolerate him. And he packs a mean punch, so that saves him some trouble. Just be careful, Judge. He walks a narrow line."

She nodded as the sheriff left her office. Tying her bonnet beneath her chin, she gathered her reticule and papers and left her office, closing the door behind her.

Disturbed by the sheriff's words, she shopped, going down her list, telling Clem Mandeville at the general store that Mr. Black Eagle would pick up the items later. As she approached Wilbur Throckmorton's dry goods store, she debated whether to push the issue or wait. Remembering the sheriff's warnings, she walked on, her head high. How could people be so spiteful and filled with hate? Would Wilbur Throckmorton turn away Jacob later?

She stopped stone-still in the middle of the boardwalk as this new worry about Jacob mushroomed. The son would face the same prejudice as the father.

"Afternoon, Judge," a voice said pleasantly, and she answered perfunctorily without seeing the person who passed her. Rooted to the spot, she stared into space, upset and distracted.

Little Jacob would face the white man's hatred of Indians. She bristled. He was one-quarter Indian with a white mother and a white grandmother. He was born to civilized people, not out on the prairie. She thought about his dark skin and eyes and raven hair. He looked as Indian as the most full-blood she had ever seen. Her worry knotted like a tangle of yarn. She could cope with townspeople who disliked Black Eagle. And he had long ago learned to deal with them or he wouldn't have a solid business. But the thought of Jacob being treated badly tore her apart. She wanted Jacob to be able to learn law when he grew up or follow whatsoever path he chose.

"Judge, you all right?"

She looked up as the clerk from the banker's office approached her. "I'm fine, Mr. Clarendon. Just trying to remember what was on my list to purchase." She moved on, feeling the clerk's curious brown eyes on her.

When she reached the livery stable, she forgot the cases she'd had, forgot the angry cry of *squaw* from Gower, forgot the sheriff's warnings. She wanted to see Jacob and hold him. And she hated to admit it, but she wanted to see Travis Black Eagle as well.

He was working at an anvil, bare-chested, a leather apron tied around him. His broad chest gleamed with sweat as he pounded on a horseshoe. Her mouth went dry and her insides clutched while heat washed over her. He looked primitive, male, and powerful—all qualities that she once would have expected to frighten her, but fright was far from what she felt now.

His head raised and his dark eyes looked into hers. Her heart stopped. Nodding, he went back to pounding on the horseshoe. Fascinated, she watched the flex of muscles in his shoulders, the bulge of smooth biceps.

"It's cooler in the office," he said with a jerk of his head.

Gathering her wits about her, she fled, hoping he hadn't noticed her stare.

"Howdy, Judge," Andrew Cain said carefully, giving her a half-hearted smile. His blond hair looked like straw whipped in a wind and she wondered if Andrew had had a difficult day. He glanced at Jacob, who was in the cradle, cooing and kicking. "Busy little fellow."

"I'll watch him, Andrew," she said, and Andrew jumped up as if he couldn't wait to escape.

"Thanks, ma'am. I'll work out front."

He fled the office, and she wondered whether he wanted to

get away from her or he had had to spend the day with Jacob and wanted to be free of the baby. Through the open door she could see Travis working. She turned her back, admonishing herself. She had to stop staring at the man before he noticed the effect he had on her.

"How's my baby?" she asked, bending over Jacob. He smiled and kicked and cooed as if he recognized her and her heart leaped with joy. "You sweet thing," she said, picking him up and holding him close. He reached up with tiny fingers to touch her chin.

Talking to him, she walked around the desk and glanced at the open ledger spread before her. The words were printed in large letters that were easy to scan.

She was accustomed to keeping books for Ellery, and for her grandfather before Ellery. Her gaze ran swiftly over the writing and columns. Startled, she looked at the figures again and glanced through the open door at Travis. The livery stable did far better business that she would have guessed. Since she had never used his services for anything, leaving the care of the animals to Ellery, she had no idea how profitable a livery stable could be, but this one was doing well indeed.

Well-enough that she realized she had married a prosperous man, although she had never thought of Travis Black Eagle that way. At least, not until she had found the boxes of money in his drawer.

Of course, the ranch might be draining away the profits of the livery stable; she had no way of knowing about that. Where was the ledger for the ranch? she wondered. If he kept such neat books here, he surely did there; yet she hadn't seen any ledgers and she had scoured every inch of the log house. She turned her attention back to Jacob, thankful to be with him again.

Black Eagle worked long past the supper hour and sent Andrew to Lathrop's cafe to bring back dinners for all of them. Black Eagle ate his as he worked and she had no idea where Andrew ate. She sat in the office with Jacob while she ate delicious hot roast and fluffy potatoes with golden gravy—her first supper in how long that was not burned to a crisp.

It was almost dusk when Black Eagle closed the livery and they drove the wagon back to the two-story stone Addoms & Glover Drug on West Sixteenth Street. Black Eagle made purchases and then drove to Clem Mandeville's general store, which was still open. The breeze had cooled, and she left her bonnet off, unbuttoning the top three buttons of the black dress that was as hot as a woolen blanket wrapped around her.

"I'll get your purchases and I have a few of my own. Want to come in with me?" Black Eagle asked her as he stopped the wagon in front of the open door of the store.

She glanced back at sleeping Jacob and shook her head. "I'll wait right here. No need to disturb the baby."

Black Eagle glanced at the saloon two doors down. Banjo music floated through the open doors and he hesitated, but then he turned and strode into the store. She sat quietly waiting, startled when two men burst through the saloon doors and staggered in her direction.

Recognizing the stringy blond hair of one and the grizzled features of the other, Crystal drew a deep breath, lacing her fingers together and staring straight ahead, hoping the men wouldn't see her.

Eight

Virgil Shank and Slim Tipton guffawed loudly. Feeling uncomfortable and prickly, Crystal glanced at the store and could see Travis just inside the open door. He was kneeling down by several large sacks of flour. On more than one occasion she had sent both Virge and Slim to jail for drunkenness, and she suspected they despised her.

"Lookee there." Virge's voice carried easily to her ears. "Can you believe someone up and married old Judge Spinster? Man must have been blind desperate for a woman."

"Hell, Virge, Judge ain't no woman. She's a stick."

A man crossing the dusty street laughed, nodding his head. Since his back was to her, Crystal had no idea who the man was. Burning with embarrassment, Crystal prayed that Travis could not hear Virge and Slim and that he would finish quickly and join her. She wanted to be off the street, out of the town, and out of the sight of men like Virge and Slim.

Man must have been blind desperate for a woman. The words cut like a knife because Black Eagle had been blind desperate. Were those two scoundrels still smarting because of the times she had sent them to jail or was she honestly that ugly to men? Common sense told her that Virge and Slim were only striking back at her, but she felt miserable and plain, a spinster-woman in spite of the paper that declared she was Mrs. Travis Black Eagle.

Man must have been blind desperate for a woman. The words played again in her mind and she felt as if she couldn't get her breath. She remembered Baltimore, remembered that horrible night when Harvey had knocked on her window and said he had to talk to her. Did men here know about her Baltimore life? She knew they didn't or she would have heard about it, too.

"'Course the man that married her is a breed. Any white woman, no matter what a sorry excuse for a woman, would be what he'd like."

"I don't know, Virge. A man would have to be crazy drunk and fired up something terrible to put up with the likes of her. Even a worthless redskin. Whoo, McGawley's old hound is better looking."

"When it comes to white women, redskins ain't picky."

Humiliated, Crystal felt on fire, wishing that they would go away before Black Eagle heard them. Even though their words were slurred, what they were saying carried all too clearly.

Black Eagle strode out of the store with his arms filled with purchases. The moment he emerged, the two men sauntered off.

Black Eagle dropped the supplies into the wagon bed and shot her a swift glance. One look in his dark, glittering eyes, and a chill ran down her spine. Then he was gone, striding down the boardwalk, and her heart jumped when she saw him heading after the two men.

Concerned by what he might do, she stood up. "Mr. Black Eagle," she called, mortified and knowing he must have heard them call him a redskin.

Virge glanced over his shoulder, said something to Slim, and they turned toward Black Eagle with their fists clenched.

How could she stop a calamity? Fighting was illegal, but there were so many fights in frontier towns that no one paid any heed unless some other law was infringed. She hated violence as much as breaking the law, and the three men were all set to do both if she didn't stop them . . . and there would be two tough fighters against her husband. Slim was tall and brawny with a barrel chest and thick arms.

"Mr. Black Eagle!" she called again, but he didn't change his stride or look back. She scrambled to get Jacob and climb down to go for the sheriff before Black Eagle ended up unconscious or in her court.

"You won't talk about my wife that way." The words were soft-spoken, but Crystal heard them and halted, rooted in shock. He was fighting because of what they said about *her*.

Virge swung at Black Eagle, who ducked, while Slim threw a punch that slammed the Indian against a wall. Both men waded in, fists pounding. She watched Slim swing his fist into Black Eagle's stomach while Virge struck a swift blow to his head.

Black Eagle hit Virge squarely on the jaw with a blow that cracked like a limb snapping, and Virge slumped to the ground. Slim jumped Black Eagle, and the two stumbled and crashed against the saloon wall.

Black Eagle spun and hit Slim, sending him sprawling in the street. Both Virge and Slim lay still.

Stunned by the swiftness of the confrontation, Crystal was immobile and terrified by how badly Black Eagle was hurt. To her relief, he picked up his hat, jammed it on his head, and strode back to the wagon. Blood ran down his jaw and there was a cut on his cheek.

She scrambled up on the seat and placed Jacob in his cradle, thankful he could sleep through all kinds of rumpus. Humiliation still cloaked her, making her burn with embarrassment. How many fights would Black Eagle have because of her? And fighting was wrong!

Black Eagle climbed up beside her and gave a swipe at his

bleeding mouth. With roiling emotions—feeling humiliated, amazed, embarrassed and angry with him all at the same time, she turned away swiftly. To her relief the horses moved forward and the wagon rolled down the street. She didn't look around; nevertheless, she knew people were staring at them. And in spite of what she'd heard him say to the men about his wife, she suspected Black Eagle's anger was over the slurs directed at him.

They rode in silence until they were well past Cheyenne and moonlight splashed over the wagon and grass. With a sudden movement Black Eagle caught her chin and turned her to face him. Moonglow bathed her face, but beneath his hat brim, his eyes were hidden in shadows. "You're angry, aren't you, Judge?" he asked tersely.

"You broke the law back there. Sheriff Hinckel could have arrested you."

"If Wade Hinckel arrested every man in Cheyenne who settled problems with his fists, the jail would stretch from here to the mountains."

Black Eagle turned back to driving the wagon. "If I had ignored those two, they would have been worse next time they saw you. They're bullies and they would have given me a harder time. Here the law is tenuous."

"It shouldn't be. Not all men resort to violence."

"Maybe not back in Baltimore; but out here, everyone is close to primitive reactions."

"It's barbaric, and this town is nothing but an abode of savages who take the law into their own hands."

"Ease up, Judge. You're going to find the law cold company someday."

"Ellery didn't resort to violence, and he probably lived here as long as you have."

"If he had resorted to violence a little more than he did, he might be alive today."

"He was shot in the chest, so he faced his killer. I think it was someone he knew."

"I know who you think it was," Black Eagle remarked in a harsh voice.

"Violence doesn't solve anything, and Ellery never used it," she repeated, thinking about her gentle brother.

"For a white man, your brother was one of the best damned knife-fighters I've ever seen. That kept him from having to resort to violence as often."

"Ellery?" Shocked, she looked up at Black Eagle.

"You didn't know that, did you?"

"No," she answered, her thoughts on taking care of the body when they brought it back. A stiletto had been fastened inside one of Ellery's boots. She had been surprised to find it, but she assumed he carried it for protection yet had rarely ever used it. "He never told me."

"I'm sure he didn't. A knife fight is a little on the wrong side of the law, too," Black Eagle stated dryly.

They rode in silence, the tension thick between them. She could feel his anger at her stance about the law, but she couldn't approve of what he had done. She still burned with humiliation over the dreadful words.

"If you fight every man who doesn't like me, you may have to fight nearly the entire male population of Cheyenne. You married a woman with a lot of enemies," she admitted stiffly.

"Crystal, those two were vermin, but they'll think twice before they talk in public about you or me again. Actually, we're both misfits," he said, looking at her. "A lot of men don't want a woman judge. That may come as a shock, but I hear them talk. I've heard the governor talk about it. He appointed you and the men of Wyoming gave women the vote and let them serve on juries and hold office because of politics. Women having the vote here is a quirk in time and their rights don't make the male citizens happy. If anyone else gives you a bad time because you married me, you should tell me, but I know you won't."

"Indeed not! You should think of your son. I don't want Jacob's father in jail for brawling—or in my courtroom," she said. She didn't want him fighting half the town and she was beginning to wonder how many fights he had already had because of the color of his skin.

"God forbid I ever face you in a courtroom!"

"For once, we both fully agree. Think of Jacob before you hit the next man."

"If I had stopped to think of Jacob, I would still have hit Virge and Slim. Judge, you're meddling in something a woman wouldn't know a thing about," he declared with a finality that made her grit her teeth.

"You broke the law tonight," she said, annoyed that he wouldn't repent. When he didn't answer, she became silent, glancing at him occasionally and wondering about him. She thought of the hateful things the men had said about him. "Do you have a lot of trouble from people around here?"

"Compared to other places I've lived, no. Some people won't associate with me and you might as well know about them. Sherman Knudsen is happy to bring his animals to me, to buy horses from me, to take my money and keep it in his bank. But otherwise, he won't speak to me."

"No!"

Black Eagle turned to look down at her. "Crystal, hasn't it ever occurred to you that people out here hate Indians? At least, some white people do. They think Indians are dirt, absolutely worthless, or else they view them as uncivilized savages."

"I know people think of Indians as savages, but I think of ones like Running Horse," she said, naming a Cheyenne chief who occasionally came to town to talk to the governor or officers from nearby Fort Russell.

"All the forts around us are filled with soldiers to fight the Indians—my people. I'm satisfied to walk the white man's road and speak his language, but it's a thin veneer and some people see me the same as they do Crazy Horse or Red Cloud."

"You're not the same at all! You have a good business here."

"Fortunately, I do. Remember, the fourteenth amendment

was passed only three years ago giving full citizenship to anyone born in the States and all territories—except Indians. We're non-people and we have no rights as far as the U.S. government is concerned.''

''What will happen to Jacob? If townspeople are that hateful to you, how will they be to him?''

''That's why I work until I drop every night. I'm trying to build enough fortune and acquire enough cattle and land that they'll have to treat him with respect.''

She knew Travis did work until late every night and then was up and working long before dawn. While she had to admire him for what he was trying to do, she knew each bit of approval she gave him made him even more dangerously appealing.

''Your efforts might not make a difference,'' she remarked, thinking that it was the color of his skin, not his possessions, that other men thought about.

''If I succeed, Jacob will get respect. Land and money are what white men idolize.''

''That's a harsh view,'' she said, wondering about his past and the hurts inflicted on him.

Moonlight spilled over his black hat and broad shoulders and played across his strong hands. Another rush of longing tore at her. If only he cared a little and they were a man and wife and baby, riding back to their home, starting their marriage together. The emptiness of her existence seemed greater than ever. Black Eagle was an energetic, virile male who had become a constant reminder of what she was missing in life.

She tried to stop that line of thought because it was as dangerous as admiring him for his struggle to win the respect of local people. She was nothing more than a business partner with him and that would never change. She had agreed to caring for Jacob. In turn, Black Eagle had agreed to paying Ellery's debts and sending her to California later, to providing a home for her in the meantime. And to leaving her body alone.

At the last thought, her nerves came alive and her untouched body ached for moments like this morning when he had picked her up in his arms to lift her into the wagon. He was warm, solid, and strong, and it had been marvelous to be carried close against his heart.

With an effort she stopped thinking about him and lifted her face to the breeze. The harness jingled while the animals kept a slow, steady pace. She looked at the millions of bright stars, and as she gazed across the rolling land, she was aware of how alone they were. She remembered Ellery being killed along this trail and shivered, glancing again at the tall man who sat so still and straight beside her. And she suspected he was fearless about the ride.

"We're very alone out here."

"Not scared, Judge?" he asked, his voice laced with amusement.

"Maybe a little."

"I don't believe it! If a grizzly came charging at us, you'd fight him to protect Jacob."

"I might, but it frightens me to think about it and I don't want to talk about such things right now."

She heard a soft chuckle. She locked her hands together, looking at his broad shoulders and feeling better because he could protect them from a lot of things.

"Is Turtle River Comanche also?" she asked, trying to get her mind off the shadows. For days she had wondered if Black Eagle and Turtle River had been friends for a long time.

"No, Cheyenne."

"Why doesn't he return to his people?"

"He can't go back to his people," Black Eagle answered in a bitter voice, and she wondered about Black Eagle. Perhaps he couldn't return to his people either; but if he couldn't, why not? Was he hiding his past, too?

"Turtle River loved a woman and fought a warrior for her," Black Eagle continued. "The warrior won her; and even though she loved Turtle River and he loved her, she had to go with the warrior who won the fight. Months before Turtle River fought for her, in a battle with soldiers, he had been shot and he hadn't fully recovered when he had to fight for her.''

"That seems unfair," Crystal said, glancing up at Black Eagle, who shrugged.

"One cannot always pick the time for a fight. The warrior mistreated her badly. He and Turtle River were enemies and Turtle River felt the warrior was hurting her to hurt Turtle River.''

"That's dreadful! Wasn't there a law or a tribal counsel who could stop his mistreatment?''

"A woman belongs to her man," Black Eagle said quietly, and Crystal twisted her fingers together in annoyance.

"The law is not much different for a white woman. As your wife, I belong to you as much as the horses and this wagon.''

"That's true.''

"That still doesn't explain why he can't go back.''

"He took her from the warrior and they ran away. She was killed later by soldiers, but Turtle River can't return. The woman was not his to take and the warrior would never have consented.''

Thinking about the stoic Cheyenne, Crystal rode quietly. "Turtle River must have loved her very much.''

"He did," Black Eagle replied gruffly, and Crystal knew his thoughts were on Elizabeth. "He says we each have one great love. I think he's right.''

Crystal stared into the darkness, feeling a hurt twist inside. She would never have one great love unless she was unfortunate enough to fall in love with her husband, and then her love would never be returned.

She looked at his dark silhouette against the backdrop of silver moonlight. Constantly, he made it all too clear he was incapable of loving again. His heart had gone to the grave with his wife.

Crystal sighed, thinking of the two lonely, stoic warriors, drawn together, both mourning lost loves. "Where did you meet Turtle River?''

"He was being held by soldiers in a prison. They accused him of stealing their horses. I helped him escape, Judge," he said dryly, reminding her that he had little regard for some of the white man's laws.

"Had he stolen their horses?"

"Yes, but they had taken his people's horses and land and killed Cheyenne women and children."

"Still, you broke the law."

"It wasn't in Wyoming, Judge, and it was long ago," he said lightly and she heard amusement in his voice.

"You broke the law."

"Yes, ma'am. Right in two. It must be nice to see all of life divided up neatly. Right here, wrong over there. Keeps you sleeping quietly at night—doesn't it?—to have such a clear conscience."

He was taunting her, stirring up the old clash of wills. And she would never admit to him that she was not sleeping quietly at night and it wasn't because of her conscience.

She became quiet and they rode in silence, yet she was aware of him at her side. When they turned the last bend and the house came in view, she felt a surge of relief to be home. The small log house already looked like a haven to her. It was her home, and she felt as if she belonged there.

"Don't disturb Jacob. I'll carry the cradle inside." Black Eagle jumped down and came around the wagon, lifting her easily and swinging her to the ground. He released her at once and turned to get the cradle. Watching him, Crystal longed for his arms to go around her, wanting to press against him, growing more curious about a kiss.

Mentally chiding herself and knowing her thoughts were taking dangerous turns too often, she headed toward the dark cabin, stepping inside to light a lamp. He placed the cradle on the floor and knelt beside Jacob, touching his head lightly with his fingers. Black Eagle's dark hair fell forward, hiding his face from view and she thought how contradictory he was, so gentle with his son, yet often so harsh with others.

He headed toward the door. "Good night, Judge," he said. "I'll sleep outside."

He closed the door behind him and she felt alone, longing tearing at her until she hurried to Jacob's side, reassuring herself with the baby that there was one person who loved and needed her. That should have been enough, but it wasn't. . . .

She stared through the open window at the dark night, thinking about Travis Black Eagle out there in the darkness with his own loneliness and pain. Had she already fallen in love with him? The moments after the fire, had he simply won her heart without his knowledge or effort? Was it possible to fall swiftly and deeply in love with a man?

She moved restlessly about the cabin, extinguishing the lamp, undressing, and taking her hair down by the light of the moon spilling through the windows. Travis Black Eagle. He had told her to call him Travis and maybe she could now.

The next day beneath a hot sun, Travis shoveled dirt, moving with a steady rhythm as he shoved the tool into the black dirt, scooped up a shovelful, and tossed it into a wheelbarrow. He was building a dam for the swift-running creek so he would have a wide pond of drinking water for his cattle and horses. At the lower end of the pond, he would leave a small spillway so water could continue downstream, but not at the rate it did now.

Zachary brought back an empty wheelbarrow and picked up the handles to the one Travis had filled, wheeling it away to dump the dirt. Travis paused and picked up a canteen to take a long drink, letting water spill down his chin and over his chest.

He watched Zachary, who was changing daily. Travis felt a mild amusement when he watched Zachary with Crystal. Zachary couldn't tear his gaze from her and was obviously suffering with infatuation, but Crystal seemed completely unaware of any effect she had on Zachary. Travis suspected if she knew, she would be distraught. She did nothing to cause such feelings; there wasn't a fraction of flirtatiousness about her.

He studied Zachary, who wore a shirt to protect his tender back from the sun and a broad-brimmed hat to shade his face. Travis could swear the boy had grown two inches since they had carried him home that first night. Travis's gaze ran over Zachary's long slender arms and he saw the bulge of muscle that hadn't been there before.

Zachary had to ache from all the physical labor, yet he had never complained or to shirked any task. Far from it. He was more than eager and willing to help, starting to work beside Travis far sooner than Travis had thought he should. Travis felt the same flush of anger that came every time he remembered how badly Zachary had been beaten when they found him. He would never allow Zachary's father to take him back without a fight.

Travis capped up the canteen and bent to dig again. Later, when Zachary appeared to get another load of dirt, Travis paused to watch him, seeing the play of muscle in his arms and looking again at the lad's height.

"You've grown."

"Yes, sir. I know I have. Those pants you gave me don't have to be rolled up as much now," Zachary said with a grin.

"It was your father, wasn't it?"

"Yes, sir," he answered, all cheer leaving his voice. "I won't ever go back."

"You're under age, and by law, he can take you home with him. There's no law to protect you."

"I won't go back." He seemed to change the subject. "I told you once before, I'd like to learn how to really shoot. As soon as I earn money for ammunition, I'd like to use your revolver to practice."

Travis studied the boy, pondering his request. Was he planning to learn to shoot better to defend himself or to revenge himself? Too well, Travis knew the trouble the boy could get into if he relied on guns.

"Zachary, do you know how to fight to protect yourself?"

The boy blinked. "I've been in a few fights. Not with my father. He's bigger."

"How big?"

Zachary wiped sweat from his brow and studied Travis, his gaze sweeping from Travis's head to his toes. "Not nearly as big as you. The top of his head would come to your chin, probably. And he's soft because he doesn't like to work. He's full of whiskey half the time."

"When we stop work tonight, I'll show you how to fight to protect yourself. Remember, you're taller now and stronger than when you left home. And you get stronger every day," Travis added quietly.

"I'd never get strong enough to stop him," Zachary said bitterly.

"You might be surprised." Travis turned back to work; but that night when they headed home, the two of them went around the shed, out of view of the house. Turtle River came to watch, rubbing down his horse and keeping an eye on Zachary.

Two nights later Travis leaned against a post at the pen and scratched the pinto's nose. Wind sighed across the plains while silvery moonlight spilled over the pen. He tried to keep his mind blank, to feel the sleek short hairs of the pinto as he slowly rubbed his hand down its neck.

"Night, boy," he said softly to the pony and turned, jamming his hands into his pockets and stepping into the shed where he picked up a blanket and went back outside. The ground was wet from another heavy rain. After Elizabeth's death he'd hated going to bed alone; now he hated the thought of going to bed with someone. It was the wrong woman. Yet when winter set in, he couldn't stay out on the ground unless he put up a tipi like Turtle River's.

Travis crossed the soft, wet ground. The smell of damp earth and wet grass filled the air. He was exhausted; the lack of sleep over the past weeks was taking a toll.

At the prospect of bedding on the wet ground he studied his house speculatively. He had to sleep if he wanted to continue to work as hard as he did. He had slept one night in the bed, waking with Crystal fully-dressed, sleeping on the far edge of the bed away from him. He hadn't known she was there until he was awake. If he slept beside her tonight, she would never know and he would be up and gone long before she awoke in the morning.

His log house was darker than the moonlit night, and Crystal probably slept peacefully. He hoped she would learn to cook; but if she didn't, he would survive. She seemed to take to the baby like a bird to the air, and that was what was important.

He strode toward the house and wondered whether she slept fully clothed every night. It would not surprise him except she was so orderly. Whether it was day dresses or nightclothes, whatever she changed into, it would cover her from her chin to her toes. He had noticed, however, that when she was hot, she unbuttoned the first buttons of her dress and he wondered whether she was even aware of what she did. He suspected that if she were made aware of it, she would keep her dress completely buttoned—even if it meant she would faint from the heat. Prim and straitlaced, she seldom laughed, but she was good with Jacob and all he had to do was remind himself of how she dealt with the baby and he was satisfied.

He stepped inside and dropped the horse blanket on the floor. Leaning against the piano, he tugged off his boots and placed them by the door. He hung his hat on a peg and yanked his shirt over his head, dropping it carelessly on the floor. Wyoming nights were cool, but he had spent most of his life out-of-doors and was accustomed to cool air. The warmer air of the house was hot and stuffy, especially on nights Crystal had cooked for hours.

He turned toward the bed. Moonlight streamed through the

window and splashed over the bed, revealing the curving mounds of her shoulder and hip.

Longing for Elizabeth struck him with such force that his knees almost buckled. He tightened his fists and clamped his jaw closed, staring at the sleeping woman in his bed, knowing she was little more than a stranger, not his love. But the shapeliness of rounded hip and tuck of narrow waist was pure woman and called up memories instantly.

Elizabeth was gone forever. How many times would he have to remind himself? He started to turn to stride outside, even if he had to sleep in a puddle, but he stopped, steeling himself. He had to go on with his life and he couldn't spend the winter sleeping elsewhere.

He brushed at his eyes, feeling the sting of hot tears. When he reached the bed, he glanced again at the judge. A sheet was pulled to her waist. He had guessed correctly; she was covered in a white gown that had sleeves to her wrists.

If he lay down carefully, he didn't think she would ever know he was there. He was hot and longed to shed the rest of his clothing, but he would have to go back outside if he did. He had to grin at the thought of the judge finding him naked in her bed. She would either faint or grab that revolver and aim it at him.

He reached the bed and halted in surprise as he looked down at her. Moonlight spilled over her, revealing her unbraided hair. Silver beams caught red-orange highlights in the mass of rich auburn hair that spread over the pillow and her arm and shoulder. The curling locks partially hid her face, the waves in the long strands a testament to the curls that could be there if she didn't wear her hair constantly pulled tight in a bun or a braid. Short curly tendrils framed her face and he supposed he had never noticed them before. The wild mane of hair was a surprise and seemed incongruous, as if it could not possibly belong to her. He couldn't take his gaze from it.

Her slender hand lay on the pillow, the golden wedding band he had fashioned for her gleaming dully in the light. He noticed that Crystal's lashes were thick and long, slightly curled above her cheek. His gaze returned to her hair. He couldn't resist and reached out and touched the locks. Silky strands slid through his fingers while he stared at her in shock, as if it were the first time he'd realized Crystal was a woman.

The white wash of moonlight bathed her face clearly, her lashes dark smudges above her cheeks. Startled, he stared at her smooth skin. He was wrong about her age. He leaned closer, really looking at her. With her hair down, she was transformed; her pale skin was smooth. The woman was far younger than he had guessed. She must be only twenty-three or twenty-four, he decided.

He straightened up, standing over her. Why hadn't she ever married? The war had taken so many men away; perhaps that was what had happened. He could remember Ellery talking about her occasionally, but he hadn't ever paid much attention to what he'd actually said. Travis reached out once more and touched her soft hair.

If she had let down that mass of hair once or twice and let the men of Cheyenne have a glimpse of it, she would have had more proposals than his to consider.

Travis sat down gently and stretched out, trying to avoid disturbing her.

The bed creaked as he straightened and shifted. Suddenly she sat up, gasping and scrambling away from him.

Nine

"Crystal," he said quickly, taking hold of her arm lightly, trying to reassure her. "It's Travis. Remember?"

She blinked and stared at him. Her face was in the shadows, yet his eyes had fully adjusted to the dark and he could see clearly her wide eyes and her slightly parted lips. Her thick cascade of hair tumbled over her shoulders and once again he was amazed by the transformation of her looks when her hair was down. She held the throat of her gown. She looked young, frightened, and *pretty*. He realized he was staring and checked the urge to reach out again and touch a silken curl. He became aware of his fingers closed around her slender wrist.

"The ground is wet and I came in here to sleep."

She nodded. "You startled me," she whispered and ran her fingers across her forehead.

"Go back to sleep," he said. She nodded, but she didn't move. He caught the faint tea rose scent that he detected so often when he was around her. The darkness and her hair falling over her shoulders changed her dramatically. It was difficult to equate the female creature only a few feet from him with the stern, black-robed judge he knew so much better.

As the silence lengthened between them, he realized he was staring again. He stretched out, turning on his side with his back to her. His ears prickled as he waited, listening to hear the rustle of her moving around, waiting for the shift of the mattress as she settled. When there was no sound except her breathing, he glanced over his shoulder.

"Dammit, there's only one bed," he said when he saw her still sitting there, staring at him. "I told you I wouldn't touch you."

"I know you won't," she said quietly. "For a few minutes I just couldn't remember where I was." She turned and lay down on her side with her back to him. He looked at her hair fanning out on the pillow and spilling over her shoulders.

"Crystal, why didn't you marry someone when you were in Baltimore?"

She twisted around to look at him and then rolled over onto her back. Moonlight spilled across her, outlining the shape of her breasts beneath her gown. He was astounded how womanly and pretty she looked. Why did she constantly hide it?

She turned her head toward the window, her fingers plucking nervously at the throat of her gown. "There was never a man who wanted to marry me," she answered stiffly, and he wondered whether his question had stung.

"Well, maybe if you had let your hair down and hadn't covered up so much, that would have been different. Why do you hide how you look?"

She glanced at him sharply, throwing her face into the shadows. "I don't."

He sighed, losing interest in the conversation and turning away from her. He should be thankful she dressed severely and kept all that riot of red curls hidden from view. Otherwise, she wouldn't have been available for him and for Jacob.

Prickly with awareness of him, Crystal stared into the darkness, wondering whether he was already asleep. She carefully turned on her side to stare at him. Moonbeams played across the bed and over his shoulder and back. His broad shoulders were solid and powerful. His black hair was as dark as a moonless night, but silvery moonlight outlined the taut muscles in his back. She watched the slight rise and fall of his ribs and knew he was asleep. He had startled her and she had come awake, uncertain whether she was in Baltimore or back in the small house in Cheyenne. The wild-looking man facing her in the darkened bedroom had momentarily frightened her, a cry locking in her throat when she recalled where she was and it was Travis Black Eagle before her.

Why do you hide how you look? She didn't hide anything. She kept her unruly hair braided as was the fashion. There were other styles; but many women wore their hair as she did, and for a judge it was seemly to look proper. And when loosened, her hair had a life of its own and was difficult to keep secured beneath bows and ribbons. She had once wanted to wear her hair with ribbons and let the curls fall freely down her back, but what had it brought her? Only humiliation and rejection.

Why had he asked her why she hadn't married? Perhaps the cruel remarks in town had raised his curiosity about her past. Her answer had been the truth, yet guilt burned inside her because she had avoided a complete answer.

She pushed her hair away from her face and looked at his smooth back, tingling, all too aware that only inches separated them. She could reach out so easily and touch him. She slid her hand toward him carefully, touching the hair that lay on the pillow. The strands were different from her own, thicker and coarser, black against her pale hand as she let them fall over her palm.

It made her breath catch to touch him, even the strands of his hair when he was asleep and knew nothing about what she was doing. Her gaze drifted down to his back and she wanted to trail her fingers over his smooth skin, to feel the hard muscles.

She pulled her hand away and turned on her side with her

back to him to try and stop the torment she was experiencing, yet suspecting sleep was gone for hours now.

She lay still in the moonlight and thought back to that night Harvey had awakened her, tapping on her window. His blue eyes were wide and his blond hair slicked down neatly. Shocked to see him, she had dressed before going outside to talk to him.

Their fathers had once been partners, and then Harvey's father had opened his own law practice. The families had decided that Harvey would marry Crystal when they were educated and grown. And it had remained that way. She expected to marry Harvey and she knew he expected to marry her. And then Harvey had gone away to school and he had acted nervous around her the few times they were together in his school years. Just before his graduation, while she had two more years of school, her grandfather had begun to talk to Harvey's father about a wedding.

Then on a cool spring night Harvey had called her out and he had told her that he regretted what he had to do, but he had fallen in love and he had his father's blessing. They would announce Harvey's engagement to Abigail Potter within the month.

Crystal could still remember the humiliation and hurt, and seeing her dreams crumble. The next day her grandmother was livid and her grandfather charged off to talk to Harvey's father and was gone for over an hour.

Crystal had begged him not to go. She couldn't bear for Harvey to feel forced into marrying her. And he was not. Her grandfather was no match for Harvey's father and he was back, saying there was nothing to be done. Harvey would marry Abigail Potter early in October.

Crystal remembered the smirks of other young ladies, the whispers behind her back at parties. Except for Ellery and herself, the last survivor of her family had been her grandfather; and when he died, she sold the house and moved to Wyoming with Ellery because if she stayed in Baltimore, she would always feel the disgrace of Harvey's rejection. She was not a woman men wanted. Her experiences in Baltimore and Wyoming had confirmed that too well.

She turned her head to look at the handsome, virile man asleep beside her. Their bargain was a good one for her. She had tied her life to a strong, ambitious man who had a beautiful baby that now was hers, too. She had a responsible, important position in town, the only woman here to have such a task. She sighed. Life should have been perfect and she should have been filled with joy. Instead, longings were awakening, yearnings that she had never really experienced. There was so much more that life could hold. She turned on her side to face Travis and reached out cautiously again to touch his hair, wondering how much regard he would ever come to have for her.

She saw little of the men that week. The next two mornings Travis was gone long before she was awake; after that he slept outside and she saw him only at supper when she saw Turtle River and Zachary.

As they sat around the supper table, Travis cut into his meat and glanced at her. "Tomorrow morning Lester Macon is coming to buy a mare and foal. I'll work around the shed so I'll be here when he arrives."

She nodded, barely hearing Travis while she watched Zachary clutching his knife and sawing the tough meat she had cooked. Would she ever master cooking enough to put a meal on the table where nothing was tough, stringy, mushy, or burned?

"I'm sorry the meat is tough," she said quietly. "I never have learned to cook."

Travis raised his head to look at her. "You will," he said quietly.

"It's good, Crystal," Zachary said, always complimenting her even as he sawed away at the thick slab. She doubted that she could do anything to displease Zachary. He seemed to accept all of them without question, trailing after Travis and

Turtle River, beginning to use some of their phrases and mannerisms. She suspected Travis might be a substitute for the father Zachary despised.

When they finished eating, they followed the same pattern they had nearly every night: Travis and Turtle River carried Jacob outside to play with him while Zachary remained behind, helping her clean. Once they had put the last dish away, he sat beside her at the piano and they played and sang for another hour.

When the baby was asleep, Travis returned Jacob to his cradle. As she sang, Crystal turned and watched her tall husband stride through the door and knew he wouldn't be back until breakfast.

The next morning she heard the creak of a wagon approaching the house and the jingle of harness. Drying her hands, she picked up Jacob and stepped outside. The men had started building the framework of a new barn. Travis set down a board and turned for the house. Her pulse jumped as she stared at him, unable to pull her gaze away.

He yanked his shirt over his head, but not before she had a clear glimpse of him striding purposefully along, bare-chested, his shoulders a solid bulwark, his black hair loose over his shoulders with an eagle feather hanging from a red headband. Sometimes she suspected he missed his former life badly.

He bounded up onto the porch and moved to her side to wait for the arrival of the wagon. He stood close enough that she could feel the heat from his body.

"That's Lester Macon coming to get his mare and foal."

"Invite him in for a cool drink and to join us for dinner. I haven't burned the biscuits yet," she said, smiling shyly at him. He looked startled at first and then the corner of his mouth lifted in a slight, crooked grin before he stepped off the porch and went to greet Lester Macon.

In minutes the two men and a boy were heading toward her, Macon and his son as blond and fair as Travis was brown and dark.

"Crystal, this is Lester Macon. This is my wife, Mrs. Black Eagle This is one of his boys, Elmer Macon."

"Happy to meet you," Elmer Macon said. He smiled as sunshine splashed across his freckled face.

"Morning, Judge," Lester said. "I believe we met when you settled a dispute recently with my neighbor over rights to the creek."

"Yes, to your satisfaction as I recall. Come have a cool drink."

They all sat on the porch, and she served tall glasses of well water and sugar cookies that were only slightly burned on the bottom.

It was an hour after lunch when the Macons climbed into their wagon with the mare and foal tied behind. Travis came back into the house with her, opening his drawer and taking out the box with the money to place the money inside he had just been paid. Crystal carried dinner dishes to a pan of water. She glanced at Travis as he put his hat on his head. Drying her hands, she crossed the room to follow him to the door.

"I'll be back tonight," he said.

"Travis," she said when he strode toward the door. Self-conscious about calling him Travis for the first time, she flushed. He swung around only a few feet from her.

"You didn't enter the purchase in your ledger."

His dark brows drew together and his face flushed. "I will later."

"If you're in a hurry, I can enter it for you."

He shook his head and started toward the door.

"Travis," she said, acutely conscious of her familiarity, yet her curiosity grew.

He paused and faced her.

"You're leaving the money here with me, so I know it isn't because of trust. Why don't you want me to record it for you? I kept all the records for my father and my grandfather in their business."

To her amazement his dark face flushed again, and his lips

thinned as he stared at her. He stood in silence, a muscle working in his jaw, and the longer he stood staring at her, the more her curiosity increased.

"I won't interfere," she added quietly, wondering if he would not allow a woman to meddle in his affairs. Yet he had no qualms about letting her know where he kept his money or letting her see his books in town.

"I haven't brought my records up to date."

"Then I can do it," she said. "I'm accustomed to that."

To her amazement, he looked uncertain. He blinked and then stared at her as if he were mulling something over.

"Perhaps it would be better to have a record of the ranch expenses," he said quietly, his face flushing again. "Right now, I don't keep one."

"You don't have any account at all?"

A muscle worked in his jaw and he stared at her with a belligerent scowl. "It isn't necessary."

"You'd know where your money is going and whether you are earning money or losing it." Scowling, he glared at her and she felt she had angered him, though she couldn't guess why.

"I know whether I'm earning or losing."

"I'll set up books for you so you can keep a record here as you do in town."

"I don't keep the one in town. Andrew does."

Puzzled by his discomfort, she stared at Travis, trying to sort out why Andrew kept a record in town yet here none was kept and Travis seemed so disturbed by her suggestion to keep an account. "Even if you don't want *me* to maintain a record, you should keep one."

"Damnation. I can't read," he admitted, his voice stiff, and his face flushed darkly again.

Startled, she stared at him in disbelief. "You were taken back to civilization. Surely they put you in school."

He shook his head. "Not for long and I missed most days. I was in a class with very young children."

She realized how painful that must have been for him to be uprooted, thrust into a classroom with small children. Accustomed to keeping records of her family's household and her grandfather's law practice, she spoke without hesitation. "I'll keep your records then. And I'll teach you to read."

"No, I think not." His scowl deepened. "Judge—"

"Of course, I can. It's not that difficult and we can spend time after the others have gone," she said, suspecting he would not want to be taking lessons from her in front of Turtle River and Zachary.

"I am too old to learn."

"Don't be ridiculous! You can't be much older than I am. You have a mind and you can learn. You should know so you can deal with people in town."

He glanced at Jacob and she could guess what was running through his mind. He nodded. "I had only a few months of the white man's school."

"It will be easier than you think," she said, smiling at him.

His dark eyes flickered and he moved close to her, reaching out to lightly touch the corner of her mouth.

"So the judge can smile," he said in a deep voice. His finger tickled slightly and he stood close, his dark eyes studying her, and she forgot their conversation and their plans, gazing up at him.

"There has been little to smile about since I came to Wyoming," she said solemnly, thinking he smiled even less than she did.

"You have a nice smile, Crystal," he said softly. "We will try the reading, but I think I may be beyond learning."

"No, you're not," she said, suddenly lost in dark eyes that seemed to pull on all her senses. "I rather suspect you can do whatever you decide you want to do," she added in a whisper, without thinking about what she was saying.

Dropping his hand to his side, he turned and left, striding across the porch and then breaking into a sprint to the barn. She stared at him from the door, watching his black hair fly as he ran. Her cheek still tingled where his finger had traced an arc and she could remember his words, his tone, and his dark mesmerizing gaze—that seemed to swallow her whole.

Don't fall in love with him! The warning danced through her mind again—sensible, prudent, a message from her brain that her heart never heard. She watched him until he disappeared from sight and then she thought about the past few moments with him and the touch that had been so slight, yet so lasting.

In late afternoon the men began to build a sturdy wooden fence around the horse pen to replace the flimsy rope one that served now.

She took down washing from the clothesline that was strung from the house to the shed. While she watched them work, her gaze was continually on Travis as he carried lumber and hammered boards in place. She couldn't stop watching the play and flex of muscles, the grace of his movements. She glanced over the three men, two powerful, dark warriors who looked so masculine and formidable and the brown-haired, fair-skinned youth that worked alongside them.

Zachary was changing, filling out and developing muscles. Thank heavens no one had come looking for him! She couldn't bear the thought of turning him over to the beast that had inflicted the beating. A new law needed to be on the books— one that protected children from such beatings. And probably one for wives, too, she thought grimly, thankful for her own lot in life. While she felt her husband was a man capable of great rage, he also was a man capable of great control and he had been good to her.

She watched him swing an axe and yearning filled her. He was good to her, but he cared nothing about her. And he was an enigma with so many unanswered questions. Why hadn't he returned to his people? Why was he at this outpost of the frontier? She had assumed he was in Cheyenne because he was still close to his own people, but that had been a mistaken assumption. He was hundreds of miles from his people. He couldn't read. He could write his name; she had seen it on their marriage license. How could he have been an officer in the army if he couldn't read? Yet that had been wartime when formalities were gone, so she could concede the possibility of an illiterate officer because she was certain he was an excellent warrior.

A week passed and she was never alone with him except for the ride into and out of town when she went to court.

One summer night after the others had gone and Travis knelt beside the cradle, gently rocking Jacob to sleep, she stared at Travis's bare, broad shoulders, nervousness assailing her.

"Travis," she said, her heart drumming, afraid she would insult him and send him storming away. "I think we should begin on your reading."

His lips firmed and he stared at her until she wondered whether she had angered him or embarrassed him. He shook his head. "We will do it another time."

"I think Jacob's father should be able to read."

Travis's chest expanded as he drew a deep breath and his face darkened like a thundercloud. He stood and she expected him to bolt from the cabin, but instead he nodded. She knew he was hot when he was shut in the house and he preferred to be bare-chested. He wore a shirt to supper each night, but shed it as soon as he moved away from the table. Now, to sit close beside him and work with him and try to avoid looking at his bare chest was going to be difficult. Trying to be brisk and keep her mind on reading, she moved to the table and pulled two chairs side by side and picked up pen and paper. He sat beside her and she was aware of their shoulders brushing, of his large hand holding the corner of the paper.

Her heart drummed and she hoped she could keep her attention on the letters instead of him. She carefully drew an A and began.

He was attentive, doing what she said, catching on quickly, and she knew it would be easy to teach him. Turning in her chair, she faced him to teach him the sounds of the vowels.

His dark gaze watched her mouth intently, and her nerves

prickled and came alive. Sitting only inches, actually touching shoulders until she'd twisted to face him, she was acutely conscious of his body. His steady scrutiny made it difficult for her to keep her mind on the simplest instructions.

"Ahh—" She mouthed the sound of a short *a* and watched when he followed her lead. His lips were finely sculpted, his underlip sensual, and her curiosity flared. What would it be like to feel those firm lips against her own?

Her gaze lowered, drifting over the magnificent chest that was only inches away, so close she could easily touch him and draw her fingers over him.

Realizing how she was studying him, her gaze flew up and met his. Curiosity was in his eyes. His gaze lowered to her mouth and Crystal thought she couldn't get her next breath.

"E. Now here are the sounds of the letter *e,"* she said in a rush, refusing to look at him as she mouthed the sounds and gave him examples in words.

"I think you do hide how you look," he said quietly, and her head jerked up in surprise. She felt the hot flush of embarrassment and touched her hair, suddenly aware of all the escaping tendrils that wantonly curled around her face.

"Of course I don't hide! That's absurd. I try to look the way a judge should look. Are you listening? Say the *e* sounds back to me, please."

The hint of amusement in his dark eyes made her nerves prickle and made her feel uncertain with him. She could cope with the stoic, disinterested male that he usually was better than she could deal with him when he turned his attention on her.

"Now, you write," she said, handing him a pen and pushing the paper in front of him. He dipped the pen into an ink bottle and traced what she had written. He started incorrectly, and she reached out to take the pen from him.

"Do it like this. It will be easier. See, start here."

She drew another capital *A* and handed the pen to him,

watching him trace over her lettering and then do his own. He tried to draw another capital *A*, but paused.

"Now I've forgotten what you just showed me," he said.

"Here, like this," she said, closing her fingers over his to move his hand. The moment she placed her hand on his, tiny currents shot through her. The contact was intense, and she could barely think about what she was supposed to be doing. Instead, she was far more conscious of his warm, strong hand beneath hers . . . big, powerful, dark.

"Damn," he said softly and tossed down the pen and stood abruptly. He inhaled, and when she met his gaze, she knew something about her touch or something they had done must have triggered his memories of Elizabeth.

"I'm through tonight," he said sharply and strode into the darkness.

She stared after him, knowing he was hurting, sorry again he had lost his love. She capped up the ink and put away the paper, looking at the scrawl of his letters and remembering the feel of his hand beneath hers.

Later that night when she lay alone in bed, she prayed it took a very short time to teach him to read because she was a bundle of tingling nerves and aching longing after spending an hour sitting only inches from him and working with him on letters.

The next night was worse. She was even more keenly aware of him, tempted to ask him to wear a shirt, yet not wanting to make an issue of it and scared it would bring that teasing amusement to his eyes that made her feel foolish. There were moments when he lost his solemnity, and then she had an even more difficult time dealing with him.

When he faced her, mouthing letters in imitation of her, her pulse raced and she couldn't resist letting her gaze roam over his chest. Smooth brown skin was taut over powerful muscles and she tingled, remembering being held in his arms, feeling his heart beating against hers.

And later, she held his hand, moving it over letters, wondering if more sad memories would send him storming from the house. Instead, he seemed to concentrate diligently on what she was showing him and carefully read the alphabet back to her, writing a few letters.

"That's good! You're progressing fast," she said, looking up and smiling at him.

His dark eyes studied her and a faint smile lifted one corner of his mouth. "The second smile is even prettier than the first," he said quietly, touching her cheek and making her blush.

"Thank you," she said, flustered. She turned to the paper. "Now, read these letters," she said swiftly, trying to keep her mind on what they were doing while her senses spun over his remark and his faint touch.

Three nights later as she rose from the piano and told Zachary good night, she went to the desk to get out pen, ink, and paper for the reading lesson. When she turned around, she saw all three men striding back through the door.

"Crystal, I told Turtle River and Zachary what we have been doing late at night."

"Yes," she answered cautiously, wondering exactly what he had told them since she had felt he wanted to keep his reading lessons from everyone.

"They know you are teaching me to read. Will you teach them also?"

Startled she stared into three pairs of curious eyes. After the first moment of surprise, she realized they were waiting quietly for her answer.

"Yes, of course! Come sit down and you can all learn."

Immediately she was surrounded, Travis on one side, Turtle River on another, and Zachary facing her. They were an avid audience and consequently learned quickly. Now that she was no longer alone with Travis, it should have been easier to deal with him; but to her dismay, it was not. She was as conscious as ever of him, and each slight contact left her more tingly than the one before. And even more disconcerting, when she brushed hands with Turtle River or with Zachary, she felt none of that tingling awareness that she did when she had even the merest whisper of contact with Travis.

Travis slammed an axe into a log and split it, then brought the axe down again. He worked methodically, flexing muscles, glad for the chance to do hard physical labor and clear his thoughts. He'd had a wagon load of pine logs brought down from the mountains, plus the lumber he had purchased in town.

He was learning to read and write and it astounded him. That part of the white man's world had been closed to him, and he had thought it would always be out of his grasp; but thanks to Crystal, he was learning. Now he felt better when he walked into the bank and he felt more certain of himself when he dealt with townspeople at his livery. So far, he hadn't done anything in town to indicate his newly acquired knowledge, but the ability gave him more confidence in his dealings.

And once again, he was pleased with Crystal. If she could teach him and Turtle River and Zachary to read, she would easily be able to teach Jacob. And Travis was learning that the stern person who was a Cheyenne judge could also be a caring, pleasant woman.

He was beginning to see her as a woman. When she tried to teach him sounds, telling him to look at her mouth, he suspected she did not have the faintest notion of the effect it had on him. Her lips looked full and soft and rosy, and more than once he had had to abruptly end the lesson. Why did she keep such a barrier up around herself? And why didn't she want to go back home to Baltimore? He remembered Ellery saying they no longer had any family there, yet she grew up there and had friends and she had to have liked Baltimore better than Cheyenne, the town she constantly referred to as a wild, waterless, windswept collection of petty criminals.

Travis swung the hammer and thought about her inflexible stance on the law. He would have to counter that with Jacob because he didn't want his son to grow up accepting the white man's rules as absolute. Some were wrong. It would be wrong to give Zachary back to his father.

Travis raised another board in place and hammered it, the sharp bang of the hammer against the nail carried away on the wind. He picked up a hinge, fitting it against the wood and looking at a bump along the log that kept the hinge from fitting flatly against the board. Searching his pockets, he remembered he had used his knife last night; it was probably still lying on the kitchen table. He strode back to the house. His sweatband was soaked and sweat ran in rivulets down his back and chest. He was in moccasins, the shoes he often preferred, and he covered the distance in swift, long steps.

He bounded onto the porch and crossed it, swinging open the door. "Crystal—"

Ten

Travis halted in shock, his gaze riveted on her. Jacob slept in the nearby cradle, but Travis saw only Crystal.

She was standing in the tin tub, just reaching for a towel, water dripping and running off her body. She was half-turned, half-facing him, and she was as naked as a newborn babe; but it was no baby he faced. Her skin was pale, flawless, covered with a silvery sheen of water.

Her breasts were small, high, and firm with rosy-tipped nipples, and her waist was tiny. He saw the enticing curve of her firm bottom and then her endlessly long legs. The woman was *beautiful*.

His jaw dropped and his breath caught.

In that one frozen second when both of them were startled into immobility, her green eyes were round and huge, her mouth open in an appealing *O*. In that brief second of time, he realized she was all woman and she had kept herself hidden more than he'd realized, but then had he ever really looked at her? Her curves were feminine and lovely, her skin pale and splendid. Her breasts could fill his palms and her long legs were shapely, perfect. A sweet rose scent hung in the air, along with the damp odor of water. It was a moment frozen in time, filled with shock and clarity, to be forever remembered.

His body reacted, startling him. Stunned, he had thought he was numb, dead to attraction, his masculinity of no importance to him. But one long look at Crystal's body and his own responded instantly. He was hard, hot, having a reaction to her that held a fiery intensity. Steeped in mourning since his dreadful loss, he had felt lifeless, but that changed in an instant as his body revived and responded.

Her red hair was piled on her head, strands falling over her shoulders. The wet locks were a deep, burnished russet, with short auburn tendrils curling around her face.

"He'e'yo'!" he exclaimed under his breath, reverting to his native tongue.

She gasped and flung her arms across her breasts to cover herself, dropping down into the tub with a splash, sending water sloshing over the sides. "Sir!"

He had already spun around, throwing up his hands. "Sorry, Crystal," he said, his voice husky. "I didn't think about you bathing. I thought you would be cleaning. I left my knife here this morning."

He spoke fast, telling her the truth, yet his thoughts were spinning. All that was clear was that one frozen second when he had glimpsed her naked. The woman was *beautiful*. He was astounded and just as shocked at his reaction to her. He needed to get out of the cabin and to hell with his knife. His reaction would be as plain to her as to him if he had to face her again. He strode outside where it felt cooler when hot air blew over him than it had in the house.

He stood in shock, forgetting where he was or what he had been doing. He glanced over his shoulder at the door that he had swung shut behind him. "Damn," he whispered, knowing she could have easily had proposals from over two-dozen males in town if she had dressed differently, taken down her hair, and turned down the appointment as judge. If men knew how she looked . . .

His thoughts took an abrupt turn. He didn't want men to know how she looked. And that included Zachary.

Stop. Travis told himself to stop such thinking. He didn't want to feel possessive about his wife in name only. He didn't want to feel any stronger about her than he had yesterday or the week before or the day he'd met her. Yet his body indicated that no matter what common sense told him, he would not forget what he had seen or be able to keep from reacting to it. He would know now what was beneath her prim, high-necked dresses and ankle-length skirts and black judge's robe.

Damnation! He wiped his sweaty forehead and moved away from the house, fighting the urge to glance over his shoulder. Conscience attacked him. He had married her and ruined any chance she would have for a decent and loving marriage to a man who adored her. He hadn't given it much thought because at the time he'd thought of her totally as a *spinster.* Everyone did. Judge Spinster. He shook his head and wiped his forehead again, fighting the images that danced in his mind. Her body was beautiful, taunting, unforgettable.

How would he sit beside her for an hour or more tonight, trying to concentrate on letters, when all he would be able to think about was how she looked when she was bathing?

And he knew she was aware of him as a man. He had caught the looks she had given him, seen her look at his chest and the pink flush of her cheeks. Her awareness had meant nothing and occasionally had given him mild amusement because beneath all her primness and spinster ways, there was a female who responded to a male.

Now he knew there was more than just a female behind her prim exterior. There was a beautiful woman with a body to burn a man to cinders.

It didn't change their relationship. No matter what his body was doing or wanted, his heart still belonged to Elizabeth and he had too much respect and regard for the judge to violate the promises he had given her.

And in spite of the looks she had been giving him, he could not imagine that the judge would be willing to have more than a name-only marriage. No matter what kind of body she had, she was still prim, particular, a spinster. She kept barriers around her heart . . . and around her body.

And even if he didn't still hurt too much over Elizabeth to forget his vows to her and seduce his wife, he never wanted to risk falling in love again. Never again would he go through the hell of losing the woman he loved. And any woman who would succumb to lovemaking would also run the risk of having a babe. And of dying from it like Elizabeth.

He went back to the barn, hammering more boards in place and trying to shove images of Crystal out of his mind—and failing.

Zachary joined him at the barn. He hoped Crystal would hereafter bar the door when she bathed. The boy was cow-eyed over her now and he had never seen her hair down, much less the rest of her. If Zachary walked in on her—Travis felt an annoying and puzzling clench to his insides. He could not possibly feel one shred of jealousy over the judge—and never could he feel it about a boy. His gaze ran over Zachary, who was still a child even though he must be over six feet now and filling out, losing the lankiness of a boy.

Turtle River appeared and they worked silently until Turtle River picked up boards from the stack of lumber at the same time Travis did. Turtle River gave him a long look. "Are you well?"

"I'm fine. It's hot in the sun."

The Indian kept his gaze on him, then shouldered a load of lumber and moved away.

What the hell had Turtle River noticed? Travis couldn't imagine, but the full-blood had the ability to pick up the merest hint of change.

Travis focused on a board and tried to shut out everything

else. Losing his concentration, he slammed the hammer against his thumb and swore, shaking his hand and glaring at the house, still shocked, unable to forget how the woman looked. She was beautiful! It astounded him. She wasn't like other women he knew, and now he wondered why not.

Without question she was one of the most intelligent women in the Territory. She said she had kept records for her brother and grandfather, and he knew that they had had a law practice which had given her the background to be appointed judge.

Realizing he was staring at the house and still shaking his injured hand, he found Turtle River watching him. The Cheyenne turned away and bent over some boards with his hammer.

The past three nights had been cooler and Travis had slept in the cabin. The judge's horsehair mattress was far more comfortable than even a buffalo robe on the ground, but now he suspected he would have to sleep outside again until the disturbing images of her body faded from his mind.

He picked up his hammer and tried to concentrate, working swiftly, tormented by a vivid image that refused to vanish.

Long after Travis had left the cabin, Crystal sat with her arms crossed in front of her, staring at the door. Burning with embarrassment, she tingled from head to toe, vividly remembering the moment he had walked into the room and halted, his jaw dropping and his dark eyes raking over her as if they were burning flames consuming her. She couldn't recall his ever coming back to the house during the day after the first week of her arrival and she hadn't given any thought to leaving the door unbarred. None of the men were at the house until night, and Zachary and Turtle River never entered without knocking.

Travis wouldn't think to knock because the cabin had been his home long before she'd become a part of it. She burned with embarrassment and thought about Elizabeth, her dainty size and her full breasts that had sometimes looked as if they might spill out of her dresses. Crystal knew she was too tall, too long-legged, too small in the bosom.

"It won't matter," she said aloud. He would forget and it meant nothing to him. He was legally her husband, for heaven's sake! She should not almost faint because he saw her in the tub. But she felt faint. The glittering, dark-eyed look he had given her had not been disinterested or impassionate. And it had not been her imagination running wild. His look had been swift, but it had been consuming and thorough.

She was hot, embarrassed, and prickly. She sponged off, stood, and toweled dry, stepping out of the tub and walking to the window. She could see him working on the new barn. He talked to Turtle River and then turned to glance over his shoulder in the direction of the house. She stepped back from the window, her heart pounding. She was acting foolishly and would feel ridiculous if he saw her watching him.

She spent the day in a fog, still remembering and tingling from the shock of the encounter, knowing she was making too much out of a moment he had probably already forgotten but would remember when he walked through the door tonight.

Tonight. She closed her eyes and clutched her arms in front of her until she realized what she was doing and dropped them to her side. Jacob was kicking and cooing, lying on a blanket she had spread on the floor, but for once he had lost her attention. How would she face Travis tonight? She blushed just thinking about his return and looking into his knowing brown eyes.

"He is my husband," she declared aloud, looking at their small one-room home. He was bound to see her undressed, just as she was bound to find him that way someday. And that thought shook her more than the others. She drew a deep breath, her body on fire.

"Land's sake!" she exclaimed. "I'm married to the man." She threw up her hands and shook her head. With a thinning of her lips, she worked swiftly, cleaning and getting out potatoes to start dinner, trying to forget the morning and not think about when he would come home in the evening.

Yet as the shadows lengthened in the afternoon, she studied herself in the mirror. She braided her hair tightly, winding it around her head, trying to look as plain and unnoticeable as possible. She clamped her jaw closed and pulled on the hot, scratchy, black woolen dress, buttoning it to her chin and pulling the sleeves to her wrists.

Jacob woke from his nap with a loud fretful cry, and for the next hour, nothing would satisfy him. She forgot the slab of meat she had placed in the oven with potatoes around it and didn't remember until she smelled it burning. She set down Jacob, stirring up another fury of protests from him. While he kicked and screamed, she yanked out the roasted meat and potatoes and surveyed their charred crust.

She ran her hand across her forehead and wanted to get the wagon and go to town to her courtroom where there was order and she could control people and cope with cases.

She was burning in the black dress and the heated house. Jacob couldn't be pacified no matter what she did. Her hair was falling around her face; supper was a charred crisp.

"Now he will forget this morning," she told herself. He will eat and leave for the night. "And you are not helping," she whispered to Jacob, cuddling him against her shoulder.

"Sweetie, what's wrong with my baby?" she asked, trying to soothe him and jiggle him. "What's the matter with my precious boy?" she cooed, patting his back as she headed outside where it was cooler. Jacob was hot and damp from crying, hiccupping yet still bawling as he clung to her shoulder.

"Jacob," she said softly, wondering if something hurt him. She stepped outside as Travis opened the door to enter. They collided, and his strong hands steadied her.

Momentarily they stood without moving. His gaze swept over her, intense, dark, and glittering. He remembered. She knew he was thinking about the morning. His dark eyes stripped away every stitch she wore, leaving her as naked as she had been this morning.

Suffocating, she couldn't get her breath. And as always, he

was bare chested, half-naked himself. Her gaze dropped and she looked at the broad chest in front of her, inches from her, and remembered being in the tub. Her breasts tightened, tingling.

"Sorry," she stammered, at a loss, looking up into his dark eyes.

"I'm sorry. I keep barging in," he apologized quietly. His attention shifted to Jacob, who was screaming lustily again.

"Ho, what's wrong here?" he asked Jacob, taking the baby from her, his hands brushing her throat and shoulder and arm. The moment he lifted the baby into his arms, Jacob stopped crying.

"Thank goodness! Nothing I can do pleases him."

"What's all this crying?" Travis asked, swinging Jacob slightly in his arms, and Jacob hiccupped.

"Your papa's home," she remarked, watching the two of them and feeling a pang that she wasn't part of the moment. She longed to step up and hug them both, to wrap her arms around baby and father. Travis laughed and she gazed at him, forgetting herself and her surroundings. How seldom he relaxed and laughed; yet when he did, he was handsome beyond belief! She was mesmerized by the flash of his white teeth, the creases that appeared in his cheeks, the fine laugh-lines that fanned from the corners of his eyes. And his eyes twinkled, a merriment dancing in them that she seldom saw.

"You say I hardly ever smile," she said quietly, touching his cheek with her fingertip and feeling his slightly bristly skin. "Yet you laugh only on rare occasions. Your laughter is very nice," she added.

His dark eyes focused on her, and there was a change in their depths. She had his full attention. More than that. He was remembering again. She wanted to swear, and at the same time, she felt hot and embarrassed again. How long would it take before they could have any kind of encounter and not think about this morning? And how long would it take her to become accustomed to living with this vital, handsome male?

She turned away abruptly, fingering the top buttons of her dress and realizing she had left them undone. She patted her forehead. It was unbearably hot and stuffy in the house and she felt Travis's eyes on her even though her back was turned as she got down plates for supper.

When Zachary walked through the door behind Turtle River, her cheerful greeting died in her throat. He wore a fresh chambray shirt that had once been Travis's. His wet hair was sleeked back from his face, but what startled her was the dark bruise below his eye and his swollen lip.

"What happened, Zachary?" She glanced at Travis and back at Zachary, whose face flushed. He grinned, yelped as the smile hurt his mouth, and shook his head.

"I didn't duck when I should have."

"Didn't duck from what?" she asked, her temper soaring. Had Travis or Turtle River tried to hurt the boy?

"Travis and Turtle River have been teaching me to fight," Zachary said happily.

"To fight?" Her temper soared even more, and she spun around. Travis was busy talking to Jacob and had his back to her. "Travis!"

He glanced at her and held up the baby. "Look at him smile!"

She glanced at Jacob and saw his big grin for his father as he held his little arms out and for a moment she almost forgot her anger, but then she looked at Zachary. Turtle River had disappeared outside.

"Why are you teaching him to fight? Of all the horrible things and it's illegal—"

"Crystal, ma'am, begging your pardon, I need to know. I like learning."

"You shouldn't fight. Violence is inexcusable."

"Zachary, why don't you take Jacob out to Turtle River," Travis said easily and handed the baby to him. Zachary scurried outside quickly, and Travis placed his hands on Crystal's shoulders.

"Out here, a man needs to know how to defend himself; and of all people, that boy needs to know how so he never has to take another beating like he'd had when we found him."

"It's sinful for you to teach him to fight," she accused, too aware of Travis standing close to her and too conscious of his hands on her shoulders. She wasn't going to win any argument with him standing so close and looking at her so intently.

"Would you rather someone like Slim or Virgil beat him into unconsciousness?" Travis ran his finger along her throat and his gaze drifted over her features. Crystal could barely get her breath.

"No, of course not," she whispered, too aware of the wild tingles stirred by his touch. He stood close, and his dark eyes pulled on her senses. She wanted to feel his arms wrap around her; she wanted him to kiss her! Disturbed by her wanton desire, she tried to move away from him but couldn't. His warm fingers drifted back and forth on her neck. "I don't want him beaten, but it doesn't seem right for you to deliberately show him how to fight. And you gave him a black eye!"

"Next time he'll know to duck," Travis said quietly. "And sometime soon, I need to show you how to use that revolver before you take it down and do some damage with it."

"Since I moved in, I have only needed it when we had the fire. I don't see why I should have to know anything else about it."

"You and Jacob are alone here, and sometimes the men and I are damned far from the house. You're Jacob's only protection and, just like Zachary, you should know how to take care of yourself."

"I can take care of myself," she protested, annoyed with him and flustered by her racing pulse. "And you're changing the subject. We were talking about the evils of your teaching Zachary to fight. How could you hit that child?"

Travis grinned, revealing his even white teeth and infectious smile. "You can't imagine how insulted he would be to hear you call him a child."

"He's a boy next to you and Turtle River," she whispered without realizing she had said anything. They stared at each other and this time it felt as if her heart had stopped although she was aware that he was gazing back just as intently at her. Silence stretched between them. Could his pulse be racing like hers?

"I think you frightened Turtle River and Zachary into skipping supper," Travis remarked finally in a husky voice.

"Surely not," she replied, but she was still caught in his dark gaze. As the moment lengthened, Travis studied her. The air all but crackled between them. What was happening? Why didn't he move? Was he as ensnared as she? Then he turned away, and she decided her imagination had been running wild.

"If we're ready to eat, I'll get the others."

"Fine," she answered, barely speaking and not caring whether she ate or not. Travis had won that argument so easily. One smile and she was as mushy as her potatoes. Annoyed with herself as well as with him, she threw up her hands.

And just as she threw up her hands, Travis reached the door and glanced over his shoulder at her. His brows arched. "Did you say something, Crystal?"

"I will never understand men or the violence they love," she snapped and jerked the lid off a pot on the stove. With a deep chuckle, Travis disappeared outside; she could hear the rumble of his voice as he talked to Zachary and Turtle River. One of the men laughed.

She picked up a knife to loosen a loaf of bread from the pan. She sliced it furiously, thinking that when she had argued with Travis, she had been softer than butter. Let them all beat each other to unconsciousness! She would stop interfering where she wasn't wanted or listened to.

Annoyed, she watched them file in while she placed a platter on the table. It held slices of steaming roast and hot potatoes. She put a bowl on the table with ears of golden corn, one of the few things she could cook without ruin. Steam rose from the thick slices of bread. Surprising her, Travis held her chair and his fingers brushed lightly across her shoulders in a brief, disturbing contact she was sure he didn't notice.

When they passed dishes of food around the table, their hands brushed. Zachary chatted brightly about the events of the day, the progress of the barn, the wild horses that Travis and Turtle River were breaking, and how patient they were. Throughout supper, she caught Travis studying her speculatively; and each time, she looked away, a flush rising in her cheeks.

Afterwards, when they began the reading lesson, she was even more conscious of him. As always, he shed his shirt and sat beside her. Turtle River held Jacob and then passed him to Travis. Why did she have this volatile reaction to Travis? A reaction the other males didn't stir. She didn't understand her own feelings, but there was no denying them, and tonight every brush against his hands was as disturbing as a brush against a flame.

All three men were learning swiftly, each striving to keep up with the other. They readily grasped what she taught them and took to reading eagerly.

After an hour they always stopped the lesson and Crystal read from Ellery's dime novels by Beadle about the West. The stories were too wild and too much like Cheyenne for her to enjoy them, but her three pupils seemed as enthralled with the stories as Ellery had been.

As she read, she was acutely aware of Travis listening, his dark gaze steadily on her. When he was concentrating, he could be as still as a stone; and now he was quiet, his long legs stretched out, her skirt slightly over his boot. She felt drawn to glance up and she met his gaze, catching his dark eyes drifting down over her and back up. She gripped her book and tried to focus on what she was reading. *He was remembering again!* She felt heat flush her face, and she kept her head bowed over the pages as she read.

She closed the book. "My voice is tiring, and I hear Jacob stirring."

"We'll stop," Travis said, standing easily. "I'll take care of Jacob, and you may have a rest. Besides, it's time for the piano."

Startled, she looked at Travis. He had never mentioned her playing and she didn't know whether he was indifferent to it or whether he enjoyed it. She and Zachary moved to the piano to play and sing; yet tonight, she was aware that Travis was listening.

She wondered how their routine evenings would change when fall and winter set in. It was late August now and Travis had started sleeping inside. He came in after she was asleep and left before she awoke; but if she stirred during the night, she saw him on the far side of the bed.

The next morning when she stepped out of bed, he was gone. She dressed, fixed breakfast for Jacob and herself, and then began to clean. Jacob was on a blanket spread on the floor inside the house. When she stepped outside to shake the counterpane, she saw a stranger riding toward the house, leading a riderless horse behind him.

Surprised, she watched the man and glanced at the barn where she expected to see Travis and Zachary working, but no one was in sight. She went inside to put down the counterpane, and then she stood on tiptoe to take the big revolver from the shelf.

Jacob was busy chewing on a rag doll she had made for him. She placed him in a large basket filled with a big pillow and carried it to the porch where she could see him while she walked down the steps to wait, keeping the revolver at her side in the folds of her skirt.

The man rode at an easy gait, but she noticed the horse was a sad-looking animal with ribs showing. The man had a rifle across his saddle.

She glanced uneasily over her shoulder again, but there still was no sign of the men. As the stranger drew near, her misgivings increased when she saw that he wore a shirt spotted with tobacco stains. His pants had tears and his hat was battered and stained. He had a sandy beard and a long narrow face that ignited a faint memory. Then she realized she might be looking at Zachary's father.

Her heart thudded and she tightened her fingers around the revolver. By law, he had every right to take Zachary home with him. But she didn't want to give Zachary up. She was torn between what she knew was the absolute law and what her heart screamed for her to do.

The man approached slowly, and when he got fifty yards away, her qualms increased.

"Good morning, ma'am."

"Hello." She wanted to snatch up Jacob, fire the revolver twice to bring Travis, and run inside. Instead, she stood her ground.

"Are you Judge Black Eagle?"

"Yes, I am."

"I'm Eb North. I'm looking for my son, Zachary North, and I've heard he's living out here on your place."

Eleven

The moment she had dreaded had come. Crystal's mind raced and her emotions warred. She wanted to raise the revolver and order the man off the place. At the same time, he had a legal right to claim his son. A man had full rights over his wife, his children, and his belongings. Short of killing, he could do with them as he pleased, and far too often, killing was excused in court.

The man waited for her response. He spit a wad of tobacco to one side, his gaze raking over her.

"I heard about you, Judge. Ask anyone in town and they say you stick to the law. And the law says that boy is mine."

She remembered Zachary's beaten body. If they hadn't found him, he would have died out on the plains. And it would have been because of this man who wanted to take him home and would probably inflict the same kind of punishment again.

"You nearly killed him," she said, hating the man and hating the law that said she had to give his son back to him. She had to follow the law. It was the strength of her life and everything she believed in.

"So, he's here. Where is he now?"

"He's working."

"And you know I can take him back with me, no matter what he's said to you. The boy lies something terrible."

"He hasn't lied to any of us," she said, stalling because she hated to get Zachary and watch him ride away. Travis wanted to know, too, when Zachary's father appeared, but she didn't want to tell him because she knew he would fight Eb North.

"You go get my son."

"They don't come in until supper time," she said, regretting the admission that she and Jacob were alone.

"You can get him if you want to. Just take that little baby and go get him. Unless you're inviting me in to wait," he said, grinning at her and making her skin crawl.

"There's no law that says I have to allow you in my house!"

"There is a law that says that boy is mine. Go get him."

She couldn't bear the thought of handing Zachary over to this man, but she had no choice. If she refused, all this odious man had to do was ride into Cheyenne, get the sheriff, and return. Wade Hinckel would have to uphold a father's rights.

Defeated and fighting tears, she turned toward the house.

"Well, well," he said, staring beyond her and taking his rifle in hand. He swung down off his horse and came forward.

When she glanced over her shoulder, her heart thudded. Zachary was striding toward them, Travis and Turtle River behind him.

They stopped only yards away. "Crystal, take care of Jacob," Travis said, moving forward.

"You can't stop me from getting my boy," North said as Crystal hurried to the porch.

Zachary stepped in front of Travis. "Sir," he said. He moved toward his father.

"Let's go home, boy," the man said, his gaze sliding to Travis. He motioned toward a gray horse. "I brought the pony for you."

Fists clenched, Zachary walked up to his father. Crystal

watched him, her gaze flicking back to Travis, who stood with his fists clenched and a muscle working in his jaw. He was poised to go after Eb North.

"Are you afraid to face me without that rifle?" Zachary asked, his words carrying clearly.

Eb North scowled and spit tobacco at Zachary's feet, splattering his boots. "Get on the horse."

Zachary stepped forward and slammed his fist into his father's stomach. Crystal gasped. "No!" Eb North doubled over, coughing, his face turning crimson.

"You little bastard," he snarled, swinging the rifle and striking Zachary with the butt, driving him to the ground; then he kicked him in the ribs.

"Stop him," she cried and raised the revolver. Travis was at her side in a flash. His fingers curved around her wrist like iron and he yanked the revolver from her hands.

"Leave them alone," he ordered grimly. "Just wait."

"He'll kill Zachary," she protested.

"Give the boy a chance."

Zachary rolled away and came to his feet, swaying, blood streaming down his face from the blow on his temple.

Eb North swung the rifle again. This time Zachary ducked, then grabbed the weapon and yanked it from his father's grasp. He flung it away and it sailed high in the sunlight and fell into the grass far from the men.

"You'll regret the day you were born," Eb said and swung.

Zachary ducked and then struck his father. He swung his right fist and landed another solid punch in Eb's middle; then he moved in, kneeing him and pounding his head. To her amazement he ducked blows and hammered away at the older man until Eb North fell and rolled away.

He scrambled to his feet and ran to retrieve his rifle. Crystal gasped as Travis strode forward, raising the revolver. "Get in the house!" he snapped without looking at her.

Eb North started to raise his rifle and aim. Turtle River pulled back the hammer of his revolver. The click was a small sound, but Eb North froze and then slowly lowered his rifle.

Crystal stood rooted to the porch, watching as Eb North stomped to his horse and hauled himself into the saddle. "You'll regret this!" he shouted, shaking his fist. His face was covered in blood. "You sonuvabitch!" He dropped into the saddle and turned the horses, urging them to a gallop.

As Zachary swayed, Crystal rushed to him. "Come inside. I'll wash your cuts."

"You stood up to him." Travis clamped a hand on Zachary's shoulder. "It won't ever be the same."

"No, sir, it sure as hell won't. Pardon, Crystal."

Crystal was relieved Zachary had not had to go with the dreadful man, yet she was certain Eb North would return with the law on his side. She put her arm around Zachary to help him inside. While Travis stood by with his hands on his hips, she fluttered around Zachary, washing his cuts.

"Are you all right?" Travis asked.

"Yes."

"There's no need for you to run."

"He might be back," Zachary said.

"I don't think he will. I saw his face when you hit him. He was surprised more than anything else. Now he knows you've grown into a man, and it'll never be the same. You can run if you want; but if you go, take one of the horses and let Crystal pack food."

Zachary nodded. "Thanks. I don't want to leave, but I don't want to bring trouble here."

"You won't bring trouble," Travis said. "We're not afraid for you to stay."

Zachary nodded and looked at Crystal, his gaze going over her features. "Then I'm staying."

"I'll go back to work," Travis said and went outside.

Crystal dabbed at his cut face. "Zachary, do you have brothers and sisters?"

"Yes, but they're all older and have run away. I haven't seen any of them for over two years."

"Sorry."

"We'll find each other. I'm close to one brother and one sister."

"There," Crystal said, stepping back. "I'm sure Turtle River will give you something to put on your cuts."

"Thanks, Crystal," he said, squinting at her with one eye and shaking his long brown hair away from his face. The other eye had puffed shut. Impulsively, she reached out to hug him, wondering how many hugs he had received as a boy.

"I'm sorry you've had that trouble."

He placed his arm around her lightly and held her a moment. "Thanks, Crystal," he repeated and stepped away, looking intently at her with one blue eye. "All three of you have been good to me."

She watched him head back to work, wondering how he would be able to do much in the shape he was in.

Jacob began to fuss and she picked him up, hugging him. "Thank heavens you'll never be mistreated. And I'm not going to allow your father to teach you to fight. I just won't allow it!"

Jacob gazed at her solemnly, pursing his lips and making odd sounds, and Crystal held him close, looking down the road and praying that Eb North never rode back for Zachary.

Saturday, late in the day, Travis appeared with Zachary and Turtle River. It was far earlier than he usually returned home and she became aware of her dishevelled appearance. Her hair curled around her face, tendrils springing free from the long braid that hung down her back. She had her red calico sleeves pushed high. Travis was bare-chested, and she suspected he was more comfortable that way. She watched him reach up and get Ellery's revolver. "Turtle River will stay with Jacob. Zachary wants to learn to shoot, and it's time you learn, too, Crystal."

She started to object, then thought about being alone with

the baby and nodded, untying her apron and leaving with a glance at Jacob, who was napping.

They walked away from the house and Travis set up bottles, standing between the two of them and showing them how to aim and fire. He gave the revolver to Zachary, who missed the first three times and then hit a bottle while Travis gave him instructions on his aim. He hit another bottle with the next shot, missed again, and then clicked the empty revolver.

Travis took the weapon to show them how to reload. Watching avidly, Zachary leaned forward. Crystal could not imagine firing the terrible thing enough to have to reload, but she watched. Then Travis handed her the revolver.

She took it carefully and held it up with both hands, her arms wavering. Travis stepped behind her to hold her arms steady.

"Now, get the sight on your target," he instructed. His voice was quiet; his breath fanned her ear. Wrapping his arms around her, he held her wrists, and her pulse raced from his nearness. She barely thought about the weapon.

"Just squeeze the trigger."

She pulled and the blast was deafening. He held her hands steady. "I missed. I don't think I can ever hit a tiny bottle."

"Yes, you will," he said quietly. "Try again."

She shot five times; then, on the sixth, a bottle shattered. Zachary cheered and Travis leaned closer to her ear. "That's good, Crystal."

She felt no elation about learning to shoot a revolver.

"Now, it's Zachary's turn."

She watched as Travis had Zachary reload and she knew he would want her to do so next. She found the weapon loathsome, but knew she should learn to use it. Her father and her brother should have used their guns instead of letting someone kill them. She looked at Travis as he handled the revolver so easily. It didn't look big in his hands.

"Let's see you shoot the targets," she said.

His brows narrowed slightly as he studied her. He picked

up the bottles and handed them to Zachary. "Toss them in the air."

Zachary threw two high and Travis tossed one. He shot all three easily and she gazed at him coolly.

"I'm not surprised."

"Part of my wicked ways, eh, Judge?"

"You know how I feel about violence."

"Yes, but you *have* expressed some yourself. I seem to recall your aiming at me *and* pulling the trigger."

She inhaled, glancing past him at Zachary, who stared at her wide-eyed, his blue eyes filled with curiosity.

"I will never hear the last of that."

"No, I don't expect you will," Travis drawled, handing Zachary the revolver. "It doesn't pay to push the judge over the edge, Zachary. Just remember that."

Zachary looked at her and she smiled sweetly at him. "Don't listen to him, Zachary. You would never push me over the edge. Only one person has done that."

Travis turned away and bent over the revolver, but not before she saw the corner of his mouth lift in a grin. Zachary smiled, but curiosity stayed in his eyes.

The barn went up steadily, and on a crisp day in September, the roof and outside walls were complete. The nights grew cooler and Crystal ordered three books—*The Last of the Mohicans, A Tale Of Two Cities* and Dickens's *A Christmas Carol*—to read through the long winter.

Travis continued sleeping outside, but he knew the nights would soon be too cold and he would be shut away with Crystal more than ever . . . unless he fixed a place in the barn to sleep. While he had no inclination to spend his nights in a drafty, horse-smelling barn, it might bring him more peace of mind than lying on a bed only inches away from Crystal.

On a sunny fall day when the wind was slight, he returned to the house about half an hour earlier than usual. By this time of day, he knew his arrival would be no surprise to Crystal. It was warm enough for the door to be open, and as he neared, he heard a peal of laughter. Startled, he listened to merry laughter. He couldn't imagine such laughter coming from the judge, but his ears did not deceive him. He crossed the porch quietly and looked in.

Crystal and Jacob were seated on the floor, Jacob propped up with pillows. A thin stream of smoke rose from a skillet and Travis guessed their supper was literally going up in smoke while she played with Jacob. Travis would have rescued the searing meal had he not looked at them again.

Seated in front of her, Jacob was making faces that made Travis grin. Jacob puffed out his cheeks, emitting a strange noise, and then chortled happily. Crystal's laughter rang out again, and as adorable as Jacob was, Travis was mesmerized by the sight of Crystal. Her blue-gingham skirts were spread around her as she sat on the floor with the baby. Her hair had been piled on her head, but locks had fallen loose, tumbling over her shoulders. She had her sleeves pushed high and the neck of her dress was unbuttoned and had fallen open. But it was her laughter that held him immobile. Her green eyes sparkled and she bubbled with merriment. Desire swept him, hot and swift. He wanted to scoop her up into his arms and take her laughter in kisses.

His body responded, and his breathing became heavy as if the air had thickened and heated. The woman was appealing, filled with a joy that made her irresistible. Only he knew he'd better resist. And his food was burning in earnest now.

"Crystal—" He crossed the room and yanked the skillet off the fire, setting it aside and stabbing slabs of meat to turn them.

"I'm sorry," she said, scrambling up.

"It's all right," he said. "It's only supper. What's my son doing?" he asked, looking at Jacob.

"Watch him. I've never seen him laugh so much. Here's your papa, love. Show him how you laugh."

Crystal made a whinnying sound, shaking her head, her curls flying, and Jacob giggled gleefully.

Grinning, Travis dropped to the floor beside Crystal and could not resist sliding his arm around her waist. She smelled of roses and was soft, her waist so tiny. She laughed merrily at the baby while Travis had to fight every inclination to pull her to him. He ached to hold her in his arms, though he shouldn't and couldn't. There was so seldom a moment like this in his life that he couldn't bear to walk away from it.

She made a silly sound at Jacob again, and the baby shook with a laughter that was infectious. Travis laughed, and so did Crystal.

"No one can resist a baby," he remarked, sneaking a peek at her again. The neck of her dress gaped open, but revealed little more than her collarbones; his imagination pushed away the rest of the blue gingham. A longing to hold her swamped him. She turned her head and gaze into his eyes. A wide smile still wreathed her face and her eyes sparkled, but her laughter faded as she looked at him.

His heart thudded because her green eyes darkened and he could see the change in their depths. His gaze lowered to her mouth, so rosy and soft. A yearning for all he had lost tore at him again. He wanted to pull her into his arms, to forget, to kiss her laughter away, taking her joy and exuberance into himself. Everything sensible inside him protested a senseless yielding to emotion. He stood abruptly.

"I'll see about supper," she said behind him, suddenly subdued and solemn.

"If you want, I'll watch Jacob for you," Travis offered, scooping up the baby and heading outside without glancing back.

Wiping his brow in the shade of the porch, he set Jacob down in the grass before he went to the pump to wash. He was aroused, something happening more often around her. He was torn between wanting her and wanting to avoid an emotional entanglement that could rip apart his heart for the second time.

As he pumped water over head, trying to cool himself and think clearly, he realized Crystal had another accomplishment to her credit—she was taking him out of the darkness of grief. He would always love Elizabeth and cherish her memory; but thanks to Crystal, the terrible pain of loss was diminishing. Day by day, Crystal's joy and optimism and companionship were melting away his hurt.

Life was better now than it had been when he'd brought her home with him. His meals were still burned and they might not ever improve, but she kept his clothes washed and the house tidy and cared for Jacob. His life was much better, but Travis didn't want to open his heart up to her or anyone other than Jacob ever again. One such devastating loss as he had suffered was enough for a lifetime.

As he dried, he talked to Jacob, letting his body cool down, unable to get the burning images of Crystal out of his mind. This was more than merely wanting a desirable woman. It was too many things—loneliness; need; constant daily contact; raging, fiery desire; and an admiration that was the bedrock of his feelings for her. He had always known she was a strong, intelligent woman. Now, to discover she was all-woman, feminine and beautiful, threatened his sanity.

"Aw, damnation," he muttered, sweeping his wet hair back from his face. "Sorry, Son. Your mama said I have to watch my language around you."

He fastened his hair behind his head with a strip of rawhide. "Someday I'll tell you all about your real mother. She was beautiful and loved you with all her heart. In the meantime, Crystal is your mama now and she loves you, too. And I suppose you love her already."

He picked up Jacob and carried him inside. Crystal was braiding her hair. She had rolled down her sleeves, buttoned her dress, and combed her hair. His gaze flicked over her, mentally stripping away the blue dress and remembering in sensual detail how she looked naked. There was no erasing that vision from his memory. Her gaze met his in her small mirror. She continued braiding without a word. As her fingers moved deftly, weaving strands of shiny hair, he had the urge to take the braid out of her hands and undo it and tell her to tie it with a ribbon.

Instead, he sat down near the table and jiggled Jacob on his knee, singing to him and struggling to avoid watching her.

That night after supper, while Turtle River held Jacob and Zachary read, Crystal found Travis watching her with that inscrutable, brooding look that she had begun to notice more often. He sat relaxed, his long legs stretched in front of him, his booted feet crossed at his ankles. Momentarily forgetting what Zachary was reading, she looked at her son. She did think of Jacob as her son, and she loved him beyond measure. Her dream of sunny California had vanished. She would never willingly leave Jacob when he was thirteen. She loved him as her own child and she wanted to be a mother to him always. He was a precious, happy baby with none of the stormy temperament of his father. Yet in fairness, she knew that Travis had had enough disasters in his life, and at an early age, to give him a volatile disposition.

She wondered what thoughts ran through his mind. She had caught him watching her more and more often. Was he regretting this alliance? With his steady gaze so often on her, something was on his mind. Zachary and Turtle River never received any such scrutiny. Or was it simply because he had walked in on her in her bath? She rejected that at once, fully aware that she did not have a body like his Elizabeth or even one that had ever caused any man a stir.

Forgetting Travis, she tried to concentrate on Zachary's reading while she watched Jacob.

Shortly, the book was passed to Turtle River, who had the most difficulty, but he had known the least when they started. Zachary had had a smattering of learning. So had Travis, but Turtle River had had none. He read slowly and carefully, struggling with new words and getting help from Travis, who sat next to him.

When they finished, all three men left. As the door closed behind Travis, she felt alone, wishing he had stayed to talk as he occasionally did. She picked Jacob up.

"Time for night-night, love. Off to bed."

Crystal changed to her nightgown and took down her hair, singing to Jacob and watching him as he played with the rag doll she had made. She dressed him for bed and put out the lamps, sitting down to rock him.

She held the baby in her arms until he fell asleep and she placed him in his crib. She would have to ask Travis to make a bed for him because soon he would outgrow his small crib. She wound a silky curl around her finger. She loved him deeply, but felt a sudden longing for another baby. Leaning down, Crystal kissed Jacob and lay down on her bed. She turned on her back to stare into the darkness. Why couldn't she have her own baby? Even in the darkness the thought made her burn with embarrassment because she could not have a baby without Travis. But the notion would not go away. They were man and wife.

The ranch was thriving and the livery stable profitable. Travis might be happy for another son. She fell asleep thinking about another baby.

October came and faded into November. The nights were chill and blustery, yet Travis still did not sleep in the house. One November afternoon, Crystal took Jacob to look at the horses. Meandering into the new barn, she saw a bed of hay with two blankets hanging on the wall beside the straw. So, this was where Travis was sleeping.

A mixture of conflicting emotions filled her. She felt relieved that he slept elsewhere because he was too disturbing. At the same time, she suffered a familiar sense of disappointment and rejection that he preferred the cold drafty barn to sharing the bed with her.

She shrugged her shoulders and turned away, but even the sight of Travis's solitary bed of hay could not dispel the now ever-present desire for another baby.

Jacob grew more adorable by the day and she yearned for companionship for him. Ellery had meant so much to her. Jacob needed a brother or sister. She brushed little Jacob's curly locks from his forehead, watching them promptly spring right back. "We'll look at the horses again," she told him, carrying him outside. The pinto waited and one of the blacks ambled over to the fence. She held Jacob near the animals so he could pet them.

One night in the first week of December, while a fire crackled and the wind howled wildly around the house, the men finished reading and stayed talking and playing with Jacob. When Turtle River and Zachary rose to leave, Travis sat rocking Jacob, telling them good night but making no move to go himself. Crystal took Jacob from him to change him and dress him for bed.

With an easy movement Travis handed the baby to her. "The wind howls. I will sleep in here tonight, Crystal."

"You have before, and I would think the barn would be cold and uncomfortable."

He shrugged shoulders clad in blue chambray. "I grew up accustomed to sleeping on the ground and in a tipi. It matters little."

He crossed the room to get the harness he was mending and moved to the table, setting a lamp in its center, while she carried Jacob to the bed to change him.

"I've been thinking it would be best to build a room onto this house. We will need more room as Jacob grows."

Surprised, she nodded, looking at his dark head bent over the table, the lamp making strands of his black hair shine. His hands were strong and capable and she watched him turn the leather in his hand.

"Another room will be good. It might be better to build two rooms."

His dark gaze met hers and his brows arched.

"A room for our bed," she said, although her face flushed

at the words *our bed* because the term barely fit. "And a room for little Jacob."

Travis nodded and bent over the harness. They worked in silence until she sat down to feed and rock Jacob. The rocker made a steady creak as she went back and forth.

"Crystal, Clem Mandeville and his wife have a party every year in December."

"I remember. I didn't attend last year, but Ellery went."

"Why didn't you go?"

"I find parties tedious," she answered, rocking steadily, her feet pumping as she found the rhythm soothing. The room was cozy and quiet, but her mind was in a turmoil because he would sleep beside her this night. And she feared she would be able to get little sleep.

"I think we should go."

"Why?" she asked, aghast, all her attention returning to their conversation. He put down the leather strap and knife in his hands and leaned back in his chair.

"Clem Mandeville is my friend. It will hurt his feelings if no one shows up."

"My goodness!" she exclaimed, dismayed. It had never occurred to her that she could hurt anyone's feelings by refusing to attend a party. This new awareness bothered her.

"Almost everyone will be there," she acknowledged. "Ellery said there couldn't have been more than ten people in town who didn't go last year," she said uncomfortably. Ellery had chided her for not attending.

"That's probably true. It's winter. The harvest chores are behind us and it's a time to celebrate. The holidays are just ahead of us."

She frowned. "I've been thinking about the holidays. You will miss your Elizabeth and I'll miss Ellery. Little Jacob won't know it's a holiday. Turtle River will not care; it is not his holiday . . . or yours. Since I doubt that Zachary has any warm memories, perhaps we should simply ignore them this year.

Next year Jacob will be old enough to know and we can celebrate then.''

Travis nodded. "We can at least have a holiday supper. I'll
bring us meat.''

"And I'll burn it." She tried to make light of her housewifely
deficiency.

"You'll learn to cook," he said encouragingly. "You're
better than when you came here."

"Thank you, but I think you exaggerate," she said, yet she
was pleased.

"Well, holidays or no, we need to consider the Mandeville's
party. I think we should attend."

She drew a deep breath, wanting to argue with him but
having no good reason to object. "You know I don't have
friends in town."

"It's time you did, Crystal," he said firmly. "For Jacob's
sake, you need to get to know the other women."

She looked at the sleeping baby in her arms and sighed.
Travis was right. They could not live in isolation, and she
should get to know the other women. Jacob would go to school
in town and he would have friends there. It would be easier
for him if she had friends there as well.

"I suppose you're right." She placed Jacob in the crib and
stroked his cheek.

"If you need to make a dress, you can get material when
you're in town Friday."

She shook her head. "I have dresses from Baltimore."

"Crystal," he said solemnly, "wear you hair down. I don't
know how women fix their hair, but wear yours with ribbons."

She stared at him with consternation. "I see no reason to do
so. They all know me as Judge Spencer."

He crossed the room to her, and her pulse jumped beneath
his steadfast look. He took her arm and led her to her oval
mirror. She looked at his reflection as he stepped behind her
and unfastened her hair, removing the pins.

Crystal felt on fire. Her pulse raced and she was aware of

each little tug against her scalp, each brush of his fingers against her. He stood too close for her to get her breath, and she suspected he could hear her heart drum. She watched his image in the mirror.

"What are you doing?"

"Taking your hair down," he answered quietly. His dark eyes held her immobile. She could not tear her gaze from his, as if looking into the darkest midnight and feeling drawn by a power she couldn't resist. *If only he had not lost his heart in grief . . .*

Yet if he hadn't lost his wife and been buried in grief himself, he would never have wed her. The long strands tumbled over her shoulders, and then he combed his fingers through them gently. Relishing each stroke of his hand, she wanted to step closer to him and close her eyes. She looked up at him, her gaze dropping to his mouth. She knew she blushed, but she could not control the heat that flashed through her. What would it be like to feel his mouth upon hers?

He placed his hands on her shoulders. "Look at the difference your hair makes. People only see you as Judge Spencer. This once, I want them to see you as a woman, Crystal. It will stop some of their cruel remarks."

"It'll never stop them," she said matter-of-factly. "People have talked behind my back all my life."

"I can't believe that," he said, frowning.

"I'll wear my hair down and you'll see!" she exclaimed, trembling because he was too close and she wanted him in a way she hadn't known a woman could want a man, hurting because she wanted people to accept her but they never had.

"If you let your hair down and look your best, you'll see a difference in their attitude toward you."

"I'll see no such thing!" she snapped. All the ribbons and silks she had had in Baltimore hadn't helped her back East.

"You wear your hair down," he said emphatically, and the matter was closed. "I'll be back inside after a while."

He turned away, his boot heels scraping the floor as he

crossed the room. He shrugged into his heavy coat, put his hat on his head, and closed the door behind him. A gust of cold air buffeted her and she stared after him in consternation. She closed her eyes, aching and yearning for more of him.

She was in love with him. His slightest touch set her heart pounding. His presence made her pulse race. Why couldn't she go back to seeing him as she once had? He was an ordinary man, like other men. Only, in truth, she knew she had never seen him as ordinary or like other men. He had always been different, always disturbed her. She just hadn't had to live with him before.

She groaned, clutching her middle, wanting his strong arms, wanting his laughter and his kisses. Instead, she stood in the empty house with a sleeping baby, the howling wind and cold coming through cracks between logs.

She changed for bed, aware he would be back some time during the night. She felt edgy, disturbed by the prospect of his sleeping inside. After a look at Jacob, she crawled beneath the cold covers and lay staring into the dark, the moan of the wind adding to her solitary feeling. The Mandeville's party was more than a week away; she was not going to worry about it now.

She fell asleep before Travis returned, and he was gone before she awakened. That afternoon as she played with Jacob, she again contemplated a baby of her own. The idea had taken root in her mind and sprouted, blossoming into a notion that she could not set aside. To have at least one more baby would fill their house with joy and fill her life. Jacob was six months old now. She watched the flames dance high in the fireplace and thought about her tall husband. Day by day, she was falling more in love with him. Perhaps she had fallen in love that moment when he had scooped her into his arms and run to the house out of the storm with her. Whenever he appeared, her pulse jumped, and she felt a tingly awareness around him that she never experienced around other men. And she wondered more about his kisses.

How could she ask him to father her baby? Every time she considered it, she grew hot with embarrassment and uncertainty. Yet daily, as she watched Jacob grow, she wanted another child.

Also niggling at her brain was the memory of Travis unbraiding her hair. He had so seldom seen her with it down, yet he must prefer it that way. Setting Jacob on a blanket on the floor, she moved to her mirror and took down her hair. What had Travis seen when he'd stood so close behind her, his fingers winding through her hair? When her unruly mane tumbled over her shoulders, she picked up the brush, pulling it through the curly, tangled locks.

She had not worn her hair down in years, and she wasn't certain she could manage to pin it properly. She had little idea of the latest styles. Finally she gave up, pinning up the sides and letting the rest cascade down her back. She studied herself, dismayed by the short tendrils that curled around her face and were impossible to catch and pin down.

She gave up, leaving it down, selecting a dress with a white cotton top and a black skirt. She changed before the men returned for the supper that she checked on repeatedly, trying her utmost to produce something somewhere between raw and burned.

When she heard footsteps across the porch, she forgot about her hair.

Twelve

She set down a pan of potatoes and whirled around.

"We're back," Travis greeted her, hanging his hat on a hook with a nonchalance that belied the intensity of his scrutiny.

Turtle River nodded and Zachary came inside. "Evening, Crystal," Zachary said and then he halted and his mouth dropped open.

"Evening. Supper's almost ready," she said, rushing to attend to Jacob, who had begun to cry.

Travis reached him before Crystal and waved her back to the table. "I'll take care of him. Go ahead with supper," he said easily, his gaze sweeping over her face and hair without giving her any reassurance that it pleased him.

Zachary still stared at her, and suddenly she wondered if he were staring because her hair was down. She looked at the roasting meat and forgot about the men as she tried to get roast, potatoes, and corn on the table at the same time.

"Crystal, your hair is pretty," Zachary said, sounding awed and still staring at her as if she had sprouted a second head.

"Thank you," she answered, pleased but wishing the compliment had come from Travis.

"It's really pretty," he said again, and she felt her cheeks flush because it was obvious she had pleased Zachary no end. She was aware in her peripheral vision that Travis watched her, too.

She couldn't imagine that he really even noticed her. He always seemed wrapped in his own world, an invisible wall between himself and others.

Through supper, she felt a hum of excitement from all the attention she received from Zachary and even more than usual from Turtle River and Travis.

After eating and cleaning the dishes, they gathered to read, and she caught all three men studying her until she felt fluttery inside. How could letting her hair down cause as much attention as she had received through supper and now? Yet something had changed. She wanted to run and look at herself again in the mirror.

Travis rocked Jacob while Zachary read, and then when Travis took the book, he passed the sleeping baby to her. While flames danced and sparks shot up the chimney, she held Jacob in her arms and listened. She would forever remember his deep voice and *A Tale of Two Cities* read beside a crackling fire. His lashes were thick and dark above his cheeks and the book looked small and fragile in his big hands. After the others had gone, perhaps she would summon the courage to ask him about another baby.

She felt nervous, self-conscious. For days she had mulled over ways to ask him, yet night after night, she let moments slip away because she could not say the words. Tonight, he stayed behind after Turtle River and Zachary left; she would never have a better opportunity.

"You took my suggestion about your hair," he said, facing her across the room. Jacob slept and the only sound in the house was the crackle of the pine logs he had hauled from the mountains. "It's very pretty, Crystal."

"Thank you," she said quietly, her heart pounding with pleasure.

"The barn is too cold and uncomfortable. Tonight I'll stay here again. I'll see to the animals and be back shortly."

She nodded, unable to broach the subject of another child. She watched him leave. She changed and put out the lamps, sliding beneath the covers, expecting to awake when the morning sun's rays spilled across the bed and find Travis had indeed slept there and gone before she was awake.

Instead, she heard the door and saw him in the shadow by the fire.

"I'm still awake," she said quietly over the pounding of her heart.

A floorboard creaked and she made out his silhouette against the window. He pulled off his boots and yanked at his shirt. She heard the rustle of clothing. Had he shed his denim pants as well? She blushed in the safe darkness of the room and lay still, pricked by a million pinpoints as his weight came down on the bed oh-so-close and yet so far from her. Only inches away, but a lifetime of feeling.

"It's a cold night. I expect snow again this week," he said. His voice was deep and quiet in the night, filling her with longing. She shifted onto her side and faced him. Was this the right time to ask him for another baby.

"Do you miss seeing your brother?" she asked instead.

"Brett? I think about him. I hope he's all right, but we each went our own ways and have our own lives."

"Were you close when you were little?"

"Yes. He's twenty-six, two years younger than I am."

"He's my age. I was very close to Ellery when we were growing up. He was my big brother, three years older than I was."

"The war came and Brett and I separated. Lord, what a stupid war it was! So many lives lost. So many of my people lost now."

"You miss your early life, don't you?"

"Yes, sometimes, but I know the Indian way. Our old tribal ways can't last. With the railroads cutting across the land, causing towns like Cheyenne to spring up, change is coming."

"How did you meet Elizabeth?"

"I was headed to Cheyenne and stayed for a time in Colorado. I met her and went back twice to see her. The third time, I married her and brought her here with me."

"Her family didn't object?"

"Her father died the year before I met her and I think her mother was rather desperate about her own circumstances. Her mother married soon after we did."

Silence filled the night. "Tell me about your early years," she said.

Her eyes adjusted to the dark. He lay on his back, his arms behind his head, and talked about his boyhood. The fire had burned low, yet the fires within her seemed to curl higher every moment. She was only inches from him. She could reach out and touch him so easily, but a wide and deep chasm might as well lay between them.

She had no idea how long they lay and talked. As she told him about Baltimore, he turned, facing her. She couldn't see him in the dark, only the bulk of his body, the curve of his shoulder. He reached out to take a lock of her hair, turning it idly in his fingers, the faint, gentle tugs on her scalp making her quiver with longing for more, for him to reach for her, for his hands to stroke her.

Now is the time to ask him, an inner voice told her. It was dark, quiet, and intimate. They had been talking easily about one topic and then another, a closeness developing she had not felt with him before. Yet she wanted to be able to see his face, to see his eyes when she asked. She didn't want darkness hiding everything from her.

Jacob stirred and began crying.

Crystal pulled on her blue wrapper and picked him up, talking softly to him. Travis lit a lamp, and prepared a bottle of milk for Jacob.

She sat in the lamplight, rocking the baby and holding him close on her shoulder until he fell asleep. Then she continued to rock.

Travis put more logs on the fire. He wore his denim pants and moccasins, his shaggy hair hanging loose over his shoulders.

"I'll put him in his bed." Travis took the sleeping baby, bending over her, pausing momentarily when their eyes met. Her breath caught as she gazed at him, his face only inches from hers. "You let your hair down. It's pretty, Crystal."

"Thank you," she said, her heart drumming, pleasure warming her more than the roaring fire.

He took Jacob from her arms and stood, still looking intently at her. "I told you it would change how others see you. Zachary and Turtle River were like two men hit by lightning."

Her joy increased. She was unaccustomed to hearing such praise; and from Travis, a compliment meant more than it would have from any other man on earth. "I don't think it was that drastic, but they did notice."

"More than notice, Judge," Travis remarked dryly and turned away, taking Jacob to bed. She watched as he bent over the baby and then leaned down to kiss his cheek.

"You're a good father," she said, taking a deep breath. Now was the time to make her request.

Her palms grew damp and suddenly the air was suffocating. Travis sat facing her, stretching out his legs in front of the fire. "Now I'm not sleepy."

"Travis, I want to ask you something."

His gaze settled on her and her pulse roared so loudly she could barely hear her own voice. Could he tell how frightened she was?

"Jacob is adorable and he's growing."

"I'm glad you love him. You're a good mother."

"That's what I want. I mean, it's what I wanted to ask you." she blundered on, hurrying to get the words out. "Although there is no love between us," she said in a rush, feeling as if she might faint, "I want to be a mother." She couldn't get her breath, yet she knew she had to go on now. "I want to have a baby. A brother or sister for Jacob."

Thirteen

Travis was speechless, stunned by her proposition. Never in his wildest moments would he have dreamed she would make such a request of him.

All his hurts and fears and caution constricted his heart. He stood up. She had asked for what he wanted to avoid—involvement. And even if his heart could remain unattached, he was not going to lose another woman and have to find a third mother for Jacob. Everything in him cried out in angry refusal, and he wasn't going to argue with her about it.

"No! That's not part of our bargain, Crystal. I will not." He yanked on his shirt and reached for his boots. "I won't go through that again. Never." He stomped into one boot and then began to tug on the other. "I'm sleeping in the damned barn," he said, wanting to get away from her, away from her request and all its implications.

Crystal came to her feet, shaking with anger, disappointment, and hurt. "Go! Just get out!" She watched as he moved across the room to get his coat. He was angry, giving no thought to what she had requested, just rejecting her instantly. Once again a man would scorn her and hurt her and there was nothing she could do about it, but this time it affected Jacob as well as her.

"I wish women could do as men do," she cried, shaking with humiliation and fury. "Before we wed you said if you wanted pleasure you would just go to the soiled doves. If a woman wants a baby, I wish there were somewhere she could go, some man she could pay to have her no matter how odious she is!" she cried, hating that she was losing control of her emotions yet unable to stop the rage and hurt boiling in her.

"Odious?" His hand halted in midair as he reached for his hat.

"Men do as they please, have the children they please, treat their women and children as they please—"

"What do you mean no matter how odious she is?"

"You know damned well what I mean," she flung at him, furious with him and hurting because it had taken all her courage to make her request after months of thinking about another precious baby.

He crossed the room toward her.

"You get away from me!"

"It isn't because I find you odious, Crystal. I don't want to be hurt again. I don't want to lose another woman and have to find a mother for Jacob again."

"Stop it!" Blind with anger, she didn't believe him. Tears streamed down her face, infuriating her even more that she had lost control. "No man has ever wanted me, not here, not in Cheyenne, not in Baltimore!"

"Baltimore? Someone hurt you—"

"You get out!" she cried and picked up a pan to throw at him. He ducked and it sailed over his head and crashed against the wall behind him. "Harvey was supposed to marry me, but he refused. All you have to be involved with me for is one night. You can't even stand that! Men do find me odious—"

"Odious? Men find you *odious?* The hell they do! Zachary is almost blind with infatuation. Turtle River couldn't stop looking at you tonight," Travis said, his voice growing quiet.

Crossing the room to her with a determined gleam in his eye, he ducked a flying tin cup that struck behind him. As she picked up a plate, his hand banded her wrist tightly. His arm swept around her waist.

"The last thing I find you is odious." He ground out the words in a husky voice. "My God, Crystal!" His dark eyes held fires as he looked into her eyes. He lowered his head, his mouth coming down over hers as his arm tightened and he pulled her against him.

Stunned, Crystal had one moment of shock before a flooding wave of hot desire burst inside her with the press of his mouth on hers. His lips were warm, tender, yet insistent. His tongue was hot and wet against her mouth. Her anger and argument went up in flames of passion.

His lips opened hers and his tongue thrust into her mouth in possession and demand. His tongue stroked the inside of her mouth, sending fiery trails that spiraled down inside her. Need and desire rocked her, waking sensations that she had never experienced. She had never known a man's kiss like his. His tongue was deep in her mouth, moving and stroking and destroying the last faint vestiges of anger, replacing it with white-hot desire.

She moaned softly, starting to wrap her arms around his neck, and then realized she was holding a plate. She let it drop and heard a crash, the sound dim in the roaring of her pulse.

His arm held her tightly while his other hand was wound in her hair, tilting her head up as he kissed her until she clung to him, her hips pressing tightly against him. She felt his arousal, stirring her more as she realized just how he was responding to her. And she felt him tremble.

She hadn't imagined it could ever be like this between a man and a woman. She had felt vague yearnings, but nothing that was like a dam bursting and flooding her, carrying her away on a rush that would never leave her where it had found her.

And if she had thought she was in love with him before, she

had no words to describe this new emotion, she loved him
. . . irrevocably, irresistibly, forever. No matter how much he
rejected her. Yet this was no rejection. It was a virile, strong
man who desired her and was burning her to ashes in his arms.

She followed his lead, her tongue thrusting against his, lights
dancing behind her closed eyes, blood pounding in her veins.
For whatever reason he had said no, it was not because he
found her odious or repulsive. And never again would she
entertain such a notion. His hands, his kisses, his body, his
maleness—all indicated he wanted her and wanted her badly.
She felt as if he would devour her and she wanted him to. Her
thoughts spun away as she was caught up in feeling, sensations
bombarding her.

Travis bent over her, kissing her, feeling her come apart in
his arms. Her hips thrust against his, her arms locked tightly
around him, and her fingers wound in his hair. She moaned
and trembled, and he felt as if he were standing in the center
of the blazing logs in the fireplace. He wanted her as much as
he had ever wanted a woman. He wanted to peel her out of
the gown and wrapper and kiss and touch and stroke every
inch of her beautiful body. His hand slid to her breast and she
moaned again. He felt the tremor that shook her; felt the taut
bud beneath his fingers, the soft breast that he cupped in his
hand.

They were going too far, too fast. Far ahead of logical thought
and cool wisdom. In a few more minutes he would be so
ensnared, he could never say no. Never. Did he want to say
no now? Torn by conflicting emotions, he knew what he should
do.

He stepped away, gasping for breath, his heart pounding.

"Crystal—"

His voice was a rasp that grated in his ears. His pulse still
roared and he hurt. He ached for the woman. He wanted to
carry her to bed and lose himself in her. To come back to life
fully and completely. Yet to come back to life and love meant

pain and vulnerability and loss. All those things were part of living.

He wound his hands tightly in her hair. Her lashes raised. Her gaze was sensual, her mouth swollen from his kisses. Fires of hungry desire danced in her green eyes, mirroring what he felt. The woman wanted to be loved.

"Crystal," he began again, his voice a rasp. "I don't ever want to go through that pain again. You know I want you. But if we become truly a husband and wife, you'll have a baby. I can't lose another wife. I can't survive it again."

The dazed, sensual look in her eyes changed as his words registered. She blinked, and her brows drew together in a frown. "That's why you said no? You're—afraid of living?"

"I won't go through that pain."

"I won't die."

He inhaled, his chest expanding. In one more minute he would be lost to words and argument. His gaze raked over her. Her open gown revealed the curve of her high breasts, and her wrapper had been pushed away. He could see she was aroused, the taut peaks of her nipples thrusting against her soft nightgown. He moved away from her: he could not resist her much longer.

"You can't promise that. Elizabeth never expected to die."

He crossed the room, pulling his coat tightly around him and reaching for his hat.

"Look at me," she cried, forcing him to turn around. His pulse still pounded. She stood with the fire behind her, her hair like flames around her head, her big green eyes on him, and he wanted to go right back and haul her into his arms. He remembered her naked, and he could barely get his breath. He ached to love her.

"I'm not Elizabeth. There's nothing dainty or delicate about me! I'm almost as tall as you. I'm strong. Not all women die in childbirth or you and I wouldn't be standing here talking."

"I won't run that risk. It hurt beyond hell." He yanked open the door and stormed into the cold, slamming the door behind him as if the devil were on his heels.

Only it was no devil. It was a desirable woman, a woman who had more facets to her than the most intricately cut diamond. A woman he admired and was beginning to like. And he wanted her to an extent he would never have believed possible. He had been wildly in love with Elizabeth, yet he had never desired her any more than he did Crystal right now. And if he bedded Crystal, he would fall in love with her. And then he would run all the risks of hurt that he had run before. "Never!" he exclaimed aloud. He had promised himself he would not open himself to that pain of loss again.

Propelled by his seething emotions, he stormed through the dark across the open ground, going away from the house, putting distance between himself and temptation. A fiery-tressed temptation that he could barely resist.

Visions of Crystal emerging from her bath danced in his mind and he ground his teeth and swore. "Dammit to hell."

He clenched his fists as he strode, wishing it were light enough to work because he would never sleep tonight.

She wanted a baby! Their baby. The shock was as great as the other emotions tearing at him. Crystal wanted another baby.

Everything in him cried out no! He couldn't go through another dreadful childbirth. If something happened to Crystal . . .

At the same time, all the maleness in him urged him to turn around and go back to the house and take her to bed . . . to bury himself in her softness, burn himself away in her warmth. She wanted his baby. This beautiful, desirable, capable woman wanted him to give her a baby. He could barely breathe. Crystal was more responsive than any woman he had known. Maybe it was her deep-rooted honesty. There was nothing coy about her. Or maybe she was starved for love. Whatever it was, the woman had responded instantly and wildly.

She was strong, passionate, fiery. He tried to conjure up another image, because thinking about Crystal just kept him hard and hot. Oblivious of the cold, sweeping wind, he strode through the night. His long legs carried him swiftly away. He was over two miles from the house when he finally felt a chill from the cold wind buffeting him. Tiny flakes of snow were flying through the air.

How could he sleep this winter with her? And damned if he wanted to sleep in the barn during the cold months. He stood on the barren, wind-swept high plains with the dark bulk of the mountains beyond his land. The wind howled over the open space and bits of straw and snow blew through the air. He could see for miles, and he could see his house and the light in the window. She was inside . . . hurting, wanting, sleep as lost to her as it was to him.

"Dammit!" He swung his fist through the air. He wanted to howl like a wolf. He would not risk her life with a baby. He couldn't bear to. Yet he was going to hurt her so damn badly that he felt her pain as well.

He hunched over, striding back to the house. He was unarmed and he shouldn't be out walking alone in the dark. Crystal wanted a baby.

And she thought men didn't like her. Some fool had rejected her in Baltimore. Travis reminded himself of his own perceptions when he'd met her. Dressed in her judge's robes or her high-necked, long-sleeved plain dresses with her hair wrapped around her head, she looked stern and plain. She had had an air of primness that he could no longer associate with her. Most of the men in town hated that she was the justice of the peace, so that made them see her in a poor manner to begin with.

No, he had to admit, that day he'd proposed, he probably had added to her feelings of rejection, telling her so emphatically that he would never want her body. She had been rejected, maybe left at the altar in Baltimore. Now he understood why she'd left and didn't yearn to go back. Didn't she realize Zachary was in awe of her? Tonight the boy had been senseless, his mouth dropping open when he walked in and saw her with her hair down. He couldn't put a coherent sentence together for ten minutes. And he couldn't stop staring at her all evening.

Even Turtle River had briefly lost his stoic composure. Travis had seen the shock on his face and the few minutes of his unabashed staring at Crystal and the absolute appreciation in his eyes.

And she probably had no idea the effect she'd had on any of them.

For his own sake and hers, Travis shouldn't have kissed her, but he had been no more able to resist than he could resist breathing.

And it had just compounded the tension between them. She wanted a baby. He swung his fist through the air again. "No!"

His shout was carried away by the wind. He hunched over again, walking, looking at the light in the house in the distance and imagining her curled by the fire in her gown and wrapper. She had been warm, so soft, curves and softness in his arms, eager. She smelled like roses and tasted like honey. And was as fiery as the blaze on the hearth. He remembered her throwing the skillet and a cup at him. A dish had smashed. The lady had strong feelings about life and she didn't hesitate to show them. And she wouldn't hesitate in bed either. He thought about her long legs, imagining them wrapped around him. With a groan he shoved the image out of his mind.

"Damnation." Would he go through the torment of hell now? Whatever he did, he was doomed. If he made love to her, got her with child, then he might lose her. If he didn't, he would be in agony and she would hate him.

One concern he would never have—she would never turn to another man for a child. In spite of her speech about wishing women could be as free as men, he knew that no matter how much she wanted a baby, she would be true to her vows. She was unyielding on her principles and as honest as nature.

He kept looking at the house as he drew closer, the light both a beacon and a temptation. A dark figure emerged from the shadows of the shed and barn and walked to meet him . . . Turtle River.

The Cheyenne fell into step beside Travis. "She is a beautiful woman."

"Yes, she is."

They walked back toward the house. "We get snow tonight, but it will blow away," Turtle River said. "It will not hurt the animals."

"We can work in the barn tomorrow if we aren't busy breaking ice or taking care of cows."

They reached the house and Travis kept going, heading toward the barn. They walked in silence until they reached the barn and Travis glanced at his friend. "Thanks for waiting. I left without my Colt."

"It's best to be armed if you roam the night." Turtle River lightly touched his side and Travis knew he carried his revolver.

He nodded to Turtle River and went inside the barn, bedding down in the straw, chilled, yet knowing wherever he lay his head, he would not sleep. He put his hands behind his head, staring into the darkness, hearing the horses moving, and knowing that if he wanted he could be in bed with Crystal in his arms.

What kind of bargain had he sealed himself into with this marriage? When he'd asked her, she'd seemed the solution to his dilemma. A perfect mother for Jacob. She was in need. He was in need. Travis had never thought he would want to bed the woman or desire her or be torn between reason and want. And he knew she hadn't foreseen her future either. When she'd agreed to marry, she had been as desperate as he.

He needed her and he could never ask for a better mother for Jacob. What was he to do?

She should understand what he was telling her. She had hurt enough over the loss of her brother to halfway understand why he didn't want to lose another wife. Was he fighting the inevitable or bringing only grief to both of them? And depriving little Jacob of a brother or sister. He thought of Brett and how close they had been when growing up. Jacob would like a brother or sister. Crystal wanted another baby. Should he take a risk on life again?

Crystal sat rocking in front of the fire. Her body tingled; her mouth still felt the imprint of Travis's kisses. She stared at the dancing flames that he had built, knowing he had built more flames than that inside her. A high wind had caught her and tumbled her across the earth and then dumped her down. Impressions and memories fell through her mind like raindrops spilling over glass.

His kisses had shattered the notion that he found her less than appealing. That was the most dazzling discovery. He had kissed her in a manner that could mean nothing else but that the man wanted her. And wanted her with his whole being.

She rocked steadily, trying to fathom her discovery, relishing it, mulling it over and over. Travis Black Eagle desired her. She would never doubt that again. Not when the man had kissed her the way he had tonight . . . as is if he had waited a lifetime for those kisses.

She *had* waited a lifetime for them, and it had been worth the wait. Never again would she look back at Harvey Goodwill with anything but a deep thankfulness that he had kept them both out of a loveless marriage. For the first time in her life, she truly felt like a desirable woman.

Yet Travis did not want another baby. She understood his hurt, understood his reluctance and fear. But if he desired her— even if there were no love in his heart—if he desired her, he might succumb to his need. And if all that stood between them was his fear of another loss, she could deal with that. She was not delicate and dainty like his Elizabeth and she had reminded him of the fact. He would think about it. She was a tall woman and a hardy one. The world was full of people delivered by women who got through childbirth and survived to raise their children.

Patience, patience, she told herself. He loved Jacob, had been close to his brother. He would see the need to give Jacob a brother or sister.

She must be patient. And in the meantime . . .

A delicious heat filled her that came from memories rather than the fire. His kisses had been headier than the bubbling champagne she had had at Baltimore parties. Always she would remember him pulling her into his arms, pressing her against him, his maleness so hard against her. He wanted her. That knowledge was magic, changing the night, making everything vivid, unforgettable.

The high plains were no longer windswept and lonesome, but filled with hope and a future. The dark night no longer held unknown terrors, but the promise of consummation, completion.

The solitary enigma of Travis Black Eagle held a tantalizing hope of his becoming her man. *Her man.*

She loved him. He might never love her back, but he wanted her and he was good to her. And they could enjoy each other's company. That was more than she had ever dared hope for.

And the Mandeville's party was coming up. For the first time she could remember, Crystal looked forward to a party. She slipped behind the curtain Travis had strung up to give her privacy and examined the dresses hanging on hooks along the wall. Beneath cotton, gingham, and calico; beneath her black woolens were three silks she had brought from Baltimore. She touched them—a red, a deep blue, and a brilliant green. She ran her hand along the green. That was the one to wear to the party. She had green ribbons and she would have to practice doing her hair.

She went back the fire, pausing beside Jacob's bed to stroke his rosy cheek, tenderly taking in his black curls and the thick black lashes above his fat little cheek. His hands were doubled in fists and he smelled soapy and sweet.

"You will have your brother or sister, my sweet baby. I promise you."

She moved back to the rocker, too excited to sleep. Tonight

had changed her life forever. Never again would she be the same woman or think of herself in the same manner as she had before.

Embarrassment flooded her again at her appalling lack of control. Hating that anger had overtaken her reason, she glanced at the pan now hanging innocently on its hook on the wall, embarrassed all over again that she had thrown it at him. And she had broken a plate. She would have to replace it at the general store when she went to town. Occasionally in her life she had lost command of her emotions, suffering afterwards, lecturing herself that she should use more restraint, try to keep a level head.

Yet how could she keep a level head around someone as volatile as Travis? The man was mercury, changing, forceful.

Her thoughts jumped right back to standing in his arms and kissing him. When the wind shook the house, she wondered how he fared in the cold barn. She hoped he was freezing. All he had to do to get warm was walk the short distance back to the house, into her arms.

He would be back. Life would settle into its routine, and now, it would be different when he slept in his own bed. Just as she would never forget his kisses, she knew he was not going to forget this night either.

Crystal finally scooted down on the floor in front of the dying fire, warming and growing drowsy, a smile hovering on her face and in her heart. After an hour she put out the lamp and climbed into bed, wriggling down under the covers, running her hand over Travis's pillow. Wrapping herself in memories of his kisses, she drifted to sleep.

A light sprinkling of snow lay across the land in the early hours, but the morning sun melted it away. The wind blew fiercely and the temperature dropped, but the day was bright and clear. Crystal fed and played with Jacob and did chores in a rosy haze, going over and over the past night in her mind.

While Jacob napped, Crystal bathed and dressed carefully in a pale-blue woolen dress that she had not worn before for

Travis. She parted her hair in the middle, catching it up on either side of her head with blue bows, letting the back fall free. As she worked, she sang and tried to concentrate on the roast she was cooking for dinner, hoping to keep it from burning or being as tough as the floorboards.

That night Travis came in with the others. He shed his heavy coat, hanging it on a hook by the door. His blue chambray shirt pulled across his broad shoulders as he stretched out his arm to drop his hat on the piano. Aware of her hair and how she looked, she tingled from head to toe. She was oblivious of the other men except to give them a smile and a greeting. Travis turned around.

"Evening, Crystal." His dark eyes rested on her briefly. It was impossible to read what was in their depths. His attention shifted to Jacob, who laughed with glee at seeing his father.

"Crystal, let me help you," Zachary said, taking a knife from her hands. "Is this ready?"

She nodded, taking the lid off a pan of potatoes. He lifted the roasted meat to a platter.

"You look pretty, Crystal," he said shyly, and she smiled at him.

"Thank you." She spooned the whipped potatoes into a bowl and set them on the table. She had labored over biscuits and she checked on them once again. They were golden brown, not as fluffy as she would like, but at least they weren't burnt.

"Let's sit down to eat," she announced, pleased that the bowls of food still steamed. She was doing better. Not wonderful, but better.

Zachary held her chair and her gaze met Travis's as he sat down. Her surroundings faded. She didn't hear the others talking, no longer heard Jacob jabbering. All she could see was her husband and all she could think about was last night in his arms.

Something changed in the depths of his dark eyes as he gazed back at her. She felt caught, mesmerized by brown eyes as dark as midnight. Was he thinking about last night, too?

He looked away and she became aware of silence and of Zachary looking back and forth between Travis and her, a puzzled expression on his face. Travis carved the roast and the conversation turned to cattle.

Her appetite was gone. She was too aware of Travis, too filled with memories. She got through supper without knowing what she or the others said, aware only of Travis's gaze continually on her.

After they ate and she and Zachary cleaned the dishes, they all gathered around the fire to read, first going over letters and words and then getting out *A Tale of Two Cities*.

By the time Travis took the novel and began to read, Jacob was sleeping in her arms. She held him close, listening to Travis, glad for a time in which she could sit and watch him openly. As he finished, his gaze raised to meet hers and her pulse jumped.

Turtle River rose, ready to leave. Travis and Zachary stood also. Although disappointment rushed swiftly over her, she reminded herself to give him time to think about her request . . . time to think about her. She never expected him to love her, but he wanted her and that was enough. As hot and fierce as his kisses had been, she suspected his desire was warring badly with his caution.

As they shrugged into their coats, she held the baby. Travis gazed back with a brooding, shuttered expression that gave no hint to his feelings. Then they were gone, the door closing behind them, but she didn't feel as alone as she had before last night.

She knew Travis was thinking about her, thinking about her request. She hummed as she straightened the room. He had built the fire high before he left, and she sat in front of it. How long would it take, she asked the dying embers, before he came around to her way of thinking?

* * *

The next afternoon as they broke ice on a pond, Zachary paused nearby and gazed at Travis solemnly until he straightened up, lowering the axe.

"What is it?"

"Well, sir, you've been mighty good to me."

"You're good help, Zachary," Travis answered.

"It's not my place to question what you do." He shifted uneasily, and Travis realized the boy had his fists clenched and was ready to fight. Startled, he studied Zachary, unable to imagine what was wrong.

"What is it? Go ahead. You can say what you want."

"It's Crystal."

Damn, Travis thought.

"I know you sleep in the barn. It's not my business to question you."

Travis held his peace. He had long ago recognized the boy's wild infatuation with Crystal.

"I figure, she must have sent you there. And if so, then I just hope you haven't hurt her in any manner."

He realized Zachary thought he might have beaten Crystal. The notion was absurd. If Zachary knew Crystal only a tad better, he would know that she would put a shot through any man who raised a hand to her. Yet he could understand why the boy had jumped to such a conclusion. He shook his head.

"Nope, Zachary. I sleep in the barn through my own choice. And it suits her, too. You ask Turtle River, and he can tell you about our marriage. Maybe it will change, but that's the way it is. I'm happy and Crystal seems happy with our arrangement."

He watched the belligerence change to bafflement.

"I wouldn't ever strike Crystal," he continued. "And I'll tell you, Zachary, Crystal's disposition being what it is, it wouldn't be healthy for any man to try to hit her. There's a difference between growing up like you had to and growing up with a family that gives you independence. You've found your own independence now. Crystal isn't hurt. You can ask her."

Zachary flushed a deep scarlet. ''Travis, I'm sorry. I shouldn't have said anything.''

''Forget it. I can understand why you would have made those assumptions, but she's fine. And she didn't send me to the barn.''

''Hellfire. If she didn't—'' He shut his mouth quickly and the red in his face deepened. ''Sorry.''

Travis went back to chopping ice, avoiding Zachary's unvoiced question. He couldn't imagine any man in his right mind sleeping in the barn if he could sleep in bed with Crystal. And Travis was beginning to wonder himself.

And at night when they sat with their reading lesson and she bent over a paper, talking to Turtle River or Zachary and explaining sounds to them, he gazed at the lamplight on her soft skin and the highlights of orange it caught in her red hair and he longed to touch her. At night, after lying awake during hours of torment, he would dream of holding her and kissing her and then suddenly losing her . . . erotic dreams that always ended before fulfillment and brought him wide awake, his heart pounding and the feeling of loss swamping him.

It was going to be a hell of a long winter.

The night of the Mandeville's party arrived. Turtle River was not going and offered to keep Jacob.

Crystal spent the day getting ready. There was sage grouse left from the night before, so Zachary and Turtle River would have something to eat. She had Jacob dressed and ready.

Travis had told her he would bathe and dress in Zachary's cabin. She was mildly surprised that they were still going to the party because Travis had avoided her for days now except at supper time and the few hours afterward when he spent most of his time playing with Jacob.

She felt fluttery, more excited than she could ever remember, because she would spend the evening with Travis. She examined herself in the mirror, wishing she had the oval pier glass that she had sold in Baltimore so she could see how her dress looked.

She smoothed it over her waist, looking at the colorful green silk with lace in the neck that dipped, but not too much. Long sleeves ended in lace at her wrists. Swags of lace banded the skirt with pink bows at the tops of the swags. She wore a pink sash around her waist. She knew many of the ladies would be in woolen dresses, but there would be silks and satins, too. She had quizzed Ellery about the party last year and she remembered his descriptions of the dresses.

When she heard a loud knock, Travis and Turtle River entered. Travis closed the door behind him. She barely glanced at Turtle River, her gaze flying over Travis and her breath catching in her throat. How handsome her husband was! Beneath his long coat, he wore a black suit with a dazzling white shirt that made his dark skin look more exotic than ever. His black hair was sleek, secured behind his head with rawhide. Black boots showed beneath his trousers.

Then she looked up to find his gaze drifting over her, and her pulse soared. He liked the way she looked, she was certain of that. His dark eyes met hers and the hunger and heat in them astounded her. She picked up her cloak and remembered Jacob.

Turtle River sat on the floor in front of the fire, talking to him. She crossed the room to tell Jacob goodbye. Turtle River came to his feet easily and picked up the baby.

She leaned forward to kiss his cheek and looked up into Turtle River's brown eyes.

"You look very beautiful," he said.

"Thank you," she answered quietly, pleased by his remarks. "You're sure you want to stay with Jacob and not go to the party? There will be children. We can take him. With all of us to watch him, he won't be a problem."

Turtle River shook his head. "The party is not for me."

She wondered about his lonely, solitary life and if he intended to go through all his life in such a manner. But then she turned, looked into Travis's eyes, and wanted to go to the party, to spend hours with Travis. He kissed Jacob, helped her with her black velvet cloak, and took her arm. They stepped outside into a cold, clear night.

Wrapped in a buffalo hide, Zachary waited in the wagon. "Ready to go?" he asked.

"Yes," she answered as Travis lifted her onto the wagon seat. For an instant she was in his arms. She slipped her arm around his neck swiftly, holding him, looking into his dark eyes and remembering and yearning for him.

Then she was seated and he was moving around the wagon to climb up on the other side. Travis threw a buffalo hide around her shoulders and another across her lap, then he pulled part of the hide over his own legs and flicked the reins.

It was cold and she pulled the cloak close about her, scooting against Travis for warmth, glad for the excuse to move beside him. He placed his arm around her, holding her tight, and Crystal felt in paradise.

They talked about Jacob and the ranch and had long moments of silence while they simply rode. The stars twinkled brightly against the dark night, and a full moon peeped over the horizon. Then they were at the Mandeville's house, where a welcoming light shone from every window.

Fourteen

Travis helped Crystal from the wagon and Zachary climbed down and walked on the other side of her. When they entered the front door, she paused to let Travis take her cloak. Travis had bought Zachary a black woolen shirt in town and he wore that with black denim pants. His hair was slicked down and Crystal realized he was still growing, a fact she had barely noticed at home.

He turned to look at Crystal, his eyes going wide. "Crystal, you look beautiful!" he exclaimed quietly.

"Thank you." She smiled at him. "You look very nice yourself."

"I'll put away the coats," Travis said, knowing Zachary did not even hear him. If Crystal didn't see the boy's adoration, she had a blind side.

Travis placed their coats on a bed in a front room. When he walked back down the hall, he saw her talking to Lester Macon and balding Theo Chaney. Travis's gaze swept over her and he felt his pulse jump. She was a beautiful woman. Why the hell she had hidden it, he didn't know. If she had let down her hair and come to the Mandeville's party last year, looking as she did tonight, she would be another man's wife now and not his. And he said a swift prayer of thanks that she had done no such thing.

Her eyes seemed a deeper green because of her green dress. Her hair was shining, and he remembered how soft the long strands had felt in his hands. The dress had a neckline a few inches lower than Crystal usually wore, still modest, but it showed pale, smooth skin. He looked at her tiny waist, and then his gaze dropped lower and he stripped away the green dress in his mind.

Drawing a deep breath, he watched two more men saunter up to talk to her and he knew that her life would change tonight. She would get more respect now, and for the next three hours, she was going to get a hell of a lot of attention.

Although he knew he should step back and let her enjoy it, his inclination was to wrap his arm around his wife's waist and hold her close to his side.

He was losing hours of sleep every night, lying awake in the freezing barn thinking about Crystal, knowing all he had to do was get up and go inside and tell her he would give her another baby.

His gaze swept over her again. She was tall, far taller than his Elizabeth. She was a strong woman, but she still had a slender figure, a tiny waist. All he had to do was remember what Elizabeth had gone through in childbirth, and the memories stopped him cold.

If he had had good sense, he would have stayed home tonight and kept her with him. It would be more difficult to forget how she looked this night. But Crystal deserved for everyone to see her as she could look. She deserved more respect and she needed to make friends with the women in town . . . although that might be a little difficult if their menfolks hovered around her all evening.

The fiddlers were playing. The Mandevilles had cleared their large living room for fiddlers and dancing, and the ladies in town had baked and brought their cakes and pies and other sweets all day long. Travis strolled through the crowd to join the group of men talking to his wife, greeting each man.

Clem Mandeville stepped up and shook hands with Travis, his gaze going straight to Crystal. Travis almost laughed at their host, who was staring at her with an open mouth. "Judge?"

"Evenin', Mr. Mandeville. It is so nice of you to have this party for everyone."

"Saints alive, Judge! I didn't recognize you."

She smiled, her green eyes sparkling. "I didn't think you'd want me to come in my judge's robes."

"Oh, hell no! Excuse me, Judge."

"It's Crystal, Mr. Mandeville."

"And you call me Clem," he said. His wife approached. "Mama, here's Travis and his new wife, the judge."

Irene Mandeville nodded to Travis and smiled at Crystal. "Evening, Crystal. I'm glad you could come and how fetching you look. I'll bet that's one of those dresses you brought from Baltimore with you."

"Yes, it is."

Travis stood idly listening, paying more attention to Crystal. The Mandevilles moved away, but Crystal was drawing a crowd. Women wanted to look at her dress; men wanted to talk to her. And Travis could see the shock on their faces. It was almost an hour before he took her arm and they made their way to the edge of the dancers.

"Evening, Travis," said a deep voice and he looked around to see Sherman Knudsen. Shocked that the man had singled him out, Travis shook hands warily, and then he realized why the sudden thawing from Knudsen.

"Evening, Judge Spencer."

Crystal smiled up at him. "Evening, Mr. Knudsen. And it's Mrs. Black Eagle now."

He glanced at Travis and then back to her. "Yes. I haven't seen you in the bank in a while."

"My husband takes care of everything."

"I saw the list of books you ordered from Clem. Enjoy reading myself and I wondered about that book *A Christmas Carol.* Phoebe likes to read, too. I thought I might order a book for her for Christmas."

"It's a delightful story. Don't you think so, Travis?"

"I've enjoyed it, but my favorite is *A Tale of Two Cities,*" Travis answered with amusement. Knudsen knew he had not been able to read. He saw a swift, curious look from Knudsen and he met it directly, feeling a strange clash between them, and then the moment was gone.

"I didn't know you enjoyed reading," Knudsen said, a chill in his tone.

"I have my wife to thank for that," Travis answered easily. "She's instructing me."

"Then you have the prettiest teacher west of the Mississippi," he said to Crystal.

"Thank you, Mr. Knudsen."

Son-of-a-gun, Travis thought, both amused and irritated. Old Man Knudsen was dazzled by his wife. But then, what man in the room wasn't dazzled by her tonight? Travis couldn't resist placing his arm lightly around her waist. He could see where Crystal would never make the stir in Baltimore that she could here. She was taller than most women, her hair too unruly to be combed down in a decorous, fashionable manner. And in Baltimore, parties would have been filled with petite young ladies in beautiful dresses. But in Cheyenne, she stood out like a swan among chickens.

There were some very pretty women in the room . . . Eloise Knudsen, Agnes Blair, Myrtle Hastings. But they were few, and Crystal was striking with her hair and height. And her imperious judge's manner. This was no simpering, shy miss; and he thanked heaven for that, though at moments her fiery disposition gave him fits.

"If you get a chance, tell Phoebe about your books and see what you think she might like. I'd appreciate it."

"I'll do that."

"There she is," Knudsen said, motioning to his wife to join them. Travis saw Eloise Knudsen looking at him, her gaze shifting to Crystal and back to him. Black haired and blue eyed, Eloise was dressed in scarlet and was the second most beautiful woman present. After he lost Elizabeth, if he could have married Eloise under the same circumstances he married Crystal, he would have been overjoyed. Now he was thankful beyond measure to have Crystal. But he had known from the first day he approached Crystal and proposed that she was a good woman for Jacob.

Eloise's mother, Phoebe Knudsen, joined them and the women talked about books and Travis walked away, leaving Crystal on her own. As he left them, he heard Crystal's voice.

"Mrs. Knudsen, I've heard you have the most delicious biscuits in Cheyenne."

"Thank you!"

"I have so much trouble with baking. My mother died before imparting to me how to acquire the skill for light and fluffy cooking."

"I'd be happy to help you sometime," Phoebe Knudsen said, smoothing her lavender silk dress.

"Thank you. I'd deeply appreciate it if you would tell me how to bake even ordinary biscuits," Crystal said with sincerity.

"I would love to. And you must tell me about your Baltimore dressmaker. How lovely your dress is!"

Travis bit back a smile and moved on through the crowd. Maybe their eating would improve after this party, although he had serious doubts as long as Crystal found Jacob more fascinating than her cooking.

He waited, watching her talk with some of the women, and then Rufus Milligan threaded his way through the crowd. As tall as Travis, Rufus could draw as much attention as Crystal. Cheyenne's bachelor attorney, Rufus was also Cheyenne's most colorful attorney. He had a flamboyant manner, flaming red hair and beard, an impressive height, and a bass voice that could achieve thunderous power. Travis always wondered why

Rufus had not become an actor, but he supposed that Rufus found law more financially rewarding and he still got to use his acting skills almost as often as on the stage. The man was also as good a marksman as the best in town. His blue-eyed gaze was set on Crystal.

Travis was amazed Rufus had not courted Crystal since their backgrounds were so similar. Yet no one had courted Crystal. And he knew Rufus did court Eloise Knudsen.

Now Travis watched as his wife went to the dance floor with Rufus and he turned her into his arms. Travis stood sipping the innocuous punch. Everyone knew that the whiskey was out on the back porch, but at the moment, Travis didn't care. He watched Crystal, aware her Baltimore background was showing tonight.

She looked perfectly at ease, dancing in Rufus's arms, smiling at him as if she went to parties every month. And Travis suspected there had been plenty of parties in her background if her father and grandfather had been lawyers.

She stood out among all the pretty ladies. Her dress was fetching, but it was Crystal who was holding everyone's attention. With her cascade of flaming hair and her big green eyes and her height, she was a striking woman. And she was enjoying herself and it showed.

His gaze swept over her again. Could she deliver a baby and survive? Was she as strong as she thought? He thought of the calves he had pulled, the horses that had foals turned the wrong way. He remembered Jacob's birth and how difficult it had been and how Elizabeth had suffered.

He didn't want to go through that again or put Crystal through it, and he didn't want to lose her. But this was tearing him apart.

The music stopped and Zachary claimed her. He wondered when Zachary had learned to dance and he saw that she adjusted to his simple steps.

She adjusted quickly and damn well. Could Crystal have taught him to dance? Travis didn't know when she would have and he felt mildly annoyed at the thought of his wife dancing alone with Zachary while he was away working. Ridiculous. He was being ridiculous. She had taught them all to read, brought order to Travis's life. She was a strong, beautiful woman, and Travis realized suddenly that as desperate as she had been upon Ellery's death, she would have managed some way on her own. Now, looking back, he was amazed that he had persuaded her to marry him.

As the evening progressed, Travis watched one man after another dance with his wife. Logan North came up beside him. "Damnation, Travis. I didn't know you married a beauty. I can't believe it's the judge. And I don't think you knew it when you married her. How could any woman change like that?"

"I didn't know it. And I think, mostly, she just let down her hair."

"And got out of those damned black dresses. Whew! Every unattached male is wishing he had looked closer at her. Even a few of us who are married. Ellery just hid her away damned well."

"I don't think Ellery had much to do with it. I think it suited her."

"Yeah. I suppose her disposition hasn't transformed as well."

Travis looked into Logan's curious blue eyes and smiled and kept his mouth shut.

"Damn, you did all right when you up and married her. Whatever her disposition is, you got yourself a prize. Man would put up with a lot to get a woman looking like she does."

"Indeed, he would, Logan." Travis thought about Sherman Knudsen being friendly for the first time when they were doing anything besides transacting business and he suspected that Crystal had the respect of more than one educated man in the room. She put the fear of God in the others.

Tom Yiblonski joined them. "She damn sure had this town fooled. Sure you haven't exchanged the judge for someone else?"

"She'll be in her courtroom next Friday and you can look for yourself," Travis remarked and listened to the song end. As the dancers came to a halt, he turned. "Excuse me. It's time I got to dance with my wife."

"Yeah," Tom said. "I'd like to get to have a dance with her myself."

Travis barely heard him, moving swiftly to her, his eyes on two men that were heading her way.

He took her hand, pulling her to him and placing his other hand on her waist. "I'm claiming the next dance with my wife, darlin'."

Something flashed in the depths of her big eyes and he saw the change come over her that shut out the world. He forgot the others, looking into a green that enveloped him and held dancing fires in their depth. The music began and he moved easily with her. In Texas, he had danced plenty himself. She was light, following his lead perfectly.

"You've dazzled the town."

"I don't know about that, but it is gratifying to find that some of those men who have been rather unkind in the past cannot be kind enough now."

"Damn fools," Travis said, grinning. "Their loss and my gain, Crystal. And I think you are opening doors for me. Which means they will open for Jacob."

Her brows arched as she gazed up at him. "Then that's very good. I suppose it's my Baltimore background in this wild place."

"That and your education and your intelligence and your beauty."

"The ladies have been nice."

"And that, is a tribute. It's a wonder they aren't all turning as green as your dress with envy. I've seen a few who are glaring at you. I wonder when Zachary learned to dance."

"I taught him."

"When?" Travis stared at her.

"The past two weeks he's come by the house in the afternoons. He told me he was looking forward to the party, but he didn't know how to dance. This is his first dance, and I think he's doing quite well.''

''Damn.'' Travis was thinking about Zachary stopping by the house. If the boy had ever surprised Crystal bathing as he had, he couldn't imagine how Zachary would survive the incident. ''He didn't try to kiss you?'' he asked, chiding himself for questioning her and disliking the tight knot in his stomach at the thought of Crystal and Zachary dancing together ... every afternoon for the past two weeks.

She laughed, her eyes sparkling and annoying him. ''Good grief, no! Zachary wouldn't try to kiss me!''

''The hell he wouldn't. Then I suppose he's honorable to the bone,'' Travis said. He was jealous ... and that was ridiculous. ''If I had been dancing around the room with you, I would have kissed you.''

Her smile vanished, and she gazed up at him solemnly. Lost in her green eyes, he moved to the music, wanting to dance her into a secluded corner and kiss her now. Wanting more than that.

Was he falling in love with his wife? The question shocked him and he stared at her, looking at her rosy mouth, her big green eyes, her smooth skin, the riot of red curls that made him want to wind his fingers in their softness and pull her face to his.

He tried to stop his thoughts, knowing in seconds he would be in no shape to stay out on the dance floor, although he was certain few would notice him. It was Crystal the others watched. And he was glad for her, glad to end some of the cruelty she had received.

Then the dance was over and immediately Tom was at his side.

''May I have a dance, Judge? Travis?''

Reluctantly, Travis released her, hearing her soft voice murmuring to Tom. Travis had another dance, and before it was over, took her to the dining room to see if she would like something to eat.

She turned an accusing gaze on him. "Phoebe Knudsen told me to sample her chocolate cake. You didn't tell me that I should bring something."

He grinned. "Darlin', you are a beautiful woman and you have stunned the locals this night. But, in truth, I think I did you and the others a favor when I didn't tell you to cook something for this evening."

Crystal laughed, a merry peal of laughter that made him want to pull her into his arms. Her eyes sparkled as she gazed at him. "I'm sure you're quite right. People have been unmerciful because I am the justice of the peace. If they discovered my cooking, I might be sent to court!"

He grinned, touching her cheek. "I like to see you laugh."

"Not as much as I like to see you laugh! I really didn't think you could when I first knew you. But you can—even if it's my cooking that's making you chuckle."

"Crystal, you do so many things that make up for your cooking."

"Do I really?" she asked saucily and his pulse jumped. He heard the challenge in her voice and saw it in her eyes. "Like what? I really want to hear you say what—besides caring for Jacob."

His laughter vanished as he looked at her and slipped his arm around her waist. "I think I'll tell you what when we're back home," he answered in a husky voice, noticing her response to his words and his tone. Her eyes darkened and her smile vanished as swiftly as his own had. That sensual, heated look came to her expression and her gaze dropped to his mouth. They were alone, and he couldn't resist. He bent his head and placed his mouth on hers, tasting her, taking her kiss, doing what he had wanted to do since the night he had stormed out of the house.

For an instant she yielded, responding to him with all the heat that she could kindle so swiftly. His heart thudded and he wanted to tighten his arms, but then she pushed him away. "Travis, for heaven's sake! We're in public!"

"I don't give a damn. You're my wife, Crystal. There's nothing wrong with a man kissing his wife."

"It isn't proper and I won't have gossip circulating that Jacob's mother is not a lady."

"Yes, ma'am," he said, teasing her and stepping away from her, aroused and wanting her. Now, he needed to get away and cool down before he returned to the party. "I think I'll get a drink. I'm sure you won't be alone more than thirty seconds."

Rufus rounded the corner and brightened. "Ah, Mr. and Mrs. Black Eagle," he said. "Try Phoebe's chocolate cake."

"I'll leave my wife to the chocolate cake," Travis said. He left, knowing Rufus would hover over her. He went to the back porch, stepping into the cold to join a group of men and get a glass of whiskey.

When he returned, he watched her dance with Rufus and saw Zachary dance past with Agnes Barnes. Zachary was laughing and talking and looking as if he were having as much fun as Crystal. Travis remembered how the boy had been when they had found him. Thank heaven his father hadn't returned with the law, although Travis would have urged Zachary to run away. But he suspected Eb North knew his days of beating Zachary were over.

Zachary passed him again. Agnes was gazing into his eyes, smiling up at him, and Travis hoped Zachary would begin to get over his feelings for Crystal. Yet that was part of growing up, he supposed.

His gaze rested on Crystal, looking at her long, slender figure again and thinking about a baby. And thinking about taking Crystal to bed. Was she slowly and with absolute certainty taking his heart anyway?

Before the night was over, he had one more dance with Crystal and then he held her arm possessively as he steered her to thank the Mandevilles, gather their coats and Zachary, and go.

Zachary offered to drive the wagon home and Travis agreed, sitting in the bed of the wagon and pulling Crystal into his arms, covering both of them with hides while Zachary wrapped in hides and hunched over the seat.

"That was the most fun I've ever had at a party!" Crystal exclaimed, cold wind nipping at her nose while she was aware of the warmth of Travis's body and his arms wrapped around her. Joy bubbled in her. She had had a glorious evening and the best part of all had been the moments alone in the dining room with Travis.

"I'm glad. You stirred up the townspeople and you made friends. Maybe a few enemies of young ladies who paid no attention to you before, although since you are a married woman, I doubt if they feel too much jealousy."

"And plenty of them watched *you* all evening," she remarked. "They looked as if they would faint for a dance with you."

"I doubt that," he said dryly. "Who was Harvey?"

"Harvey Goodwill," she said, realizing she could talk about Harvey now without feeling anything but relief and gratitude to him. "We were pledged to wed by our families, but Harvey went away to school and fell in love and broke the engagement only months before it was to be announced to the world. He wed a very wealthy young woman, so his family was quite pleased, but it broke relations between our two families. Otherwise, I would be in Baltimore, married to Harvey. Or, even if we had never yet married, I would still be in Baltimore. At the time it was humiliating, but now I'm glad."

"Crystal, were you in love with him?"

"No, not ever."

"Ah. Then you weren't heartbroken over the broken engagement, just hurt pride."

"That's right," she answered easily.

"And your family? Your mother and father?"

"By that time I lived with my grandparents. My grandfather was an attorney," she said, settling in Travis's arms and laying her head back on his shoulder while she talked. She could smell the fresh scent of soap on him and his warmth enveloped her. Her legs were against his and she loved being held close in his arms.

"My father was one also and worked for my grandfather. They were in the same firm. Harvey's father was a partner as well, but he opened his own firm. There were six attorneys. My grandfather drank heavily and so did my father, something passed down from father to son. One day an irate former client accosted my father on the street. Mother and I were with him. The man pulled out a gun and killed my father."

"Damn. How old were you?"

"I was twelve. It was just like Ellery—if my father had been armed, he could have protected himself. The man was wild. Anyway, then I started going to the office to help my grandfather. Soon the other partners were gone, except for Charles Allbloom. I learned to keep books for them, and I began to read Grandfather's law books. On days he was sober and not busy, he would talk to me about law. That's how I learned what I know. If I were a man, I could be an attorney."

"I suspect you could, Crystal."

"My father and grandfather could not cope well with adversity. The women in my family were the strong ones, although not physically strong. When I was seventeen, Mother got pneumonia and died. Then my grandmother died two years afterwards. Grandfather died when I was twenty-four. I sold what was left and came out here."

"I'm glad you're here," Travis said quietly. His fingers played with her hair and stroked her throat, her nape, her ear. His touches tingled, building a blaze of longing in her.

"I agreed to go to Phoebe Knudsen's for a tea a week from Sunday, so we shall have to go back to town and you will have to keep Jacob."

"That's fine. Ah, Crystal, they will accept me now because of you."

"I don't think everyone will. There were a few people very cool to me tonight."

"If it was only a few, then you have jumped a barrier that I have known all the time I have been here. Feelings run high toward half-breeds."

"That's great foolishness. You lead the same kind of life they do."

"My skin isn't the same color."

"And I find the color of your skin fascinating," she said shyly.

"That's the first time I have been told that!" he replied, his warm breath fanning her ear. Then his tongue flicked over her ear. Desire flashed hot within her, and she sucked in her breath. Heat coiled, drumming with her pulse, and she twisted around to look up at him. In the darkness, she couldn't see the expression in his dark eyes. He was only inches away, and then his head came down and his mouth met hers.

Wrapping her arms around his neck, Crystal moaned softly. He shifted her onto his lap and her heart thudded as he leaned over her and kissed her, his mouth brushing hers so lightly, tantalizing and teasing. She flicked her tongue over his and then his mouth was demanding, hard and hot, making her heart race.

All too soon, she felt the wagon halt and Travis released her. He stood, pulling her to her feet. He jumped down from the wagon and then swung her to the ground.

"I'll put the wagon away and take care of the horses," Zachary said. "I had a very good time. Thank you for taking me with you."

"You're welcome," Travis said easily. "I'll be there in a minute to help you."

Disappointed, Crystal tried not to react. She wasn't going to let anything mar an evening that had been wonderful beyond belief.

Travis took her arm and headed toward the house. Before they reached it, the door swung open and Turtle River greeted them. "Welcome back. Your son sleeps quietly, and we had a good evening."

"Thanks for staying with him," Crystal said. "We had a good evening, too. I had a wonderful time!"

"I thought you might," he said. "You're very pretty tonight, Crystal."

"Thank you," she answered, wondering about Turtle River's solitary life and wishing he had agreed to go to the party with them.

"Now I'll go." He pulled his coat close around him and strode into the night while Travis followed her inside and closed the door.

A fire still burned brightly in the fireplace. Travis's fingers brushed her nape as he removed her cloak and tossed it aside. He turned her into his arms and she gazed up into eyes so dark they caught the firelight in their depths. His desire burned as brightly as the flames and her heart pounded. She wanted him and she loved him. This tall handsome man who was her husband now, even if in name only. Their lives would be forever entwined, and she could wait because she knew he wanted her, knew he was standing here now, torn between what he wanted and what he feared.

Travis pulled her into his arms and kissed her hungrily. She was a beautiful, appealing woman, his wife. All he had to do was take her to bed and he would have a full, complete marriage.

Yet he wasn't ready; he wasn't certain. He had sworn off love, but he was falling in love with her as surely as the winter was moving toward springtime.

He hadn't wanted to love her; didn't want to love her now, yet there were so many reasons to. And tonight had added more reasons to love her, moment upon moment as he had danced with her, watched her, held her in his arms on the ride home. He knew he was falling in love with his wife.

He bent over her, his tongue going deep in her mouth. This woman had been hurt by men, hurt and humiliated by others, yet she was so strong, so caring. She had never been courted, never had times like tonight.

And then he stopped thinking. She was soft, pliant, eager for his kisses, returning them with a passion that made him forget everything except her. He ran his fingers in her soft hair, feeling pins fly and ribbons fall free. His hand drifted to her back and twisted the buttons, unfastening them while he kissed her. Her tongue was in his mouth and he shook, trying to keep from yanking the green dress off her shoulders and peeling it away completely.

Finally it loosened and he pushed it off her shoulders, bending down to trail kisses along her throat. He slipped off her clothing, shoving down her chemise, cupping her high, firm breasts in his hands. Soft, so very soft. His thumbs circled her taut peaks and she moaned, her fingers digging into him and then sliding over his chest, down along his hips, down to his thighs.

He growled deep in his throat, aching, trembling with need. He wanted to take her, to shove himself deep into her, join with her. He leaned down, and his tongue flicked over her nipple.

As sensations flooded her, Crystal cried out. And above all, she was aware it was Travis who was kissing and stroking her. Her love, her life. The barriers between them were coming down, surely, steadily. Her heart pounded with desire, with eager anticipation, with a womanly sureness that she was wanted by her man.

And then he straightened up. His eyes, black as night, focused on her. "Crystal," he said in a rasp, cupping her face with his hand. He kissed her hard and then straightened to look at her again.

"You're winning. I got what I wanted when you married me. You're going to get what you want someday."

"I can wait until you're sure and until you're not afraid."

"I'll be afraid. That won't ever go," he said fiercely. "And if I love you, I'll be damned terrified."

Hearing the emotion in his voice, she knew this brave warrior who had fought so many battles and who had been an officer in the army during the war was petrified of loving and losing again.

She stood on tiptoe, winding her arm around his neck, her bare breasts pressing against his coat and shirt as she kissed him passionately. She leaned back to look at him.

"I'm very much alive, Travis. And I intend to stay that way."

He shook his head. "You can't know that. I've seen too many men go into battle with that attitude, Crystal. And I've carried their bodies away later."

He pulled her dress and chemise up on her shoulders, brushed her mouth so lightly, lingering, brushing his lips softly over hers again.

"Oh, my woman," he whispered. He straightened, his dark eyes boring into her, before he turned and went to the door. He paused to look back at her. Then he was gone into the night, closing the door quietly behind him.

She swung out her arms and spun in a circle, then danced around the room, remembering being in his arms, waltzing with him, kissing him, relishing the glorious evening with him! The moments in the dining room had been special . . . the moments in the wagon . . . the moment in his arms on the dance floor. She hummed a tune as she pirouetted by herself. Seeing one of his jackets hanging by the door, she took it down and held it, her feet still moving gracefully in time with an unplayed melody.

When she finally curled in bed, her body ached with longing for him to finish what he had started tonight.

But he was changing. So swiftly changing. He wanted her, perhaps cared for her. He was good to her. She smiled, snuggling down beneath the covers and thinking about him as she drifted to sleep.

Travis shifted on the cold straw. He was freezing—and at the same time burning. His body was hot with need for Crystal. For a woman. Any woman, he thought angrily, but then he knew that was not so. One tall, brave, red- haired woman who had tried to shoot him, who had married him in desperation, who had thrown pans at him, and whose kisses were scalding promises of wild passion. All-woman, desirable, intelligent, challenging. She had been beautiful tonight, so damned poised, leaving the town shocked and dazzled, opening doors for him and for Jacob. Travis wanted to storm back to the house and take her. He wanted to resist her and use some reason and caution.

He sat up, gazing into the darkness while anger churned in him. She had been brave marrying him. Maybe he should be braver and get her with child.

He laughed in the darkness at himself. Hell, he sounded as if it would be a chore to bed Crystal. He wanted her to an extent he couldn't believe and it would never be a chore in any manner. She would burn him to ashes.

How many sleepless nights would he spend before he could live with his decision? He lay back down, recalling the evening and all he had learned about her. She had had to care for her grandfather just as she'd cared for Ellery. He guessed she might have cared for her entire household. That would be no surprise.

Travis settled in the straw, trying to think about the livery business and his ranch and get his mind to the point he could fall asleep, something he was doing less and less of lately. Thanks to Crystal.

The next day was clear and cold. As Crystal hung out wash, knowing it would freeze but the wind might still blow it dry in time, she turned to rush back to the house. She scooped up Jacob, who was bundled up, his tiny face showing, his nose fiery red from the cold.

She saw someone approaching the house. Her heart jumped and she thought of Zachary and Eb North. She hurried her step, rushing to get the revolver, but stopped on the porch when she recognized the rider. She stood in the wind as she watched

Sheriff Hinckel ride up and she remembered that dreadful day when he had brought Ellery's body home to her.

"Afternoon, Crystal."

"Sheriff Hinckel. Want to come in? There's a pot of coffee."

"Thanks. How's the tyke?"

"He's fine," she said as he followed her into the house. She set Jacob down, removing his mittens as she offered what hospitality she could. "Take off your coat and hat. I don't suppose you came out here to talk to me?"

"Nope," Wade said, removing his coat and draping it over a chair. He looked around him. "You've made a nice place here."

"Thank you."

His blue eyes met her gaze. "I rode out to see Zachary North."

Fifteen

She had known as soon as she'd seen him that he wanted Zachary.

"I was hoping you wouldn't ever come. Something's wrong with a law that says a child belongs to a parent no matter what the parent does to that child."

"Yeah, I agree, but that's the law."

"The men are working. If I fire a couple of shots, they'll come in."

"Sit down. I'll go fire the shots." He strode outside and she heard two quick blasts that she knew would bring them running. As the sheriff returned, she poured a steaming cup of coffee for him.

"Crystal, I'm not taking the boy back with me."

Startled, she turned. "You're not? Then why'd you come?" She set down his coffee and stared as he pulled out a chair and sat down.

"Just to tell him his pa was shot and killed."

She thought about Eb North. "Then Zachary doesn't have to worry about him ever again?"

"That's right.

"It's a dreadful thing to be glad a man has died."

Hinckel shook his head. "Some men ain't worth spit. I guess we won't have to worry about Zachary being torn with grief." Hinckel paused, and in the silence she thought about what the news would mean to Zachary. "He seems like a nice young fellow."

"He is," she said, smoothing Jacob's curls and giving him a spoon to play with.

"The sage grouse is abundant this year. Suppose you folks have been eating it regularly."

"Had some last night."

Crystal talked with the sheriff until they heard a horse and Travis came bursting through the door, bringing a gust of cold wind with him. He looked tall, powerful, even more broad-shouldered in his coat. He yanked off his gloves and crossed the room.

"Afternoon, Travis," the sheriff said, standing to shake hands. Travis's eyes narrowed.

"He hasn't come for Zachary," Crystal said quickly.

"That's right. Just came to tell him his pa is dead. Shot in a saloon fight last week."

"Thank heaven," Travis said quietly, looking at Crystal. "We were afraid you'd come to take Zachary back to his father."

"Man wanted me to come get the boy, but I've heard about Eb North. And Turtle River told me about Zachary. I told Eb North if he wanted the boy to go get him hisself. I know it's my job," he said, looking at Crystal, "and I know you might not approve, Judge, but Turtle River said the boy could have died."

"He would have if we hadn't found him," Travis said. "He's down at the barn. We can go tell him about his father."

Crystal got Jacob's coat and quickly bundled him up again. She glanced up to find Travis watching her. "Where are you going?"

"With you. I don't think Zachary will be sad, but I think I should go."

"He won't be sad," Travis said. He held her coat for her and when he pulled it around her shoulders, his hands lingered and his fingers brushed the side of her throat. She was conscious of him so close behind her. Every time they were together, he brushed against her and he touched her constantly. And they were together every day. The steady, slight contacts were building up fires in her that made her long for his arms around her and his hands moving over her.

Travis swung Jacob into his arms and they left, closing the door. She hurried to keep up with the men's quick strides, and in minutes, they entered the drafty barn. Horses snorted and pawed the ground. Zachary was hammering boards in place, building a horse stall in the still-unfinished barn. He had shed his coat and hat and pounded diligently, but glanced up and saw them coming. He lowered the hammer and stepped out of the stall, looking from Travis to the sheriff.

"Hello, Sheriff," he said cautiously, his eyes shifting across the barn. Crystal followed his gaze and saw the rifle propped against the wall.

"Afternoon, Zachary," Sheriff Hinckel said, extending his hand. Zachary shook hands with him, and Crystal could see the tense set to his shoulders.

"Son, I've got some bad news to bring you about your family. Your pa was shot and he died last week."

Zachary gazed beyond them as if looking into his past. "That isn't bad news," he stated harshly. His gaze swung back to the sheriff and his blue eyes were filled with anger. "Who did it?"

"Lester Fennell shot him at Stokely's Saloon. Sorry."

"You don't need to say sorry," Zachary said. "I'm glad he's gone. And there's nothing there for me to go back home to. Not ever. Before he died, I'm glad he stopped by here, and he knew I would never come back home." Zachary focused on the sheriff again. "Thanks for riding out and telling me."

"Come up to the house and stay for supper," Travis offered, but Wade shook his head.

"Thanks. I want to get back to town before nightfall. It's blue in the north and another storm may be coming in. I'll let you folks get back to work."

Travis turned to walk with them back toward the house. When they stepped outside, Crystal looked at the darkening northern sky that looked the color of blue steel and she shivered, suspecting they were in for a bad storm.

The holidays loomed ahead and she could not resist thinking about a special dinner for everyone. As far as gifts, there was little she could make. She had never mastered needlepoint and crocheting. She was sadly lacking in such arts as cooking and sewing and she knew it full well. If they thought her cooking was bad, they should see her sewing.

Travis draped his arm casually across her shoulders and she walked close beside him. When they reached the house, Sheriff Hinckel mounted up and talked a few minutes to Travis before bidding them goodbye. Travis placed his arm on Crystal's, and they stood watching the sheriff ride away.

"Now we don't have to worry about Zachary."

"I hope he isn't always bitter."

"Crystal, he has plenty to be bitter about. You've seen his scars."

"I wonder why he doesn't go back to see his mother."

"I've heard him talk a little about her. She was almost as bad as his father. And you heard him. He said there was nothing for him to go back for."

Crystal shivered and shook her head, unable to understand such treatment of children and deciding she would write a letter to the governor about the law that gave parents full rights over their children no matter how much cruelty they inflicted. Laws could be changed and this was one that needed change.

They went inside and Travis lifted Jacob high. Jacob squealed with laughter and Travis swung him around, laughing with him. She looked at father and son and then at the father. How

handsome he looked when he laughed! It changed him from
the hard man he seemed so much of the time. She hung her
muffler over her coat and stuffed her gloves in her coat pocket.

Travis placed Jacob on the table and shucked off his son's
coat.

"Want coffee?" she asked

Travis shook his head and set Jacob on the floor and gave
him the rag doll, which he promptly put in his mouth.

"You saw the sky. I think we're in for a snowstorm. I'd
better keep working before it hits." He headed toward the door,
but when he reached her, he leaned down to brush a kiss lightly
across her mouth. Then he straightened and left.

Surprised, her lips tingling, Crystal followed him and moved
to the window to watch him stride away. His coattails flapped
around his long legs and his hat sat low on his head; his arms
swung at his sides. She touched her lips lightly. A fleeting kiss,
yet it was the first time he had kissed her goodbye. Her pulse
raced from his kiss and from the knowledge that he was touching
her more and more, kissing her lightly more often. How long
would it take before he could let go of his fear of losing a
woman in childbirth and the grief that he kept wrapped around
him like a blanket torn by the wind?

Yet she understood why and how much he hurt.

Christmas came with a blanket of snow over the ranch. The
day before, Turtle River knocked at the door, his hands filled
with deer meat.

"This is for dinner tomorrow. I know you have a turkey,
but I thought we could have both."

"Thank you! I hope I can cook it without burning it beyond
recognition."

"We don't have to recognize it, Crystal," he replied with a
smile. "Just be able to slice into it. Perhaps if I watch Jacob
tomorrow, then you won't have trouble cooking it."

She ran her hand across her brow. It had been a busy morning and Jacob had been fussy, unusual for him. "I don't know whether I will ever develop into a cook."

"You have already improved and you have changed since you came here."

She looked into his warm brown eyes. "This has been a good place for me."

"It's good for him. His heart was ripped to shreds, but you are mending it and this is good and as it should be."

"He doesn't let anyone close enough to mend much," she answered quietly. Turtle River shook his head.

"No, he mends. I can see it when he works. I see it when he is relaxed. He is my friend, just as you are, and your marriage is good. I thought it would be good. Give him time."

She nodded. "I hope someday you find someone to love again," she said quietly as he walked to the door. He wore a buckskin shirt and she wondered what kept him from freezing, yet he never seemed bothered by the elements. He shook his head and looked at her as he reached for the knob.

"No. It is not in the future that I walk with another. My road is alone or near friends."

"That can change."

He shook his head. "This is my life." He closed the door behind him and she watched him through the window. He had none of the swift, purposeful stride of Travis, but walked quietly as if he had the day to wander, yet she knew he was headed somewhere and would be there almost as quickly as Travis could.

She hoped he was wrong about himself, but he had a way of seeing things others didn't see. He was a quiet, strong man, so good to her and to little Jacob. And he deserved more than the lonely life he led.

For Christmas, they all kept their agreement to forget gifts, except for Jacob. Crystal tied a large red bow above the fireplace. Along the mantel she scattered the delicate ornaments she had so carefully wrapped and brought from Baltimore. Although it was not a holiday Turtle River or Travis had known most of their lives, they seemed ready for a feast and a celebration.

They had a huge wild turkey and the deer meat, and Crystal was determined to cook their supper without burning it. She had received valuable hints from Phoebe and Eloise Knudsen, and on the past three Fridays, during her luncheon recess, she had left her courtroom and hurried to the Knudsen's house to have a cooking lesson from Phoebe. Eloise was younger than Crystal, yet she and Crystal discovered they shared a mutual interest in books. Eloise joined Phoebe and Crystal in the kitchen for the Friday cooking lessons.

Now Christmas day was sunny, snow sparkling, and the men gathered at the log house while tempting smells filled the air. Crystal had risen before sunrise. She had bathed the night before and washed her hair, and for this festive occasion, she wore her red silk dress, tying her hair behind her head with a ribbon.

The moment Travis came through the door and his dark gaze swept over her, she could see the approval in his expression. Then he crossed the room to her. He wore a white shirt and black denim pants and had his hair fastened with rawhide. He tilted her chin up.

"Merry Christmas," he said in a husky voice.

Her heart thudded and her lips parted, her breath catching as she looked up at him. "Merry Christmas, Travis."

He leaned down, his mouth brushing hers lightly in a sensual, slow touch that ignited fires in her. She closed her eyes, slipping her arm around his neck.

His arms banded her waist and he pulled her close, his mouth covering hers gently, teasing as he slipped his tongue over her lips and into her mouth. Crystal moaned softly, returning his kiss until they heard a knock at the door.

When Travis released her, she opened her eyes. Feeling dazed, she found him watching her intently, his eyes darkened to blackness and pulling on all her senses. He touched her mouth with his fingertips and then hurried to the door. She straightened her dress, trying to pull her wits together, knowing she must look like a woman kissed senseless.

Turtle River and Zachary entered, bringing cold air in with them, and Jacob began crying, holding up his arms and wanting someone to pick him up.

During the next hour Crystal and Zachary played the piano and all of them sang, Travis's and Turtle River's deep voices blending with Zachary's tenor and Crystal's lilting soprano. As she played and sang, Travis stood on the other side of the piano, watching her with his dark eyes that always seemed to see right to her heart. And while she didn't know whether he would relent and give her the baby she wanted, she knew that he was changing. Some of the barriers were gone. He was friendlier with her and more open and more physical. He flirted; he kissed her often, and he touched her constantly.

She frequently caught his brooding gaze on her. He watched her with speculation and she wondered what ran through his mind. How many times had she caught his eyes sweeping over her body and she wondered whether it was with desire or, perhaps, reflection about her ability to carry and bear a child.

He adored Jacob and held him in his arms while they all sang. Jacob tried to sing, blowing bubbles and making strange noises that were drowned out by the adults.

She looked at the handsome men surrounding her and marveled how her life had changed, remembering the exciting Christmases in Baltimore when there had been presents and food and friends calling, yet in spite of the celebration how often she had felt lonely. She recalled the quiet Cheyenne Christmas with Ellery. They had presented each other with books. Now here she was out on the high plains with three strong, handsome men and a baby. How her life had changed! She looked into Travis's dark eyes as she sang and she felt a tingle and that singular awareness of him that shut away the world. Everyone else vanished from mind. All that was left was a virile, exciting man who was looking at her as if he loved her. And today, his look made her heart race more than ever.

Turtle River kept an eye on the roasting turkey and deer, and then it was time for her to get their dinner on the table. As always, Zachary helped while Turtle River and Travis played with Jacob, who was a full six months old and could pull himself up and stand for minutes at a time.

They sat down to a feast with hot biscuits, blackberry jelly, and a jar of relish given to Crystal by Eloise Knudsen. The turkey was golden brown, only slightly dry, and the deer meat was smothered in sauce and not too tough to chew. But it was her biscuits that Crystal prized. They were golden, fluffy, and not in the least burned. Perhaps she *would* learn to cook.

The men heaped compliments on her and ate until she felt satisfied that they had truly enjoyed their holiday dinner. Then they all gave Jacob presents and he looked pleased with each gift, happy to have something to chew on.

Turtle River gave him a wooden rattle he had carved. Zachary had ordered a large ball for him. Travis presented him with a rocking horse that he had made. Crystal had ordered a new shirt for him and a child's book of verses that he tried to chew until she retrieved it. Andrew Cain had sent him a small toy steam engine.

They watched Jacob play with his gifts while Crystal and Zachary cleaned the kitchen, and then all of them went back for more singing. As the short hours of day faded, they ate sandwiches of the remaining biscuits and cold turkey or deer.

Travis built up the fire and they sat around it while they read. They started *A Christmas Carol*, and after each man labored with a turn, they asked Crystal to read to them. Travis sat close beside her and wound his fingers in her hair while she tried to concentrate on the story.

She felt Travis's fingers stroke her nape, and it was difficult to sit still and act as if she felt nothing. The constant feathery strokes of his warm fingers were erotic and stole her attention from the story spinning in the night.

She didn't know what ran through his mind or what his casual, light touches were doing to him, but they were setting her aflame. She loved him, completely, desperately. Yet again, she reminded herself to have patience. He was her lawful husband. He would not leave her. She glanced at him, remembering his telling her that if he wanted pleasure he would go to one of the soiled doves; she knew she didn't want him to do that. She wanted him for herself, for the deep love she suspected a man and woman could have between them. He had been faithful and true to Elizabeth. He never would have been so crushed and hurt, never would have said he was numb if he had turned to other women when he was married to Elizabeth.

His fingertips trailed slowly, lazily drawing circles across her nape. Crystal took a deep breath. She wanted to move over onto his lap, to place her arms around him, to feel his arms around her. Instead, she sat still, trying to keep her thoughts on her reading.

Jacob began to fuss and Travis stood at once. "I'll get a bottle."

She passed the book to Zachary to read while she held the fussing baby. Travis returned to take Jacob from her, leaning down and giving her one of his long, intent looks that only she could see. And every time she gazed into his eyes, she could feel the tension between them. The air had a sizzle and the sparkle of the new-fallen snow outside. Only this sizzle and sparkle were silent, invisible, but a million pinpricks to her nerves.

She handed over Jacob, his big eyes going to his father. She had already changed the babe to his nightclothes. Tucked in the crook of Travis's arm, he drank his milk and then went to sleep.

When the men stood to pull on their coats, Travis didn't reach for his and her heart missed a beat.

Sixteen

When he closed the door behind the men, he turned around to face her. His hands rested on his narrow hips and he gave her a level look. "Crystal, I have not changed my mind."

Disappointed, yet curious why he hadn't left with the others, she waited in silence.

"I am getting damned tired of sleeping in the cold barn."

"That's fine," she said, trying to hold back a smile. She would have him close to her; and every time they were close and spent time together, her case became stronger and the barriers he kept around himself became weaker.

"Would you like another cup of coffee?"

"Yes, and this time I will lace it with some whiskey," he said, taking a bottle off a high shelf. "Want some, Crystal?"

"No, thank you," she answered primly, not missing the flash of amusement in his eyes.

"Have you ever tasted alcohol?"

"Champagne once or twice at parties in Baltimore. No whiskey."

"And so, I'm sure you don't approve."

"Just don't teach your son such habits. After years of caring for my besotted father and grandfather, I find nothing appealing in demon whiskey."

"If there's a demon," Travis remarked, shaking a blanket out on the floor in front of the fire and sitting down cross-legged, "it is not whiskey, but cold. Hell has to be frozen over. I feel I have not slept peacefully through a single night for a year."

"That's your own doing," she said lightly and received a scowl from him.

"Come sit down beside me."

Humming a tune, she sat near him, turning her back to the fire, tucking her skirt beneath her. The red silk billowed out in front of her. She set her cup of steaming coffee on the floor beside her and felt the heat from the fire on her back. The flames threw an orange glow over him, highlighting his prominent cheekbones, leaving his cheeks in shadows. She could see the firelight reflected in the darkness of his eyes, and the depth of his midnight eyes danced with fires. Anger or desire? Or both?

She wondered what would happen if she put her arms around him and drew him to her and kissed him. She was tempted to try, but she wanted him to let go of the barriers of his own accord. She needed him to want this marriage with his heart and soul, not because she had used her body to win him over . . . though it might come to that to get him beyond his fear of losing another wife in childbirth.

Patience, patience, she reminded herself. He was changing, slowly, but changing. She remembered how cold and angry he had been the day they had married. How hurt he had been. He had been in agony and grief, but he had come out of that, so she could wait. She glanced at him to find him watching her. He reached out to take the end of the red silk ribbon holding her hair. He tugged it loose and her hair cascaded across her shoulders and back.

Travis stared at her, emotions warring in him. The minx was teasing him, telling him it was his own fault if he spent miserable, sleepless nights. Hell, it was the fault of death and loss and a strong woman who wanted more from him than he could give! She looked like the barn cat who'd caught the mouse. Had the Mandeville's party given her that much confidence?

The fire made her hair look even more red and caught the golden highlights in the long strands. Her green eyes were sultry, dancing with a desire that heated him. It was hell to stay out in the drafty barn, but he knew it was going to be the torment of hell to stay here beside her and not make love to her. He wanted her. He wanted her now and totally. But he didn't want to love again, didn't want her to get with child. He shouldn't have spread the blanket before the fire and sat down with her. He shouldn't have done a million things he had done lately—touching her, kissing her, holding her close beside him.

He shifted, turning his back to the fire and looking away from her while he sipped the hot coffee, clinging to the cup as if it were a lifeline. And she had the good sense to keep quiet. If she had been one of those chattering females, he would be up and gone.

He was aroused, rock hard, aching to love yet torn. And always, he came full circle to the same decision he'd made last summer. He would not love again. Not ever. He didn't want to lose her in childbirth.

"Don't you ever fear anything?" he asked, his voice threaded with anger. She slanted him a mischievous look that made him draw a deep breath. Her straight brows arched and a faint smile curved her mouth.

"Of course, I do," she replied. "I was shaking so badly that day you came to the house to propose that it was a wonder I didn't fall right down in front of you."

"Hell, no. You tried to shoot me. That isn't exactly total fear. Most women would have been screaming and hysterical."

"I detest losing control, and screams and hysterics would not have helped in the slightest."

"I think I like it when you lose control. Though thank heaven, the gun wasn't loaded,'' he added dryly and she blinked, a faint flush tinting her cheeks even pinker.

"I'm sorry about that. I'll always regret it, but I was desperate and I had no idea you had Jacob in your arms."

"You didn't see him?"

"No. For goodness sake! All I could see was you and your anger and your dark eyes."

He finished his coffee, but his desire for her did not die as the fire burned down. The silence between them lengthened until, humming, she rose and moved around the room, putting out the lamps until the fire was the only light left. He watched her walk around him, ignoring him, looking happy, and he realized she looked far happier than when she'd come to live with him.

She sat back down, facing the fire, her back to him. Her skirt billowed as she pulled her knees up and wrapped her arms around them. "I sit here a lot at night and get warm before I go to bed." Her voice was soft, seductive, sliding over him and taunting his stretched nerves.

If she were unhappy over his rejection and refusal to father a child for her, she didn't show it. Far from it, he thought. She looked happier every day that passed. It annoyed the hell out of him because he was growing more miserable with each new day.

No, that wasn't totally true. Today had been a good day, and she had gotten him through a holiday that he had dreaded. He was healing, his grief becoming a thing of the past. Today had been good; yesterday had been good. A lot of days were very good. It was the nights that were torment, moments away from her when he was torn with thoughts about her, longing for her.

"Oh, hell. Come here, Crystal."

He pulled her into his arms and leaned down to kiss her. Her lips were soft, opening to his, her tongue stroking his. His pulse roared and he wanted her, ached for her. He pulled her onto his lap and held her with one arm while his other hand went to the row of buttons that ran down the front of her bodice.

He twisted them free while he kissed her, hungry for her softness and warmth and passion.

He pushed away her dress and then leaned away. He removed her chemise, gazing at her breasts in the firelight. He cupped her small, high breasts, flicking a glance at her. Her eyes were closed, her lips parted; her hands wound in his hair, her fingers moving, tugging slightly, stroking his nape. Her right hand drifted down to unbutton his collar and her eyes opened lethargically, desire flaming in their green depths.

She pulled his shirt over his head. He released her to shrug out of it and then cupped her breasts and flicked his thumbs over her nipples, drawing circles, watching her as her eyes closed again and she moaned. Then she looked at him. Her gaze was direct, honest, and hot. She wanted him as much as a woman could want a man, and her desire showed in her clear green eyes.

She wound her arm around his neck and leaned forward, tilting her head up to kiss him. He felt her soft bare breasts against his chest, her slender body in his arms. He kissed her hard, the kisses wild, both of them wanting each other desperately.

She pushed away, and it startled him. He had never known her to stop him, and she wanted a baby. Puzzled, he looked at her as she scooted away from him and stood up. With tantalizing deliberation, she pulled up her dress.

"We'll stop. I don't want you stomping off to a cold barn or roaming the windy night. And I don't want you to love me until you are certain of what you want. And you're not yet. You may reach the point where you can't say no. But I won't. I don't know passion fully, so I can stop and tell you no."

"Crystal, I keep coming back to the same impasse—"

"I know you don't love me and you won't; but when you come to bed, I want you to feel that you're willing to get me with child. You have to live with your fears about losing another wife." She smiled at him, her lips curving invitingly. "I think you'll come to agree with me. I can wait."

"What I went through was pure hell. And it was for Elizabeth as well."

"I know it was," Crystal replied solemnly. "But that tragedy doesn't have to happen again. Maybe you should sit here for a while and let me get to sleep before you come to bed. That way, we can keep from touching each other."

He wanted to yank her into his arms and kiss away her maddening reason and calm. Yet he knew she was right. He was not ready, not as long as he feared pain and loss.

He sat quietly, listening to her clothes rustle, sounds that tormented him as his imagination worked wildly. He listened to clothing sliding over her, dropping, until he would have welcomed the cold barn. But not for long. He thought about Crystal. She was virginal, had never known a real courtship, might not have known any courtship with the fellow in Baltimore. She was being cheated,

Was she right about being strong and able to bear children? She didn't know the answer to that any more than he did. Elizabeth had expected only the best.

He stretched out on the blanket and fell asleep in front of the fire, only to waken in the middle of the night to a cold room. He came awake at once with a soldier's ability to pull out of a deep sleep instantly. He placed more logs on the fire, building it up again. Then he picked up the blanket and crossed the room, looking at Crystal, whose hair was flung over a pillow.

He pulled off his boots and shirt and slipped beneath the covers, wanting to pull her into his arms. He could smell the sweet scent of rosewater. He couldn't resist reaching out to wind his fingers in her hair, and he thought about the prospect of another baby. And of loving her. Maybe he already did.

He stared at her in the darkness, exploring the depth of his feelings for her. How strong did they run?

Travis turned on his back, recalling their moments together, knowing half the day now his thoughts were on Crystal instead of on the ranch or the livery stable. If she had another baby, she would have to give up her justice of the peace office.

How deep did his feelings go for her? If he had to leave her now, would he care? He would care a hell of a lot. It was no longer a matter of having a mother for Jacob. It was far more than that, and she was becoming vital to him.

He turned his back to her, staring into the darkness. He hadn't wanted to love again, but he might already be deeply in love with her.

For the next two months into February, Travis was in torment. Unable to concentrate on his work, over and over, he would find his thoughts drifting to Crystal. Crystal, walking down the street toward the livery stable from the courthouse, her chin high, a slight sway to her hips that he found fascinating. Crystal, her green eyes sparkling when she greeted him or Jacob. Crystal, playing with Jacob, laughing, her hair tumbling around her face, looking dishevelled and appealing.

When he was off in the distance, feeding cattle, he could see the bright flame of her hair as she hung wash on the line. At night, he watched her sleep after tormenting nights of lovemaking that always stopped too soon . . . her kisses, her breasts filling his hands, her green eyes darkening with passion like storm-tossed seas.

He had sworn he would never love again, yet here he was, tied in knots by a headstrong, determined woman.

Devil take it! He pounded a horseshoe, sweating in the heated room in spite of the cold day while he thought about Crystal, and knew it was another hour before she would be through at the courthouse.

Since the Mandeville's party, people had grown friendlier. At least, some people had. The Knudsens accepted Crystal fully and that helped with others, but there were still plenty who would never associate with a half-breed no matter who his wife and friends were.

He paused, staring at the blazing fire and seeing only her while he debated what course to follow. Jacob was eight months old and becoming more of a joy every day. He had taken his first wobbly steps and now had a vocabulary of several words. Another baby would be good, and good for Crystal since she wanted one badly.

An hour-and-a-half later, Travis wiped sweat from his face as he looked through a window and saw Crystal heading toward the livery stable. He put down his tools and watched her. Standing with his hands on his hips, he looked at her slender body and the skirt that covered her long legs. She wore a bonnet on her head and a black cloak that swirled around her. She was covered from her head to her toes, with only her face showing, yet his pulse jumped and he mentally whisked away all the layers of clothes.

He wanted the woman damned badly. He would like another child, but he was so frightened about losing her.

Rufus Milligan rode up beside her. She smiled up at him and Travis clenched his fists, wanting to stride outside and tell Milligan to keep moving. Rufus Milligan would not be half-demented trying to make such a decision as whether to bed Crystal or not when she desperately wanted it. Nor would any other man in town except Will Barnesdall, who had lost a wife in childbirth.

"Hellfire!" Travis snapped, returning to the anvil. She had him in knots, muttering and swearing to himself.

He saw Andy watching him with curiosity that was no stronger than the curiosity he often saw in Zachary's eyes.

Then she swept in the door. Her nose was red, her cheeks pink, and he wanted to wrap his arms around her and kiss her.

"You should rescue Andy. I think our son has worn him to a frazzle."

She smiled, her eyes sparkling. "Where is my baby?" she asked, sailing past him as if he were part of the fixtures in the room. He heard her cooing and chattering with Jacob and he swore again beneath his breath. "Damn, damn, and double damn."

"Travis, what's wrong?"

He looked up at Andy. "Nothing I can't fix," he snapped. "Get some money out of the box and go get us all supper at the cafe."

Crystal appeared in the door. She was in one of her black dresses, her hair wound around her head; but he knew too well how she looked most of the time to see the stern judge that he used to see.

"We're eating here?"

"Yes. I'll stay until about nine. I told Zachary and he's taken the wagon."

She smiled. "I'm glad you gave him today without work and let him ride into town with us."

"Crystal, he can take off any day he wants," Travis said dryly. "He just doesn't get paid when he doesn't work."

"I know, but he feels he needs to work. All he talks about is Agnes. I think he's falling in love."

"Do you really?" Travis asked, amazed at his shrewd wife who was so blind when it came to men.

"So, you knew this long ago?"

"I think he fell in love with Agnes Blair the night of the Mandeville's party. At least he no longer is blind in love with my wife."

She laughed merrily. It annoyed him and he knew his reaction was unreasonable. "That's absurd, Travis. If he even remotely was attracted to me, it is over. Frankly, I don't really think he ever was."

"Crystal, you can count on it. And I saw Rufus stopping to talk to you."

"Rufus has become downright friendly." She shook her head in bewilderment. "He used to be very unfriendly. But then a lot of people have become friendly."

"A lot of men."

Her smile broadened, and she turned her attention to Jacob.

He wiggled to get down and she took him into the office and closed the door. Occasionally Travis heard her laughter ring out and he wanted to put his work aside and join her.

All the way home, Zachary talked about Agnes Blair. Riding high on the wagon seat, Zachary drove while Travis, Crystal and a sleeping Jacob rode in the bed of the wagon. Travis held her close to him and Jacob was curled in his other arm. Halfway home, Travis could no longer resist and leaned over to kiss the corner of Crystal's mouth. She turned her face and his mouth covered hers, and Zachary's words about his day with Agnes were lost.

"Crystal, what do you think?" Zachary asked loudly.

She pushed Travis away, and he raised his head.

"Crystal?" Zachary repeated.

Travis ground his teeth but refrained from telling Zachary to shut up. Didn't the boy have any notion that Travis wanted to kiss his wife and stop being bothered with conversation about Agnes Blair?

"Tell me again, Zachary," Crystal said patiently, showering light kisses on Travis that made him tighten his arms around her. He set Jacob on a blanket and covered him and turned to pull her onto his lap, rearranging the blanket around them while she and Zachary discussed the next time he could take Agnes out.

"Crystal, I want to order a locket for Agnes. Will you go with me and help me get the right thing?"

"Yes, I will," she said, closing her eyes while Travis tried to kiss her.

"When do you think you can go?"

She pulled away and Travis wanted to poke Zachary in the back; but he suspected Zachary was so wrapped in thoughts about Agnes, he would think the jab was an accident.

"Next week would be fine if you want to go to town. Or next Saturday. Eloise Knudsen asked me to come over. She's having Agnes and Myrtle and some friends for lunch."

"If I can get away, Saturday would be good," Zachary said.

Travis pulled Crystal back to him, tightening his arms around her and brushing her lips with his.

"Crystal, I want to write a poem to Agnes. Will you help me with it."

"Why don't you do that later, Zachary?" Travis asked politely, and Crystal shook his shoulder, frowning at him.

"Oh, I've already thought of the first lines. Listen, Crystal. *Agnes with your eyes so brown; you are my love, you are my crown.*"

Travis held his head, and Crystal shook her finger at him.

"How does that sound? Is it all right?"

"I don't quite understand why you call Agnes your crown," Crystal replied sweetly, feeling Travis's fingers slipping beneath her cloak to stroke her nape.

"She makes me feel like a king."

Travis choked, and Crystal shook her finger at him again. "I think that's fine, Zachary."

"Crystal, could we ever invite Agnes and her family to the ranch?"

Travis growled deep in his throat, and he heard Crystal's soft laugh. "Of course, we can. Won't that be fine, Travis?"

He thought about Elwood Blair, who was friendly enough, but into hardware and that was all he could discuss. And Travis knew Mrs. Blair did not approve of him. She barely spoke. "Yes, that's fine, Zachary," he answered perfunctorily, wondering if there was anything that would shut Zachary up so he could go back to kissing Crystal without the damned interruptions.

"I can help you cook. What do you think would be best?"

Travis leaned his head back against the wagon and played with Crystal's hair, winding it around his fingers and then tracing the line of her jaw, the curve of her ear, while she and Zachary discussed food. If he wanted his wife to himself, he supposed he would have to wait until he reached home and could shut Zachary out and bar the door.

It seemed eternity until he lifted down Jacob and swung

Crystal down with his other arm and told Zachary good night. As soon as he placed Jacob on his bed, he turned to look at Crystal. She had taken off her cloak and was unwrapping her muffler from her neck.

He unbuttoned his coat and dropped it on the floor, tossing his hat on a table. "Crystal, I've been waiting all night," he said in a husky voice and reached for her, pulling her into his arms to kiss her hungrily. Too soon she would stop him, but for the next few moments he could kiss and fondle her freely and he had been waiting and dreaming of this time all day long.

The next week as he rode across the cold land, checking on his cattle, his thoughts still on Crystal, he knew he wanted to take the chance on another child. She wanted one, and surely he wouldn't lose two wives in that manner.

The possibility terrified him, but he couldn't go through life like this. And his control around her was pushing closer and closer to the edge. Soon he was going to lose it, and then what he felt would no longer matter.

He would tell her his decision. He thought what he felt for her was a lot of things—respect, desire, friendship, but not the soul-deep love he had known with Elizabeth. But Crystal hadn't required that of him. Only to give her a child. And that he could do. He turned his horse and looked back over his shoulder at his house in the distance. Smoke rose from the chimney. Tonight he would tell her.

Dark came earlier than usual, the northern sky growing bleaker and blacker. Then after night fell, a raging blizzard struck. The temperature dropped and the wind tore at the house and the world was a swirling white that drove the men inside early. They shed snow-crusted coats and hats and ate several helpings of her steaming stew. Travis kept the fire roaring, but beyond the bright firelight, the room was chill.

"I will be back after I see about the horses," Travis said, pulling on his coat and hat and gloves. He left with the others, but at the door he paused. "I'll be freezing when I get back. Set water on to warm for a bath, would you?"

She nodded and closed the door behind him. He bent forward in the wind, running to catch up with the others.

He worked in the biting cold, his fingers becoming numb as he checked gates and made certain the horses were safe inside the barn. He saw the smoke spiraling up from Turtle River's tipi and from the narrow chimney of the small cabin where Zachary lived. Both men had fires going.

He pulled his collar high and stepped out of the barn, fighting the wind as he closed the door. He tucked his chin down and headed back to his house while the gusts and squalls whipped him. When he stepped inside, Crystal looked up. Travis drew a sharp breath.

She sat in the rocker in front of the fire, her long legs curled under her. Her hair was a fiery halo around her head and she wore her gown and her wrapper. The tub was placed on the other end of the hearth, a screen in front of it. While Crystal bathed during the day when he was away, he bathed at night when she was there, so he had made the screen to give them privacy.

"Thanks for readying a bath."

"I've already bathed," she said. "You'll have to share the water, but it's quite hot."

"I feel like ice clear to my bones," he remarked, knowing it was a bald lie because all he had to do was stand and watch her and he would heat to an inferno.

He stood in front of the fire, tugging off his buckskin shirt. He turned to look at her and his heart drummed as he gazed into her wide green eyes. Her gaze lowered, drifting over his chest, and he saw the change in her expression from cozy longing to burning desire.

"Are the animals all right?"

"They'll be fine if this storm doesn't last too long. That's when it gets bad. When they can't eat is when it's dangerous," he answered perfunctorily, his mind on her. Her hair spilled over her shoulders and he remembered its softness. He crossed the room, taking down the bottle of whiskey. He held it out to her. "Want some?"

"No, thank you. Not ever."

"Crystal, if you have a drink sometime, it does not mean you will turn into a sot like your father and grandfather."

"Perhaps not, but I see no reason to partake."

"That's fine with me. I didn't want to wed a drinking woman, God knows."

Her eyes narrowed. "That was a criteria?"

"Yes. I asked you at the time. I wanted someone intelligent, capable, dependable, trustworthy, kind. You seemed to be all of those things."

"Thank you," she said, smiling mischievously at him. Setting down the whiskey, he crossed the room and placed his hands on the rocker arms on either side of her.

"I'd give what I earned Friday to know what is running through that mind of yours."

"I'm not certain you saw any such qualities at the time. All you wanted, Travis Black Eagle, was a live, breathing woman who was caring and whom you could browbeat into matrimony. There has never been a day any man, including you, has given a whit about a woman's intelligence."

He wound his fingers in her hair, rubbing her head, and tilting her face up. "That's not so, Crystal. I'm thankful Jacob will have a mother with intelligence."

"Only because you had no intention of ever having to kiss me when you entered into this bargain."

He released her, moving his hands to her waist to pull her up into his arms. "If I had intended to kiss you, you'd still be wrong. Flat wrong. I couldn't bear a flighty, silly woman or a timid rabbit who would cower when I raise my voice, no matter how pretty she was.''

"If you had found such a woman and she had been a beauty and would have married you, I would never have known you and you cannot possibly convince me otherwise. Although, I find it refreshing to know that I have not lowered myself in your estimation by my loss of temper.''

"See, you have boxed me into a corner. Either I admit that I am happy with your tossing pans at me or I admit that beauty is more important than intelligence.''

"So, which is it?'' she asked, her voice growing husky and her gaze on his mouth as she ran her fingers lightly over his bare chest.

"If we carry on this conversation one minute longer, my bath will go to waste,'' he drawled in a rasp. He moved away from her, piling the fire high with logs. He picked up his drink and stepped around the screen. He was aroused, wanting her and not wanting to take time for a bath, but tonight was important and she deserved time and a long, slow loving. And he suspected she had no idea of his change of feelings.

Now that he had capitulated, he wanted her so badly he could barely breathe when he thought about her. It still struck terror into his heart to think about her going through childbirth. It was a cold, sheer terror such as he had never known on a battlefield, not once, even in the midst of hand-to-hand combat. But he decided that was partly the impetuosity of youth and the anger that had burned in him toward the soldiers who had taken him from his people.

This was a cold, stark fear that he would lose her as he had Elizabeth. And that Crystal would suffer. Travis couldn't look back. The past was done and over, but he prayed that this night was not leading him into the same hell again. All the same, Crystal deserved her chance to be a woman and a mother and he was not going to stand in her way.

He sneered at himself for thinking about it as if it were a sacrifice on his part. He was so eager, he shook. And he was already hard, hurting, and he had been aroused too many times during the day and tonight.

He stripped, stepping into the hot tub and sinking down, wanting to get Crystal and pull her in with him. But he had sworn this first night he would love her long and slowly as she deserved.

Crystal rocked, listening to him splash, imagining him naked, but her imagination only carried her so far. She was abysmally ignorant of men and their bodies, knowing basic anatomy, but nothing about Travis and how he looked beyond his waist. Nor would she know when he emerged from the bath. She expected him to dress in fresh pants and join her as he had so many nights lately.

She pulled the wrapper close beneath her throat and listened to the wind howl and thought about their conversation. Intelligence, indeed! If Zachary cared that Agnes Blair had a thought in her head, it didn't show in his hours of raving about her big brown eyes or her curly golden hair.

Crystal smiled at the thought of Zachary. He was incredibly smitten, and she hoped Agnes did not break his heart. Agnes seemed sweet enough, but Crystal suspected Agnes's parents had higher aspirations for her than a boy like Zachary, who had nothing of his own and was still wearing clothes given to him by Travis.

Still, he was saving his money, and within the month he intended to buy a horse from Travis. She rocked and gazed into the fire, contented to have Travis close at hand. She longed for his kisses, wanted more than kisses from him, but she kept reminding herself to wait. *Patience, patience* . . .

He was changing. She knew that and she knew he wanted her more each day because he showed it in so many ways. She heard deep splashes and then a rustle. He was drying and would dress and join her.

He came around the screen finally, and he was wearing his denim pants and moccasins and was bare-chested. The firelight gave orange tints to his dark skin and highlighted the bulge of hard muscles in his chest and arms. Her mouth went dry as she looked at him.

All her quiet satisfaction transformed to a burning need. She wanted to be pressed against his hard, lean body, to feel his strong arms band her, and to have him kiss her into ecstasy.

His dark eyes that enveloped her in a blackness that was hot and consuming. She couldn't take her gaze away and the air all but crackled between them as the tension grew tighter.

Without taking his eyes from hers, Travis crossed the room with deliberation. Once again he leaned down to put his hands on her waist and pull her up to face him. She placed her hands against his chest. His heart pounded swiftly and fiercely and she knew he wanted her with the same intensity that she wanted him.

"Crystal," he whispered, his voice a deep rasp. "I've come around to your way of thinking."

Her heart clenched. A tremor shook her as she clutched his arms and stared at him.

"If you want a baby, then I'm willing to try to give you one."

Seventeen

Crystal stared at him as his words poured over her. Joy spread in her. Fulfillment. Love. So many things she had dreamed of, once thought impossible to know in her life. Now he held them out to her. Travis. He would make love to her. His heart might still be locked away, but she suspected he couldn't lock all of it away. This tall man whom she loved with all her being was going to give her so much. She slipped her arm around his neck as she gazed into his dark eyes and met a steadfast, clear look.

"You're sure?"

"As much as I ever will be. Yes."

She pulled his head down, brushing his lips with hers.

He groaned, his arm tightening around her, pulling her against him while his mouth covered hers and opened hers. His tongue thrust into her mouth in a hot, silky demand.

He held her tightly, his strong arms solid and sure. She kissed him with all the love and joy of her being, knowing she would get a part of him this night that would belong to her forever.

As they kissed, his hand roamed over her back and then

pushed away her wrapper. He stepped back, taking her gown and pulling it over her head.

Travis sucked in his breath. Firelight bathed her body in a golden light that fell over her pale skin and rosy nipples, the red curly triangle between her thighs. His fingers roamed over her lightly while his gaze lingered, moving down her long legs and back up.

"You're a beautiful woman, Crystal," he whispered.

Her fingers tugged free his pants and then he stepped back to shed them. He stood before her and her green eyes were heavy-lidded, sensual. She stroked him, curving her fingers around his throbbing shaft until he caught her wrist.

"Not yet. I want to love you, and if you touch me like that, I can't keep my control." He bent his head to kiss her, pulling her to him, feeling her bare flesh against his, relishing every sensation that he had waited too long to know. How right it seemed to have her in his arms!

He bent his head, cupping her breasts, their softness marvelous in his hands. He flicked his tongue over her nipple, heard her gasp of pleasure as her fingers wound in his hair. "I want to pleasure you for hours, Crystal," he said softly, knowing he would never last hours, but hoping he could last long enough to bring her to a quivering peak of need before he possessed her.

Crystal felt his tongue circling her nipple, his hands splayed on her hips as she clung to his shoulders and then let her hands drift down over this body that was a marvel . . . hard, muscled, virile, so incredibly different from her body, and so handsome. She wanted to touch and discover and kiss all of him; but every time she began, he caught her hands and stopped her. His kisses were driving her out of mind.

A fiery sensation burned in her. An ache she had never known drove her to thrust her hips against him. She wanted him in her, wanted completion, yet she didn't want him to ever stop what he was doing now. She moaned softly as he took her nipple in his mouth to suck and bite so gently, a sweet torment.

And then he knelt in front of her, his tongue sliding down over her flat stomach, down lower. She gasped with pleasure as his hands stroked her thighs and she moved her legs apart for him. And then his warm fingertips trailed along the inside of her thighs and Crystal thought she would melt into a boneless, quivering mass of flesh.

Instead, she clung to him, her eyes closed, her lower lip caught in her teeth as she was rocked with more sensations, amazed by what he was doing to her, wanting him to keep on forever.

His tongue trailed where his fingers had been inside her thigh. He picked her up and laid her on the blanket spread on the floor in front of the fire. And then he knelt, moving between her legs, watching her as he drew his fingers along her thighs and then touched her intimately between her thighs. She felt his fingers on the core of her femininity, felt him caress and rub her. Sensations exploded from each stroke and then his tongue was there and she opened her eyes once to find him watching her.

His manhood was dark, full and hard and she knew how badly he must want her, yet she couldn't tell him to stop loving her now. His dark eyes were filled with a look she couldn't fathom except for a desire that overwhelmed her, a desire that looked as if he could devour her completely with his hands and mouth and tongue.

She closed her eyes, her hips arching against him. Winding her fingers in his hair, she cried out, and he took her to the brink and over, pleasure rocking her wildly. He turned her on her stomach to trail kisses and caresses all over her from her nape to the soles of her feet. Then he came back up the length of her legs with his tongue until she rolled over and sat up.

"I have to kiss you!" she said, her voice a strangled hiss. She placed her mouth on his and then her hand curled around his shaft. He was hot, ready, and she moved away, pushing him down and moving over him, watching him as he was watching her.

She bent to take him in her mouth, stroking this tip of manhood that was velvet beneath her tongue and then taking him in her mouth and hearing him groan, feeling his hands tugging in her hair.

With a cry he sat up and moved her, pushing her down gently, moving between her legs. "I can't wait. I told you that you couldn't touch me if you wanted me to keep my control."

"I hope you lose all your control, because you took mine away long ago," she said, stroking him.

He was on his knees between her thighs, his proud manhood stiff and ready, his dark eyes burning with desire for her. She pulled his hips toward her and he came down. The tip of his shaft touched her lightly, yet it was agonizing torment because she wanted more.

She cried out, arching beneath him to meet him, tugging at his hips and winding her legs around him. She raised her head slightly to kiss him and then her head fell back as he kissed her hard and his shaft entered her slightly and withdrew.

She cried out again, wanting him more with each slow, deliberate thrust as he drove her to a blinding, mindless need.

Travis tried to check himself, tried to tease her into such a frenzy she would forget the pain of the first time. Her hips were arching against him. She clung to him and cried out with each thrust. But the control was costing him. Sweat poured off his body and he could feel his restraint slipping away. It had been too long for him, too impossibly long and she was fire and warmth and softness and wild passion in his arms.

He entered her, feeling the obstruction, thrusting hard and sliding deep into her satiny heat. She enclosed him, taking him with her out of pain and fear and grief into ecstasy.

They moved together, her cries dim beyond the roaring in his ears of his own hot blood pounding in his veins. The woman was wild, her long legs squeezing him, her hands stroking his back, his buttocks. He kissed her hard, wanting all of her, wanting her warmth, her love, her womanly self. He had starved himself, but would no longer.

"God, Crystal!" He ground out the words and pumped his seed into her, making her truly his woman at last.

Crystal arched beneath him, crying out and clinging to him as rapture burst over her with release. She felt his shudder, and his swift spilling of his hot male essence excited her as much as everything else he had done. She was locked in an embrace with him, his arms holding her, his body united with hers. She gave her body and her heart and her soul. She was his completely without reservation in every manner, whether he wanted her that way or not and whether he realized it or not.

This was a deep binding that would last the rest of her life, and she intended to have a long life . . . and children. This strong man's life force was part of her body now.

In rapture, she held him, pleasured beyond all dreams, loving more deeply than she would have ever thought possible.

And she knew women throughout time had taken the risk of babies for their men out of want . . . for the men . . . and for the precious babies.

She clung to his broad shoulders, loving his strength. They were one in more ways than he could ever guess. His weight came down on her, heavy, male, so incredibly marvelous.

She loved being in his arms. Her body was satisfied, complete, and he was still inside her, still joined with her. He trailed kisses along her cheek and temple, down to her mouth and then he kissed her long and hard before he rolled to his side with his legs entwined with hers, taking her with him.

"Ah, Crystal. Do you hurt?"

She kissed him. "Never. I am so happy I could fly right off the roof."

He chuckled. "I hope to hell you don't. The cold would sober you up before you got to the roof. Ah, darlin', I wanted it to last longer for you. I wanted to love you all night."

"I'm happy. And I don't know how we could have lasted a lot longer."

He kissed her, holding her close. She could feel their hearts beating together. He stroked her back, lifting her hair. "Crystal, I know you're right. Everything in me says you are right about childbirth, about Jacob, but it was such hell."

"That time of your agony and loss is in the past, Travis. This will be right," she said with unfounded certainty. Everything seemed so incredibly right, right now.

"I hope, darlin'. Heaven knows, it couldn't be any better. You're quite a woman, Judge Spencer!"

She laughed and stroked his jaw and his eyes darkened, change flickering in their depths. He eased away and rolled off the bed, bending to pick her up.

"What are you doing?"

"I'll bet that water isn't icy cold yet. It's been sitting in front of the fire."

"Travis!"

He chuckled and climbed into the tub, holding her in his lap.

She caught her hair, twisting it swiftly and holding it on top of her head. "Travis, I don't want my hair wet."

"You just hold it, darlin'. Hold it right there and let me enjoy myself," he said, sitting back and settling her with her legs astride him.

She blushed beneath his direct stare. His gaze roamed over her. He was aroused again. His hands drifted freely over her and she closed her eyes. "Travis. I can't keep holding my hair. Either we get out or you'll have a woman with a cold, wet head on your hands."

He stood, water splashing and sloshing as he set her on her feet in front of him and pulled her into his arms to kiss her. She released her hair, winding her arms around his neck, her heart thudding.

His kisses were a hot demand as he bent over her, one arm holding her tightly against his naked body, his other hand stroking her back, sliding down over her behind.

She moaned, amazed desire would rekindle in both of them so swiftly.

"This time, love, I can take the time you need. I want to kiss you for hours and drive you wild before we love," he whispered in her ear, his warm breath tickling her.

Joyously she held him, kissing him, her hands trailing over his strong body, memorizing textures and shape. She paused to look up at him, a long, searching look. "I love you," she said.

"Ah, darlin'—"

She placed her fingertips on his lips, stopping his words. "Don't say anything. I didn't ask for anything in return. What we have is enough, Travis. You're very, very good to me. We'll have a good union."

She looked into his dark eyes, unable to fathom what he felt. She didn't want false words or reasons he couldn't give his love again. She just wanted what he had already given her, that was enough of himself. Yet she could tell him her feelings. She would not do it again, but he should know. He should know with one look at her. She thought her feelings should be as plain for all to see, as Zachary's were for Agnes Blair, but that might not be the case.

She pulled Travis's head down, placing her mouth on his and ending any conversation between them.

This time he kept his word and it was a long, long time later when he moved over her and took her away to rapture with him.

The next morning she moved languorously, a tantalizing warmth at her breast. For a moment she thought she was dreaming of their lovemaking, of Travis's tongue on her nipple, his hands moving over her. But then she opened her eyes and discovered it was no dream.

His dark head was bent over her, his big hand cupping her breast while his other hand stroked her legs. Sleep-filled, warm, she came awake at once, reaching for him and pulling him to her to kiss him, and their loving started all over again.

Jacob's insistence on eating got them out of bed. Travis dressed swiftly and made flapjacks while Crystal washed and dressed and finally helped him. They fed Jacob and then, as he played happily with a stack of pans, Travis pulled Crystal into his arms to kiss her.

They gazed at each other, a smile curving her lips. Travis thought about the night. She had been all he had expected and more. She was wildly passionate, completely giving and responsive. And their course was set with no turning back now. He didn't have regrets, but he would never shake the lingering fear for her.

He looked into green eyes alight with joy. And love. He remembered her declaration that he couldn't honestly return, but was amazed at the depth of his feeling for her. Although it ran deep, was what he felt truly love? He wasn't certain. It was not the blinding infatuation Zachary felt for Agnes. As swiftly as that thought came, another followed. How different was he from Zachary when it came to a woman taking his attention and his thoughts? He thought about Crystal all day and couldn't wait to get back to her at night.

"It's good, Crystal. So good," he whispered and kissed her hard. She held him tightly and returned his kiss, and he wanted to forget horses and cows and take her right back to bed. And if it hadn't been for Jacob banging pans together, he would have, but they would have no peace or privacy with Jacob awake.

"I'm building some rooms on this place as soon as the weather warms enough to start. We need a bigger house."

She smiled up at him, her eyes twinkling. "I hope you're not getting another bed."

"Hell, no. If I spend another night in the barn, you'll be there with me."

"You could have been in here sooner. I've been waiting."

He stroked her throat, touched her hair. He didn't want to leave her. And he had thought a night of love would quiet all the hungry fires that had been burning him lately like the flames of hell, but instead, he wanted her more than he had last night.

"I won't be able to think or work today because of you, lady. I'll be as sappy as Zachary, besotted with you, crazy to get back to you."

"I do hope so!" she replied saucily, standing on tiptoe and drawing the tip of her tongue across his lower lip.

He groaned and wrapped his arms around her to kiss her hard and long again, wondering if he could ever get out of the house and ten feet away from her today.

"I can't get enough of you, Crystal," he said finally, as breathless as if he had run for hours.

"Good! That's delightful to hear because I feel the same and I want you to come home to me."

"If we didn't have little Jake to take care of—' "

"But we do and he can make his presence very well known. 'Course in the middle of the day, he always sleeps, so if you happen to be nearby—"

Travis pulled her close and kissed her again. "I'll be here."

He left swiftly, closing the door behind him. A gust of cold air hit her and she hurried to the window to watch him stride away. Her handsome, strong husband, who had loved her senseless all night long! She placed her hand on her stomach and prayed they had a baby from the union. How she loved Travis! She had never known how much a woman could love a man and she had never dreamed what it would be like to be made love to. She blushed, thinking about the night, but a smile curved her mouth and she felt a delicious anticipation of his return.

The evenings that Travis had once looked forward to now became a tedious waiting for time to pass. Where once he had anticipated the reading time, listening to Crystal play the piano and sing, now he couldn't wait to get it over and tell Zachary and Turtle River good night and shut the door behind them.

Then he could take Crystal in his embrace and make love to her long into the night. Until then, he had to sit and read and listen and talk and quietly share her with others and try to keep his hands halfway to himself.

He wanted to touch her all the time. She was soft, sweet-smelling, fetching. She set him on fire doing nothing but sitting with a book in her hands. Her green eyes would meet his across the room and the world would vanish and he would think about their lovemaking.

The last week in February he came home to find her looking stricken when she turned to greet him.

"What's wrong?"

"I'm having my monthly. I'm not expecting a child."

He smiled at her, relief washing over him. "Crystal, having a baby doesn't always happen instantly."

"I don't see how it could not have happened!"

"It just doesn't. Life isn't that way. Patience, love. We'll work on it," he said kissing her. She kissed him in return, but then moved away and wiped her eyes. "Crystal, that's the first month. That means nothing." He kissed the nape of her neck until she turned and wound her arms around him and kissed him. When he released her, he gazed down at her, and at last she smiled.

"That's better," he said softly, hearing a step on the porch. She moved out of his arms and he sighed, knowing the others would be with them for hours and he wouldn't get to love her the way he wanted to this night anyway.

Zachary invited the Blairs to Sunday dinner. Travis suspected it was a strain on the elder Blairs, and he knew Crystal was terrified about her cooking.

They sat down to a roast and potatoes. The gravy was thick and lumpy, but the biscuits were edible and carrots were something even Crystal didn't ruin.

Mrs. Blair had brought an apple pie that was marvelous, so

the meal ended on a good note. Zachary and Agnes had eyes only for each other, but the Blairs were reserved and not too friendly. They spent a couple of hours and then left, Agnes riding into town with Zachary, who had borrowed Travis's wagon.

Travis closed the door behind them. "I don't think they will ever allow her to wed him if it gets that far."

"I don't know how you can say that now. They both are very young."

"Elizabeth was only eighteen."

"Well, you were more than eighteen."

"They don't approve of Zachary and I doubt if it helps that he works for me."

She placed her hand against Travis's cheek. "I'm sorry when you have to deal with prejudice."

Travis gazed down at her, thinking about her justice of the peace status, wondering how sympathetic she would be if she knew all about his past.

"It is not as bad here as it has been other places and other times. And there is nothing I can do to change it."

"I pray Jacob does not have to endure much of it."

"He'll learn to deal with it just as I have. We have little choice." Travis glanced at Jacob, who was sleeping.

"If Agnes is that shallow, then Zachary is better off. Love should bridge differences and different pasts."

"Do you think so, Crystal?"

Startled, she was surprised by something in his voice that made her curious. "Yes, I do," she said, sensing a double purpose in his question. He sounded as if he were talking about the two of them, yet that was absurd because they had no problems about their pasts and their different cultures.

As she watched him, his brown eyes darkened. Travis unbuttoned his collar and tossed it aside. He pulled his shirt over his head and reached out to draw her to him. Her pulse jumped when he leaned down and brushed her mouth lightly with his.

"I need you," he whispered, his hands drifting over her,

unfastening buttons, removing ribbons and pins, kindling a blaze deep inside her.

She ran her hands over his broad chest, marveling in his hard, strong body, aching for him, and knowing his need for her could never be any greater than her need for him.

Nights became bliss, followed by stolen afternoons when Travis rode home for an hour while Jacob napped. And the next month when Crystal reported she was still not carrying his baby, all he could feel was immense relief.

In April the days became nice enough for Travis to commence building a room onto the house and Crystal had him around more than ever. Construction was temporarily halted because of cows calving and new foals, land that needed to be tended. They had to get animals ready for market, and the reading lessons ceased because the men became so busy with spring chores. Jacob was ten months old, toddling and jabbering with new words each day. Crystal felt invigorated by spring, wanting another baby, so deeply in love with her tall husband.

It was a cool spring night when she stirred and awoke and found the bed empty beside her. She sat up and looked around the room. Moonlight bathed it, and the house was empty, save for her and Jacob, who was sleeping soundly. She slipped out of bed and pulled on her gown and wrapper and went to look outside, wondering where he was and why he was gone.

Eighteen

Crystal returned to bed, puzzled because he had never been gone during the night since he'd stopped sleeping in the barn. Or if he had, she hadn't been aware of it.

When he came back to bed and pulled her into his arms, she wound her arms around his neck. He raised slightly to look down at her, his black hair framing his face. He was naked, his body warm, hard against the length of hers. His shaft pressed hotly against her, and she knew he desired her.

"I woke up and you were gone."

"I couldn't sleep and went for a walk."

"Why—"

His mouth brushed against hers and desire flamed low within her. He brushed his lips over hers again, so light, so tantalizing, and then his tongue touched her lips. She moaned and pulled his head down, kissing him as his mouth pressed hers and his tongue went deeply into her mouth. He moved over her, and she forgot about his inability to sleep.

* * *

The next day when Travis left for work, Zachary caught up with him. "Travis, I've wanted to ask you something."

"Go ahead and ask," he said, feeling springtime in the air. The grass was greening and the winter had not been harsh enough to hurt them. Calves were dropping and it looked like it would be a good year. And Crystal was not yet with babe. He knew she was disappointed each month, but he could not keep from being enormously relieved.

"I'd like to keep working for you."

"I'd like for you to."

"What I want—I'll pay for all of it because I've been saving my money."

He glanced at the tall boy walking beside him. Zachary was raw-boned and gangly, but all lean strength with his hard ranch work.

"Zachary, what do you want to do?"

"I'd like to build on to my house. It's rather small."

"It's damned small," Travis remarked, wondering why Zachary suddenly wanted more room. He was rarely in the little cabin, spending his days at work and his early evening hours with them.

"I'd like to build on because I want to ask Agnes to marry me."

Startled, Travis glanced at him. "You're sure? You're still young."

"I'm real sure," Zachary said. "I'll be eighteen this year."

"It's fine with me if you build on. I'll pay for the costs of the materials, since it's on my land and it stays if you quit."

"Whillikens! Thanks! That's great."

"You'll have to talk to Agnes's father."

"I plan to. I know her mother wants her to marry someone in town, someone who has land or a business. I'll get my own place someday, but I like working here. You pay me well, and it's good to work with you and Turtle River. I'm learning."

"How old is Agnes?"

"She'll be eighteen a month after I am. That's old enough to marry."

"Her parents will have to approve."

"I know they will," Zachary said, staring solemnly ahead. He glanced at Travis. "I know I'm not much in lots of ways, but I love Agnes and I'll be good to her. And God strike me dead if I'm ever a man like Eb North."

"You won't be."

"No. I'm honest and hard-working and I love her. I hope that's enough."

"I wish you luck."

"Thank you."

"When are you going to talk to Mr. Blair?"

"I'll go by when we're in town Saturday and see him if I can."

They reached the horse pen, and the bay walked to meet Travis as he entered the pen.

"Thanks, Travis."

He nodded as Zachary mounted the pinto and turned away from the barn. He watched the boy ride away and hoped he didn't come home with a broken heart. But if he did, he was young and he would mend.

Travis thought about his own eighteenth birthday. A hell of a cry from Zachary's. Wanted for murder. Travis turned to look at the house. The past was better left dead and buried. As much as Crystal cared for him and as close as they had become, her rigid view of the law would see only one thing—her husband the outlaw.

He mounted up, his thoughts on his brother Brett, on the past, on the future.

Two nights later Crystal woke, disturbed by a faint creak of the boards on the porch. She turned to Travis and stared at emptiness. Swiftly she grabbed up her wrapper and stepped out of bed. She saw him crossing the ground, his long stride carrying him swiftly and purposely toward the barn. If he were a man unable to sleep, why was he striding away as if he had to be somewhere in the next few minutes? And he looked as if he carried something beneath one arm.

What was worrying him that he wasn't sleeping? Why the jaunts away from the house in the dead of night? He didn't act like a man in the throes of worry. Nor did he seem unhappy with her. Far from it. Curiosity gnawed at her. What was Travis doing and why was he keeping it from her?

She leaned against the window and stood watching as he disappeared into the barn . . . and did not come out. Puzzled, she stayed at the window until her legs grew tired. Maybe he had gone there to sleep and she would stand until dawn before seeing him again. Yet she couldn't give up and go back to bed. And she didn't want to leave Jacob alone and go to the barn. Nor did she want to take the baby out into the night.

She pulled a chair to the window and sat, watching and waiting. Finally she returned to bed and lay awake, worrying about whatever he was concealing from her. When he stepped through the door, she watched him move around and saw his arms were empty. Whatever he had carried to the barn, he had left there.

And then he was in bed beside her, pulling her into his arms.

"Travis, where have you been?"

"Out walking," he said, kissing her, and once again all the questions she had intended to ask were gone like smoke in the wind. The next morning she faced him over the breakfast table while Jacob still slept.

"Why aren't you sleeping?"

His dark eyes were inscrutable. "Just restless. Maybe worried about you."

"Me? I'm fine."

"I know, but I worry."

She sat on his lap and slipped her arms around his neck. "Then stop worrying. I love you, Travis Black Eagle, and you're not going to lose me."

He gazed at her solemnly. "I hope you mean that, Crystal. I hope with all my heart you mean that," he said so earnestly her heart missed a beat. What about his feelings for her? How deep did they run now?

She leaned forward to kiss him, a slow, wet, lingering kiss that made him tighten his arms around her and carry her back to bed.

As he dressed to go, she lay in bed watching the ripple of muscles in his back and she remembered how smooth the skin on his back was. Love for him surged in her while fears about his jaunts outside at night were a torment. Pulling on her wrapper, she crossed the room and slipped her arms around his waist.

He grinned, his teeth white against his dark skin, and she gazed up happily at her handsome husband. "What's this? Back to bed again? Crystal, my knees are almost too weak to hold me up now, and I have more than a full day's work ahead."

"We're not going back to bed. I'm just hugging you before you go. And stop worrying about me."

His grin vanished and she saw a shuttered look in his expression that she hadn't seen since their first months together. "Crystal, I—" He stopped, staring at her, and then he bent his head and kissed her hard.

Her heart thudded and she returned his kiss passionately, all the love she felt for him welling up in her. He had given her so much, a full, rich life, a son, joy, endless hours of loving that drove her wild, a home and a future and hope for another baby. She loved him to the depths of her soul and she wondered if he had been on the verge of declaring his love for her. And if he had, why was it so hard for him to do so?

She didn't care. She had enough of him now. Lord knows, he acted like a man in love.

He released her. "Damn, you make me want to go right back to bed. I can't get enough of you, woman!"

"I hope you never get enough of me," she said.

"I'm getting out of here while I can still walk. I have to go to work."

"You go, darlin'," she drawled, "and just think about coming home to me."

He inhaled, his chest expanding; and instead of giving her one of his teasing answers, he gave her a hard look and touched her chin. "Lady, that's all I do think about."

He left and she stood in the open door and watched him stride away, wondering why he was so tied in knots. What had he been about to say to her? One thing, the man cared for her. Maybe more than he could acknowledge, but that farewell had sounded like a man in love if she could judge by her own feelings. Her joy was tempered by an instinct that made her feel something was amiss. Something was coming between them and she couldn't fathom why or what.

On Saturday, Travis drove her to town in the wagon to have lunch with Eloise Knudsen and her friends. Zachary rode with them to purchase his new horse and then ask Agnes's father for her hand in marriage.

After lunch, when Crystal left the Knudsen's and returned to the livery stable, she wondered how Zachary had fared and she was anxious to be with Travis and Jacob. Nights in Travis's arms were magical and she was looking forward now to going home.

As she reached the livery, Zachary rode up. He wore the new black suit he had ordered and his hair was combed down and parted neatly in the center. One look at his white face, and she guessed he did not have good news.

She shaded her eyes and looked up at him.

"Mr. Blair wants us to wait a year." Zachary's hands were knotted on the reins, his knuckles white. "A year, Crystal! I'm in love with Agnes and I know I shall be always." He dismounted, his face in a scowl.

"Nineteen is not an old age," she said, disappointed, but not surprised.

"Hellfire, Crystal! Sorry. I love her and I want her to be my wife. And she loves me. She's home crying now."

"Zachary, if she loves you, then both of you can wait. She won't change and love someone else. And they haven't said no. They just asked you to give a year to waiting."

Her pulse jumped because she could see Travis through the open door. He raised his head and smiled at her and she smiled in return.

"See, dam—sorry. See what you two have. Marriage is good. Both of you are happy."

"Yes, we are," she said. Travis moved away from a stall and came to meet her, handsome in a chambray shirt and denim pants that hugged his slim hips. He brushed her lips lightly with a kiss. Jacob toddled after him and he swung him up in his arms. Jacob held his arms out to her.

"Mama, hug."

She wondered if she would ever stop thrilling to hearing Jacob call her mama. He went into her arms and hugged her, wrapping his little arms around her neck. He smelled like hay and horses, but she hugged him and was glad to be back with him. He smiled at her with a big grin that showed his tiny baby teeth.

Travis watched her and then draped his arm across her shoulders. "We're busy today. I've bought two horses and sold three, so business is brisk, besides the horses brought in for me to board and the ones I need to shoe. Andy will not be back until late."

"I can help," Zachary said, going inside.

Travis watched him. "The boy is a help. He wants to learn everything he can. I'll hear from him, but how did it go for him with Agnes's father?"

"Mr. Blair wants them to wait a year."

Travis watched her with smoldering fires in his brown eyes. "That one year will be eternity to Zachary. I don't want to wait the rest of the day to get you home to myself," Travis added in a husky voice, touching her collar, brushing her throat with his fingers. His hair was fastened behind his head, leaving the planes and angles of his face more stark and handsome.

Feeling a rush of longing, she leaned closer against Travis until Jacob wiggled to get down. She set him on his feet.

"I'll walk down to the general store. I can take Jacob with me."

As Travis nodded, she took Jacob's hand. They set off down the street and she could feel Travis watching her. Turning, she waved, feeling a strange tingle and wondering about the long looks he had been giving her lately.

That night she came awake in bed as she heard the door close. This time she was awake instantly and turned to look at the empty bed. Once again when she looked out the window, Travis was hurrying to the barn and he had his arms full. What was he doing?

Something was incredibly wrong. Travis was slipping out every night and not sharing with her why or what he was doing.

There was only one way to find out. She could not bear to leave Jacob alone in the house. Stepping onto the cold floor, she dressed swiftly in one of her black woolen dresses and pulled on her shoes and cloak. She gathered up the sleeping baby, who didn't wake, and wrapped him in a small blanket. Holding Jacob close, she emerged into the cold, clear night.

At the barn her pulse speeded up. She could see a light beneath the door. She stared at the thin sliver of yellow light, suddenly wondering whether she should turn and run back to the house and never discover what he was hiding from her.

Her life was good—more wonderful than she had ever dreamed possible. Travis was marvelous; their loving was ecstasy. Jacob was adorable, and the future looked promising. She had a dreadful premonition that whatever Travis was hiding, he was hiding it from her because he knew she would not like it.

Crystal stood immobile, torn between a need to know and the strong feeling that discovery might be a Pandora's box that would destroy her marriage.

Yet she had to know. She remembered her drunken father and grandfather and how they had ruined lives. She had to know what Travis was keeping from her. She moved forward cautiously, stepping close to the doors.

Only inches from the barn door, Crystal heard Travis's deep voice. Shocked, she stared at the door. Someone was staying in their barn. Travis was slipping out at night to see the person without telling her. What were they doing? Were they planning something they didn't want her to know about?

Puzzled, wondering about her volatile, inscrutable husband, she leaned against the door. Their voices were muffled, but it was another man and they were arguing.

Anger that he would hide something from her filled her and caution went up in smoke. Impulsively, she reached for the handle and tugged the barn door open and swept inside.

Nineteen

Shocked, Crystal halted. Travis stared at her. He was bent over a man with a roll of bandage in his hand. Seated on bales of straw, the man had a bloody wound in his side that looked dreadful. Travis had obviously been changing the dressing.

While they both stared at her, she looked into two pairs of dark-brown eyes belonging to two dark-skinned men with black hair. The other man's hair was cut shorter and he was thicker through the shoulders, but he was as powerful as Travis and blatantly handsome. They had the same firm jaw, the same nose. She guessed instantly that this was Travis's brother. He wore black denim pants and dusty black boots. He smiled at her, a wide, charming smile that surprised her and tempted her to smile right back. Except she was too filled with fury to smile.

"Why are you hiding in the barn?" she asked Travis.

"Oh, hell," he said. As the two men exchanged a look, the injured one stood. He swayed and sat down.

"Crystal, I want you to meet my brother Brett. Brett, meet my wife, Judge Black Eagle." The way Travis stated her title, she surmised the wound in his brother's side was a gunshot or knife wound and the man was on the wrong side of the law.

Stunned, she stared at Brett, who flashed her another charming smile. "Ma'am, I am delighted to meet you." His words were slurred, and she saw that he was in terrible shape. "Don't be angry with my brother. I needed a little help and I'll move on tonight. No one will ever know I passed through here."

"You need a doctor," she said.

"There's no damned doctor in Cheyenne since your brother's demise," Travis said. "They're trying to get a doctor, but in the meantime, there isn't one except for Doc Chaney, the vet."

"Couldn't go to one anyway."

"Shut up, Brett."

She stared at the two of them and then focused on Brett Black Eagle. "You're running from the law."

"That I am. If my brother will just bandage me up again, ma'am, I'll be out of here and you'll never be bothered by me again."

"You're not in any shape to travel," Travis said, grinding out the words as he checked Brett's wound. As she watched him work, her anger churned. His brother was a desperado, wanted by the law and harbored in their barn. It went against everything she believed in and stood for and had sworn to fight. She should turn Brett Black Eagle in to the law.

"You're an outlaw."

"You could say that, yes," Brett answered.

"I swore to uphold the law."

"Crystal, this is my brother. Would you have turned Ellery away?"

She stared at Travis. His dark eyes were like two knives cutting into her. She hated the question because it was ridiculous. Ellery had never broken the law.

"Look, folks. I don't want to come between husband and wife. Just let him bandage me up, and I'll get on my horse and ride out of here. Just minutes, ma'am, and I'll be gone."

"He's been hiding here in our barn all this time?" she asked
Travis, ignoring Brett.

"He's been here nights so I could feed him and change his
dressing and take care of him. During the day, he's been hiding
down along the creek."

"And Turtle River and Zachary knew about him?" she
asked, her anger that she had been deceived still growing.

"Turtle River knew. He helped clean the wound. He was
shot, Crystal."

"Doing what?" she asked Brett and looked into wide, dark
eyes that were the same color as Travis's but held none of her
husband's fire.

"Your Honorship, I don't think you really want to know."

Her fury soared. "Yes, I do want to know!"

"Crystal, take Jacob home and we'll talk when I get there,"
Travis ordered.

She gazed into his eyes and felt the clash that she used to
have with him when she first met him. She turned away.

"Ma'am—"

She glanced at Brett.

"I'll say it again, I'm sorry to have caused trouble. Don't
blame Travis. He's a law-abiding citizen and he couldn't help
it if I rode in and asked for his help. And I'm glad to have met
you, Judge, and glad to have seen Travis's boy."

She tugged open the barn door and stepped outside, pulling
it shut behind her. Enraged, she stormed back to the house.
She wanted to get a horse and ride for the sheriff. The man
was an outlaw, harbored at her own house! And Travis had
hidden him. She paused as she crossed the porch and looked
at the dark barn. Travis had let his outlaw brother stay. He
knew how she would feel about it. He had gone against her
wishes and hidden his brother. A deception if there ever was
one.

"Hellfire and damnation, Brett," Travis swore as he bent to
wrap the bandage around his brother.

"Sorry."

Travis straightened and looked into his brother's eyes. "I'm glad you came to me for help, but it's hell to pay now. I don't know how she knew where I was. She was sound asleep when I left."

Brett chuckled. "Your wife must not sleep well if you're not right beside her. You got yourself one pretty woman there."

Travis glanced down at his brother and wrapped the tape tight across his wounds. "I knew her over a year and half and was married to her before I saw that she was pretty. You take one look at her and realize that."

"You're going blind if it took you that long to see it."

"Well, it'll be hell now. Crystal can only see things as absolute. It's either right or it's wrong."

"She doesn't know about Texas?"

"No, she doesn't." Travis finished and stepped away. Brett stood up and pulled on his shirt. He strapped on his gunbelt and reached for his coat. With care he pulled it on.

Travis studied him. "You stay right here."

Brett shook his head. "I've caused you enough trouble tonight for a lifetime."

"You can't go until you heal. You need rest and you're safe here. I'll keep Crystal from going into town, and you stay here until you mend."

"I'm a hell of a lot better than I was when I came. I'll be okay, Travis. You get back to your wife. You're going to have to do some mendin' with her."

"Brett, don't go."

Brett grinned and reached out to hug Travis. "Don't hug me back. My ribs can't take it."

"Dammit, I don't want you to go. You might have a U.S. Marshal on your trail."

"He won't find me and he sure as hell doesn't know to look here." Brett settled his hat on his head and looked at Travis. "Just remember, no matter what you hear, I didn't kill Abner Kendrick. Outside the war, Travis, I haven't ever killed anyone.

Robbed a hell of a lot of places; but in all those robberies, there were no killings."

"I believe you," Travis said. "And I wish you'd at least stay tonight and sleep. Go at dawn if you have to go."

"You go home and tell her I've already ridden out of here. You won't see me again until I can live like you do." He looked at Travis solemnly. "You were the smart one. You always were. It took me a long time to see it, but I'm tired of the life of an outlaw. I'm tired of running, of never having a woman like that to come home to, of never having a child. That's a fine-looking boy you have."

"He and Crystal are my whole world," Travis said, thinking about Crystal and knowing she was hurt and angry. He was certain her anger would outweigh her hurt.

"I'm ready to settle. I'll go off somewhere like you have and start all over with a new name and a new life. And when I get honest enough and settled enough, Travis, I'll let you know."

Travis felt a knot in his throat. Even though it had been years since they had seen each other, he loved Brett. Time and the years of separation simply fell away and vanished as if it were only last week he was riding with Brett.

"Dammit, I wish you'd stay. And I hope you mean what you say about starting over. I've never once regretted it. Far from it, Brett. I'm damned thankful for this life."

"I know. I was on my way to Idaho and going to begin again when this happened. I didn't kill the man."

"You can take one of the blacks if you want. Then you'll have two horses and you can switch off if necessary."

"I'll be all right. I've got a good horse."

Travis nodded. "You have the food I brought. Crystal's no cook, but it's food."

Brett grinned. "If she were in my bed, I wouldn't give a damn about her cooking."

Travis smiled. "I don't. She's good to Jacob and that's why I married her."

"If that's the only reason, your mind is unhinged. I'm beginning to worry about you, brother. Now go back to her and start making peace."

They gazed at each other a long moment and then Travis turned and left. He knew by the time he reached the house Brett would be gone.

As he crossed the porch, he glanced back at the darkened barn. He knew it was empty, the lantern extinguished and Brett riding away. Travis said a quick prayer for his brother and then one for himself. Taking a deep breath, he opened the door. First thing, he checked for Ellery's revolver and, to his relief, saw it was on the high shelf. A lamp was burning, but Jacob was back in his bed. Crystal stood in front of the fire and her green eyes held their own fires of rage.

"He's gone, so you can calm down. You won't see him again."

"How could you bring him here and keep it from me!" She shook with anger, and he glanced past her to see what was within her reach that she might toss at him.

"I didn't bring him here. He came on his own. He's my brother and he was wounded and I wasn't about to turn him away."

"Then why didn't you tell me? You deceived me."

"I didn't tell you because you only see right or wrong. You see no excuses, no possibilities of circumstances. And I knew it would upset you to have him here."

"Yes, it would upset me. A criminal under my own roof when I'm the justice of the peace and sworn to uphold the law! And right now our district judge just died of pneumonia, so I am the *only* law in these parts!"

"There's the sheriff; and you're not creating law, you're just ministering justice, Crystal. Brett is on the run, but he's gone, so it no longer matters."

"It matters. Who's after him? Should we expect a posse? Has he killed someone? I should have asked more questions about your family, except you wouldn't have told me the truth."

"No, I wouldn't have because you have a closed mind when it comes to law." He looked at his tall, beautiful wife and wished she would just listen and give a little.

"I believe people should do what's right. That's pretty simple. What's he done and who is after him?"

Travis had anticipated the question and feared that the answer would wreck all that had been building between them. But he would not lie to her about Brett. A cynical voice inside him reminded him that he had as well as lied to her about himself.

"A man was shot and killed and other men have tried to hang the guilt on Brett because he was new in the area. And maybe because of the color of his skin," Travis replied. He didn't want to go any deeper into it because it would only stir up Crystal more. Abner Kendrick was a stockman who'd fought his neighbor Whit Odell constantly over water rights. Brett had said that one of Odell's men had shot Kendrick and then tried to pin blame on Brett, but there was no need in going into it with Crystal. If Brett got away, the incident would die down and be forgotten, wiped out by the next killing. With the regular occurrence of shootings on the frontier, this killing would fade quickly from people's minds.

"He has robbed and stolen in the past, but now he's wanted for a murder that he didn't commit," Travis continued, "and a U.S. Marshal might be after him."

She closed her eyes and rubbed her temple. "A marshal! A U.S. Marshal may ride in here and discover that I have harbored an outlaw."

"Crystal, he will discover no such thing unless you tell him. And I'm asking you to keep it to yourself and give Brett a chance. He's tired of the life he has led—"

"Oh, please! How often do men say that when things are going badly or they have been caught!"

"I think he means it. He wants to start over and uphold the law. He wants a chance, Crystal."

"How can you believe that if for years, he's robbed and

done heaven knows what else? Damn you, Travis! How could you hide him here?''

''I'm asking you not to tell the marshal, or any lawman. No one has to know Brett is my brother or that Brett was here at all.''

''I can't promise any such thing! I've sworn to uphold the law.''

Travis stared at her. They were getting nowhere. He jammed his hat on his head. ''I'm not wanted here, so I'll leave. Good night, Crystal.'' He closed the door behind him and strode into the night, heading back to the barn.

Crystal shook with fury. She sat in front of the fire, rocking, trying to calm herself, yet every time she thought about Brett Black Eagle, her anger soared. A U.S. Marshal would show up here trailing him. And Travis expected her to help hide his brother. An outlaw was an outlaw—outside the law—and should have to pay the penalties.

She watched the logs she had put on the fire until they burned down to ashes before she finally had calmed enough to feel drowsy again. She went to the cold, empty bed and felt a pang, torn between wanting to be in Travis's arms and furious with him for harboring his outlaw brother.

She didn't see Travis again until he returned home with the other men at the end of the day. The moment he stepped through the door, her pulse jumped. As soon as they ate, Turtle River and Zachary left to go back to work. While Travis played with Jacob, he watched her with hooded eyes and an unfathomable expression.

Her anger still simmered. ''If your brother returns, will you tell me?''

Travis stared at her for a long time before he nodded. ''All right, Crystal, I'll tell you; but you know it will only cause a bigger division between us.''

''If a marshal comes, I can only tell the truth.''

She saw the chill settle on Travis's features and knew she had angered him, but he might as well know what she would do. He stood abruptly. "I don't understand how you see only the law, the right or wrong, and not the person or the circumstances. More than one man has been hanged for a crime he didn't commit."

She raised her chin. "The law might err, but your brother is not completely innocent."

"No, he's not. But he's going to change."

"I don't see how you can possibly believe him."

"Sometimes you just have to have faith in people." He strode past her and got his hat and coat and left, and she knew she would not see him again that night.

The next night he left when the other men did and she supposed he was sleeping in the barn again.

As she began to see less and less of him, she missed him in so many ways. She hated to admit it, but she was aware of it constantly. Her husband became a stranger to her again, and hopes for a baby vanished.

The second week in May, Crystal dressed for court. She wore her hair tied behind her head with a black ribbon and she felt fluttery about the ride into town with Travis.

He had withdrawn from her, the old barriers coming back up as if they had never vanished. Yet she had her own barriers, too. She couldn't let go of her anger over Brett. And she knew part of Travis's anger and aloofness was because she would not agree to keep silent about Brett if a marshal appeared. No matter how I looked at it, she could not keep quiet about an outlaw.

She heard the wagon and went outside to see Travis jump down from the wagon seat. Longing hit her like a physical blow. He came around the front of the wagon and her pulse jumped again. He was dressed in his black denim pants and a black shirt, and his black hat was pulled down on his forehead. He looked formidable, handsome. In spite of his coolness, she was glad to be with him. He came forward and took Jacob from her arms and his fingers brushed over her, making her heart race.

Travis set Jacob in the wagon and then picked her up. Her hands rested on his forearms and she felt the flex of his hard muscles.

The moment his arms closed around her, his dark eyes met hers and she couldn't get her breath. Yearning for him tore at her and she hated that something had come between them, yet she couldn't give up her beliefs.

He set her on the wagon seat and went around to climb up beside her. While they rode in stiff silence, she was aware of him beside her. She ached to touch him, to place her hand on his arm, but it would solve nothing. And she felt as if disaster were hanging over them as she waited to encounter the marshal. Each trip into town, she thought she might see the marshal or hear he had been there, but so far there had been nothing.

Travis lifted her down in front of the courthouse while Jacob clung to the side of the wagon and watched her.

"See you later, Judge," Travis said in a cool, flat voice.

She merely nodded and waved at Jacob. "Bye, bye, love," she said to him as Travis walked around the wagon and climbed easily up the wagon seat to drive away. He didn't look back as she waved to Jacob and he waved to her.

When she entered the courthouse, one of the first persons she saw was Sheriff Hinckel. "Morning, Crystal. How's the family?" His blue eyes were wide and friendly.

"Fine. Little Jacob is growing so fast."

"You'll be chasing him all over the ranch before long."

"I suppose."

"I had to toss Virgil in jail last night for shooting up the Golden Bear, drunkenness and generally stirring up trouble, so he'll be in your court today."

She groaned as she reached her door and opened it. "He is a dreadful man, and I'm sure he despises me."

"He probably does," Sheriff said blandly. "They had a killing up north of here. Virgil saw it."

Crystal looked back at him. The sheriff was standing in front of his open office door. "A murder?"

"Yep, a rancher, Abner Kendrick. It's in our jurisdiction." That sent a chill down her spine. "Who did it?"

"Virgil said one of Kendrick's men did the shooting. He was a drifter probably—only worked one day for Kendrick. Shot and robbed him."

She stiffened, listening to Wade Hinckel talk about the shooting. She should tell the sheriff that they had harbored the killer. She was becoming part of the crime if she didn't tell.

"Virgil and some others heard the gunshot and saw the man robbing Kendrick. The hombre got away for now. I've got a deputy looking for him. He probably was an outlaw passing through the Territory."

"Which deputy?"

"Raymond Parnell. He's a good man for the job ... a tracker."

"There's too much fighting and shooting," she said woodenly, her mind on Travis and his renegade brother. She went into her office and closed the door.

Murder. In this jurisdiction. Brett Black Eagle couldn't have ridden far with the wound he had. He was wanted for murder and they had given him aid and shelter. Travis's brother had killed a man.

Her fury returned that Travis could turn such a blind eye to the law, brother or not. She thought about Ellery, but then shoved the notion aside because Ellery had not been an outlaw. It was not a consideration to compare how she would feel about her brother to how Travis must feel.

And if Deputy Parnell caught Brett and brought him back, she would tell the truth. They had hid him at the ranch.

She opened her door and then went to her desk, ready to begin her morning tasks and look over the docket. She heard footsteps and Sheriff Hinckel reappeared in the doorway.

"I sent Deputy Larson to get us some coffee, Crystal. And

Virgil offered me all his faro winnings if I'd let him go this morning so he wouldn't have to appear in court.''

She shrugged. ''I told you—the man doesn't like me.''

''Yep, I suppose. I didn't take the money,'' the sheriff said with a chuckle. ''I'll keep an eye on Virgil in the courtroom. He's in a sour mood.''

''I may be, too.''

Sheriff Hinckel grinned and went striding down the hall. She turned to look out the window. Instinct told her that Brett Black Eagle was the drifter wanted for murder. She felt torn between hoping for Travis's sake that Brett got away and thinking Brett should pay the price for his deed. She remembered his cocky, charming smile and wondered how many times he had used that smile to smooth things over and get himself out of trouble.

And then, unaccountably, she wondered about her husband's past. Had Travis come to the Territory because he had something to hide? Then Deputy Larson came through the door with coffee for her, and she forgot about the matter.

Travis led a customer to a pen with five horses. ''Take your pick. They're all good mounts,'' Travis said, eyeing the horses and knowing which he would choose.

The man pushed his hat to the back of his head and moved closer, touching first one horse and then another, looking at the sorrel's teeth. Travis waited patiently as the horses moved around. Behind him Jacob sat playing in the dust, piling dirt on his short legs. Travis knew Crystal would have scooped him up instantly, but Travis saw no harm in Jacob getting a little dirt on himself. He thought about Crystal and his insides knotted. When she'd stepped outside this morning, she had looked beautiful . . . fresh and full of energy. Tall, slender, regal-looking, she had walked to the wagon, and he had wanted to meet her and wrap his arms around her and kiss her.

Instead, he had had to stand and watch her, the chasm between them growing wider as more time passed and they could not make amends. Beneath his anger, he hurt. He knew it might be stubbornness, but no more than hers. Where the law was concerned, Crystal wouldn't yield an inch. The pain was steady and so damn hurtful that he knew for sure he was in love with his wife.

What he had sworn he would never do again, he had done: He had fallen in love with his wife. He loved Crystal; he needed her in too many ways. With the horses milling around him and Jacob jabbering, Travis closed his eyes and could see and hear only Crystal. He remembered her in his arms, her green eyes dark with love and desire.

He stiffened and opened his eyes, looking at the pen of horses and trying to get his mind on his work. Instead, it slid right back to Crystal. He was in love with her. He loved her desperately, as much as he could love a woman.

He had never intended for it to happen, had fought against it. But now there was no going back to the way he had felt before. He wanted to shake her for her stubborn views on law and right and wrong. He believed Brett. Besides, his brother would have admitted the truth to him, no matter how damning. He might lie in court, but he would not lie to his brother. And Travis would bet his life on that.

Travis glanced at Jacob, whose dark skin branded him Indian. His midnight hair did as well, but it was thick with curls and showed less of his Comanche heritage. There was no denying the color of his skin. Travis hoped people would become more accepting as Jacob grew older. Crystal had already opened doors for them that had been shut to Travis.

While he ached for her, he felt assured that she would not turn her anger on Jacob. She was as loving as ever to his son, as if there were nothing else happening in their lives that was tearing them apart.

He turned his head, looking down the street toward the courthouse, imagining her there in her black robe, sternly meting out her sense of justice. He wanted her in his arms and he wanted to tell her he loved her. But he didn't want her to turn his brother in to the law. Damnation.

"I'll take the sorrel," the stranger said to Travis, who shook on the sale, his mind still on his fiery-haired wife who was the judge.

Crystal sentenced Virgil to two days in jail, banged her gavel, and dismissed court. She was relieved to escape the courtroom. Always before, she had found satisfaction in her work, but this morning she could not. Her mind kept going to Travis and his glacial dark eyes, the stubborn set of his jaw and the disagreement between them. How could the man be so stubborn?

She rubbed her forehead and stepped into her tiny office, where she removed her robe. She straightened her hair and black dress and felt suffocated by the walls, so she went outside. In sunshine she stood and looked down the street. She couldn't see Travis's livery stable, but she knew it was there. He was there. She could imagine him working. He was probably so busy, he gave no thought to her. Or if he did give her a thought, it was an angry one.

Still seething over Travis, she didn't feel like eating. She wanted to close up and go home. Instead, she had a docket for the afternoon. Before she returned to her courtroom, she stopped at Sheriff Hinckel's office.

"I fined Virgil for contempt of court this morning. He threatened me and I don't think he'll ever do anything, but he was angry."

"I'll talk to him. It's time Virgil moved on to another town. He's given us enough grief. He's smart enough to avoid causing anyone too much trouble who might pull out a gun and get rid of him. Right now, he's back there snoring away."

A gun blasted. As she looked into Sheriff Hinckel's blue eyes, she saw the surprise that she felt. He raced past her, pistol at the ready. She hurried after him into the hot sun. She blinked, feeling the warmth splash over her. A crowd had gathered and she looked to see what was causing the commotion. Her heart stopped and then thudded back to life.

Twenty

Two men rode toward the courthouse. One wore a badge and led a horse. His face was covered in cuts and bruises and his shirt was bloody; one hand has wrapped in a bandage and a kerchief was tied around his head.

The man on the second horse had his hands tied behind his back. His face was a bloody mess, black hair hanging over half of his face. His shirt was torn and blood-soaked, his side a deep crimson. She looked at the unrecognizable bloody features, looked at the long black hair, his broad shoulders and his blood-soaked side and knew she was looking at Brett Black Eagle.

A crowd was gathering on both sides of the riders. Men shook their fists and tossed rocks at Brett.

"Hang him!"

"Killer!"

She saw Slim Tipton yelling with Gomer Tarkington beside him.

Chilled, she dashed down the street. She was two blocks from the courthouse before she remembered she was supposed to be in court. Glancing around, she saw ten-year-old Theo Garrison, his blond hair like a stack of straw on top of his head.

"Theo! Come here. I want you to get down to the livery stable and tell Travis Black Eagle that Brett has been caught and is in jail. Can you do that?"

"Yes, ma'am."

"Good. I'll leave a silver dollar for you on my desk."

"A dollar! Yes, ma'am!"

"You run all the way."

"Yes, ma'am!"

She watched him race down the street and she wanted to go, too. In spite of her feelings about Brett, she hurt for Travis. And she worried about what he would do when he saw his brother. Brett was soaked with blood and had to be in bad shape. He looked as if he had been beaten badly.

She rushed back to the courthouse, pausing at Sheriff Hinckel's door. He stood behind his desk, deputies around him, but immediately came to her side.

"Excuse me, a minute, men," he said, taking her arm and leading her down the hall away from the crowd. "Did you see the prisoner that was just brought in?"

"Yes."

"He's Brett Dancer. He was—"

"Dancer?"

"Yes, why?" His eyes narrowed. "You sound surprised. Do you know this man?"

She debated, but there was only one answer. "Yes, I think I do. It was hard to tell because he was so bloody."

"Has he been in our jail and your courtroom before? I don't remember him."

"No, he hasn't."

His eyes narrowed again. "How do you know him?"

"I think he's my brother-in-law," she said stiffly, exactly as Travis had predicted.

Hinckel's brows shot up. "Dancer is really Brett Black Eagle?"

"I think so. I told you, it's difficult to tell."

"I guess he gave a false name to protect Travis. Come here and look at him, Judge."

She didn't want to confront Brett; and although she expected Travis to appear at any moment, she could not imagine what he would do.

"Sheriff, I'm supposed to be in court."

"It can't start without you."

"What's he done?" she asked, dreading the answer.

"He's killed Abner Kendrick."

"No!" She closed her eyes and sucked in her breath as her head swam. Her worst fears were coming true.

"Sorry, Crystal. Feeling is running high. I'm swearing in more deputies in case some of Kendrick's men try to lynch our prisoner without a trial."

"You mustn't let that happen!" Crystal cried. More than anything she detested the lawlessness of men taking justice into their own hands. A lynching was the total absence of justice. And Travis would fight them to the death. Her hands were ice as she locked her fingers together and stared at the sheriff.

"If it turns out he is Travis's brother, both of you'd better let him go by the name Dancer and not claim him. I know Travis probably won't turn his back on his own brother, but when there's a killing, tempers get hot. According to Whit Odell, this Dancer was passing through, got a job with Kendrick, then robbed and killed him."

"Travis will stand by his brother," she said woodenly. "He would defend Brett with his last breath."

"I'll go tell Travis."

"He should know already. I sent Theo Garrison to tell him."

"I hope Travis doesn't try anything foolish. I don't know what kind of feelings he has for his brother—I didn't even know the man had a brother—but if they're close, Travis had better not try to get him out of jail and away from here."

"He won't," she said firmly, but she had no idea what Travis would or would not do. She was terrified he might try to free his brother and get killed in the attempt. But if he did that, he would have to run, too. She thought of Jacob. Whatever happened, she knew Travis would think of Jacob. But what he thought was best for Jacob might not be what she thought was best.

"See if you recognize him, Crystal."

She hated to go with Wade and stared at him, wanting to rush back to her courtroom and avoid identifying the man. "You're sure his name is Dancer?"

"That's what he said."

She heard someone swear and then she recognized a deep voice.

"Wade!" Travis bellowed.

"Your husband's here," the sheriff said under his breath. "You don't need to identify the prisoner for me. Travis is going to."

The sheriff moved away from her and she turned to see Travis standing at the other end of the hallway. He was wearing his revolver and he stood with his feet spread apart, his fists clenched, and he looked ready to fight. Her heart thudded as his gaze stabbed her. He looked as if he thought she had turned Brett in.

She raised her chin. She regretted that his brother was a prisoner, but it was Brett's own doing. And if he'd committed the crime, murder was a horrendous deed that had to be punished. But in spite of her defiant look at Travis, she was terrified what he might do and what might happen to him.

She remembered how he had crossed the room without pause when she'd held a revolver aimed right at him. At that close range even a complete novice could not have missed, and yet Travis had never hesitated or blinked. And he had asked her if she ever feared anything! Yet if he had been that fearless with a pistol aimed at him when all he wanted to do was propose marriage, to what length would he risk himself now to save his brother?

Her guess terrified her, and she wondered whether she would soon be a widow and Jacob fatherless.

"I was told you have my brother in jail." His voice was icy, making Wade draw a swift breath and blink in surprise.

"We have a man who says he's Brett Dancer."

There wasn't a change of expression in Travis's features. He merely nodded. "He's my brother. Why is he in jail?"

"For killing Abner Kendrick."

"Did he admit to that?"

"No. Whit Odell said he did it."

"Can I see him?"

Hinckel nodded and motioned to him. "Come with me."

Crystal wanted to talk to Travis. More than that, she wanted to see that he didn't pull his revolver right now and try to set his brother free. The moment Sheriff Hinckel had said the name Brett Dancer he had known it was his brother.

Even though her courtroom was waiting for her, she had to see Travis when he came back from talking to Brett. She waited, and listened.

She heard Travis yelling and Wade Hinckel yelling back; Travis was in a rage over Brett's condition. At the force of the swearing and shouting, she speculated that Travis himself might soon be behind bars.

She ran through the sheriff's office, past startled deputies.

"Ma'am. Your Honor," Deputy Thomas said, trying to block her path, but she pushed past him and ignored him, racing to the jail in the back. She stepped inside the hall and saw Wade Hinckel unlocking a door and her heart thudded. She expected Travis to pull his revolver and take Brett. Instead, Travis stepped inside where Brett was sprawled facedown on the floor.

"Deputy!" Hinckel yelled, glancing around to see her. Geoffrey McDougal appeared behind her.

"Sir?"

"Get water and bandages and something for these wounds. This man has lost lots of blood."

"Sir—"

"Deputy!" Wade roared, drowning out the starting of an argument. She could imagine his deputy wondering why they should patch up a man who was likely to be lynched before dawn.

"I'll help."

"I thought you were supposed to be in court."

"You said it can't start without me."

"Go on, Crystal," Travis said in a cold, harsh voice as if he were talking to a stranger he didn't want around. She looked into his glacial dark eyes and felt his fury and she left hastily.

The afternoon was a blur as she heard one case after another. There was no more commotion from the direction of the jail. When she finished the docket, she rushed to her office to shed her robe and then tore down to the sheriff's office.

He was seated behind his desk, writing on papers spread beneath his hand. Deputies still stood beside him, but it was a different group of men. Two stood at the front window, and she wondered what they were watching.

"How's your prisoner?" she asked, stepping inside.

"He's not in good shape. Travis has sent for Turtle River to let that Injun doctor on him. He's already had the new doc out."

"We have a new doctor?"

"Yep. Just in time for all these shenanigans. Name is Sam Mason. He came by and worked on Dancer. Doc said if Dancer gets through the night, he'll survive. I don't know about that. Besides his condition, Parnell said he thought sure we'd have a Kendrick hangin' bunch come get Dancer. They can try, but they're not going to do it while I'm sheriff."

"I hope not!" she said fervently.

"Your Honor, you know you're the only law in this part of the Territory right now and we can't wait for a new district judge. You'll try the case."

Stunned, Crystal stared at him. "I've never tried murder, and the man is my brother-in-law."

"Well, now you're going to try it," Hinckel said, giving her a squinty-eyed look and getting a stubborn note in his voice. "I can't keep this man here weeks without a trial. He'll be dead without any due process. He's gonna hang, anyway, but we're going to do it right. I don't want a lynching on my record. The governor has already told me he doesn't want it on his, and it would ruin you as a justice of the peace."

She stared at him in consternation. He was right, but she didn't want to judge Brett.

"Don't up and resign on me," Hinckel said, studying her. "I don't see you as a coward, so I don't think you will."

"I don't know that much about a murder."

"You have your law books. Did your father or grandpa defend accused murderers?"

"Yes," she said, barely able to get out the words. If she tried and sentenced Brett to die, her marriage would be over. She would be sentencing Jacob's uncle to death. And if she let Brett go, she would not be able to live with herself.

"I just can't take the case! I'm a relative."

"Judge, listen to the crowd. That's a lynch mob out there."

She could hear the shouting and she felt like ice. She would judge Travis's brother ... unless the mob stormed the jail and tried to lynch him. She couldn't bear to think about the consequences—Travis would defend his brother to the death.

"Crystal," Wade said patiently, as if she had not heard him the first time, "you have to take the case. You don't have a choice. I don't care if it is your brother-in-law. There isn't anyone else, and if we wait, he'll be lynched."

She looked beyond him. "Where's Travis?" she asked.

"He's back there, still with him. The boy's in bad shape."

"How did he get in bad shape?"

"He didn't want Deputy Parnell to bring him in. He's been shot and he took a beating. He gave a little back. The deputy don't look so great hisself."

She remembered Parnell's cuts and bruises, but they had been nothing compared to Brett's condition. Indeed, Brett had been in bad shape when he'd left the ranch. And he wouldn't have left if it hadn't been for her.

"Can I go back and talk to Travis?"

"Yes."

She swept past him and turned the corner going to the cell. Brett was on the wooden bed, covered in a blanket. In spite of his dark skin, he looked ashen. His eyes were closed, one eye puffed shut. His face was cut and swollen. She looked up into Travis's eyes; they cut into her like knives.

"How is he?"

"Go on home, Crystal." Travis averted his stony gaze. "I'm staying here. One of the deputies will accompany you and Jacob home." His voice was laced with anger and contempt.

She looked at him, kneeling over his bother, and she ached with him. He had had too many hurts and losses in his life. He needed someone at his side now, yet she couldn't be the one; she couldn't defend a murderer.

"Come home with me," she said, wishing with all her heart he would. Travis gazed at her again, a long look that she met with a direct, level gaze of her own. She held her breath as she waited for his answer.

"No. He's my brother." Travis crossed the cell to her. As he looked at her, the iron bars between them, she could all too easily imagine Travis getting himself into trouble over his brother. "He's innocent, Crystal."

"Oh, Travis! They all say that! Every man that comes before me says he's innocent."

"There's no reason for Brett to lie to me. He never has, and I don't think he'd start now. He didn't kill Kendrick."

Of course Travis would want to believe his brother, but so few men who had committed crimes admitted it. Even under the most blatantly guilty circumstances, most men proclaimed their innocence.

"This isn't the first time your brother has been on the wrong side of the law. You told me he's robbed."

Travis's jaw tightened, and a muscle flexed as his eyes

became even more glacial. "He's never killed, he said, except in the war. I believe him."

"You're his brother."

"I know he's telling me the truth."

"Come home with me," she said quietly, her heart missing a beat. Courts, relatives, laws, and lawlessness all seemed less important than Travis and their marriage. Jacob needed him; she needed him enough to ask him again.

Something flickered in the depths of his eyes, but he stared at her with a cold, dark look and shook his head. "Go home. I don't want you here, and Jacob should be home."

"I don't want Jacob fatherless."

Travis's brow arched. "Spare me, Crystal. You're capable of taking care of him; and now if you were available, more than a dozen men would marry you."

She stared at him and knew she was going to have to tell him the sheriff's demand. "Travis, Sheriff Hinckel said I'm going to have to try this case. There isn't anyone else to do it, and if we wait, Brett might be lynched."

"Oh, God!" Travis sounded pained. He shook his head and turned his back on her, shutting her out.

She stared at the broad, unyielding shoulders that had carried too many burdens. She loved this tall, strong man who was hurting badly. Half of her clamored to run to him and stand by him through this. The other half of her could not shirk a duty that had to be carried out.

He looked so incredibly alone. She reached out her hand tentatively and then withdrew it. He didn't want her touch. He wanted what she couldn't give. Yet how badly she wanted to go to him! To be the wife he needed.

Fighting the sting of tears, she turned away and left, hastily wiping her eyes before passing through the sheriff's office. He stood up when she entered and fell into step beside her.

"I'm going home now."

"I'll send a couple of deputies along. You and your baby shouldn't be out there alone."

She glanced at him. "The anger toward Brett won't spill over on Travis, will it?"

"I've told my deputies—as much as we can, we're not going to spread the word that Brett's his brother. Dancer did him a favor by using a false name. The less people know about the relationship, the better. Right now, most people know they're both Injun, but that's all."

She nodded. It'll get out soon enough."

"Crystal, we need to have this trial as fast as we can. Travis has the livery stable; he's a good farrier, and he has his ranch. People have accepted him. But you know, around here, there's some bad feeling by some of the folks about Indians."

"That shouldn't have anything to do with it."

"Well, it does. People want Brett to hang. I've already talked to Clarence about prosecuting Brett Dancer. Travis has already talked to Rufus about defending his brother."

"Rufus is going to defend Brett?" she asked, startled because she hadn't thought Travis liked Rufus. And she didn't think Travis could afford Rufus. Then she remembered the boxes of gold. Yes, he probably could afford the flamboyant, expensive lawyer.

"Yes. Surprised me that Rufus would take the defense. I didn't think there was much good feeling between Rufus and Travis. Rufus charges pretty high, but Travis is probably willing to pay."

"We'll have to post notice, have the arraignment—"

"Crystal, cut the formalities as much as you can. Get down to basic law or we'll have a body hanging from our scaffold without any law putting him there."

She nodded. "This is Friday. We'll have to wait at least until next Wednesday so I can post notices. We have to have the arraignment, although I can move from the arraignment into the trial if I have to."

"You have to. Make this trial Tuesday at the latest. I can't hold off a mob long."

"I don't want to do this," she said, thinking about Travis.

"I want to get him legally tried before there's a lynching."

"Since I have to try him, I'll get a room at the hotel so I don't have to go back and forth to the ranch. I can get Zachary and Turtle River to keep Jacob for me. I don't want Jacob here if there's any chance of violence."

"Good idea. And your staying at the hotel instead of the ranch will be better. I can give you protection. You should be safe from violence—unless you turn Dancer loose, but I can count on you to do what's right."

She walked toward the door with Sheriff Hinckel at her side. She would do what was right, but it was going to mean the end of her marriage to Travis, a marriage that—briefly—had been paradise. Now, looking back, her marriage had ended the night she'd discovered Brett.

"I've put out the word and posted notices that no one is allowed into the courthouse packing iron except my sworn deputies."

"Thank heavens! That's one crumb of good news."

"Jed and Elgin will ride home with you."

"Thank you," she said to Deputy Larson and Deputy Thomas. Both men smiled politely, sandwiching her between them. "The wagon is at the livery stable and Jacob is there. I'll be back in the morning, Sheriff."

"Then you boys just stay the night at their place. It's warm enough to sleep in Travis's wagon and you accompany her back to town."

"You don't need to do that. Turtle River can come with me."

"Judge, let me handle this before someone else gets hurt."

Nodding, she turned to go. As they walked past the building, she looked back over her shoulder at the barred window where Travis and Brett were.

Travis sat across the cell from his brother, his back against the wall, his knees bent, arms resting on his knees as he watched

Brett's chest rise and fall while he dozed. He heard voices and looked up as Wade Hinckel and Rufus Milligan appeared.

Rufus looked cool and citified with a black suit and black hat. While Travis felt a flare of the old animosity, he was glad to have Rufus take the case. Rufus was quick-witted and smooth-talking, a showman. And the prosecutor for the court was Clarence Hoyt, who hated Indians but was not as articulate as Rufus. Clarence could hold his own against several of the other local attorneys, but he hadn't done well in the past when he was up against Rufus.

Travis knew Rufus didn't like him, but Rufus liked money and Travis was paying him exceedingly well. He unfolded and offered his hand to Rufus, who shook it with a strong grip.

Travis looked into Rufus's cool, blue eyes and felt good about having him defend Brett. A deputy brought a chair inside, placing it near the bed where Brett lay.

"Thank you, Wade. I'll call when I'm ready."

"Want to leave, Travis?"

Travis shook his head. "It's up to Rufus."

"You can stay."

Travis nodded to Wade, who left them alone and locked the door behind him. Rufus sat down beside the bed, pulling his chair as close as possible to Brett. He glanced at Travis.

"It would help if he could talk to me. Can we wake him?"

"I'll try." Travis moved close and leaned down, looking at Brett's mangled face. One eye was swollen shut, his mouth swollen and cut. He had a cut across his temple and another on his cheek; and every time Travis looked at his brother, his anger grew toward Parnell. "Brett."

Brett's eye fluttered open and he stared into space, then he focused on Travis. "This is Rufus, your attorney. He'd like to ask you questions."

"If you can, just wave your hand for a yes. Hold up one finger for a no. Can you do that?"

Brett waved his fingers.

"Good. Now, did you kill Abner Kendrick?"

"No, I didn't," Brett whispered.

"I have heard a version of what happened from Deputy Parnell, who got it from Whit Odell. If you're able to talk, I want to hear what happened. Did you work for Abner Kendrick?"

"Yes. I just hired on four days before the shooting."

"I heard it was one day."

"No."

Travis hunkered down to hear Brett's voice, which was barely above a whisper.

"I'd been traveling west and I didn't intend to stay in Wyoming Territory long. Kendrick was looking for men to break horses, and I signed on. I had just worked there four days when we were out on his land near the Odell boundary. There were three of us and we had four wild horses. Kendrick sent the other two men after some more wild horses. While I was with Kendrick, Whit Odell and two of his men rode up." Brett paused and Rufus waited quietly until Brett was up to talking again.

"Odell and Kendrick got in a fight. One of Odell's men drew on him and shot Odell. They claimed I did it and was robbing him when they rode up. They're lying."

"Who were the men with Odell?"

"I heard them called Slim and Virgil."

"Damnation!" Travis exclaimed. "That's Slim Tipton and Virgil Shank. Those two are scum."

"Do you know which one shot Kendrick?" Rufus asked.

"The one called Slim."

"You have no other witness?"

"No. It's my word against theirs."

Travis rubbed the back of his neck. He believed Brett, but he didn't think anyone else would, even though Whit Odell was a troublemaker and everyone in the Territory knew it. And Virge and Slim were worthless, constantly in trouble, absolute liars.

"Have you ever committed a crime?"

He waved his fingers. "Robbed a train in the Territory. Union Pacific carrying gold. Lots of robberies."

"Did you get the gold from the Union Pacific?"

Brett waved his hand.

"Do you still have the gold?"

He held up one finger.

"Do you know where it is?"

He waved his hand again.

"Ahh," Rufus said, and Travis wondered if Rufus had just set his own sights on that gold. Wherever it was, it should go back to the railroad, but he doubted if Brett saw it that way.

"Had you ever been in jail before?"

Brett waved his hand.

"How many times?"

Brett held up two fingers.

"Twice. What for?"

"Robbery," he whispered. "I have never killed a man. Except during the war as a soldier."

"Is there a price on your head?"

"One hundred dollars until the Odell shooting."

Not much for reward money.

"What happened after Kendrick was shot? Did he die then?"

"Yes. His men heard the shots and rode back. Odell had drawn a gun on me and told them that he and his men were nearby and heard a shot. He said they rode to see what was happening and found me as I was trying to rob Kendrick. They said I had shot and killed him. Kendrick's men took me prisoner and Odell said he would go with them to take me in to the sheriff in Cheyenne, but they said it wasn't necessary. During the ride, I got away from them. I was shot in the side, but I escaped."

Brett lay still and quiet and Travis thought he had lapsed into unconsciousness, but after a few minutes his eye fluttered open. "I didn't kill Kendrick or rob him. But Odell and his men are going to swear I did."

"I'm your lawyer, Brett. I'm damned good. Expensive, but good. You're sure that's the way it happened?"

"As God is my witness. Bring a Bible and I'll swear on it."

"I'll settle for your word. Tell me if I have it right."

Travis stared out the window as dusk settled, listening to Rufus retell Brett's story. Brett was coherent and Travis thought it a good sign, that his health had taken a turn for the better. It was the wound in the side that was dangerous, but it had not hit vital organs.

He wondered about Crystal. He knew Wade had sent at least one deputy with her. Would she be in danger if the town tried to lynch Brett? Travis didn't think so. She would be on their side.

Glancing at his brother, Travis felt a tight knot in his chest. They had gone years without seeing each other, but during all their early years he and Brett had been close. He didn't want his brother to hang and he believed his story. He turned around as Rufus finished his summary.

"Is that right?"

"Yes," Brett whispered, and Travis moved so that he could look at Brett.

Rufus stood up. "I know you're hurting, so we'll stop, but I wanted to hear the facts from you. I'll do the best I can for you, but this is going to be tough because it's your word against theirs and you have a price on your head. You're a man with a record, but I'll do what I can."

Rufus gave Travis a long look, and Travis felt frustrated. Brett's story sounded false, and no one would believe him with witnesses who would swear they saw him kill Abner Kendrick. If he hadn't had a past record, a price on his head, he might have stood a chance with his word against the likes of Slim and Virge. But Brett would be viewed as more of an outlaw than two local men who kept their crimes to petty misdemeanors, drunkenness, and brawling—things not even considered crimes by most men in town. No, people would not believe Brett's story. Crystal didn't even believe it, and she was going to try the case. She would hang Brett if she could.

Travis looked at the rise and fall of Brett's chest. His good eye was closed again. "He's asleep or lost consciousness," Travis said.

"This may cost you more."

"Whatever it takes." Travis shook his head. "My brother isn't lying. I'd bet my ranch and my livery stable on it." He looked into Rufus's searching blue eyes and gave him back just as direct a stare.

"His past is going to go against him. Some men hate outlaws with a feeling that's overpowering," Rufus remarked.

Travis thought about Crystal and nodded. He understood.

"And you know without my telling you, there's bad feeling about Indians. That's going to go against him."

Travis nodded again, his frustration and anger growing.

"And you would bet everything your brother isn't lying?"

"I'll bet you my livery stable right now if you want to match it with something."

"No, I don't. Whether he's telling the truth or not, I'm his attorney and he's innocent until proven guilty. If I get him off, you'd better get him out of town quickly."

"I agree," Travis replied grimly. Brett's chances of getting off were almost nonexistent, but Rufus had had some amazing verdicts. Travis watched Rufus go toward the door.

"Wade told me that my wife will judge the case."

Rufus turned, his brows arched, a look of incredulity on his face.

"They're going to let your wife sit in judgment on her own brother-in-law?"

"She's the only law in this part of the territory right now. Wade doesn't want to wait and have a mob lynch his prisoner."

"What about Clarence? He agrees?"

"I'm sure he'll be glad. Crystal is mule-stubborn about law."

A smile wreathed Rufus's face. "By thunder!" He straightened his hat on his head. "I'd better get ready for the news-papers. I'm beginning to see a ray of hope."

"Don't get your dancing boots on," Travis drawled dryly. "My wife is an absolute stickler for law,"

"She is your *wife*. To my immense disappointment I did not take a good look at your lovely lady when she arrived in Cheyenne. Now it is too late, because she is very much in love with you. Very much in love."

"Not so damned much in love that she'd turn a blind eye to justice."

"Ah, you don't even know the depth of the lady's feelings. Your wife loves you."

The words hurt badly. Travis inhaled, thinking of what he had lost a second time. "There is no one who can come between Crystal and what she thinks is right," Travis said, feeling as if a fist had closed around his heart. His wife might have been falling in love, but not now. Now there was a divide between them that grew wider daily, and Brett's trial was going to be the final separation. "Whatever she felt for me will make no difference."

Rufus frowned. "I've seen how the lady looks at you, heard how she talks about you. Maybe you don't know how much your wife is in love with you." He studied Travis, who clamped his jaw closed.

"I just know what she feels for law."

"I've never met the woman who will judge with her head instead of her heart."

"Rufus, you're wrong. You have met one. When I went to talk to her before our marriage, I burst in on her. She pulled a revolver and squeezed the trigger and I would be a dead man now if Ellery had kept his revolver loaded."

"Damnation! Now I really regret I didn't get to know her when she moved here. Well, we'll see."

Travis felt a swift stab of anger tinged with jealousy. His marriage was falling apart, and Rufus was already half in love with Crystal. He would have yelled at Rufus to get out, but he was Brett's only chance.

"I'll go now. You're paying me, and I want to earn my money." He turned his back to Travis. "Sheriff!" he yelled.

Travis heard boots scrape the floor and a jingle of keys as Wade appeared.

Travis stepped out, too, and walked down the hall with the two men.

"A crowd is gathering, Rufus," Wade said. "You're his attorney and you're not going to be popular, either. You ought to go out the back door. I had a deputy bring your horse around to the back and I have deputies standing guard all around the building. If you're leaving, Travis, you ought to go the back, too, although right now, no one outside of this office knows he's your brother, except Crystal and whomever you've told."

"I'll stay. If you have to fight off a mob, I want to help."

Wade nodded. "Can't say that I won't welcome you. I'll swear you in so you'll be official and no one will wonder. The only connection most folks will see is you're an Indian and he's an Indian."

"I'll be back tomorrow," Rufus said. He strode toward the back door while Travis went into the hall and looked out the front. Torches burned outside and he could see men standing in small clusters. Right now everyone was orderly, but that could change fast.

Saturday morning, Crystal gave last instructions as Zachary stood with Turtle River. She had their word they would not let Jacob out of their sight for a minute.

Deputy Larson carried a satchel filled with her things. Sandy-haired Jed Larson was stocky, striding out to the wagon with a rolling gait and climbing up easily. She gave Jacob one last hug and handed him to Turtle River.

Elgin Thomas held out his hand to help her up and then he climbed into the back. Missing Travis, feeling very much alone, she turned to look at Jacob. He waved his tiny hand at her and called goodbye.

"Mama, bye! Bye, Mama!"

She waved back and blew him kisses and thought about her son. He was as much her son as if she had given birth to him. She would tell him about Elizabeth, but Crystal felt as if Jacob were her own. She loved him totally. Just as she loved his father.

While Jed Larson drove, she gazed into the hazy distance and she wondered what lay ahead in Cheyenne. All through the past sleepless night, a premonition of disaster had filled her. With each mile closer that they drew to town, her concern grew. She knew Travis would defend Brett to his death. Tears stung her eyes because she loved her husband desperately.

When they were within sight of the courthouse, her hands were knotted into tight fists. She saw the crowd of men gathered in front of the courthouse. Had Brett survived the night? And had Travis?

Then a shot rang out and the clusters of men suddenly formed one mass, some with guns held high as they stormed the courthouse.

Twenty-one

Jed Larson halted the wagon and Crystal stood up. As the crowd surged toward the courthouse door, Sheriff Hinckel stepped outside and fired his rifle. The blast reverberated in the air and everyone halted.

Deputies with guns drawn poured out behind the sheriff and spread out in front of the courthouse. Her heart missed a beat when she saw the tallest man move to Wade Hinckel's side. Travis's black hat was pulled low over his forehead and he stood tall and straight with his rifle in hand. There were angry shouts, but the sheriff quieted the mob.

Slim Tipton was in the crowd. "Hang the redskin!" he yelled, waving a rifle.

"Men, go home, so no one gets hurt. We'll have a trial Monday morning," Wade Hinckel shouted.

Monday. He had told her Tuesday! Her thoughts spun. In two days she was going to have to sit as judge for Brett Black Eagle. And her marriage would never be the same. She remembered how she had felt when she'd thought Travis had killed Ellery. She had wanted Travis to hang for the deed. And it

wasn't going to matter to Travis that there would be a jury to
render a verdict. He would still hold her just as much responsible
since she would preside at the trial.

She watched as the crowd began to disperse; a few men at
first, and then gradually the mob broke up. Travis turned his
head and gazed in her direction, but she was too far down the
street to know whether he was really looking at her.

"Judge, if you'll sit down, we'll go ahead."

She took her seat in the wagon once again, her icy hands
clutched tightly together while they rode closer; then she knew
for certain that Travis was watching her. Her pulse drummed
and she was dismayed at the impasse they had reached. Brett
Black Eagle had killed a man. Brett should hang for his crime.
And they would have a trial day after tomorrow.

Justice was swift on the frontier, especially when a mob
prevailed and there was no trial at all. Even though sunshine
spilled over her, she felt chilled to the bone. They rode past
the courthouse while men clustered on the street.

"Hang him, Judge!" a man yelled.

She rode, staring straight ahead until she could no longer
resist turning her head. She gazed into Travis's eyes and, even
at a distance, she felt his anger and his worry for his brother.
She guessed that few knew yet that Brett was Travis's brother.
And she prayed they wouldn't know. When Brett was sentenced, what would Travis do?

Although she entered the courthouse through the back door,
Travis was waiting for her. "Can we talk?"

She nodded, and he fell into step beside her. She was aware
of him at her side—his height, his silence, the tension between
them. And in spite of their differences, longing tore through
her.

As soon as they entered her office, Travis closed the door.
Nervous and filled with dread, she removed her bonnet and
faced him. She could feel his anger coming in palpable waves
across the narrow room, and she remembered that first confrontation she'd had with him. Travis, angered, was formidable;

yet beneath all that controlled rage festered pain. He hurt over his brother, and she hurt for Travis. Deep down, below all the other churning emotions, she missed him and the closeness and rapture they had discovered. She loved him, and her love was strong.

"Crystal, get yourself off this case."

"I can't," she said, her voice strained. "Surely you can understand that I don't want to be the judge for Brett."

"I can't understand any damn such thing! You could get off if you wanted to."

"No," she replied wearily. His anger was blinding his logic. He should see why she had no choice. "If we delay Brett's trial, what do you think those men waiting outside will do? Thank goodness, nobody knows you're his brother. Travis, go back to the ranch."

"I'll never do that," he snapped, "and you wouldn't either if it were Ellery. Wade said you're going to stay in town until the trial is over."

"Yes, I'll be at the hotel."

"Then we both have rooms there."

Startled, she frowned. "You took a room?"

"I want to stay here with Brett. I'm a deputy now, and the sheriff might need me."

She barely heard the last, focusing on Travis's taking a room at the hotel and worrying that he might live there for a long time to come. He could easily get Turtle River to run the ranch for him and go back to working all week at the livery stable. However, she didn't think he would stay away from Jacob.

"Brett's innocent, Crystal."

"I know you want to think that. I take it he lived through the night."

"Yes. He's tough."

So are you. She looked at the muscle flexing in his jaw. He was tied in knots over Brett and over the clash between them, although this division could not possibly cause him the anguish she suffered. He had never said he was in love. She had never really known the depth of his feelings. But she knew the depth of her own, and this arrest was destroying what was between them.

"In this nation, in any of its territories, a man is innocent until proven guilty."

"I know that, but they are going to prove him guilty so fast."

"You shouldn't jump to that conclusion," he warned her. "My brother is innocent."

"Travis, there are witnesses."

"Virgil and Slim," Travis said, the utmost contempt in his tone. "How reliable do you think either of them is?"

Crystal was startled to learn their identity. No one had told her, even though she had just sentenced Virgil. Was it only yesterday?

"They're not reliable," she granted, "but they're also not desperadoes. Your brother is an *outlaw.*" Why couldn't Travis see that when a man was on the wrong side of the law, he had to pay for what he had done?

"An outlaw, yes," Travis replied in a tight voice laced with fury, "but not a murderer. Brett has never lied to me."

She stared at Travis in exasperation. Neither one of them would ever convince the other. "I hear you hired Rufus." She longed to cross the room to her husband, just to touch him. He looked tough, all the barriers back between them, a gulf that widened each time they were together. His broad shoulders were a bulwark. She missed him, his strength, all they had had together. The trial was tearing them apart, and before long, it would effect Jacob. Yet the worst was still to come.

"Yes, Rufus took the case. He gave Brett more fair-mindedness than you have," Travis snapped and whirled. In an instant he had slammed the door behind him.

He was gone so swiftly, it startled her and left an aching void. She stood immobile, recalling every hurtful word he had said. She had no choice. His brother could be lynched.

Getting ready for Monday was a nightmare. She went back

to the hotel Saturday night, wishing she had waited until Sunday. The town was in turmoil.

Men mingled in the street in front of the courthouse. They burned torches and gathered in clusters until late in the evening. Although they gradually dispersed, she suspected most of them had gone to saloons, where they might become more unruly than ever.

Sunday, Turtle River rode into town to check on Brett, and when she saw him pass her office, she hurried after him. Dressed in buckskins with his hair in a long braid, Turtle River headed toward the back door, pausing only when she called to him.

"How's Jacob?"

"He's fine. Misses his mama, but he's just fine."

"And Brett?" she asked, "Are you still treating him?"

"He's recovering." Turtle River stared into the distance. "He did not kill Kendrick."

"You, too?" she asked. Had Turtle River's loyalty to Travis made him blind to the truth? Could he actually believe Brett innocent?

Turtle River's dark eyes focused on her. They held none of the chilling anger of Travis's dark gaze. They were direct, and she knew Turtle River felt strongly about his belief. "The man did not kill."

"You only have his word."

"On occasion, a man's word is sufficient. I will watch little Jacob." He strode outside, into the mob.

That night she could not sleep, but stood in the darkened hotel room, observing the men that milled in front of the courthouse. Was Travis inside? Or was he here in the hotel only a short distance away from her?

Occasionally, she had seen him from her window. He was tall, easy to spot, his long-legged stride making him noticeable in a crowd. Turtle River had said Brett was better. As she stood in the open window, feeling the swift gusts of wind that carried the smell of rain, she saw Travis once again.

Her pulse jumped as she watched him cover the distance

from the hotel to the courthouse. Along with a long, narrow board, his rifle was in his hand. His long legs crossed the ground swiftly until he disappeared inside the courthouse. Deputy Black Eagle. Had he become a deputy so he could wear his revolver into the courthouse when regular citizens could not? The notion made her blood chill.

"No!" she whispered, praying he wouldn't go wild if Brett were sentenced to hang.

Travis strode down the hall of the courthouse, straight to Crystal's office. At the door, he paused and looked up and down the hall. Despite the unusual number of deputies, no one paid Travis any heed. He went inside her darkened office and closed the door behind him, letting his eyes adjust to the light.

A heaviness filled him. This was Crystal's room, her domain, and her scent still clung in the air. Roses. He missed her so much it was shattering. He leaned against the wall and closed his eyes, remembering her laughter, her kisses.

Groaning, he straightened and moved across the room, but when he reached Crystal's desk, he stopped and ran his fingers over the smooth wood. This was where she worked; her hands had touched this surface. He had slept only a few hours at a time, and his nerves were ragged. He had gone over and over the possibilities of the trial.

If Brett were found guilty—and Travis expected he would be—Travis had only one course open to him, he would get Brett free and away from Cheyenne.

He clenched his fist. He loved Crystal to the depths of his soul. She was a strong, vital woman and he needed her for life. She was ecstasy in his arms, joy immeasurable. He needed her and loved her, and he had never told her that he loved her. Now it was too late, because he also loved his brother and would not let him hang for a crime he did not commit.

As a deputy, he could carry his revolver into the courtroom, and he had already slipped a pistol to Brett. Indeed, his brother was well-armed, for Turtle River had given him a knife as well.

Travis's insides knotted at the thought of leaving Crystal . . . and his son. Tears ran unheeded down his cheeks. He was going to lose the two people he loved most in the whole world, because he couldn't let his innocent brother hang.

Travis wiped his cheeks. He adored Jacob. And Crystal, who would raise their son. She would give him the right training. He would be able to read and cipher, and he would learn the law when he was grown. She would take care of him, educate him, and adore him.

Travis raked his arm across his face in an effort to control his emotions. Tomorrow, and each day afterwards until the trial concluded, Turtle River would leave Jacob in Zachary's care and wait with a change of horses just outside Cheyenne. Travis would have two good mounts ready at the back of the courthouse for their escape from town. Once they had exchanged horses, Turtle River would escort Crystal home, where he would help and protect her and care for Jacob. Travis thought about her wide green eyes, her softness.

She would know he would not be back. He wished he had told her he loved her. Just once. She knew it anyway—how could she not know it? Yet he wanted to say the words to her. He looked at her chair. A white linen kerchief lay on her desk and he picked it up, detecting her familiar rose scent. He tucked the kerchief beneath his shirt near his heart. He touched Crystal's chair.

If only she hadn't cared about the office of justice of the peace. If only she had been like other women—but then she wouldn't have been the woman he had fallen in love with. He was running out of time. If he didn't go, someone might remember seeing him enter Crystal's office and not come out.

Travis crossed the room quietly. He wore his moccasins and could move without a sound. He wore his Colt revolver with five chambers loaded with cartridges. The revolver was cocked, the hammer on the empty chamber.

Crystal's office opened into her simple courtroom. He strode to the table where she would sit, and he knelt down. Placing his rifle on the floor beside the board he had brought with him, he leaned beneath the table. He picked up the board and jammed it underneath the table, wedging it against the short six-inch boards that formed table skirts below the tabletop. He carefully laid his rifle on the board.

Crystal's legs would be beneath the table, but she would never discover the rifle or see the board wedged there to make a narrow shelf for his weapon.

He stood, looking at her chair and seeing her and her big green eyes.

He clenched both fists. He was going to lose Crystal and Jacob this week, for he, too, would become a fugitive. Even if he tried to settle and start a new life, Crystal would not join him. Her adherence to the law was too rigid. Actions were either right or wrong.

Travis retraced his steps through her office and into the hall. He headed for the sheriff's office, and no one paid any particular attention to him. He was ready for the trial.

Monday, Crystal was up before dawn and dressed with care, tying her hair behind her head. As always, she reached for the black woolen dress that she usually wore to court. Instead, she took the blue woolen. She would be covered with a black robe, so whatever she wore would not show, and the day would be grim enough without wearing more black.

The sky was as stormy as the courthouse with black clouds boiling on the horizon. She was icy, filled with dread. She had loved her job as justice of the peace. It was frontier justice; Cheyenne was only a few thousand people, yet she felt she was helping establish law and order. Now she was going to have to hold the trial for her brother-in-law, for Travis's brother whom he loved. Would this be the complete destruction of a marriage that had become the most wonderful thing in her life?

Brett's trial would be quick. A scaffold stood behind the jail, and she was terrified what Travis might do to help his brother.

She wanted to resign and ride home to the haven of the ranch, where Jacob waited. But if she did, the trial would be delayed, with possibly disastrous consequences for Brett. Besides, even if she resigned and rode home, Travis would stay to protect his brother.

The high wind tossed bits of dried grass and dust into the air. Ignoring calls to her from the crowd, she hurried to the courthouse and stepped inside. The moment she entered her office, Wade Hinckel followed her inside and closed the door behind him. His blue eyes were filled with determination.

"Judge, don't recuse yourself."

"I have to let all concerned know I'm related to him."

"I don't give a damn if you don't. . . . You and Travis will be safer that way. You saw the mob out front. We have to get on with this trial."

"I'm worried about Travis if his brother is found guilty."

"Don't worry. I've already ordered three of my deputies to close in on him. For his own sake, I'm going to lock him up. It isn't legal, but it'll keep him safe."

She closed his eyes as relief made her weak. "Thank you! I'm terrified for his safety. You know he'll be wild to protect his brother."

"We're ready. I won't let him into the courtroom with his gun. And Crystal, when this is over, you're going to have to hide him and get him out of town. Maybe for a long time."

She nodded, her terror increasing because she couldn't imagine them taking Travis prisoner without a dreadful fight. "You know he fought in the war. He was a captain."

Wade's brows drew together as he frowned. "No, I didn't know that. Out here men don't talk much about their pasts. Well, I know he can shoot. But I don't think he'll shoot men he knows who are only trying to hold him. We'll get him locked up behind bars as fast as we can. If he has to hand over his weapons before the trial begins, he won't be able to cause much trouble.''

"He's also a Comanche. I don't know—"

"Oh, hell!"

"What's wrong?" she asked, startled by Wade's frown and exclamation.

"Comanche. The best. Or the worst, depending on how you want to describe them—best damn cavalry there is. They're the best or meanest fighters on the plains. Damn. I may not wait until a verdict to lock him up . . . a Comanche!"

"I wish I had never taken this job!"

"I thought you liked being justice of the peace more than anything else," Wade said, focusing on her.

"No," she answered bluntly, wishing she were home with Jacob and did not have to make the decisions that faced her today.

"I don't want to have to hang a man and I don't want to have to hurt a friend. And Travis is a friend. You be careful, Judge. The only person enjoying himself today is Rufus. He's ready for a fight and looking forward to it. I don't think he has any case, though."

Wade turned and left, and she was alone. Dread filled her. It was almost time to put on her robe and go into the courtroom, yet all she wanted to do was go home. Go home with her handsome, dashing, impetuous husband, who had coolly walked up to her when she'd held a gun on him. She covered her face with her hands, fighting against shedding tears.

On the other side of the building, down the hall, Travis paced Brett's small cell while Rufus had last words with his client. Rufus turned to Travis.

"When we're handed a verdict, if it is *not guilty,* you need to get your brother to hell and gone as fast as you can."

"I've already made plans."

Rufus nodded. "Keep calm, but then I don't need to tell you that. We should go now."

Travis clasped Brett on the shoulder. "You're a tough one,"

he said, marveling at Brett's recovery. "I wasn't sure you'd make it away from our barn that night."

"Don't talk about my being at your place," Brett said quietly. "No one knows. It'd be better if no one ever knows you're my brother."

"I'm not worried."

"Don't tell people, Travis. They don't know you by any name other than Black Eagle. Don't claim kinship."

"Let me worry about that."

"Promise me. Keep it quiet. I'll be happier. You and your family will be safer."

"Until after the trial, I promise."

Brett nodded as a deputy appeared.

"I'll see you in the courtroom," Travis said, clamping his mouth shut grimly and leaving the jail. In the hallway, he glanced at Crystal's office, but it wasn't the time to go declare his love. She wouldn't believe him now.

Wade Hinckel and Jed Larson moved close on either side of him. Wade held out his hand. "Sorry, Travis, but I need your rifle and revolver."

Mildly surprised, Travis handed the rifle over. "I thought the deputies were keeping their arms."

"All of them are except you, since you're kin to the accused."

It was useless to argue, and Travis handed over the revolver from his holster.

"Any knives?"

Travis bent down and removed a knife from his boot. "When do I get them back?"

"When the trial is over. I don't want any weapons in this courthouse except on specific deputies and myself."

Travis nodded and glanced across the hall at Raymond Parnell, who stared at Travis with a cold gaze. Anger burned inside him, but Travis kept his features impassive. Parnell had beaten Brett badly after he had taken him prisoner, and Travis knew

Parnell hated Indians. By now, Parnell had learned that Travis and Brett were brothers.

He turned his back on Parnell and strode into the courtroom, thankful he had the hidden rifle, a revolver beneath his shirt at the small of his back, and a knife in his other boot. He hated to break Wade Hinckel's trust, but he had no choice if he were to save Brett.

Elgin Thomas served as bailiff and announced court was in session, Judge Spencer presiding. All rose to their feet as she entered, and her gaze went straight to Travis, who sat directly behind his brother on the front row. Travis's dark eyes cut into her sharply. His expression was impassive, but she could feel his anger in waves as strong as gusting winds. It was an effort to tear her gaze from his.

Between her table and the rows of benches filled with spectators were two smaller tables, one for the prosecution, the other for the defense. A chair was beside her table where witnesses could sit to give their testimony.

The benches were filled with spectators and reporters. Rufus Milligan always drew a crowd. Armed deputies guarded the doors and were posted throughout the courtroom. She was thankful Wade had not allowed any other weapons into the building.

When she entered the room, Brett rose to his feet and stood, and she was astounded by his swift recovery. The gunshot in his side alone should have kept him flat. The family resemblance showed clearly, even though Brett had braided his hair and it hung down his back in a long pigtail while Travis had his black hair caught behind his head with a strip of rawhide.

And again, she realized how tough the Black Eagles were. Brett looked far better. The swelling had gone down in his face, although he was still covered with dark bruises and angry cuts and welts. He wore a fresh white shirt, a black coat and tie, and black pants which she recognized as Travis's.

Brett stood beside Rufus, who looked handsome in a fancy white suit. How he kept it white in Cheyenne, she couldn't imagine. His thick red hair was combed smoothly down. His blue eyes sparkled with eagerness. He looked confident and successful, whereas Clarence Hoyt made no such appearance. He merely looked angry and tired. Usually, Clarence presented a winning case, but when he was up against Rufus, he rarely did well. This time, however, the odds lay with Clarence.

"Be seated," the bailiff instructed as he called the court to order.

"Before we begin," she said, once again looking at Travis and hurting, "I want to go on record to disclose my relationship to the defendant, Brett Dancer." In the next few minutes, she was going to destroy both Travis and Jacob with Cheyenne society, just when Travis had begun to win more of them over. But to have a fair trial, she had to reveal her relationship, even though it meant letting the town know Travis's relationship to Brett.

Travis focused on her, his dark eyes like daggers going into her heart. She took a deep breath. "If anyone so desires, I will recuse myself. But due to the lack of a district judge in the Territory at present and the delay it will cause if I do not sit as judge, I will preside . . . but only if all parties agree. Here are my connections with the parties of the case: the defendant, Brett Dancer, is related to me by marriage. He is my brother-in-law and the brother of my husband, Travis Black Eagle."

A stir arose in the courtroom, and she banged her gavel for order.

"Judge," Clarence said, rising to his feet, "the prosecution has no desire for you to remove yourself from this case. We waive any objection to your presiding in this instance."

"Thank you, Mr. Hoyt." Rufus rose and she gave him her attention, expecting a welcome opposition. "Mr. Milligan."

"The defense likewise waives any objection, Judge Spencer."

Surprised, she stared at him. She had been certain Rufus

would demand another judge. "Would the attorneys please approach the bench?"

Both men came forward and she stared at Rufus. "Mr. Milligan, are you certain you want me as judge?"

"Yes, Your Honor." Rufus gazed blandly at her.

"Do you think that's wise for your client?"

"I think so," he whispered firmly. "And my client agrees. We think you will be fair."

"I am more than satisfied to have you, Judge Spencer," Clarence said.

"And so am I," Rufus reaffirmed.

"All right. You had your chance." She watched them walk back to their seats and she looked at Travis, whose stormy countenance was fearsome. She remembered the day she had heard Andrew's case and how terrified she had been then of Travis. He was no less intimidating today.

She banged her gavel. "We shall have the arraignment." She held the paper in front of her reading the legal charge of murder. "The defendant, Brett Dancer, is hereby arraigned on the charges of wilful and premeditated murder, this crime being committed against the peace and dignity of the Territory of Wyoming." She looked up. "How does the defendant plead? Guilty or not guilty?"

His dark eyes met her with a straightforward, steady gaze that looked honest, but she knew how treacherous men could be in the courtroom when they were on the wrong side of the law. And Brett was an outlaw. An outlaw who was destroying her marriage as surely as he must have destroyed a life.

"Not guilty," he replied in a strong, clear voice above the angry grumble in the courtroom. She banged her gavel.

"Is the prosecution ready to proceed? Can you present sufficient evidence to show that the defendant should be bound over for trial?

"Yes, Your Honor."

As Clarence called his first witness, she was aware of Travis's steady gaze on her. It was disconcerting, yet she was doing the job she was sworn to do.

The first witness was Slim Tipton, who glared at her before he testified. His brown shirt stretched tightly across his beefy shoulders. The shirt was as stained as ever, and Crystal wondered whether the man ever bathed or washed his clothes.

He was sworn in and Clarence asked Slim to recount what had happened. Slim told of hearing a gunshot and riding with his employer, Whit Odell, and another employee, Virgil Shank, to investigate. They had found outlaw Brett Dancer bending over the body of Abner Kendrick, who was dead from a gunshot wound.

Crystal listened to the damning eyewitness testimony of Slim, Virgil Shank, and Whit Odell. She knew that Travis did not believe them, but they had sworn under oath to tell the truth. However, as far as she knew, of the three men, Whit Odell was the only truly law-abiding citizen.

There was no question that the testimonies of the witnesses were enough to hold Brett for trial. "It is the court's ruling that the defendant should stand trial for the murder of Abner Kendrick," Crystal declared, only too aware of Travis's proximity to her.

"The court is required to provide sufficient time for both the defense and the prosecution to prepare their cases. However, both sides have expressed their willingness to waive the normal interval between arraignment and trial in the interest of justice. Is that correct, Mr. Hoyt?"

"Yes, Your Honor."

"And Mr. Milligan? For the record, do you agree to proceed directly to trial at this time?"

"Yes, Your Honor."

"Then we will proceed with jury selection."

"Your Honor," Rufus said, coming to his feet. "The defense at this time wishes to waive our right to a trial by jury. We'd like to request that the defendant, Brett Dancer, be judged by Your Honor."

Stunned, she stared at him. Then her gaze slid to Travis, whose eyes were fiery, a muscle clenching in his jaw, and she knew he did not agree with Rufus's request.

"We will have a ten-minute recess. I want to see the attorneys in my office." She banged her gavel and left the room, but her back tingled and she was conscious of Travis watching her every step of the way.

Once Clarence and Rufus had entered her office, she banged the door shut.

"Rufus, you've lost your mind to give up a trial by a jury! I don't want to make this decision. The man is my relative!"

"All of us know you will be fair and impartial. A jury of local men will be no such thing. You know many of them hate redskins. They have a violent dislike for any man with Indian blood, even if he is completely law-abiding. Ask your husband, if you don't believe me."

He spoke only the truth, but she was horrified by the prospect of rendering judgment on Brett.

"I can't do this. I've never tried a murder case. As justice of the peace, I shouldn't have to do this."

"But these are desperate times in a desperate place, so you will and you'll do a fine job. Don't you agree, Clarence?"

"As a matter of fact, for what is probably the only time in this trial, I do agree with you, Rufus," Clarence replied, studying Crystal. "Your Honor, all parties are satisfied with your fairness. I understand your great reluctance to sentence your brother-in-law to hang; but if we don't get on with this, that mob is likely to storm the courthouse. A lot of innocent men are likely to get hurt, and Brett Dancer will be lynched and hanged anyway."

"If that weren't the case, I would resign right now," she said fervently. To her own surprise, she meant it. This job that used to be her whole life and had been so thrilling and challenging was now a block of granite around her neck. She no longer loved being the justice of the peace. She wanted a home with Jacob and Travis; but because of this job, she would never have that home with them as once she had. She would never win the love of the man who had completely taken her heart.

Hot tears stung her eyes, and she struggled for control. It was going to be difficult to be fair and she didn't want this decision to be hers alone. "I think you're making a mistake. If I free him, they'll want to hang me."

"I don't think so," Rufus replied easily. "Everyone knows you are hard on outlaws and everyone knows you are fair. And Wade will protect you if I get my client off." He leaned closer. "You know damn well your husband will protect you."

"I don't know that anyone can protect a person from a mob."

"This is difficult for you, Judge," Clarence said, "but we all know you'll be fair."

Both men had to have seen her tears, and both looked satisfied. She wanted to shake her fist at them, especially when one look at Clarence's pleased countenance showed he expected to win this case swiftly and with little effort.

"Very well. We'll return to the courtroom."

Once again, Crystal declared court in session, and Rufus rose to his feet.

"Your Honor, I would like to request that any witness who will testify will remain out of the courtroom except for his testimony."

"Any objection, Mr. Hoyt?"

"No, Your Honor."

She nodded. "Witnesses are excused until called. Bailiff will show them where to wait. Deputy Parnell, you will remain with the witnesses."

They filed out of the room. When Elgin Thomas reappeared, Crystal started the proceedings, inviting Clarence to present his argument and tell what his evidence would show. Next Rufus gave his opening statement, which emphasized the lack of actual eyewitnesses to the murder. The only evidence came from those who had come upon the scene after the fact.

Clarence called the prosecution's first witness, Whit Odell, and Crystal studied the tall, gaunt man with weathered skin who was ushered into the courtroom from the waiting room. He ambled to the front and was sworn in. She listened to his monotone testimony. He had heard a gunshot and found Kendrick dead, Brett Dancer robbing him.

At midday, Crystal adjourned for lunch and hurried to her office, having her meal sent in because she wanted time alone. Whit Odell's testimony had been damning. He had described finding Kendrick sprawled on his back, shot through the heart, with Brett bending over him, going through his pockets.

When the trial commenced again, Rufus called Whit Odell back to cross-examine him.

"When you rode up, was the defendant holding a revolver?"

"Yes, he was."

"Earlier, Mr. Odell, you said he was not holding a revolver because his hands were filled with the deceased's possessions."

"I guess he wasn't holding a revolver."

"You *guess?* Is it just a guess?"

"I don't remember if I said that earlier," Odell replied, rubbing the back of his neck and frowning.

"Perhaps you don't remember now."

"Objection," Clarence said, rising slowly.

"Overruled."

"Was the defendant holding a revolver when you rode up?"

"No, he was not."

"Tell us again where the body was when you reached the scene."

"Kendrick was sprawled on his back, shot through the heart. His arms were flung out."

"Was he armed?"

"Of course."

"And he hadn't drawn his revolver to try to protect himself?"

In the pause that followed, Whit Odell's gaze shifted beyond Rufus. "I don't know."

"I would think it would be only natural for any man who

is armed and suddenly faces a man who draws a revolver to draw his own weapon. Wouldn't you think so?''

"Maybe he did have his sidearm in hand," Odell replied, shifting in his seat. "It all happened so fast, I don't remember."

"Mr. Odell, either he did or he didn't. Which is it?"

"He did, now that I think about it."

"Did you hear two shots?"

"No, just one."

"So, Kendrick held a revolver that he did not fire to protect himself."

"He probably didn't have time."

"No more questions," Rufus said, returning to his seat.

Clarence rose to his feet and called Slim Tipton to the witness stand. A deputy escorted Slim into the room. He moved to the chair beside Crystal's desk and was sworn in.

He sat down, facing the courtroom. His testimony backed up Whit's until Rufus began to question him along the same lines he had quizzed Odell.

"And when the three of you rode up and found the man who is accused of shooting and killing Abner Kendrick, did he threaten you?"

"No," Slim answered, frowning and sounding uncertain.

"If he had just killed a man, he had nothing to lose. Why would he simply turn himself over to the three of you?"

Slim looked puzzled. "We outnumbered him. We'd drawn on him."

"You rode up with guns in your hands?"

"Yes. We'd heard a gunshot."

"Was the defendant armed?"

"Who?"

"The defendant—the accused, Brett Dancer."

"Black Eagle? Yeah, he had a gun."

"Did he drop it?"

"Yeah, when we told him to."

"No more questions, Your Honor."

Slim looked worried, and no wonder. Rufus had asked the

same questions of Whit Odell and Whit had first said Brett was
not holding a gun, then yes, he was, and then no, he was not.
The two men were not telling the same story. Did that mean
all three were lying? She glanced at Brett, who was as stone-
faced as Travis.

The next witness, Deputy Raymond Parnell, related how
Brett had fought him when he'd tried to arrest him.

"And what other charges have been brought against Brett
Dancer?" Clarence asked.

Rufus was on his feet at once. "Objection, Your Honor. This
trial is about a murder. Anything else is irrelevant."

"Sustained."

Clarence interrogated Parnell about his difficulties appre-
hending the defendant, and then he sat down. Rufus had no
questions.

It was far enough into the afternoon that Crystal adjourned
court for the day. Tomorrow, they might well have sufficient
time for the remaining witnesses, any cross-examination, and
the summations. And that was what Wade Hinckel had hoped
for. The sooner this trial was over, the happier he would be.

Before she left the courtroom, she caught a glimpse of Travis.
He was staring at her, his dark eyes stormy, and she could still
feel his coiled anger.

Tomorrow or, at the latest, the next day would mark the end
of the trial . . . and the end of her marriage as well. Now he
couldn't legally annul it, and she doubted he would try to take
her away from Jacob or Jacob from her. Travis would put Jacob
above all else, before his own feelings, and she was thankful
for that. She longed to be home with Jacob, to hear his laughter.
And she ached for his father, wanting Travis more than she
would have dreamed possible. Too clearly she could remember
the nights in his arms, his ready laughter, his loving.

With a groan, she entered her chambers and shed the robe
of office, pulling on her bonnet swiftly. Elgin Thomas escorted
her to the hotel. Ignoring cries to hang Brett Dancer, she hurried
across the street.

"Hang the redskin!"

"Hang the Injun, Judge!"

"Squaw woman, don't turn him free!"

She did not look around, but rushed headlong for the hotel, feeling as if she had turned to ice. Thankful to reach her room, she closed and locked the door.

Ten minutes later, she heard a knock and opened it to face Travis.

He swept past her, bringing cool air as if he had rushed upstairs from the outside. Dressed all in black, he strode across the room, tossed his hat on a chair, and turned to face her. The simple bed stood behind him, reminding her of the bed they had shared at home, and she wished they could be whisked back to that time and place.

She felt the tension; she was torn between the intimidation of his anger and a deep longing to throw herself into his strong arms and to hold him against the pain that was coming.

"Crystal, my brother is innocent."

"You heard the testimony today. The witnesses saw him robbing Abner Kendrick's body," she said patiently, although exasperated that Travis could be so blind to his brother's wrongful deeds. He was going to be hurt; she prayed it would not be a physical hurt. She was scared of what he would do when Brett was found guilty. And he was going to hate her. If he ended their marriage and took Jacob from her, could she survive?

"The witnesses' stories didn't agree. You heard them as clearly as I did. Whit said one thing and Slim said another. How can you believe either one?"

"A trial is a search for the truth. I have to believe one side or another. Whit Odell is a reputable citizen, and he's never been in trouble with the law."

"Not that's known around these parts, but he's fought plenty with Abner Kendrick. They have been at each other's throats for the past three years since they both settled here. And a lot of people knew about their fights. They have shot at each other before."

"I have to go with the evidence presented in court. That Whit Odell and Abner Kendrick didn't like each other does not prove your brother innocent. It's beside the point. If the men have argued and shot at each other, perhaps Rufus will bring it out, but it has little bearing on this case."

The tension between them had not decreased, and she wished he could think clearly and look at the case objectively. Arguing did not improve their situation, and tomorrow she would deliver the final blow to their relationship.

"Crystal, my brother is innocent. Give him the benefit of the doubt that the law requires."

"I am!" she snapped.

"No, you're not. You judged and condemned him before he ever walked into your courtroom."

"I'm listening to the case as it's presented," she said, her voice tight with anger, her fists clenched as tightly as his.

"Dammit, give Brett a chance! Just because a man will rob does not mean he'll murder."

"Travis, he crossed the line between right and wrong long ago."

He glowered at her, his jaw tight. "I'll not let him hang!"

Stunned, she stared at him. "Don't threaten me," she warned. "I could have you arrested right now to prevent you from interfering with justice!"

"*Justice!*" he spat. "You're not giving him justice."

"You'll be taking the law into your own hands if you try to save him." She couldn't resist crossing to him. She gripped his arms; and the moment she touched him and felt his warmth, she trembled, thinking only of Travis and how she longed for his love and their marriage. His dark eyes were as uncompromising as black stones, and she could feel the tension in his hard muscles.

"Don't try to rescue Brett!" she pleaded, holding his arms. "Please, don't. Think of Jacob. Your son's future will be at stake."

At her touch Travis inhaled. Her scent enveloped him; her

touch was devastating, and her big green eyes seared him. His
pulse drummed, and he could not keep from reaching for her.
He pulled her into his arms and his mouth came down hard on
her soft lips. He ached to take her to bed, to love her until she
was quivering, yielding in passion. And he wished he could
make her yield in her judgment.

I love you. The words welled up inside him, but he held
them back. If he spoke of love now, she wouldn't believe him.
She would accuse him of using her to get Brett free.

Crystal clung to him, feeling his hard, solid strength against
her. Her heart pounded violently, in unison with his. She loved
him completely; no matter what came between them, she would
love him always. Tears spilled down her cheeks, but she didn't
care. For this one moment in time, she wanted to hold him, to
return his wild kisses, to let her love pour over him. Even if
it could not last. Before the week was up, her marriage would
be over.

She pushed against his chest and pulled away, her heart still
pounding. She could barely get her breath and she wanted to
curl right back into his arms.

"This won't solve anything," she said harshly.

"Give Brett the benefit of the doubt," Travis implored. His
voice was husky, filled with anger and pain.

"He's an outlaw. And you will be to if you try to help him
escape."

"A man should have a chance and not be hanged by someone
else's lies."

"Whit Odell is as much a law-abiding citizen as you and I
are."

"Now, perhaps. You have no idea about his past."

"A man's past is as much his present as it is his past."

"Not on the frontier. If you sentence Brett to hang, I'm
taking him out of here."

"Then you'll throw away everything you've worked to
achieve. You'll throw away your decent life, Jacob's future,

the ranch, your stable. Don't do it, Travis. Don't cross that line.''

"Crystal, I'm more a wanted man than Brett," he said in a cold, flat voice. "I'm John Dancer Black Eagle. Black Eagle is my Comanche name. John Dancer is the name my mother gave me when we returned to civilization. And I'm wanted for murder in Texas.''

Twenty-two

She stared at him, unbelieving. Her head spun, and she was unable to comprehend his words. "You . . . wanted for murder? You killed a man?"

"Yes, I did," Travis replied. "He raped my mother and he beat her. I heard her screaming. As I fought with him, he drew a revolver and shot at me. I shot back. I was the better shot."

"He shot at you. That's self-defense."

"But no one would have believed me. We lived in a small town beside a fort and Indians were despised. Brett and I fled."

"Why Brett? How was he involved?"

"He was just there. That's one reason I know he wouldn't lie to me. My brother knows my past. My mother told us both to go because they would hang him, too, if he stayed behind. So we fled and joined the Confederacy. By the end of the war, Brett had grown wild. He had a gang of men who rode with him; they had robbed during the war. . . . War can cover a multitude of sins. I didn't want that life. I couldn't go back to Texas, so I got as far away from there as I could. I took the name Travis Black Eagle and settled here."

Astounded by his story, she had nothing to say. He continued fervently, beseeching her.

"Crystal, my life in Wyoming gave me a second chance. Brett is ready to lead an honest life and he did not murder Kendrick. Give him that same second chance at life I had. He's telling the truth."

She barely heard his request, her mind still reeling from his revelation. "You're wanted for murder."

His face became glacial. He withdrew from her, his jaw clamping shut. "Yes, I am."

"And you trusted me enough to tell me . . . knowing how I feel about the law."

"Yes," he answered grimly. "I've always trusted you."

"Is there a price on your head?" she asked.

"Yes," he admitted in a flat, harsh tone. "John Dancer is a wanted man."

"You know I can turn you in."

"Yes, I do," he replied solemnly.

"That's why you've never gone home."

"I would've brought trouble to my people. The price on my head is far bigger than that on Brett. I would have had to stand trial for murder." Travis studied her as the seconds passed. "You think about what's right, Crystal," Travis said, picking up his hat and placing it on his head. "Just do what's right and stop judging Brett beforehand."

As soon as he closed the door behind him, she collapsed, weak-kneed. Travis had murdered a man and fled. And gotten a second chance.

She sat in stunned immobility for the next hour and then, decisively, she reached for her cloak. She hurried back to the sheriff's office and found him working at his desk, papers littered around him. His tan shirt was rumpled, stained with tobacco and coffee, and she could see the strain of the murder was wearing on him. He rubbed the thick brown stubble that covered his jaw.

"What can I do for you, Judge?"

"I want to talk to the prisoner."

"It's against regulations."

"What isn't in this trial?" she snapped. "We're rushing through it so a mob won't hang him. His sister-in-law is the judge."

"All right. I'll take you back to his cell," Wade said tiredly, keys jingling in his hand. "I hope the whole damn thing winds up tomorrow." His blue eyes had smudges beneath them, and she'd never seen him so down.

When Brett saw her, his brows arched and a charming smile broke forth like sunshine through the clouds. "Well, darlin' sister!" he exclaimed and came to his feet as if he were greeting her in his living quarters and there was no terrible wound in his side.

She stepped inside the cell. Brett wore the white linen shirt he had worn in court and the black pants. He smiled, a dimple showing in his cheek, and she waited while Wade locked the door behind her and left them alone. Of everyone involved in the trial, Brett looked the least concerned. Each time she saw him, he looked better and stronger and more self-assured.

"Have a seat," Brett said with a flourish of his arm. "To what do I owe the honor of this visit?"

"You're not on trial in here and what you say to me now wouldn't matter in a courtroom. I want an honest answer from you. Did you kill Abner Kendrick?"

His smile vanished, and a silence stretched between them. "Would you believe me?"

"I want to hear your side," she said simply.

"No, I did not kill Kendrick," Brett replied, holding up his right hand. "I swear I did not."

"What happened?"

"I worked for him. I was alone with him when Whit Odell, Virgil Shank, and Slim Tipton appeared. Whit and Abner argued. Slim pulled out his revolver and shot and killed Kendrick. They have their story, but what I'm telling you is the way it really happened."

''What did Whit and Abner argue about?''

''Water rights. Abner's creek crosses Odell's land. Kendrick had dammed it up and cut off Odell's water.''

''Did you tell Rufus all this?''

''Yes, he knows it. Rufus is not through presenting my case.''

''You swear you're telling me the truth?''

''I swear.''

''You've robbed people?''

''Banks and trains. I've robbed a lot and for a long time.'' He took her hand in his big, callused hands. She looked down at dark-skin and strong hands that held hers so gently. ''Judge, I'm sorry to have brought all this trouble to Travis and to have caused a rift between the two of you.''

Brett pulled her to him, his arms holding her loosely. She stood stiffly in his arms, despite the threat of tears. He was the wrong man, a man who was almost a stranger, and she could find no solace in his embrace. She wanted Travis's arms around her. She wiped her eyes and stepped away.

''Sorry. I just wanted to hear you say what happened.''

''I didn't kill him. I've done a lot of things that were wrong, but I didn't do this. I shouldn't have stopped to see Travis, but we used to be close. . . . I didn't want to bring trouble to him.''

''Why didn't you work for Travis?'' she asked, curious.

''He knows me. He knows my past. He's honest and leading a decent life. I didn't want to upset his life.''

''He told me about Texas.''

Brett nodded. ''After the war he tried to get me to start a new life, but I was wild and young and not ready to settle. I wouldn't listen. . . . I should have.''

She looked into his dark eyes, wondering if he were telling the truth, almost convinced that he was. ''I'd better get back.''

She heard voices and Wade appeared with Travis at his side. His black eyes tore at her heart, and a tremor shook her. She wanted to reach out and grasp him, to hold him again, but his look was enough to keep her away from him. He looked like a man holding a tight check on rage.

Wade Hinckel unlocked the door and she stepped out. Without a word Travis walked into the cell. She fled, tears glistening in her eyes. She rarely cried, but today she couldn't stop.

Travis was a wanted man. A man who had put that past behind him, started over, and made a new life. He had murdered a man, but it had been in self-defense. Perhaps the distinction between right and wrong was not as clear-cut as she had thought, but she still believed in justice and law. And she was beginning to believe Brett.

Blindly, she rushed back to the hotel. Travis had killed. Yet he was a good person. And even though he had killed in self-defense, he was wanted by the law. He had started his life over and it was good and he was law-abiding.

She, too, had started over by coming to Cheyenne. Her marriage to Travis had given her a second chance at life.

She shut herself into her room and buried her face in her hands. She had been given a second chance. Travis had made a second chance for himself. All he asked was the same opportunity for his brother.

Could Brett have killed Kendrick? Three people said he did. Whit Odell, whom she knew nothing about, and Slim Tipton and Virgil Shanks, who couldn't be trusted from one hour to the next.

She rubbed her head and moved restlessly around the room. If the case were damming and she condemned Brett to hang, would Travis risk his life to save his brother? Of course, he would.

An onslaught of rain came in the night. Lightning streaked the sky, and thunder boomed ominously. Impervious to the weather, Crystal felt numbed by the storm of circumstances. She had been so sure that Brett was lying, but now every truth she'd always relied on lay in question. Travis believed in his brother's innocence, so did Turtle River; but in her experience, any man facing the gallows would try to save himself. Still, the witnesses' stories did not match.

She lay on the bed and stared into the darkness, picturing Travis and nothing more.

In the quiet dawn Travis crossed the street. The sun's pink rays shot up across the eastern horizon. The air was clear and fresh after the rain and small puddles of water still stood in the street. Dressed in black, Travis strode into the jail to see Brett.

In the courtroom, he chose a bench in front where he could face Crystal. And where he could get to his rifle quickly. His revolver remained in place inside his coat at the small of his back. Turtle River waited with horses. Travis had the fastest horses, his bay and one of the blacks, tied in back of the courthouse. But he felt as if his heart would be torn from his body within the next few hours. He loved Crystal. He loved Jacob. He clenched his fists and wondered whether Crystal would feel a compunction to turn him in for the murder in Texas.

People began to file inside, and then it was time for court to convene. As the bailiff urged all to rise, Crystal entered.

The proceedings continued, and after lunch, Brett finally took the stand to tell his story. Aware that Travis's gaze constantly rested on her, Crystal listened intently to Brett's testimony. He caused such a stir when he said Slim had shot Kendrick that she had to have several men removed from the courtroom.

Rufus called three more witnesses: a man who worked for Whit Odell and two who had worked for Kendrick. All three testified that Odell and Kendrick had fought bitterly over water rights and that Odell had threatened Kendrick before and shot at him on two different occasions.

Finally, the lawyers gave their summations.

"Judge, we have three witnesses who testified to seeing the accused, Brett Dancer, robbing the body of Abner Kendrick only minutes after the three men heard a shot fired. They might as well have been upon the scene the entire time. Their testimony is conclusive. Other witnesses who worked for Abner Kendrick testified to leaving him only a short time earlier, leaving him alone with the accused, Brett Dancer. All these witnesses heard the fatal shot. Whit Odell, Slim Tipton, and Virgil Shank were the closest and got to the scene within minutes and found the accused, Brett Dancer, holding belongings of the deceased and standing over the body. He was the only man present, the *only* man with the opportunity and the means to kill Abner Kendrick. His motive was robbery. We have the word of three *sworn* witnesses. The prosecution believes the evidence shows conclusively that the accused is guilty of murder. I rest my case.''

Rufus had his turn. He paced the courtroom, beginning in a quiet voice. ''Judge, the three witnesses were actually not present at the time of the shooting. It is a matter of their word against the word of my client. Yet, let us look at their testimony. Mr. Odell contradicted himself, saying the defendant was not holding his revolver and then saying that, yes, he was holding his revolver and finally saying, no, he was not holding his revolver. He concluded that the defendant was not holding his revolver,'' Rufus repeated, *''contradicting the testimony* of the next so-called witness, Slim Tipton, who said my client was armed.

''Judge, this is not the only contradiction and inconsistency. The testimony of one witness had the deceased lying facedown while other testimony had him on his back. My client claims one of these witnesses is actually the man who fired the fatal shot.'' Rufus looked at his audience and his voice rose in volume.

''While that man is not on trial here—only my client is on trial—the court has to determine who is telling the truth. These so-called witnesses for the prosecution do not have the same story. It isn't small details that are getting twisted, but major elements that a man should remember in dire circumstances that end in murder.''

Rufus faced the judge, his voice ringing. "My client is telling the truth! He is an innocent man and his accusers do not have matching facts, a particular the court cannot overlook. The testimony does not make sense. My client was with two hands who worked for Abner Kendrick. When Abner Kendrick sent those men away, Kendrick was left with my client, Mr. Dancer. It would be senseless to pull a gun and kill his employer then when witnesses could easily place my client and Abner Kendrick together. My client would have to have known the shot could be heard for miles. What did he have to gain? Not as much as if he waited for his week's pay! If he intended robbery, he would have taken advantage of safer, more lucrative opportunities. He had been working there several days. And his story is consistent," Rufus exclaimed, gesturing accusingly at Slim Tipton. His smooth voice had escalated to a shout. "Whereas the so-called witnesses have not had the same story any two times!" He surveyed the courtroom audience, his hands gripping the railing between observers and participants.

"It is general knowledge that bitter feeling existed between Abner Kendrick and Whit Odell and between those men and their hired help. My client, however, was new to this area and harbored no such animosity. He would have had nothing but good feelings for the man who employed him."

Rufus turned to the judge. "Your Honor, we are relying on the testimony of men who have been known to lie in this very courtroom, testimony that is not consistent and therefore suggests fabrication and lies. Do not sentence an innocent man so that other men may escape punishment. My client is innocent. The crime as related by these so-called witnesses is not logical, and my client truly had no motive. It would have been a poor time for robbery.

"This man, Brett Dancer is innocent!" Rufus shouted. "Listen to the truth." He paused, his gaze moving from Crystal to the courtroom. "The defense rests."

Clarence gave a brief rebuttal, reminding the judge that

although the witnesses to the murder might have forgotten a few facts, their stories were basically the same.

Then it was up to Crystal.

She adjourned the court for an hour and went to her office, where—under guard—she would not be disturbed. She paced the room, re-examining the faulty testimony. None of it matched completely, and at least two of the witnesses were unreliable.

She gazed out the long, narrow window and reached a decision, questioning whether she was being guided by her heart or her head. She would give Brett Dancer his second chance. She would set him free, even though she might be placing her own life in danger. She squared her shoulders and returned to the courtroom.

Travis stared at her coolly. He looked at ease. A glance at him and no one would think he was set to spring into violent action, but she had no doubts. Wade Hinckel had placed himself across the aisle from Travis. Jed Larson sat beside him.

She banged her gavel for quiet and looked at the serious faces of her all-male audience. "I have heard the evidence presented and noted that the witnesses did not always agree. The parties in question had fought over water rights. It is the testimony of one man against three, but the three witnesses have not told convincing stories."

She saw the slightest change in Travis. His chin raised, and he stared even more intently at her. And she heard the grumble that ran around the courtroom.

"Therefore, I hereby declare Brett Dancer *not guilty* of the murder of Abner Kendrick!"

Pandemonium broke loose. Men shouted and rushed forward. Travis sprang to action, knocking down Jed Larson and slugging Wade Hinckel. Travis spun and lunged for his rifle, firing it to stop the angry surge of a mob toward Brett. Brett already had one foot out a window and his revolver drawn.

Travis stepped to one side of the desk, his rifle aimed at the crowd, while Sheriff Hinckel regained his feet and yelled for everyone to keep calm. The sheriff raised his rifle, and two deputies moved forward, guns drawn.

Travis grabbed Crystal around the waist and yanked her with him. He shoved her to Brett, who lifted her out the window, took her hand, and yelled, "Run!"

Brett fired his revolver into the air and a crowd outside, moved back. Firing over the crowd again, Travis rushed behind Brett and Crystal as they dashed around the courthouse. A shot shattered a window beside Travis while the mob shouted and surged behind him.

Brett mounted the black. Travis swung Crystal up on his bay, holding her close while men spilled around the corner. Travis and Brett both fired into the air, and the crowd stopped. A shot lifted Brett's hat from him head and sent it sailing into the dust.

"Get out of here!" Wade Hinckel yelled, stepping in front of the mob and waving his rifle at them.

"I resign!" Crystal cried, hoping the sheriff heard her.

Then all words were lost as Travis and Brett urged the horses to a gallop and raced out of town. She couldn't talk because of the wind tearing at them and the pounding of hooves. After they had ridden out of town, Crystal glanced behind her. No one was riding after them, so perhaps Wade Hinckel and his deputies had stopped the mob.

While she clung to Travis, they galloped away from Cheyenne. The wind tore at her, but she hardly noticed. The trial was over. She was with Travis, his strong arms around her.

When he slowed, she raised her head. Turtle River waited ahead with three more horses. Travis motioned to him, and Turtle River fell in with them, leading the horses. They continued at a gallop until they were farther from Cheyenne, and then the men slowed the lathered horses. When they reached a creek, Travis dismounted and lifted her down, his dark eyes filled with a warmth she hadn't seen since the night she'd discovered Brett.

"Thank you," he said.

Her heart drummed. "They'll think I found him not guilty because I'm your wife."

"You believed Brett?"

"Yes, I did. If he's lying, he fooled me. It's done now, forevermore."

"I wasn't lying, Crystal," Brett said solemnly, moving close to her and giving her a brief, light hug. "Thank you. I'll never rob again. I'm heading for Idaho and I'll buy some land and some cows and try to do something good to make up for all I've taken from people." He gazed at Travis. "Thank you, brother. I didn't mean to bring so much trouble to you."

"Just make a good life, Brett, and it'll have been worth all the trouble," Travis said, hugging Brett.

"I will. I should've listened to you long ago."

"When you get settled, let us know where you are. You're a free man in Wyoming."

"Brett Dancer doesn't exist any longer. I'll take the Black Eagle name like you."

"Keep your first name. It's easier. You'll remember to answer people," Travis advised, a hint of mirth stealing into his eyes.

"From this moment on, I'm Brett Black Eagle. I'll send word when I get settled, and you folks are to come visit. I'm ready to enjoy my relatives. I want to know my little nephew."

"You be careful," Travis said. The two men stared at each other in silent communication, and then they clapped each other on the back.

Mounting his horse, Brett turned to say goodbye to Turtle River, but the Cheyenne insisted on riding with Brett until nightfall.

Beneath sunshine and a blue sky, Crystal looked up at her tall, handsome husband and her heart drummed. His midnight eyes were filled with warmth and love. He pulled her into his strong arms and his head lowered to kiss her hard and long.

She clung to him, her heart pounding with joy. How right

it was to be in his arms! She hoped nothing again ever came
between them. She needed Travis and his strength; she wanted
his love and attention. And she adored Jacob. Life without the
two would be no life.

His kiss deepened and his hand stroked her until the urgency
became desperation. His hands slipped over her breasts and
desire flashed white-hot within her. She had dreamed of him,
wanted him, needed him for so long. And been so terrified she
was losing him forever.

He raised his head to look at her and she saw the raw desire
in the black depths of his eyes.

"My woman. I can't survive without you," he said in a
voice that was merely a rasp. He shook and his reactions melted
every bone in her body. He yanked off the black robe.

"There's one thing this is good for," he said, spreading it
on the ground. He tossed away hairpins as he kissed her. She
felt the tugs on her scalp, knew when her hair fell around her
shoulders.

Spring winds danced around them, but Crystal was oblivious
to anything except her husband. He peeled away her dress and
tossed aside his shirt. As he removed his shirt, a white cloth
drifted to the ground. Crystal bent down to pick it up and
looked at him, her brows arching.

"You have my handkerchief."

"You left it on your desk. It was a part of you that I could
keep close to my heart," he replied solemnly.

"Travis," she whispered, shaken by the depth of his feeling.
"My handkerchief!" She slid her hands over him while he
continued to undress, taking off his cotton pants, removing all
his clothing, and pulling her down.

He stretched on the robe and pulled her over him, settling
her on his hard shaft. She gasped and cried out, her eyes closed
tightly while sensation carried her away.

She moved, feeling his hands on her breasts, stroking her.
Then his fingers moved between her thighs and the wild building
intensified. She heard him cry her name while she cried his in

return. She moved with him, a timeless, ageless rhythm that bonded them, body and soul.

"My love!" she cried.

His hands clutched her hips and she felt the burst of release as his hot seed spilled into her. She was carried over the brink, ecstasy tearing her apart until she fell across his chest and both of them gasped for breath.

She came down to earth, to the reality of winds blowing over them, of Travis's warm, gentle hands stroking her back and bottom. He kissed her temple, lifted her heavy hair away so he could see her face.

"This is wanton," she gasped. "Anyone could come along."

Travis held her face with his hand, his eyes revealing such need that it took her breath away. "I was afraid I would lose you," he whispered, and then he kissed her hard. He rolled her over so he was on top of her while he continued to kiss her.

"I love you, woman. More than I ever dreamed it was possible to love a woman, I love you."

She thought she would melt with bliss. "I've waited my whole life for this. Oh, Travis, I'm so blessed! I love you!"

He leaned down to kiss her and in minutes he was aroused again, wanting her with a need that ran deep and sure and would last a lifetime.

In rapture, she clung to his strong shoulders, her hips arching to meet his maleness, wanting completion, wanting the union that bound them intimately, so thankful to have her marriage mended and hear his declaration of love.

She never knew how long they were there on the plains, loving wildly, not caring about the world, but finally, she pushed him away and stood, knowing they must go home.

"Zachary will be wondering what happened. If a mob had come after us in anger, they would have appeared by now. And caught us."

Travis grinned as he watched her dress. He drew on his boots and then picked up the black robe. "That's the best damn use for this thing.'' He squinted his eyes at her. ''Did I hear you yell something back there at the courthouse about resigning?''

''Yes, you did,'' she answered. ''I no longer find the job challenging and enthralling.''

He framed her face with his hands and gazed into her eyes in a thorough scrutiny. ''You're certain you want to give up the appointment?''

''I'm very certain. I'll have to stay until the governor finds someone—''

''I suspect he will find someone damned fast,'' Travis drawled. ''You won't be safe in town for a while.''

''I think I will, but there's no need to argue the point. I would rather stay on the ranch anyway.''

''I want to hear you say that again. Every morning. I want you on the ranch, Crystal. I want you home. I don't want to worry that someone is going to be angry with you over a decision and take out their anger on you.''

''We need to send word again to town, to both Wade Hinckel and the governor.

''Good. Woman, I have other plans for you.''

Her pulse jumped at the look in his eyes. He mounted up with ease and swung her up with him, holding her close and turning the horses for home.

Travis and Zachary took turns keeping watch through the night in case any of the angry mob decided to look for Brett, but no one appeared. During watch the second night, Turtle River motioned to Travis to follow him. They entered the barn and Turtle River closed the door, lit a lantern, and moved to a stall.

Travis watched, his curiosity growing as Turtle River dug through a pile of straw to reveal a large box.

''Your brother said to give you this when Crystal was not around and when he was gone. He said it was gained illegally, but there's no giving it back now. You're to have it for the trouble he caused. Use it however you wish.''

Travis hoisted the box and was surprised by the weight, even though he thought he knew what he would find. He set the box on a barrel and raised the lid. Gold.

"He shared some with Zachary and with me, so you don't need to share yours," Turtle River remarked. "Just use it and know that your brother is a good man."

Travis replaced the lid. "For now, part of it will stay hidden right here in the barn. When I can get to town, I'll give some to Preacher Nealy for his church. If Crystal got wind of this, she would have me riding all across the States to try to find the true owners. But I'm not giving up my life here to do that. Just pray that the good Lord restores what was taken to those people." He hid the box back beneath the straw.

"I suspect your brother will spend the rest of his life trying to do good deeds to make up for his wild years. Guilt is a wild horse to ride."

Travis replaced the box and they extinguished the lantern, returning to the dark night to stand watch.

Three weeks later in May, Travis hammered boards in place, finishing the addition on his house. Halfway through the morning, he saw a rider approaching. He went inside to get his rifle.

Crystal saw him, her green eyes widening as she bathed Jacob.

"Someone's coming."

"Are you going to call the others?"

He shook his head. "No. It's a single rider." He went outside and continued hammering boards in place until the man neared and Travis realized it was Wade Hinckel. Going back to tell Crystal, Travis waved and saw Hinckel return the wave.

Wade dismounted and shook hands with Travis. "Good to see you. I thought I'd better come talk to you folks. You haven't been in to your livery stable."

''No, I reckon not,'' Travis drawled. ''I thought the reception in town might not be good yet.''

''Afternoon, Crystal. My, the little fellow is growing.''

Crystal smiled warmly, and Travis moved to her side and slipped his arm around her waist. He pulled her close to him and suddenly wanted Wade Hinckel to state his business and go so Travis could have his wife to himself. He was falling more in love with her each day.

Inviting Wade inside, Crystal put on a pot of coffee. As they sat at the table, Wade's blue eyes rested on Travis. ''I guess your brother is gone.''

''He never came home with us. He rode away that afternoon.''

''Good idea. Lots of high tempers at first, but a new witness has surfaced—Rupe Peters. He saw several men with Kendrick before the shots were fired. That calmed a lot of men down because it backed up your brother's story.''

''So, Brett was telling the truth!'' Crystal exclaimed. ''Thank heavens, I ruled as I did.

''Dammit,'' Travis said, anger coiling in him. ''Why didn't Rupe come forward sooner?''

''Scared to. He was afraid of Whit Odell. Anyway, it settled some of the men down who were worked up. Most of them don't want to hang the wrong man. I thought you ought to know. Now you can come back to work at your stable.''

''Sure?''

''What's absolute out here? But it should be as safe as it was before the trial.''

''Good. Thanks. Did you ride all the way out here to tell me that?''

''No. I also want to talk to Crystal.''

She raised her head in surprise, her green eyes widening. ''What is it?''

''You haven't been in to hear your cases.''

''I tried to tell you when we left town, I'm resigning.''

"I heard what you said, and I know you haven't come back to town, but I need to have it officially in writing."

She removed two sheets of paper from a cabinet and handed them to the sheriff.

"Here's what you need. My official resignation. There are two copies. One for your office, one for the governor."

"Judge, you were good at your job. And you drew some families to Cheyenne. I know the governor is going to ask you—I think he'll ride out here himself to try to persuade you—and I'm going to ask you: Will you finish off your term? Please."

"No, I won't," she said, feeling Travis's eyes on her.

"Just a little while. Only a few—"

She shook her head. "No. When I left the courtroom that day, I wanted to resign. I don't ever want to go back or try a case. If you desperately need me, I'll come in this week and next while you find someone else to take over. I've sacrificed enough for that job. I know my own feelings."

"I'm sure you do." He smiled and leaned back in his chair. "In that case, we might as well enjoy ourselves. We're having a boxing match tonight," he told Travis. " 'Course, there will never be another one like John Hardy and John Shaugnessy. One-hundred-and-twenty-six rounds."

"That's barbaric," Crystal commented. "And I hope that day goes down in history for the planning of Cheyenne's first public school instead of everyone remembering a fight!"

Travis grinned and squeezed her shoulder. "Darlin', it's just something you'll never understand."

"Indeed not, and if you gentlemen will excuse me, I'll tend to Jacob and get supper. Talk all you want about fighting."

Travis grinned as she moved away. Crystal listened to the men talk about things they enjoyed while she put a roast in the oven and played with Jacob. She thought about the job she was giving up. She would never miss it. It had been wonderful when she received the appointment, but now she had other plans for her future. Her gaze slid to Travis, who was watching her. His dark eyes made her pulse jump. God willing, they would have another baby. She longed to be alone in Travis's arms, where each night was pure rapture.

That summer Travis shipped his first load of cattle to the East. When he received payment, he came home early one afternoon. Crystal saw him riding toward the house from Cheyenne. He led a riderless horse behind him. Looking very much the Comanche, Travis wore a headband, an eagle feather in his black hair. The sleeves of his blue chambray shirt were rolled high and he wore buckskins.

"Papa's home, love," she told Jacob, who got up and ran as fast as his short legs could take him to the porch. She took off her apron and smoothed her blue-gingham dress, glancing at herself in the mirror before she went outside.

Travis swung his long leg over the horse and dropped to the ground. He lifted heavy bags off his mount and she noticed that the horse he was leading was loaded with bags.

Travis's dark eyes sparkled as he dropped the bags and picked up Jacob to hold him high and greet him. She heard the clink of the bags when Travis set them down and Crystal's curiosity jumped. Then she forgot about the bags as Travis set down Jacob and pulled her into his arms to hug and kiss her.

Dazed, she looked up at him when he released her. "You're home sooner than I expected."

"I took my payment for the cattle in gold." He hoisted a few of the bags onto his shoulder and they went inside, where he dropped the bags on the table. She stared at them.

"You made that much money?" she asked, stunned as he opened the first bag and poured it onto the table. Jacob climbed onto a chair and reached pudgy fingers out to pick up a handful of gold coins that glinted in the light.

"My heavens!"

"Crystal, the cattle market is booming. The stockmen are

talking about forming a club, and we're going to need one. Look at what we made!''

He left and returned with three more bags that he set on the floor by the table and she sat down, breathless, unable to grasp that he made such a fortune from selling his cows.

"How could anyone pay that much?"

"Cattle are in demand. I have to take out Turtle River's share and Zachary's share. And now, maybe the Blairs will pay more respect to him."

"My heavens!" Crystal leaned forward, examining the pile of coins. "Turtle River lives in a tipi. He doesn't need one of these coins a year."

Travis laughed and leaned across the corner of the table to kiss her. "We can build a house in town."

She considered the option. "If you want," she agreed slowly, "but I'm content to stay here."

"Someday, Jacob will go to school. It might be easier to have a house in town as well as here."

"I suppose," she reflected. "Travis, I'm amazed."

"I'm surprised myself. All the long hours and hard work have paid off. Of course, a lot of this will go right back into the ranch. I want to get another bull and keep improving our stock. And if you'd like, I'll take you and Jacob to Saint Louis and you can buy new dresses and get Jacob new clothes."

She laughed and shook her head. "I don't think we need new clothes yet. Jacob will soon, but I don't. But a trip with you sounds like great fun."

"I'll even take you back to Baltimore if you would like to go."

She smiled and moved to sit on his lap. "I don't really care, Travis. Baltimore was so long ago. It's not part of my life now. I just want to be with you."

He slipped his arms around her and pulled her close, kissed her, and the money was forgotten.

* * *

When Travis finished the additional room on the house, the men built another room onto Zachary's small cabin. With Travis's and Turtle River's help, Zachary built a buckboard.

Crystal blossomed, looking prettier than ever to Travis. She had two new dresses and was learning to sew, but it was going as slowly and disastrously as her cooking.

In the middle of July he came in to find her wreathed in smiles. Dressed in a new blue cotton, she raced across the room and flung herself into his arms. He braced his legs and caught her, lifting her up as he kissed her. Desire flashed white-hot in him at her exuberant welcome; and when he released her, he wanted to lock the door and take her to bed.

"That will make me want to get home more than ever," he said softly, his hand stroking her throat.

"Travis, I think I'm carrying our baby!"

Twenty-three

"Oh, God, Crystal!" Travis wrapped his arms around her and pulled her against him, holding her tightly so she wouldn't see the terror that clutched at his heart. There was no way he could share her joy. He had expected this, knew she had wanted another baby, but the reality hit him like a huge fist plunging into his middle.

He lost his breath, unable to get his feelings under control. She had become a part of his life, like air and sunshine. There was no way he could face a birth calmly or with any degree of certainty. He clamped his jaw shut until it hurt. She wriggled in his arms, then pulled his head down so she could kiss him.

He kissed her as if it were the last kiss they ever would share. His tongue plunged into her mouth and he held her tightly until she pushed gently against his chest.

"Travis." She looked up at him with a puzzled frown. "Oh, no!" She framed his face with her hands, so warm and soft. "Travis, the very first time when we loved, you knew this could happen."

"I know," he acknowledged, his emotions tearing at him.

He didn't want to ruin her joy, and another baby would be grand; but he was terrified. He wound her hair through his fingers. "You're my world, Crystal," he said in a rough, husky voice.

"Travis," she whispered, standing on tiptoe and pulling his head down so she could gaze directly into his eyes. "I love you. You're not going to lose me. I prom—"

He placed his hand over her lips and kissed the word away. "You can't promise," he reminded her. "Not when it's something you have such little control over."

"I feel so strongly about this baby. And I'm a strong woman. I'm a big woman."

"You're tall, Crystal, but you're slender with slender hips. There can be so many complications."

"Don't worry," she chided.

"We could move to Saint Louis," he suggested frantically. "There would be lots of doctors there to choose from."

"You can't run your business from Saint Louis!" She stared at him with worry clouding her eyes. He hated that he was ruining what should be one of the most joyous moments of their marriage, but he was too scared to think clearly. He looked at her shining eyes; her joy was unmistakable. She was his life and he couldn't bear the thought of losing her. He ran his fingers through her auburn hair, feeling its softness and relishing its flaming color.

"I can sell the livery stable and pay Turtle River to run the ranch. I'd want to keep the ranch because the cattle business is booming."

"So is the livery business. There's no need to sell out and move somewhere else. Cheyenne has two doctors now; both of them are good. It'll be all right."

"You don't know." He spun away from her, rubbing his forehead. "Damnation, I know I'm ruining this for you."

Crystal watched him pace across the room, distraught. She slid her arms around his narrow waist. His dark eyes were trouble-filled, clouded with fear. "I'll be all right. Babies are born every day."

Travis looked at her, and she saw the change in him as his fear was replaced by a love so overwhelming that her heart missed a beat. He wrapped his arms around her and pressed her against his chest. She clung to him.

"I need you, Crystal. I love you."

"I love you, too, Travis. And this will be good. This baby will be such a delight." She leaned back and placed her hands on his cheeks. "Let go of your worries."

"I'll try," he answered grimly.

She stood on tiptoe to kiss him and then smiled at him.

All through supper, Crystal caught Travis staring at her. Once she saw Turtle River watching Travis, and she knew that Turtle River had noticed the undercurrents.

She passed a bowl of steaming carrots and tried to eat what she should. Their baby! Another precious baby. A brother or sister for Jacob. He was toddling now and growing more adorable to her with each stage of his development.

She was filled with a humming excitement, but shortly after they started eating, she noticed Zachary was barely eating. Zachary, not eating? He had waded through the worst of her cooking, chomping down every burned bite. Yet now he merely pushed his food around his plate.

"Zachary?" He looked up. "Is something wrong?"

He glanced around the table and his face turned a deep crimson. "I wasn't going to say anything until I knew for certain, but I've asked Agnes to marry me this summer and I talked to her father again. He said he was pleased with my progress in opening an account at the bank, buying my own mount, and the buckboard and he knew I had built on to my house here on the ranch. He's going to discuss it with her mother and give me an answer Friday."

"Oh, Zachary, if it's what you and Agnes want, I hope her father consents to let you marry!" Crystal said.

"I wanted to wait to tell everyone."

"This is Wednesday. You'll know Friday. Friday isn't far away," she encouraged him, and Zachary gave her a weak smile.

Hugging her own secret news close to her heart, Crystal forgot about Zachary until late that night when she lay in Travis's arms. "When shall we tell the others?"

"Not until you are absolutely certain," he admonished. "One more month—although I imagine Turtle River has already guessed."

"My husband, I am so happy! Oh, Travis, it's marvelous!"

He pulled her close and kissed her, but he didn't reply. Then she remembered Zachary. "Travis, I pray that the Blairs give Zachary their consent."

"We will know without a doubt by the way he rides up toward the house," he noted. "We will not have to wonder."

"That will leave Turtle River more solitary than ever."

"Turtle River does as he damn well pleases."

"If you hadn't needed a mother for Jacob, you would have done exactly what Turtle River is doing. Look how solitary and alone you would have been and what you would have missed in life."

"Everything wonderful," Travis said, pulling her close against his chest and showering kisses on her. Crystal clung to him, closing her eyes and raising her mouth for his kisses.

Friday afternoon, Crystal remembered Travis's words when she heard a gunshot. She went outside, and Travis ran around the house, his pistol drawn.

"Well, hellfire," he said, tucking his pistol into his belt and placing his hands on his hips. Following his gaze, she saw it was Zachary, riding wildly and waving his hat and yelling. She had to laugh and Travis joined her, shaking his head.

"He will be unlivable until he gets his Agnes married to him and living here. And probably daft for another year after the wedding!"

"He's in love."

Travis slipped his arm around her waist. "And so am I. That makes two of us who can't think straight and forget to do what we should because we're in love with our women."

"Is that right? I didn't know I had that effect."

"The hell you didn't! Let's go inside and I'll show you."

"You will do no such thing!" she said, pushing against him. "Here he comes."

"He doesn't have to say a word."

"But he's going to and you're to be polite and listen to him."

"Yes, ma'am, Judge. I hope he doesn't start in on any of his damned poetry to Agnes."

"He's too excited for that."

Zachary reined in near them and looked down with a wide grin. "She's marrying me! Agnes is marrying me one month from today!" He gave a whoop and jumped off his horse. "I'll get to work, but I wanted to tell you."

"Congratulations, Zachary," Travis said, shaking the boy's hand, and Crystal hugged him. She was happy for him, happy for herself and Travis. She let her hand slide to her stomach and felt a glow of joy. Their baby. As Zachary rode to the barn, Travis put his arm around her and they headed back to their tasks. She heard Jacob cry.

"He's awake." She hurried to the house and Travis let his gaze run over her. She seemed to feel better than he would have guessed possible. She glowed with happiness, but he couldn't shake his fears and worries.

Several nights later, when Travis came in, she was in her gown and wrapper, knitting a baby blanket.

He picked her up and sat down with her on his lap. Crystal slipped her arm around his neck.

"I've been thinking, Crystal. Now's the time to build that house in town that we've talked about. This baby is due in

April; we could still have snow. I don't want you out here where a doctor will have a long ride to get to you or weather might keep him away altogether.''

"We have talked about a house before," she said, knowing it might be wise to build one because she might have to live in town part of the time when Jacob started school.

"If we could get one built by the holidays, that should be in time."

She laughed. "I don't think you can have one built that quickly, but I think you can have one before April. And furniture—"

"We'll manage," he said.

"Which means you will bully and bribe some people to get what you want."

"Is that right? You can't ever accuse me of bullying you into anything. A little bribery perhaps. Crystal, I remember a promise about paying your way to California—"

"Only if you and Jacob and all our children go."

"All our children? Oh, damnation, don't say that now."

She grinned at him. "Very well, but maybe you should plan on building a sizable house."

"Little did I know that my life would never be peaceful again."

"Ah, but it's exciting, isn't it?" she asked, tilting his chin up to kiss him.

In August, Agnes and Zachary were married outdoors on the ranch on a warm, windy afternoon with a party afterwards. Crystal helped Agnes dress and brush her hair, pinning it high on the back of her head and letting the blond locks cascade down her back. She wore a blue-and-white dimity dress and looked radiant, her brown eyes sparkling and her cheeks pink.

"You look beautiful."

"Thank you. So do you, Crystal."

Crystal gazed at her reflection in the mirror. She had on a

new blue organdy dress that she had ordered from Saint Louis and blue ribbons in her hair. Her gaze ran down her figure and she felt the familiar rush of excitement. They still had not announced the new baby, and she wondered how long she would remain slender. She touched her stomach lightly, smoothing the deep-blue silk sash to her dress.

"Crystal, I think I shall faint, I'm so excited."

"Nonsense, Agnes," Mrs. Blair said, combing Agnes's hair. "Stand still."

"I'll join the others," Crystal said, slipping away and leaving mother and daughter alone.

The weather was perfect with a blue sky and bright sunshine. Crystal had tied satin bows on the posts along the porch. The couple stood in front of the young spruce for the ceremony.

As Agnes stood beside Zachary, Crystal held Travis's hand and looked at the boy who had been so pitiful when they'd found him. Now he was a handsome young man with his brown hair slicked down and parted in the center and his new store-bought black suit.

As Zachary and Agnes repeated their vows, Crystal looked up at the tall man at her side and recalled the day that they, too, had said vows. His dark eyes rested on her, and she wondered if he were remembering also.

Crystal played the piano for half an hour, and afterwards, Mabel Smith played while couples danced across the grassy yard.

Travis took Crystal's hand, pulling her to him to dance. He had shed his coat and rolled up his white shirt sleeves, and Crystal thought he was incredibly handsome. She gazed up into his dark eyes, moving in time with him, and everyone around them faded away. Travis's brown eyes held her, pulling her into dark depths that wrapped around her like a silken cloak. Love and desire sparkled in their black orbs.

He danced her around the corner and then leaned against the house, wrapping his arms around her. He bent down to kiss her, his mouth opening hers.

Crystal clung to him and returned his kiss until their hearts were pounding and they were breathless. She pushed gently against him.

"We have to go back. After all, we're giving this party." She tried to replace a lock of hair that had fallen. "Now, look at me! Everyone will know we've kissed."

"They'll know I'm a man in love with my wife," he said in a husky voice, leaning forward to trail kisses on her throat. "I wish they would all go home so I can have you to myself."

"They will soon enough," she said, taking his hand and leading him back to the crowd. "I'm glad Agnes married Zachary. They seem so happy."

"I'm glad she married him, too," Travis remarked dryly. "Maybe now he will gradually get his wits back. Although I'm not certain he's any worse than I have been."

"Is that right? Whatever would cause you to lose your wits?"

"My beautiful, green-eyed wife," he whispered, pulling her closer.

She pushed him back. "Don't do something that will shock the Blairs."

"Next week the builder is starting our new house in Cheyenne."

"And you think it'll be done by the holidays?

"Yes," Travis answered. He was paying extra to get it done before winter set in, but he wasn't telling Crystal. He wanted her moved into town before the bad weather.

At the end of September, Travis walked through the framework of their new house. It was a two-story Victorian with two parlors, a large kitchen and a dining room, an office and library, four bedrooms and two bathrooms, and Travis wanted everything in it to please Crystal. He would give her the world if he could. He climbed back into a new buggy and headed toward the general store where he had left Crystal. He was deeply thankful she had resigned her justice-of-the-peace job, a task now taken over by Elgin Thomas.

He spotted Crystal heading toward the livery. He felt a rush of pleasure at the sight of her and mild annoyance that she was walking when he had told her he would be back to pick her up. Jacob trotted at her side, and he knew she had slowed to walk at his pace. She wore her new green woolen dress and a matching hat with feathers and she stood out in the Cheyenne crowd like a flower among dried grass, although fancy clothes and elegant houses were becoming the norm as the cattle business boomed.

He pulled up alongside her and jumped down from the buggy.

"I thought you would wait for me to pick you up," he said, sweeping Jacob up into his arms and lifting him into the back seat of the buggy.

She tilted her head, looking up at him from beneath the green hat brim, a twinkle in her eyes. "How is our house?"

"Progressing nicely. I think we will be in it by the end of November."

"November! You keep moving the date up. Does the builder know this?"

"Indeed, he does. I'll show it to you."

"I can't believe we shall have such a wonderful home. We have to order more furniture or else we'll be living in empty rooms."

"We won't do that," he said, lifting her into the buggy. He climbed up beside her and headed toward the livery.

"I thought we were looking at the new house."

"In time. I want to show you something first."

He stopped in front of the livery, and when they went inside, he asked Andrew to take Jacob. Andrew pushed his blond hair out of his face and picked up Jacob, carrying him out to the horse pen. Travis led Crystal into his office, closed and locked the door.

"Travis?"

He pulled her to him, tilting up her face and leaning down.

"I've been waiting all morning," he said in a husky voice. He kissed her, his arm tightening around her waist. He wanted her with an intensity that was growing instead of diminishing. He wanted to take her right here in the office.

He pushed away her hat, not caring about pins that fell or locks of her hair that tumbled down. His hand slipped down over the woolen bodice and he found her buttons, twisting them free swiftly while he kissed her. His hand slipped inside her bodice and he growled, deep in his throat, frustrating by the clothing she had on. He pushed at it, finally freeing her soft, bare breast in his hand.

She moaned and clung to him, her hips pressing against him, letting him stroke and kiss her until they both were losing control. She pushed away from him, staring at him with ragged breath. "We have to stop."

"I love you, woman. I need you."

"I love you," she replied, kissing him again and then straightening her clothing. "Now, when we get ourselves back together," she said firmly, trying to ignore her racing pulse or the longing to throw herself right back into his arms, "you will take Jacob and me to look at the new house."

He didn't answer and she turned to see him staring at her with eyes black with desire. "Oh, Travis—"

"I know. We have to wait, but I don't want to. I want to kiss and touch you now." He turned and left the office and she sank into a chair, shaken by the force in his voice, amazed that she had won his love so completely.

The fall was warmer than usual and she enjoyed the days on the ranch, knowing she would soon be moving to town. Each day was a joy with Travis and with Jacob, who was growing quickly. They ordered furniture, planned the house, talked about the new baby, but Crystal knew that Travis was growing more worried with each passing week.

At the end of November they moved into town. Travis packed

the wagon, but drove her in the buggy. Travis carried Crystal inside and set her down in the front hall. Jacob ran on short, chubby legs through the rooms, but Crystal barely noticed him. She was awed by this beautiful house that had her piano, a beveled oval glass in the front door, and a beautiful mahogany bannister on the staircase. The front parlor was filled with new furniture, as was the back parlor. It was a two-story house, and the largest bedroom was theirs. Crystal was dazzled, overjoyed, and she couldn't help but remember the small house she had lived in with Ellery and the simple one-room she had shared with Travis at first. Now, they would have a truly beautiful home with wonderful furnishings.

"Travis, thank you," she said softly, reaching to take his large hand in her two smaller hands. His skin was dark against hers, and she raised his hand to her mouth to brush it with her lips.

Travis looked at her head bent over his hand and he wanted to wrap her in his arms and hold her forever. Each month she came closer to the birth of their child, and each month his terror deepened. Yet she seemed healthy, full of robust energy, confident.

He picked her up to carry her into their bedroom. "Here's our room," he said proudly. A four-poster mahogany bed was covered in their red-and-white-and-blue quilt. A rocking chair stood in the center of the room, a dresser and chifforobe to one side. There was a new oval pier glass.

He stood her on her feet and wrapped his arms around her, gazing at her with love in his eyes. "Welcome home, Mrs. Black Eagle."

Crystal stood on tiptoe to kiss him. "Thank you for building this house for me and for hiring Caterina to help me with the cooking and cleaning. And this year, we will have a real celebration at Christmas time."

"I don't care what we do as long as you're all right," he said in a husky voice.

"I'm fine," Crystal replied, wishing she could kiss away his fears.

Travis dismounted and headed into the livery stable. He had turned the ranch over to Turtle River and had not been there for over two months. Now it was the third day of April and his nerves were already stretched raw. He didn't want their baby to come while he was away at the ranch. His boots crunched snow and he glanced at the sky. He checked constantly on the doctor, wanting to make certain he was in town, available and ready.

And he couldn't be reassured by Crystal's vitality because Elizabeth had been fine up until she went into labor. He paced the office, trying to get his mind on business, yet constantly thinking about Crystal. It was time for the babe, yet she didn't look ready.

He didn't care how she looked, he just wanted the baby here and Crystal all right. He stepped into his office and shrugged off his coat, brushing snow away. He crossed the room to his desk and picked up the letter that had arrived two days earlier from Brett. A sweeping scrawl covered the thick white paper.

"Dear Brother, I have bought some land and am settled. I had planned to head north, but instead, found myself going south. I am in the mountains of New Mexico, but a good place for cattle. I have land in a valley that is rich in grass and water. I want you and Crystal and little Jacob to come visit. Better you come here than I return to Wyoming Territory. I heard you cannot get statehood because you allow women to vote. Am certain your wife will be strongly in favor that women retain that right to vote. Hope all is well with you and yours. Here is the way to my place. Brett."

Travis dropped the letter on the desk and knelt to pray, something he had not done in a long time. He gave thanks for Crystal, praying for a safe delivery for her and their baby. He gave thanks for all he had—for Jacob and for the safety of his brother.

He stood, touching Brett's letter and hoping his brother had settled and found a good life . . . as good as he had found with Crystal. Travis raised his head to look out the window at the snowflakes swirling through the air. He didn't want to lose this life.

"Morning, Travis," Andrew said, stepping into the office and shedding his coat and hat. "We have three horses waiting to be shoed. I'll get the fire going."

Travis looked down the street, edgy. He would feel that way from now on until Crystal delivered their baby.

That night he swept into the house, pulling her into his arms the moment he hung up his coat. "I hate being away from you," he said before he kissed her. She smelled liked roses and was soft, her full stomach pressing against him.

"Did you write your brother today?"

"No, I'll do it tonight," he said, scooping Jacob up into his arms. "How's my boy?"

"See," Jacob said, holding out a toy dog and Travis carried him into the back parlor to play with him. He missed the ranch, but he wouldn't leave Crystal now, and he sat on the floor in front of the fire to play with Jacob.

After a delicious supper of baked chicken cooked by Caterina, Travis and Crystal sat in the parlor until it was time to put Jacob to bed. Travis hoisted him to his shoulders and carried him upstairs for a bath, a story, and then bed.

As soon as Jacob fell asleep, Travis came back downstairs where Crystal sat reading a book. Her auburn hair was caught up with blue hair bows on either side of her head and it tumbled down over her back. She wore a deep-blue dress and he thought she looked prettier than ever. There was a serenity and quiet joy about her now that had been absent in the first year of their marriage.

He placed his hands on the arms of her chair and leaned close to her, gazing into her eyes.

"Do you know how many times I have been thankful you married me?"

Her smiled broadened. "I don't believe there was even one time in those first months. Especially at supper time"

"*Au contraire,* darlin'. I was thankful the first day. Before we were even married. I remember how you took Jacob from me and quieted him down. You were meant to be a wife and mother, Crystal."

"I have told you that on me than one occasion."

"I am thankful."

"And I, too. You are quite the best husband. Particularly in bed."

He bent to kiss her throat. "Don't start that when I can't love you the way I want to."

"It won't be long before you can."

He went quickly to the desk and pulled out a ledger to make entries of the day's business. They sat in silence while he worked and wrote Brett. Crystal remained quiet, her head bent over her book, the fire making her hair a fiery halo around her head. He stared at her, captivated. And then he realized she was holding the book in her lap, but she wasn't turning any pages.

He had seen Crystal read before and she was a fast reader. He put down his pen and stared openly at her, noticing that one of her hands gripped the arm of the chair tightly enough that her knuckles were white. The clock ticked steadily on, and still she did not turn a page.

"Crystal, are you all right?"

She raised her head and looked at him with a calmness that was deep. "I'm fine."

She bent over the book and turned the page and then sat without moving for another ten minutes.

"Crystal—"

"I think I shall go upstairs to bed." She stood carefully.

His heart thudded as he rose to his feet. He crossed the room to her and tilted up her chin.

"And maybe it is time to get the doctor," she added quietly. "Now, Travis, keep calm. Our baby is on its way."

Twenty-four

Travis's heart lurched and he felt as if ice water had been dumped on him. "I'll get you to bed. Dammit, how long have you known?"

"Not long," she answered with serenity.

"Why didn't you tell me sooner?"

"Because I didn't want you worrying any sooner than necessary."

"I'm sending Andrew for the doctor." Since Andrew and his wife live only two blocks away, he wouldn't have to be gone as long from home.

"You have time to go get the doctor."

Travis picked her up, holding her with care as he climbed the stairs. In the bedroom, he yanked back the quilt and sheet.

"Travis, please get some towels to put in the bed."

He ran to do as she instructed while she changed into a gown. As soon as he had helped her into bed, he bent down to hold her hand and kiss her lightly. "I'll get Andrew and be right back."

Forgetting his hat and coat, Travis raced outside, charging through the snow to the Cain's small house. He pounded on the door until it swung open and Andrew stood there.

"Travis?"

"We need the doctor. Can you get him?"

"Yep, I will. Right now."

"Good. I'll go back with Crystal. If for any reason he can't come at once, get the other one. Let me know if one of them isn't coming within the hour."

"I will. Good luck," Andrew called after him as Travis turned and ran back toward his house.

Travis was frozen with terror. How long had she been in labor? She had sat so quietly all evening. What agony had she gone through in silence just to keep him from knowing that the time had come? Just to keep him from this panic and terror?

He raced home, barely stomping snow off his boots before taking the stairs two at a time to join her. He burst into the room. Crystal lay propped against the pillows, her legs bent, knees in the air, a sheet across her. Her hair was fanned out behind her and she clutched the sheet, but she looked serene and she smiled at him.

"You might have to deliver this baby," she said.

Panic shook him as if a fist had slammed into him. "I can't."

"Of course you can. I've seen you deliver foals and calves."

"Are you all right?"

"I'm very much all right," she said.

"That damned doctor had better get here."

"If he doesn't, Travis, you can do this. Go get a knife washed and get ready to cut the cord."

He fled, doing what she told him, his hands shaking. He was numb with fear, but aware that, so far, this was not like the time with Elizabeth, who had been racked with hideous pains. Crystal looked far more composed than he felt.

He heard a knock at the door and ran to answer it, swinging it open to face the blond physician who suddenly looked like a child himself, far too young to have the knowledge and be responsible enough to deliver a baby.

"Thank God!" he exclaimed even as doubts assailed him. "Come inside," he said, curbing the urge to grab the man and rush him upstairs to Crystal.

"How is the patient?" Sam Mason asked, shedding a snowy hat and coat.

"She's upstairs in labor."

"Well, I'll go see about her. No complications, so far?"

"No," said Travis, wondering if Crystal would let him know if there were complications. "I'll show you where she is. Thank you for coming so quickly."

"I believe there was a mild threat to my well-being if I didn't," Mason commented dryly.

Travis didn't care what the man thought. He raced up the stairs. Crystal's eyes were closed, her lower lip caught in her teeth.

"Crystal," he whispered, rushing to the bed.

She looked at him and then relaxed. He wiped her perspiring forehead as Dr. Mason entered the room and closed the door.

"You boil water, Travis," the doctor ordered.

"I'll be right back."

"You can wait in the other room," the physician remarked dryly. "I think fathers merely cause trouble."

"I—"

"I'll call you the minute the baby is here."

Crystal caught his hand, kissed it, and smiled at him. "Go on."

He stared at her, looking at how calm she was, yet she had just started her labor. He brushed her lips with a kiss and left, going downstairs to put on a pot of water for coffee and a pan of water for the doctor. He got out the whiskey bottle and tipped it up to have a long drink, suspecting it would do little to calm his nerves.

He paced the floor, moving back upstairs. There was not a

sound from their bedroom. He poured another large drink of whiskey and threw it down, feeling it burn.

The upstairs door opened. "Mr. Black Eagle," the doctor said, and Travis's heart and breath stopped.

Twenty-five

Travis couldn't move, but stared at the smiling doctor.

"You have another son. You may come in now. I'll wait downstairs."

Travis stormed into the room. Crystal was still propped against the pillows, her hair spread behind her head and over her shoulders. She held a baby in her arms and she was smiling at him.

Travis couldn't move. Worries of the past year left him unable to put one foot in front of the other. Worries and shock. She had already had their baby. She looked radiant, her green eyes sparkling, her rosy mouth curved in a triumphant smile.

"Travis," she said, patting the bed.

Stunned by her ease at delivering the baby, he crossed the room, and then the dam of control inside him broke. "Oh, Crystal!"

He sat down, knowing he should be careful with her, but unable to resist holding her in his arms. "You're safe! I love you . . . love you," he whispered, burying his face against her throat, unable to control the tears of relief and joy that fell over his cheeks. "You're safe."

"I'm very safe," she said. She stroked his head. "I'm fine and our baby is fine."

Travis held her, trying to gain control of his emotions and wanting to reassure himself that she was all right. "I can't believe you've had this baby. I've worried for so long, and in minutes, the baby is here and you're smiling." He raised his face and wiped his eyes as he looked at her.

Crystal's heart thudded with joy. She had never dreamed it possible for this strong, powerful man to love her to such an extent to turn him to tears and into a quivering wreck. Yet she loved him that much in return. She smiled at Travis, wiping his cheeks, feeling the rough stubble that was wet with his tears. She looked down at the baby in her arms. "Look at him. Perhaps we should name him Brett after your brother."

"Or Ellery after yours," Travis said, touching the baby's cheek. "Look at all his red hair. Ellery Black Eagle is fine with me." His hand wound in her hair. "I can't believe it was this simple."

"Maybe I'm meant for childbirth," she said with a mischievous grin, confident that never again would he be as worried.

"You're meant for love," Travis said, pulling her into his arms, careful of the baby. "What a surprise for Jake in the morning." He leaned down to kiss her.

Crystal wound her arm around his neck, joyous with the love she had found in his strong arms, thrilled with the family they would have together. Love filled her; her joy was complete.

Dear Reader:

The independent spirit of the prairie women of the early West is a fascinating topic to me. This novel was fun to write because of the historical background of the unique women's suffrage in Wyoming Territory that almost cost Wyoming its statehood. I enjoyed writing this novel and would love to hear from you if you enjoyed reading it.

My next novel will be *Comanche Passion,* moving the setting south to Texas where a Comanche scout for the army crosses paths with a beautiful Confederate smuggler.

Please send any correspondence with a self-addressed, stamped envelope to: Sara Orwig, P.O. Box 780258, Oklahoma City, Oklahoma 73178-0258.

ROMANCE FROM JANELLE TAYLOR

ANYTHING FOR LOVE   (0-8217-4992-7, $5.99)

DESTINY MINE   (0-8217-5185-9, $5.99)

CHASE THE WIND   (0-8217-4740-1, $5.99)

MIDNIGHT SECRETS   (0-8217-5280-4, $5.99)

MOONBEAMS AND MAGIC   (0-8217-0184-4, $5.99)

SWEET SAVAGE HEART   (0-8217-5276-6, $5.99)